THE
SHORT FICTION
OF
RUDOLPH FISHER

THE
SHORT FICTION
OF
RUDOLPH FISHER

EDITED AND
INTRODUCED
BY
Margaret Perry

CONTRIBUTIONS IN AFRO-AMERICAN AND
AFRICAN STUDIES, NUMBER 107

Greenwood Press
NEW YORK • WESTPORT, CONNECTICUT • LONDON

Library of Congress Cataloging-in-Publication Data

Fisher, Rudolph, 1897-1934.
  The short fiction of Rudolph Fisher.

  (Contributions in Afro-American and African studies,
ISSN 0069-9624 ; no. 107)
  Bibliography: p.
  Includes index.
  1. Afro-Americans—Fiction. I. Perry, Margaret,
1933-   . II. Title. III. Series.
PS3511.I7436A6 1987   813'.52   86-29580
ISBN 0-313-21348-8 (lib. bdg. : alk. paper)

Library of Congress Catalog Card Number: 86-29580
ISBN: 0-313-21348-8
ISSN: 0069-9624

First published in 1987

Greenwood Press, Inc.
88 Post Road West, Westport, Connecticut 06881

Printed in the United States of America

The paper used in this book complies with the
Permanent Paper Standard issued by the National
Information Standards Organization (Z39.48-1984).

10 9 8 7 6 5 4 3 2 1

Dedicated to the memory of Rudolph Fisher
and his late sister, Pearl Fisher

CONTENTS

ACKNOWLEDGMENTS

I would like to thank, first of all, Mrs. Rudolph Fisher for her strong encouragement that I compile and edit this book. When she and I and the late Pearl Fisher, sister of Dr. Fisher, discussed the formulation of this book over tea in the Fisher apartment on Edgecomb Avenue, the notion was ill-shaped but visionary. Now a portion of the task is complete.

My thanks to the late Pearl Fisher, who believed in my credentials for producing this book.

My gratitude is extended to Dr. Robert France, who granted my leave to work on this project when I was still at the University of Rochester, as well as to the University of Rochester English Department for its support, and to Helen Craven who typed the original manuscript.

The following are also thanked for their cooperation: *Atlantic Monthly*; *Crisis*; the Schomburg Center for Research in Black Culture; the New York Public Library; the Astor, Lenox, and Tilden Foundations; and Brown University.

My appreciation to Vice President Richard P. Baepler, Valparaiso University, for his encouragement and support during the final phases of preparing this book; to Michelle Carver, the Center for Research Libraries (Chicago), and to Penny Sippel, production editor at Greenwood Press, for their kind and concerned help.

It was this encouragement and support that enabled me to produce this book.

INTRODUCTION

The short story as we know it today has a brief history as literary history goes; the short story of today is an American form, " . . . the only major literary form of essentially American origin and the only one in which American writers have always tended to excel."[1] Edgar Allan Poe was the first writer who had the courage to try to define the form; indeed, in reviewing Nathaniel Hawthorne's *Twice-Told Tales*, Poe was announcing to the world the emergence of a form that Americans have dominated since the nineteenth century. In placing the short story next to the art of poetry, Poe also anticipated such a writer as Eudora Welty who, in a recent television interview, stated that the short story writer "writes from the lyric impulse." Indeed, the short story writer nearly sings a story to the reader, and the art of the form is as demanding of the writer as is the crafting of a poem. There is a relationship also, it seems, between both of these forms through the ancient Greek word for dance-and-song, the *Molpé*, which was choral dancing in a ritualistic fashion, a song and dance full of meaning. It is significant to note Gilbert Murray's elaboration upon the definition of this ritual: "The dance, of course, was not like our dancing. At times it may have been something with fixed steps and movements; *at times we know that it was mimetic, trying magically to bring about some effect which it imitated* [my italics]."[2] Without the magic, but with art and knowledge of genre, it seems that Rudolph Fisher was trying to accomplish what all short story writers have attempted to do: to bear down upon incident, character, and situation in order to widen the reader's view and comprehension of the human situation.

On another level, the short story has also been quite dependent upon the market; even Poe lamented this fact when he was unable to get his stories published in book form. In our own century, this economic aspect of the history of the short story has continued until the recent availability of numerous "little" magazines as well as several book-length competitions for collections. The history of the Afro-American short story has been shaped even more by the economic aspect of the market.

When *The Negro Caravan* appeared in 1941, the editors remarked about the short story and the Negro writer:

> The short story as a literary form in America has always been intended primarily for popular magazine publication;... In this medium, more than in others, the Negro author faces the dilemma of the divided audience. With the exception of the journals [*The Crisis* and *Opportunity*] of two Negro organizations... and a few fugitive publications, there have been no magazines with a primarily Negro audience in which writers could place their short stories.... The necessity for magazine publication has affected the Negro short story profoundly.[3]

The editorial policy of each of the Negro-run magazines, especially *The Crisis* under the leadership of W. E. B. Du Bois ("all art is propaganda"), hampered the artistic development of the Afro-American short story. Too often the moral was more important than the totality of the story—the blending of characters and action, the action growing out of the conflicts, and the varying intentions of the characters. For example, Jessie Fauset, a mediocre if prolific novelist, was able to publish short stories that should never have appeared in print. Once again, the editors of *The Negro Caravan* were sensitive to the weaknesses of the Negro short story writer and observed: "In few of these stories is there humor or deft characterization or psychological understanding; these elements are sacrificed to the burning message."[4] In such a world, the stories of Rudolph Fisher outshone the rest in his practice of the short story in its traditional mode. He was also published frequently in non-Negro publications, such as *Atlantic Monthly* and *McClure's* and, thus, was able to reach a wider audience of short story readers. It seems, therefore, to the writer of this book that Fisher may be the Afro-American writer who attracted the dual readership of white and black devotees of the short story, not Langston Hughes, as was proposed in *The Black American Short Story in the 20th Century*.[5]

It is not surprising, finally, to note how little information has been devoted to Fisher's short fiction. Indeed, the central metaphor of black invisibility can be said to have been operating when critics expounded on the short story in America. Fred Lewis Pattee (*American Short Story*) may be forgiven, since he published his book in 1923 and had only Paul Laurence Dunbar or Charles Chesnutt to consider. But one cannot hold the same tolerance for someone like Ray West (*The Short Story in America, 1900–1950*), who published in 1952, or Arthur Voss (*The American Short Story*) whose book, published in 1973, includes information about nearly every minor white writer (e.g., Mary Murfree, whose pen name was Charles Craddock, or Henry Cuyler Bunner) but does not include even a paragraph or two about Langston Hughes, Richard Wright, James Baldwin, or Ralph Ellison. Obviously, Fisher would not have surmounted the neglect given to these better known Negro writers. In *The American Short Story* (1964), by William Peden, there is at least some acknowledgment both in the text and in the accompanying bibliography that blacks write short stories.

The purpose of this book, however, is not to argue with short story critical history, but to present all of the published short fiction of Rudolph Fisher, including some observations and critical comments. It was hoped that some of Fisher's unpublished fiction would also appear in print for the first time, but permission to do this was denied.

The primarily descriptive introductory essay attempts to cover the salient points of Fisher's life and to place the stories within the context of Fisher's literary canon. As for the stories: They speak for themselves, and the number of notes appended to many of them have been kept brief and, hopefully, pertinent. Some notes include information that helps the reader to see Fisher's stories in the context of the times during which he lived (e.g., note 3 for "Miss Cynthie"). We have changed single quotations to double in the dialogue in some of the stories for consistency in style. The precise time in history, as well as the spirit of the place—Harlem—were significant elements in Fisher's fiction; indeed, they were perhaps the reasons he felt impelled to capture his world within the strictures of the short story form. Full of wit, irony, humor, and some acerbity, Fisher has enriched the world of literature in a medium Frank O'Connor has called our "national art form."[6]

NOTES

1. William Peden, *The American Short Story* (Boston: Houghton, Mifflin, 1964), 1.

2. Gilbert Murray, *The Classical Tradition in Poetry* (New York: Russell & Russell, 1927), 34.

3. *The Negro Caravan* (New York: Dryden Press, 1941), 10.

4. Ibid., 13.

5. P. Bruck, ed., *The Black American Short Story in the 20th Century* (Amsterdam: B. R. Grüner, 1977). This book, a collection of essays, is one of the two books that is devoted exclusively to this topic and, therefore, it is a welcome addition to a much neglected area in Afro-American literature. The other book is Robert Bone, *Down Home: A History of Afro-American Short Fiction from*

Its Beginning to the End of the Harlem Renaissance (New York: G. P. Putnam's, 1975).

   6. Frank O'Connor, *The Lonely Voice: A Study of the Short Story* (Cleveland: World, 1963), 41.

THE
SHORT FICTION
OF
RUDOLPH FISHER

THE BRIEF LIFE AND ART OF RUDOLPH FISHER

Rudolph Fisher, born in Washington, D.C., on May 9, 1897, was the son of Reverend John W. Fisher and Glendora Williamson Fisher. Fisher was brought up mainly in Providence, R.I., where he completed his studies at Classical High School in 1915 with high honors. While at high school he was a member of the debating team.

In 1915 Fisher matriculated to Brown University where he majored in English and biology. He was elected to Phi Beta Kappa and to the honorary fraternities Sigma Xi and Delta Sigma Rho. He won the Caesar Misch Prize in German and the Carpenter Prize in public speaking. When he graduated in 1919 he was elected by the faculty to be the Commencement Day speaker; he had already been the Class Day orator. To be sure, Rudolph Fisher demonstrated early those superior intellectual and social qualities that were to be reflected later in his stories and novels.

Following graduation, Fisher remained at Brown during the next academic year in order to get his M.A. Then he attended the Howard University medical school where he graduated with highest honors in 1924. After a one-year internship at Freedman's Hospital in Washington, Fisher went to New York City where he was a Fellow of the National Research Council for two years, specializing in biology at the College of Physicians and Surgeons of Columbia University. With this excellent background, Fisher started private practice in 1927. Later, he specialized in roentgenology and opened an X-ray laboratory. Fisher died on December 26, 1934 after his third operation for an intestinal ailment. He was survived by his wife, Jane Ryder Fisher, and a son, Hugh, who died in 1964.

Fisher's first story to be published, "City of Refuge," which appeared in *Atlantic Monthly* during February 1925, was written while he was still in medical school. A chronology of his published stories is given on p. 26. In addition to some stories that were never published, Fisher wrote two plays, "The Vici Kid" and "Golden Slippers," which were never published or produced. A dramatized version of his novel, *The Conjure Man Dies*, was produced posthumously by the Federal Theatre Players as their opening production at the Lafayette Theatre in New York on March 11, 1936.

According to Fisher's sister, the late Pearl M. Fisher: "Like·most writers, Dr. Fisher's ambition was to write the great Negro novel. His plan was to write a trilogy based on African backgrounds, life in a new land, and the modern social order as reflected in the lives of several generations of a Negro family."[1]

Langston Hughes noted that Fisher was a talented amateur musician, and it is true that he arranged some Negro spirituals which were never published. Hughes also captures part of Fisher's personality in this passage from his own autobiography:

> The wittiest of these New Negroes of Harlem, whose tongue was flavored with the sharpest and saltiest humor, was Rudolph Fisher. ... he was a young medical doctor and X-ray specialist, who always frightened me a little, because he could think of the most incisively clever things to say—and I could never think of anything to answer. He and Alain Locke together were great for intellectual wise-cracking. The two would fling big and witty words about with such swift and punning innuendo that an ordinary mortal just sat and looked wary for fear of being caught in a net of witticisms beyond his cultural ken.[2]

In a published version of the radio interview that took place after his mystery novel, *The Conjure Man Dies*, was published, Fisher does sound witty, intelligent, and sharp-witted—a thoroughly nice sort. Almost with tongue-in-cheek he says about the models for his fictional characters: "The Negro detective, for example, is suggested by an acquaintance of mine on the force. . . . There are perhaps a dozen in Harlem alone, one of whom is a lieutenant. . . . And the physician has an actual model."[3] Indeed, the physician appears to fit closely the description of Fisher, himself, but he was too fun-loving to admit this in a direct manner.

The interviewer on this WINS program, Miss Blizard, asked Fisher a question crucial for one's understanding of his point of view. The question: "What do you feel about Harlem as a cross-section of Negro life?" The reply: "I feel that Harlem is far more than that. Harlem is the epitome of American Negro life." Later, he said: "I intend to write whatever interests me. But if I should be fortunate enough to become known as Harlem's interpreter, I should be very happy."[4]

"Harlem's interpreter"—an expressed desire and a goal he achieved in all of his fiction as well as in his articles. The reading public responded to Fisher's role as a reflector of the life in the nation's black capital. One newspaperman wrote: "De Maupassant used Paris for his chess-board, while Fisher moves his dusky pawns over the field of Negro Harlem, a location quite as interesting as 'dear Paree.' "[5] At last, the reading public would be entertained with literature that reflected the informing spirit of the Afro-American race—the cultural *temenos*[6] sustaining the unique character of black life from country to town to city, in particular, Harlem. The model of life—the white life—was to be just another version of real life rather than the version that would overpower the black reality of living. Sometimes, of course, the evil or injustice evolving from what whites *could impose* upon blacks is treated with satiric strokes by Fisher, for example, in "High Yaller." Still, in his portraits of life in Harlem Fisher seems to have realized what Octavio Paz observed when he wrote about the majority and minority in Mexico: "Without otherness there is no oneness."[7] Fisher was, indeed, "Harlem's interpreter."

The revelation of life in Harlem and of its inhabitants by Fisher won the praise of many who had a genuine interest in the Negro. Mary White Ovington, the chairman of the board of directors of the N.A.A.C.P., wrote: "More than any other present day writer, Rudolph Fisher, to my mind, correctly interprets the Negro of today—his habits, his ways of thought, his idiosyncrasies."[8] Fisher's fascination with Harlem came with the times, and his only regrets seemed to be the effects of white incursion into Harlem's places of entertainment. He hoped that whites would venture to explore more than this obvious part of Harlem and learn to understand black life in general: "Maybe," he wrote, "they are at least learning to speak our language."[9] Not really, but as long as the writings of Rudolph Fisher exist, everyone, black and white, can learn to enjoy the sights and sounds of Negro Harlem during the 1920s. Despite what happened to him there, Harlem was the city that King Solomon Gillis first viewed with wide-eyed joy and fascination, saying he "Done died an' woke up in Heaven." It was a little of everything, and Fisher's canvases faithfully paint the people and places in its mosaic of dark and light hues.

The short stories of Rudolph Fisher have a sense of literary history behind them, for he ploughed in the same fields as the masters of this art, for example, Poe, Nikolay Gogol, and Henry James. There are times, indeed, when it seems that Fisher went from studying the nineteenth-century writers directly to his desk to write, ignoring contemporary practitioners. In an earlier review of Fisher's work, I noted that "Both stories ['City of Refuge' and 'Miss Cynthie'] illustrate Fisher's ability to transform life into art through control of characterization, plot, and diction, and insistence on a single effect at the story's conclusion."[10] Fisher was a traditionalist in form, then, but he was also one in point of view in his themes and in the values he stressed through the major characters he created. One might also venture to say that Fisher often wrote in the mode of dramatic comedies, eschewing tragedy even in the stories that end unhappily.

As Gilbert Murray states in *The Classical Tradition in Poetry*, Fisher wrote comedy in the classical sense as having at its core "a union of lovers." This re-creation of acts and emotions, or *mimesis*, moves from conflict to resolution within the very special milieu of black Harlem. The overall impression of Fisher's use of the short story form is one of engaging the reader in a positive, comic view of life which arises from the lyric impulse of wishing to sing mainly about triumph, about the possibility of being saved or renewed. Once again, to quote Murray: "Tragedies end in death. Comedies end in marriage."[11] He is not talking about a legal matter; rather, Murray is alluding to the joy that is issued from a harmonious end to the strife and conflict within the imaginative work. To allude to another treatise that concentrates upon poetry—and how well such examples serve Fisher's work—it seems he is seeking not only the melody but also the harmony, as Percy Bysshe Shelley wrote in his famous *Defence of Poetry*. One is always conscious of an ordered universe in Fisher's world; he writes about the ruptures that are brought on by disharmony—the disjointedness that must be replaced at the denouement by order.

Some important nonliterary elements in Fisher's stories should be noted because he emphasizes them consistently. He was a satirist and a social historian through the medium of the short story; thus, we have an accurate portrait of Harlem during the 1920s, whether or not one feels this is the function of imaginative literature. Fisher portrays the life of the "rats" and the "dickties"[12] as well as the criminal element and the ordinary wage-earner. We see how life is played out in the cabaret and at rent parties, and we witness the city version of religion, a religion struggling to recapture the joy and spontaneity of the "down home" mode of expression. As a critic of the city—the city as duper, the city as destroyer of the immigrated black—Fisher's stories act out the ritual of ruin some men and women suffered. The family unit is disrupted, as in "The Promised Land" or in "The South Lingers On"; others, seeking safety and freedom, like King Solomon Gillis ("City of Refuge"), find that exploitation, confinement, and racism are not limited to the South. In the "City of Refuge," Gillis encounters a new sort of racism, one that is explored in several Fisher stories: the prejudice of black against black, particularly the Afro-American against the British West Indian.

The relationship, or, more aptly, the animosity, between the American black and the West Indian black is portrayed sharply in several of Fisher's stories; indeed, this topic is the major element of conflict in "Ringtail." Sociologically, there were several reasons for this real and sometimes imagined dislike between the two groups. To many American blacks, it seemed that the West Indians were arrogant about their "British" background, and many West Indians, like Cyril Sebastian Best in "Ringtail," lorded this so-called advantage over American blacks. Also, it appeared that the West Indians who immigrated to the United States fared better economically and in a shorter length of time. As one character in "Ringtail" says: " ' . . . they stick too close together an' get ahead too fast. They put it all over us in too many ways. . . . same as ofays an' Jews.' " There was also the "Back to Africa" movement, which, carried on with parade and pomp, electrified the masses with a thesis none of them wanted in reality. Going back to Africa and "chasing monkeys" was not the dream of American blacks, and detractors had a ready-made phrase to coin about Marcus Garvey, leader and symbol of this abortive movement, "Monkey chasers." Garvey's fellow West Indians fell victims to the same appellation, and it is used privately to this day by many American blacks (and probably less privately in non-bourgeois society).

Strains of satire, light in most cases, lurk among the descriptions of life in Harlem. The picture of Cyril Sebastian Best ("Ringtail") is satirical, particularly at the opening when he is parading in his finery. Fisher mocks the concerns of the "dickties" for the false trappings of bourgeois habits, such as the So-and-So's Supper Dansant described in "Fire by Night." He mocks the fragility of the dickties further in this story when, at the height of a brawl at the "dansant," the women scurry to save their fur coats from invading pool hall scavengers: "girls who had saved for two years to buy seal wraps; wives who had wheedled for months to get a caracal like Mrs. Jones; women who had undertaken payment for their Persian lambs by instalments." Religious hypocrisy is exposed in "The Backslider," and there is even a hint of satire in the minor appearance of the Goldman brothers in "Miss Cynthie."

The imagery of a world of confinement and darkness—the black world on earth, not hell (although that is one point, i.e., that Harlem frequently is hell)—is Fisher's fictional domain. Sometimes no value judgment is implied in the painting he presents, for example, from "Ringtail," "The pavement flashed like a river in the sun"; however, usually there is an undergirding of Fisher principles and points of view in his images and figurative language. A large proportion of Fisher's imagery derive from his use of similes and metaphors: "the thoughts that gathered and throbbed like an abscess were suddenly incised" ("High Yaller"); the "roadster...snorted impatiently" ("Dust"); "A young bronze giant" ("Guardian"); the "ambulance gong was like receding derisive laughter" ("Ringtail"). In a comprehensive sense, the image we have of Harlem is one of "a stage upon which one looked as from an upper box" ("Guardian"). Fisher places Harlem in an open-air theater for the reader to view the high and low and the very fine Seventh Avenue as well as Lenox Avenue—"the boulevard of the unperfumed." In painting scenes with colors as well as with sound, Fisher gives the reader what Mammy, in "The Promised Land," sees from her window: "a screen upon which flashed a motion picture oddly alive and colorful." Often Fisher invests inanimate objects with human traits (e.g., the "key-board grinned evilly" from "Guardian") to indicate a point of view, the author's moral stance. The blacks frequently living in "hencoops," the whites downtown living in "kingly dwellings," the good and the bad, the common and the uncommon, the city itself—all are on a stage set up by Fisher to perform roles in a pageant of contrasts and disharmonies that will eventually end in an orderly resolution. It is difficult to categorize Fisher's treatment of the rent party phenomenon, whether it is sadness or satire when he writes, in "The Promised Land," "You provide music, your friends provide advertisement, and your guests, by paying admission, provide what your resources lack." Certainly, Fisher understood that the underlying reason for this northeastern version of the shindig was exploitation in most instances—paying more than a fair price for apartments. In any case, Fisher was unable to avoid the satiric touch from time to time in order to point out the meaninglessness of certain habits and concerns in the black community.

In highlighting the special qualities that composed the life in Harlem at every stratum, Fisher dramatically portrayed the obsession blacks had with their color. He turned this self-interest into an artistic mode that had moral as well as social implications. It has been noted by another critic that Fisher used color to identify good and bad characters: "the lighter the skin color the lower the moral character of the individual."[13] This differentiation is made in other of Fisher's stories, notably in "Blades of Steel" and "High Yaller." Fisher offers readers a gallery of good guys and bad ones, usually clearly designated by skin color, dark equaling good and yellow equaling the low-down cad. Consider, for example, the following characters:

> His coarse granular skin was dingy yellow and scarred. ("Fire by Night")

> Heredity had managed to withhold his rightful share of pigment

even from his hair, which was pale buff. His eyes were gray, their lids rimmed red.... the buff hair was woolly, the nose flat with wide nostrils, the mouth big, bordered by so-called liver lips, unbelievably thick. ("Blades of Steel")

Eight-ball ... was as dark as it is possible for skin to be, smooth and clean as an infant's ... the nose was broad but sharp-ridged, with sensitive nostrils, the lips thin and firm above a courageous chin. ("Blades of Steel")

Bus Williams' jolly round brown face beamed down on the crowd. ... but the cheese-colored countenance of Fessenden Baxter ... was totally oblivious to *She's Still My Baby*. ("Common Meter")

In between the absolute dark and light, we have women who are "amber" ("Common Meter"), "red-brown" ("Guardian of the Law"), or "golden-skinned" ("Miss Cynthie"). The women, in any case, are never black. The darkest woman of importance in Fisher's short stories is Effie Wright in "Blades of Steel," who is described as having an "almost luminous dark complexion called 'sealskin brown.' " With this obvious attention to color, Fisher reflects the self-consciousness of the decade toward the various shades of "blackness."

If one reads all of Fisher's stories at once, it might appear that the frequent conscious reference to color tends toward the paranoid. Indeed, the times were like that: self-discovery on the part of blacks and fascination as well as revulsion on the part of whites for the black world. It was a time, as Langston Hughes wrote, "when the Negro was in vogue," and a parallel fascination was attached to the contrast between white and black, especially skin color. Fisher was a literary portrait artist of his world and the times; therefore, his insistence upon emphasizing color consciousness is his way of being an accurate recorder of life as it was. As an American realist, this verisimilitude, embellished by the romantic imagination, accomplished the writer's aim: to entertain through an art with which the reader could identify.

The pernicious effects of color prejudice are unfolded as the primary subject in Fisher's 1925 story, "High Yaller." He goes the full length of demonstrating the effects of black prejudice toward a young Negro woman who has blue eyes, "fine lips ... delicate, high-bridged nose ... [and] white cheeks.... " In the end, she passes to the other side. At the beginning of the story, this young woman, Evelyn Brown ("nothing brown about her but her name!"), is discussing her plight with a fellow-worker, Jay Martin, who—incidentally—is dark brown. He is the admirable male character; the one to despise, Jimmy MacLoed, is a mulatto, lazy, amoral, and ungentlemanly. As they sit and talk, surrounded by dancing blacks, Evelyn and Jay are described as "two refugees"— an apt appellation for both by the time the story concludes. As a foreigner in her native land, Harlem, Evelyn takes the ostensibly easier path of passing. By escorting Evelyn for two weeks, in his role as the one who will make her acceptable to other blacks, Jay becomes disinherited and also is victimized when he is picked up by the police for going around with a "white" woman. In present-day America, even recognizing the deep-rooted prejudices of both blacks and whites, the preoccupation with skin color in a story like "High Yaller" may appear to be exaggerated and unrealistic. The present-day reader, however, must place his or her person in a period when skin color was an important issue. Even though, as E. Franklin Frazier points out, "During a decade or so following the first World War, in both northern and southern cities education and occupation increasingly supplanted family background and a light complexion,"[14] the color of one's skin was still a compelling matter in terms of social acceptance. Wallace Thurman's novel, The Blacker the Berry, albeit weak structurally, is another piece of Harlem Renaissance literature that treats this subject at great length. The subject of skin color was a preoccupation with many people during the 1920s, and Rudolph Fisher was one writer who was quite adept at capturing the power and effects of this topic.

It cannot be said that Fisher accomplished every goal he attempted in his short story writing, for there are some structural and linguistic imperfections that do not go undetected. In his balanced and sane approach to the difficulties in life, Fisher wanted to demonstrate the effects of illusion on individuals. People continually misread the motives of self and of others, thus scattering the seeds for conflict. Therefore, we have the necessary elements for a good story—action, reaction, and resolution. If the exposition complements these elements, then the production proceeds as it should to a successful ending. This did not always occur, however, in Fisher's stories; there are some apparent weaknesses.

One weakness, which appears to be derived from Fisher's occasional desire to preach or educate, is that of author intrusion. For instance, in "Dust," it seems, first, that Fisher is writing for a black audience, and, second, that he is not writing so much as preaching. This is one of his least effective stories because he succumbed to the urge to teach rather than to entertain; he did not move toward the effect he wanted; he commenced with it and rode it to death. Also, the insistent personification interrupts rather than helps the action; e.g., "the roadster jumped forward like a cruelly spurred horse, then laid back its ears and flattened itself out in a wild, headlong, heedless run." The reader nearly forgets this is a car. But Fisher's touch for irony is not lost, for the title of the story represents the futility of the main character's hatred. In a way, this person is very much like Ralph Merrit (in Fisher's novel The Walls of Jericho), who has a rabid hatred of whites. In "Dust," just as in the novel, the main character is shown the foolish and unpredictable results of prejudice and hatred: it is, as the character's girlfriend says, "such bitter fun."

Adopting the role of the totally omniscient author, of course, allowed Fisher to write as he pleased. Still, he was good enough as a short story writer to understand the necessity of removing unneeded words, the necessity of keeping the movement "tight"; yet, more than once, he placed himself as writer into the middle of a story. The naturalistic excess in describing Dirty Cozzens in "Blades of Steel" illustrates this point:

> So had heredity handed him over to environment, and environment had done its worst; had put sly cunning into the eyes, had distorted the lips into a constant sneer, had set the head at a truculent forward thrust on the large, lank body. With its present evil face, his was a head that might well have adorned the sceptre of Satan.

The same sort of excess, if more controlled, can be seen in this passage from "Ringtail":

> You need not stand on the opposite side of the Avenue and observe the disdain with which the Rosina looks down upon her neighbors. You have only to pass between her distinguishing gray-granite pillars with their protective, flanking grille-work and pause for a hesitant moment in the spacious hall beyond: ... To reach the elevator you must make between two lordly, contemptuous wall-mirrors, which silently deride you and show you how out of place you are.

Briefer, in "The Backslider," but also obtrusive, is the speculative section that follows the young man's expulsion from church:

> Whither may that man go on whom God had turned his back? To the Devil, sooner or later. It happened in Harlem, as elsewhere, that God and the Devil are neighbors—it is but the briefest step from the One to the other.

The same precision required by the fisherman in the drop of his line and in its tug and withdrawal when a fish is caught is required in the selection of the words for and the shaping of a short story—no matter how long it is (consider the length of some of James' stories!).

Another weakness was a general style of writing by formula, making a Fisher situation and/or ending predictable and sometimes too slick or facile. As one critic has written about "Common Meter": "To the cynical modern reader, the outcome is possible only in a fairy tale. The winner is the most noble and upright character, the jazz musician who prizes rhythm above all else and the man whose skin is darkest."[15] Of course, this conforms to Fisher's basic comic style, which anticipates the "happy ending." Then, the chance that the black escort in "High Yaller" would select the same theater that Evelyn Brown, now passing, would be in is stacking the deck in favor of the author's proving his point. Or, consider the insistence on an unhappy ending for the good guy in "Ringtail" hanging on the chance that the man would get crushed by the elevator in a building where he knew his enemy worked. Or, finally, consider the complete rescue scene in "Guardian of the Law," where a culprit waits around to be captured (would snuff in the eyes stop a really bad guy?), and an old grandmother's simple story is believed. All things are possible, yes, but there is also the need for imaginative complexity even in stories that are intended to be optimistic. On the other hand, how beautifully Fisher achieves this type of ending is demonstrated in a story like "Miss Cynthie," where the reconciliation between the ages grows naturally out of action preceding the story's ending.

Generally, however, Fisher went swiftly to the heart of his story—moved the reader into the conflict, clearly pointed to the cast of characters and their features, and concluded the story tidily—no doubt left in the mind of the reader concerning the meaning of the tale. Some stylistic stiffness in Fisher's expository mode sometimes impeded the smooth movement of the story, but this was an authentic feature of his writing. He was a decorous descendent of writers who wrote for "ladies and gentlemen," and this manner of writing frequently vitiated the effect he wished to produce. Take the following two examples, one brief, one longer:

> With Sam's blow he staggered back, shook his head as if in vigorous denial that any such thing had happened, then lunged precipitately forward. *The next moment saw him and Officer Sam embracing each other with enthusiasm* [my italics].
>
> Here they were indeed, a breathless Judy and *two looming envoys of the law, one black, one yellow, both extremely interested* [my italics]. ("Guardian of the Law")
>
> She was about to answer when a sharp, indecent epithet rent the wall of noise that had until then isolated them. Looking involuntarily up, Jay saw two youngsters, quarreling vituperatively. They were too close to be ignored, and, since dancing was at its height, no one else was about.
> "Excuse me a second," he said, rising before Evelyn could protest. ... The evident aggressor was a hard-looking little black youth of indefinite age,—perhaps sixteen actual years, plus the accumulated bonus of worldly wisdom which New York pays its children. He grew worse, word by word. ("High Yaller")

What these weaknesses demonstrate—primarily in his use of the Harlem version of black idiomatic language, self-conscious and often inflated—is Fisher's surrender to the heady expectations and aspirations of black writers during the 1920s. The Negro had been so poorly portrayed in the past that there was a genuine effort on the part of the Harlem Renaissance writers to correct the image of blacks in literature. Fisher was one writer—and it must be remembered that he was a full-time practicing physician—who attempted to portray all strata of Negro life, from the "rats" to the "dickties," and he achieved this goal more than any other writer (including Countee Cullen, who attempted to do this in his novel, One Way to Heaven). Certainly, Fisher's last short story to be published in his lifetime, "Miss Cynthie," leads one to postulate that he was moving closer to the real art of short fiction writing. As Robert Bone has noted, " 'Miss Cynthie' constitutes . . . a psychological as well as an artistic triumph. Published in the shadow of impending death, it testifies to Fisher's inner growth and aggravates our loss of his maturing powers."[16]

The importance of "Miss Cynthie" in the canon of Fisher literature does not obscure his lesser tales; but, this story is the exemplum of Fisher's overriding concern for the motifs of love and reconciliation, of harmonious union between opposing elements, and for that "union of lovers" in the most boundless sense. To say that "Class consciousness is perhaps the single most consistent theme in Fisher's work"[17] is to mistake the means with the goal. Other themes also blend in with Fisher's major concerns, such as the futility of prejudice (the irony of it, the waste), or the effects of the lure of the city upon people and the city's power to destroy individuals. Added to these themes is Fisher's employment of language to undergird the characterizations and settings. This wholeness of themes, characterizations, settings, and language exemplifies the concerns of Rudolph Fisher to render the life he witnessed and lived in the transformed manner of mimetic art through the short story.

Fisher is predictable and consistent in his language, descriptions, exposition, and dialogue. He uses words of confinement frequently, e.g., hencoop, airshaft, underground railroads, suffocation; he uses a religious vocabulary by having characters acutely aware of sinfulness; and finally, in his special forte, or, as some would have it, weakness, he uses the language of black Harlem, in Fisher's own words, "Contemporary Harlemese." As a glossary to his novel, The Walls of Jericho, Fisher explained the words used frequently by the blacks of this ghetto in the making. There is a certain amount of quaintness in some of the words, such as bring mud (to fall below expectation or disappoint); other words continue to have current use, such as hiney (the hindquarters); others have passed into oblivion, such as Martin (jocose designation of death); others, like *Freeby*, have been integrated. Some of the more frequently used words in Fisher's stories, however, were used to denote color, race, or position in society, e.g., fay, ofay, jig, boogy, rat, and dicky. Walter White disagreed with some of Fisher's definitions and argued that *boogy* is not a contraction of Booker T., but is "a Negrofication of the familiar 'boogaboo,' " and that *ofay* "is Aframericanization of the French 'au fait' and comes into Negro use from New Orleans."[18]

It may be partially due to Fisher's background as a minister's son that his language and moral tone represent a traditional Protestant, black-oriented religious viewpoint expressed through various characters, mostly through older women but also, as in "High Yaller," through one younger black in his twenties who represents the homey virtues of hard work and traditional family values.

The usual character, however, who epitomized the Protestant ethic was the black mammy archetype presented in varying situations in Fisher's stories: the nearly silent mother in "High Yaller," Mammy in "The Promised Land," Grammie in "Guardian of the Law," and Miss Cynthie in the story of the same name. There is some variety in their points of view, however, from Mammy's complete rejection of the city, to Grammie's sure, shrewd knowledge and acceptance of the city as her home. In the middle, there is the best realized character Fisher created in short fiction—Miss Cynthie.

The preserver of values in a world of chaos has been a traditional role given to women, especially by writers who have developed from a strong Christian background. Among Fisher's black contemporaries, this tendency is evident in the work of Langston Hughes and Countee Cullen, for example, Aunt Hagar in *Not Without Laughter* and Mattie in *One Way to Heaven*. In Fisher's work there is, one senses, a writer of gallantry and gentility overseeing his own productions. As guiders of moral principles, the women in Fisher's stories are direct in their pronouncements about right and wrong. As Miss Cynthie says, "Always mind the house o' the Lord—whatever you do, do like a church-steeple: aim high and go straight." Even a woman on the margin of respectability, such as Lil, the entertainer at the Rodent ("The Backslider"), preserves a sense of integrity and aids the protagonist to eschew the first downward step to thievery and possibly much worse.

In two stories, both weakened by a contrived plot, "Blades of Steel" and "Guardian of the Law," the women are portrayed as the helpmates of men who have the physical strength to protect themselves but are held in compromised situations. In "Guardian," it is the grandmother who—incredulously—creates a situation that saves her grandson from disciplinary action within the first six months of his career as a policeman. In "Blades," the woman helps her beloved twice in the same day; yet she performs her ultimate saving act in a manner that keeps her man immune from the criticism that he is unable to save himself from on his own. Indeed, a sense of oneness is attained between the man and woman—a state that might not have arrived as quickly without the conflict the man faces.

Two other grandmothers are quite differently portrayed; one has dimension, the other does not. Mammy, in "The Promised Land," is unbending and unyielding in her religion. She hates the city for what it has done to her grandsons, and she is unable to control her anger and sorrow against the steel and granite which seem to have been transferred from the buildings into the hearts of her grandchildren. In a poignant outburst, she cries: "New York. Harlem. Thought all along 't was d' las stop 'fo' Heaven. Canaan hitself. Reg'lar promis' lan'. Well, dat's jes' whut 't is—a promis' lan'. All it do is promise. Promise money lak growin' on trees—ain' even got d' trees." As a vessel for the faith and good life, Mammy suffers and is unable to "save" her grandsons.

On the other hand, Miss Cynthie represents the strong example of virtue and the principled life that spreads a delightful aura and downright good humor to all who encounter her. Miss Cynthie knows that evil lurks everywhere, but she also knows that where there is bad, the good is nearby for those who seek it. As she says when arriving in New York for the first time: "First trip any place, son. First time I been over fifty mile from Waxhaw. Only travelin' I've done is in my head. Ain' seen many places, but I's seen a passel o' people. Reckon places is pretty much alike after people been in 'em awhile." She represents a unification of moral and religious principles and common sense. As old as she is, she has the capacity to accept different codes of behavior and styles of life, as long as they do not offend basic and immutable God-given tenets. This is why she is able to bridge the generational gap she perceived first as an irreparable breech to mend. It is through revelation that a transformation occurs in Miss Cynthie, a revelation necessary for the reconciliation between the old and the new to be effected.[19]

The setting comes close to being the determining factor in the breech-alienation-reconciliation between David and Miss Cynthie. Actually, the setting operates as the valve that opens the floodgate of doubts Miss Cynthie has been carrying with her since before her arrival. From this point, it is a synthesis of the landscape and the underlying meaning of it—the vision of the Afro-American's past nourishing the descendants of those black toilers in the fields of slavery. The black person's durability is portrayed, as well as the race's love for joy and gaiety. Still, it is the poetry of singing and dancing—Molpé in its clearest form—that casts a spell upon the old woman and reawakens a sense of the past and present fusing: a vision facing her of "a series of harmonies," with a chorus singing before the sun, "the two, as if emanating from a single source." God-made, God-enriched.

But Fisher imposes the artistry he has as a writer moving toward the complexities that enrich a piece of fiction—disruption and dislocation of the quick adjustment to an alien situation. Miss Cynthie is made aware again of where she is when "The very music that had just rounded out so majestically now distorted itself into ragtime." Miss Cynthie must go through another trial, a greater one than being in the theater itself which she entered reluctantly, "like an early Christian martyr." She must witness her beloved grandson, the man she wanted to be "a preacher or a doctor" or, at least, an undertaker, perform his flashy dance and song routine. The wildness of the scene shakes Miss Cynthie to her soul's depth, for she sees him "turned tool of the devil, disciple of lust, unholy prince among sinners." It is only when she discovers the racial and spiritual connection, the link between the past and the present, that an inner transformation occurs, and Miss Cynthie realizes that the gifts of God to her, indeed, have been transmitted to David. And he, in his art, spreads the seeds of his past in a new form—a dance and song that is joyful in its celebration of the rituals of black life. If what David performs is authentic, then it is not untrue to the heritage he carries within himself. The reconciliation between David and Miss Cynthie, then, represents an authentication of the black life practiced in the city—a modus vivendi that is an extension and reshaping of the Southern agrarian life that is the Afro-American's veritable homeland.

The total integration of all elements into the writing of a story like "Miss Cynthie" is not exemplified in the other stories, with the close exception of the mystery story "John Archer's Nose," which illustrates the genre. But Fisher demonstrates efforts to control the components of a good story; his very facility with language sometimes hinders him from achieving his total design. With varying degrees of success, three other early stories by Fisher illustrate his major preoccupations that culminated in the publication of "Miss Cynthie."

Two stories published during 1927 in *McClure's Magazine*, "The Backslider" and "Fire by Night," are both undergirded by the religious life and beliefs of blacks, challenged by the putative glitter of Harlem. The all-encompassing keystone to his motifs, however, love and reconciliation, are integral to these stories. In both cases, the reconciliation is redemptive: in "The Backslider," the battle is with the self; in "Fire by Night," the conflict has the added dimension of healing a rift between a father and son. The technical problems in narrating the stories center around Fisher's use of coincidence, particularly at the end of "Fire by Night." Both stories start similarly, in Fisher's Harlem-personified mode—the church in one story, the club in the other. The woman in each story is the catalyst that spurs the lost soul into an action that leads him back to his true self, to God, and to a meaningful relationship with loved ones. Fisher stresses the significance of the old-time values that need not become lost in the big city; indeed, these values are the link with the past, with the South that sustains and nourishes the transplanted Negro. This is the meaning, in fact, of the group of sketches that Fisher entitled, "The South Lingers On,"[20] where "he has shown Harlem to be, not the fun city of downtown white thrillseekers, but, actually, a transplanted Southern community, bigger and brassier, of course, but still essentially a slice of the South."[21] In other words, the spirit that informs the literature of Fisher is both the visible and invisible history of the black man's past.

Not every Fisher character gets redeemed, of course; even so, there is an upbeat quality about the end of most of his stories. This occurs in Fisher's often-reprinted story of a newcomer's experiences in Harlem—"The City of Refuge." This is another of his stories, even at this early stage in his writing career, that demonstrates Fisher's concern with the shape of the genre. The action and complication of the situation mount to a climax in a carefully orchestrated series of scenes in six sections. It is a story of being duped by man and the city; it is a story of entrapment. And, once again, the language Fisher uses points directly to the outcome of the story; for example, when Gillis tells Mouse Uggams he will be in Harlem "Till I die," Gillis symbolically announces his own doom. After he is arrested by the police, even though Gillis is happy that one of them is "cullud," he is figuratively dead to the sort of life he had dreamed for himself.

The fate of Gillis is prefigured in the opening passage of the story when he is "swept blindly along for a time, and at last abruptly dumped." When Gillis finds he has been blind to the true character of Uggams, who literally dumps him, and has become a victim of the city, no longer a refuge of safety, he holds on to the only optimistic element in his capture—his being taken in by a "cullud" policeman. Despite this somewhat upbeat closing, Fisher has not romanticized Harlem for the reader: It is Gillis who is duped yet undefeated. But the reader is given clues all the way through the story that point to a view that the writer has no illusions about the Harlem of the King Solomon Gillises of this world. For example, the description of where Gillis has a room places him in his proper Harlem milieu: "in a room half the size of his hencoop back home, with a single window opening into an airshaft. . . . an airshaft: cabbage and chitterlings cooking . . . waste noises, waste odors . . . pollution from bottom to top—a sewer of sounds and smells." This description, from section II of the story, ends symbolically with Gillis' saying, "Even got cullud policemans!" just as he marvels the same at the end when he is carried off from the cabaret. Interestingly, this same section starts with the plan, by Uggams, to trap Gillis; he is a man surrounded by enclosures.

"City of Refuge" demonstrates Fisher's concern for the tidy progression of a tale from beginning to middle to end; six sections of the story each lead Gillis closer to his fate. Just as he emerges like Jonah from the whale into Harlem (after being in the "hell" of the subway), he is caught at the end in a cabaret, which is another hell—and truly the place for the lost victims of the city, such as Gillis.

The end of "The City of Refuge" reflects the tendency of the modern short story, starting in the 1920s in fact, to place the protagonist in a situation where he receives some illumination to the truth of his actual plight—a mini-epiphany, as it were—a moment of obvious reversed fortunes but without the insight into his own flawed character as one would have in Aristotelian tragedy. There is passivity in King Solomon's acceptance of his "mistakes"; that his character has weaknesses does not occur to this protagonist, however. In this fashion, Fisher was certainly part of the mainstream of short story writers during his period of creativity—a time when there was, in short story writing, an underplaying of plot, reversals, total change, or complete insight into the self (or a need to do anything about an internal problem when it was discovered). In part, then, Fisher was writing in the mode of his contemporaries. The fact that "The City of Refuge" has a comic rather than a tragic ending, also, does not lessen the emotional poignancy of Gillis' situation, unless, of course, the reader finds untenable Gillis' naïveté and gullibility.

Any body of literature speaks for itself better than an explicator, just as the source of a waterway determines its basic character before it flows and eddies to distant and diverse places. The short fiction of Rudolph Fisher stands on its own as examples of a genre conceptually emphasizing a unified impression, a concept adhered to by Fisher.[22] His world was a realistic one, also, even though it was not unknown for him to use the dream. Still, it is not a dreamworld, or one beneath the surface of reality that he paints; rather, Fisher brings reality into the dream and ignores the concept of submerging the conscious into the truths of the subconscious. His is a very straightforward, rather uncomplicated world.

There were the unhappy results of prejudice, to be sure, but not at the level of tragedy. Even though Fisher pursued a form not greatly practised by a large segment of his contemporary black writers, Fisher was not an artist who was haunted or lonely; he did not dredge up tales, no matter how poignant, infused with, in Frank O'Connor's words, "an intense awareness of human loneliness."[23] Yet, Fisher captures the varied spirit of the Negroes who lived or came to Harlem during the 1920s—harnessed the informing spirit that was a combination of the religious and the secular.

The shared tradition of life-styles, language, habits, interests—whatever gave a sense of uniqueness to black life, transposed into a city setting—became material for Fisher's art. Even Harlem was more than a city within a city, became many characters, was personified and transformed into its varied guises—saint and sinner, trickster and holy man, "rat" and "dickty." As a place personified, the city becomes the character that disappoints or destroys the ordinary black who has migrated there. As a destroyer of a family relationship, it is depicted in "The Promised Land"; as a dupe to the innocent, it pervades many of Fisher's tales, in particular "The City of Refuge." In attempting to escape the confines of southern black life, King Solomon Gillis seeks salvation in Harlem only to be caught in the vise of ineluctable entrapment set by the parasitic persons created by such cities as New York. As a refuge from poverty and oppression, New York fails Gillis; as a city where blacks still have more opportunity than in the South, however, a ray of optimism prevails.

Optimism is integral to the fiction of Fisher—a bourgeois-based belief that an optimistic philosophy of life, a firm Christian faith, and a clear comprehension finally of human needs and motives can result in a harmonious conclusion to life's inversions. Because Fisher's aim was to be instructor as well as interpreter, this adoption of a positive and sanguine attitude gave him a limited point of view and made some of his work press too hard upon "a willing suspension of disbelief." Rather than demonstrating alienation from or despair with his group, even when satirizing his race, Fisher chose to construct his stories around moral principles that served to emphasize the redemptive spirit. As in the case of all writers, of course, the choice was his to make, but the choice vitiated the effectiveness of his avowed wish to be an interpreter of his people.

The intent of his writing, however, cannot be overlooked at any time, and, because he kept his aim clearly in mind, he succeeded. In a sense, he made the leap from individualizing his artistic concerns to informing about a group experience in his literary corpus. He sought to apply universal qualities to a special group and, thus, tamed "The artist's struggle with his vocation . . . a version of a universal human struggle: of genius with Genius, and of genius with genius loci (spirit of place)."[24] And in demonstrating a manner of bond between his characters and their setting, Fisher captured the cultural temenos of that black capital.

What we have in Fisher's stories, then, is a polished portrait of the varied life in Harlem written in a quick, sometimes witty, sometimes satiric, sometimes acerbic style. The conflicts between social and moral questions inform many of Fisher's stories ("The Backslider," "High

Yaller," or "The Promised Land") which highlight his aim to be not only entertaining, but enlightening as well. The social historian works hand in hand with the creative artist; the man of conscience stands behind the stories. A descendant of Emerson, Fisher stresses in his stories the notion that the God-loving, God-fearing person can triumph over adversity. If the short story is, as Mark Schorer has said, "an art of moral revelation" (whereas the novel is "an art of moral evolution"),[25] Fisher accomplished what he wished as an artist practising this literary genre. His keen observations of life and manners in Harlem, couched in a literary form, demonstrate his very American concern for probing the flaws in our character, flaws that he felt could be ameliorated. The personal conflicts of his characters illustrate—once again, a major American concern—the problems stemming from belief versus action; a testing, it seems of the theory of the American way of life versus the reality of how life is acted out day by day.

Unlike many of the white writers during the 1920s (e.g., Sherwood Anderson and Ernest Hemingway), who frequently had protagonists who were unattractive and second-rate, Fisher for the most part eschewed this sort of character in a principal role and emphasized the redeeming features of the good guy. (One prominent exception is "Ringtail," where it is not clear, it seems to me, what attitude Fisher has or what the precise point of a story such as this one is, where the main character certainly succeeds in evildoing.) But, in each case where there is a repugnant individual in a Fisher story, a contrasting figure is in the balance to represent the author's moral point of view. This, too, is an essential element of his art—to make sure that nothing is left to reader inference: Characters, setting, theme, point of view, and resolution of the plot come together in a conclusion calculated tidily to furnish a panorama of Harlem by a master interpreter of black life in this mecca of multicolored inhabitants.

NOTES

1. Biographical information written by Miss Fisher for the Schomburg Collection is in the Rudolph Fisher file (microfiche) at the New York P. L. Schomburg Center for Research in Black Culture.

2. Langston Hughes, *The Big Sea* (New York: Hill & Wang, 1940), 240–41.

3. John Louis Clarke, "Mystery Writer Is Interviewed over the Radio," *Pittsburgh Courier* (January 21, 1933).

4. Ibid.

5. The Cameraman, "Colorful 'Movies,' " *New York Amsterdam News* (September 7, 1927).

6. A "mode of associations" between a people in a certain place. See also the concluding portion of this section, in particular the discussion before note 23.

7. Octavio Paz, The Other Mexico: Critique of the Pyramid (New York: Grove, 1972), 75.

8. Mary White Ovington, "Book Chat," N.A.A.C.P. Press Release, September 21, 1928.

9. Rudolph Fisher, "The Caucasian Storms Harlem," American Mercury 11 (August 1927): 398.

10. Margaret Perry, Silence to the Drums: A Survey of the Literature of the Harlem Renaissance (Westport, Conn.: Greenwood Press, 1976), 112.

11. Gilbert Murray, The Classical Tradition in Poetry (New York: Russell and Russell, 1927), 38.

12. "Rats" ("Antithesis of dickty"—Fisher; a lower class person); "dickty" (a "swell; High-toned person."—Fisher). Fisher put these definitions at the end of his novel, The Walls of Jericho.

13. Thomas Friedmann, "The Good Guys in the Black Hats: Color Coding in Rudolf [sic] Fisher's 'Common Meter,' " Studies in Black Literature 7 (Winter 1976): 8.

14. E. Franklin Frazier, Black Bourgeoisie (New York: The Free Press, c1957), 198–99.

15. Thomas Friedmann, "The Good Guys in the Black Hats."

16. Robert A. Bone, Down Home: A History of Afro-American Short Fiction from Its Beginning to the End of the Harlem Renaissance (New York: G.P. Putnam's Sons, 1975), 159.

17. Oliver Louis Henry, "Rudolph Fisher: An Evaluation," Crisis 78, no. 5 (July 1971): 150.

18. Walter White, "A Fine Novel of Negro Life," New Statesman 5 (August 1928): 7.

19. It is interesting to note that Fisher originally intended the relationship between David and Ruth to be questionable—unmarried but living together, or married without public awareness. The manuscript version at Brown University does not make this absolutely clear, although it appears to imply they were not married and that Miss Cynthie, noticing this, just winks at the notion. Fisher, or his editor, must have realized how uncharacteristic it would be for Miss Cynthie to ignore such a relationship, as well as illogical for David to risk this type of situation when he was faced with getting Miss Cynthie to approve of his profession.

20. Rudolph Fisher, "The South Lingers On," Survey Graphic 53, no. 11 (March 1, 1925): 644–47. The same sketches, minus the second one, appeared in Alain Locke's The New Negro under the title of "Vestiges: Harlem Sketches."

21. Arthur P. Davis, From the Dark Tower: Afro-American Writers 1900–1960 (Washington, D.C.: Howard University Press, 1974), 100.

22. Let it be clear that I am not saying that more contemporary or enlarging theories for the short story do not exist; for Fisher's work, however, they do not. Also, I should stress, perhaps more than I have, that wholeness and harmony were his aims, which may not always be the same as unity of effect but nevertheless appear to be in Fisher's stories, or so it seems to me.

23. Frank O'Connor, The Lonely Voice. A Study of the Short Story (Cleveland: World, 1963), 19.

24. Geoffrey Hartman, "Toward Literary History," in Beyond Formalism

(New Haven: Yale University Press, 1970), 372. Since I am not a literary historian, I am indebted to Robert Stepto and Henry Louis ("Skip") Gates for introducing me to this concept.

25. Mark Schorer, ed., *The Story, A Critical Anthology* (New York: Prentice-Hall, 1950), 433.

THE UNPUBLISHED STORIES

The four manuscripts of unpublished Fisher stories, located at Brown University (in Archives, John Hay Library), demonstrates the same fictional concerns one finds in his published material: the city as destroyer ("Lost Love Blues") and duper ("Across the Airshaft") or false promiser ("The Lindy Hop" and "Lost Love Blues"); Harlem as a black metropolis where, as King Solomon Gillis observed, "black was white" ("The Man Who Passed");[1] the problems between age and the view of youth ("Lindy Hop"); the innocent country black, like Gillis, confronted with the complexities and hardness of city life ("Lost Love Blues"); the importance of the black mammy archetype in Negro life ("The Lindy Hop"); and the criminal element in Harlem ("The Man Who Passed"). The tone is also typical of Fisher, optimistic and upbeat, and the good characters succeed over the bad. There are no surprises in these stories.[2]

The weakest of these stories is "The Man Who Passed"; Fisher seems to have created too artificial a situation. In reading the story, it is hard to believe in the plot Fisher has constructed; the reasons causing the events are not really plausible. A white reporter is assigned to write an in-depth article about Harlem by posing as a Negro. If the protagonist, Perryn Joel, possessed the personality of Carl Van Vechten, or even had an interest in Negroes, one could believe in Joel. This thin, unreal character, who knows nothing about Negroes and who does not particularly like them, is found out right away by a black Joel approaches for information about renting a room. This black, the same Tom Edwards readers find in "The City of Refuge," is still involved in questionable enterprises that an undercover policeman, which if Joel were one as is first suspected, would be interested in. To call attention to a parallel, a character in "The Man Who Passed," resembling Mouse

Uggams ("City of Refuge"), says to Edwards, "You got a head, chief," just as Mouse says nearly the same to Edwards, "Chief, you got a head, no lie." Joel's contact with Edwards is too pat, and the same can be said of the end where a favorite Fisher device is used—the female as the agent of rescue helps Joel; she also serves to reflect Fisher's traditional bias about the role the woman plays in life. As the young woman, Roanne, says to Joel on the day after his frightening adventures: "What I did last night, any woman would do without stopping to think." Her basic goodness simply does not permit her prejudiced and hating heart to become a party to the group of men who devise a setup for Joel so he can be killed. At the end, when Joel prepares to leave Harlem, both he and the girl have had a link removed from their individual chains of prejudice. Joel leaves by subway, the way countless blacks have found their way to Harlem, leaves a little awkwardly as he "fumbled in his pocket for a nickel."

Fisher found better ways, to be sure, to demonstrate the variety and richness of Harlem than to use a white outsider such as Perryn Joel. In "Lost Love Blues," the reader is confronted immediately with the vibrant local color of a hot Eighth Avenue broiling "under Negro Harlem's sun." One suspects it is hotter there than in the rest of New York City. This love story illustrates how Harlem fails to fulfill the promise of those who come seeking happiness there. A young couple from Waxhaw, Jed and his wife, with the warm, spicy name of Cinnamon, are the protagonists of this tale. The city seems not only to diminish them as persons but also poisons their relationship instead of making them happy. Jed cannot keep a job, which finally drives Cinnamon to an outburst of anger she regrets almost immediately, but she and Jed must go through more trials before the breach is healed. Their reconciliation is complicated by a setup manufactured by their landlady, Addie, and her jaundiced-colored husband, Strut. Once again, a setup, too pat for credence, is contrived, but Jed falls for it and learns nearly too late the erroneousness of his thinking. (Years later Fisher used a similar situation in "John Archer's Nose" in which a grief-stricken father seeks revenge from the person responsible for selling a poison potion.) That Jed accidentally hears Strut brag about the frame-up (without first being sure that Jed is dead) is no less credible than the end when Cinnamon's voice, singing "Love Lost Blues," keeps Jed from shooting Strut. The happy ending ignores the deeper problems—life in Harlem and the actual stability of the marriage relationship—and focuses on the elements of luck and chance.

This is true, too, of the story entitled "Across the Airshaft," in which right and justice triumph through coincidence and luck. The effective opening—the mood is established objectively through the actions of the protagonist—is quickly dispelled by the plot that unfolds. A rent col-

lector, Rip Halliday, has been robbed of his day's collection, and he is
certain his boss will not believe the truth. As Halliday enacts a scene
in his mind of his future encounter with his boss, the woman in the
room "across the airshaft" attracts his attention. Her tale of woe, which
he hears and sees acted before his shamelessly curious eyes, moves
him to forget his own troubles and leads him to aid her by tossing
money, unseen by the distressed woman, "across the airshaft" on to
her bed so she can pay her back rent to her evil landlady (whose name,
Devlin, comes close to sounding like devil). Before the girl can act upon
his generosity, the villain enters: a man who is sent by the landlady to
get the young woman started in crime and prostitution. The hero, however, after finding out that this man is the same one who held him up,
interferes and rescues the woman and the stolen money, and the two
of them run off unharmed to the lower part of Manhattan. There, in a
restaurant, they discover one another, discuss their situations, and,
presumably, start falling in love. A job will be opening in Rip's office,
so the young woman will soon have a job through Rip's good services.
Everything ends tidily and properly because the hero and heroine are
honest, honorable people. Evil surrounds them but does not contami-
nate them as it has the innocents from Waxhaw: Those who have grown
up in the city and have escaped the evil (like Jay Martin in "High
Yaller") are Fisher's models of conformity, a model that reaches its
apogee, perhaps, in Linda of *The Walls of Jericho.*

One disconcerting feature of "Across the Airshaft" is why Rip had
never noticed this young woman before this incident. During the story,
he hears everything that is said in the room. This flaw may be one
reason the story was not marketable.

The dialogue is good; Fisher usually succeeds in this area of his craft,
although sometimes conversation between good people is stiff and too
conventional (e.g., at the end of "Across the Airshaft").

Extensive changes were not made in these three stories; indeed, "The
Man Who Passed" has the air of an abandoned story, with its three
crossed out titles. "Lost Love Blues" is kept in a professional typing
service folder, and the word "market" is written in pencil on the cover,
but the handwriting more closely resembles Pearl Fisher's handwriting
than Rudolph Fisher's.

The last of these unpublished manuscripts, "The Lindy Hop," appears in two typed interpretations and one handwritten manuscript,
which served as an interim copy for the revised version. The first version is in a professional typing service folder and apparently was sent
to either a magazine or to a reader of some kind, for penciled comments
by an unrecognizable hand indicate some dissatisfaction with the dance
hall scenes and the ending. In an attempt to date the story, my conjec-
ture is, based on knowledge of Fisher's addresses which appear on

both typed manuscripts, that the first version was written ca. 1928 and the final one was worked on between that year and 1933 or even possibly as late as 1934, the year when Fisher died.

The two versions vary significantly, above all in the ending which is greatly improved in the final copy. The ending still is not entirely satisfactory, however, because the moral animosity of the grandmother is undercut by her own dramatic behavior of dancing at the story's conclusion. Her near heart attack acts as the symbol of her granddaughter's fate if she pursues the career of a "dance hall gal," trading her talent for tickets from men some of whom will later demand more than a dance. The views of age and youth clash, but the wisdom of the old wins in much the same way as old craftiness succeeds in "Guardian of the Law."

Fisher clearly captures the setting of the music hall and the restlessness of the young, their frenzy and vulnerability, as well as the gaudy pretentiousness of the music hall building. The final version also emphasizes the link between the past and the present, the authentication of the shared heritage—in this instance, again, as in "Miss Cynthie," through music and the dance. As Fisher writes: "Five hundred pairs of eyes set themselves on that strange collaboration, in which there was some meaning and purpose beyond the figure of the moment." So, there is harmony and reconciliation at the end in a story that contains Fisher's strongest features of good characterization, effective dialogue, and a sure and vivid handling of scene and setting.

These four unpublished stories offer the Fisher scholar a deeper, if not broader, view of his work as a short story artist. Even in the weakest of the four, "The Man Who Passed," many of Fisher's constant and consistent concerns and features are present: the delineation of the variety of Negroes one finds in Harlem (in color as well as in type), the subtle relationship between the criminal and noncriminal elements in Harlem, and his traditional handling of the female character.

There is, nevertheless, a great deal of work to be accomplished before Rudolph Fisher's work is completely known to scholars. As his sister wrote in the obituary she submitted to various institutions, "Even during his last illness in December of 1934, whenever his strength permitted, he worked on a story which had been requested by *Esquire* depicting the exploits of a Negro soldier during World War I." This story, "War Hero," is in the possession of Fisher's widow, written in pencil on crumbling yellow paper. Whatever fragment survives will be of great interest to Fisher scholars. It would be useful, as well, to have a printed edition of each version of "The Lindy Hop" to study the changes Fisher made in closer detail. In other words, this collection of stories and the comments upon them is far from being a coda to productions of this nature. The latch of the gate for this area has still other keys somewhere out there for opening into this fertile field.

NOTES

1. This manuscript has three titles, two that can be read easily—"The Man Who Passed" and "False Face"—and one in pencil that looks as if it could be "Incident in Harlem." All three titles have been crossed out. "The Man Who Passed" will be used in this discussion.

2. The main discovery of the manuscript material has been cited in the discussion of "Miss Cynthie" (see note 19 of the Introduction).

Since "The City of Refuge" was Fisher's first published story, written when he was in medical school, I am assuming that "The Man Who Passed" is a later story. It is not dated, however, and may have been written at the beginning of Fisher's writing career. Certainly, he never again used a white as the focus of a story.

THE PUBLISHED STORIES

CHRONOLOGY

1933:   "Ezekiel Learns"
              (*Junior Red Cross News*, February)

              "Guardian of the Law"
              (*Opportunity*, March)

              "Miss Cynthie"
              (*Story*, June)

1935:   "John Archer's Nose"
              (*The Metropolitan: A Review*, January)

The City of Refuge

Confronted suddenly by daylight, King Solomon Gillis stood dazed and blinking. The railroad station, the long, white-walled corridor, the impassible slot-machine, the terrifying subway train—he felt as if he had been caught up in the jaws of a steam-shovel, jammed together with other helpless lumps of dirt, swept blindly along for a time, and at last abruptly dumped.

There had been strange and terrible sounds: "New York! Penn Terminal—all change!" "Pohter, hyer, pohter, suh?" Shuffle of a thousand soles, clatter of a thousand heels, innumerable echoes. Cracking rifle-shots—no, snapping turnstiles. "Put a nickel in!" "Harlem? Sure. This side—next train." Distant thunder, nearing. The screeching onslaught of the fiery hosts of hell, headlong, breath-taking. Car doors rattling, sliding, banging open. "Say, wha' d'ye think this is, a baggage car?" Heat, oppression, suffocation—eternity—"Hundred'n turdy-fif' next!" More turnstiles. Jonah emerging from the whale.

Clean air, blue sky, bright sunlight.

Gillis set down his tan-cardboard extension-case and wiped his black, shining brow. Then slowly, spreadingly, he grinned at what he saw: Negroes at every turn; up and down Lenox Avenue, up and down One Hundred and Thirty-Fifth Street; big, lanky Negroes, short, squat Negroes; black ones, brown ones, yellow ones; men standing idle on the curb, women, bundle-laden, trudging reluctantly homeward, children rattle-trapping about the sidewalks; here and there a white face drifting along, but Negroes predominantly, overwhelmingly everywhere. There was assuredly no doubt of his whereabouts. This was Negro Harlem.

Back in North Carolina Gillis had shot a white man and, with the aid of prayer and an automobile, probably escaped a lynching. Carefully avoiding the railroads, he had reached Washington in safety. For his car a Southwest bootlegger had given him a hundred dollars and directions to Harlem; and so he had come to Harlem.

Ever since a traveling preacher had first told him of the place, King Solomon Gillis had longed to come to Harlem. The Uggams were always talking about it; one of their boys had gone to France in the draft and, returning, had never got any nearer home than Harlem. And there were occasional "colored" newspapers from New York: newspapers that mentioned Negroes without comment, but always spoke of a white person as "So-and-so, white." That was the point. In Harlem, black was white. You had rights that could not be denied you; you had privileges, protected by law. And you had money. Everybody in Harlem had money. It was a land of plenty. Why, had not Mouse Uggam sent back as much as fifty dollars at a time to his people in Waxhaw?

The shooting, therefore, simply catalyzed whatever sluggish mental reaction had been already directing King Solomon's fortunes toward Harlem. The land of plenty was more than that now: it was also the city of refuge.

Casting about for direction, the tall newcomer's glance caught inevitably on the most conspicuous thing in sight, a magnificent figure in blue that stood in the middle of the crossing and blew a whistle and waved great white-gloved hands. The Southern Negro's eyes opened wide; his mouth opened wider. If the inside of New York had mystified him, the outside was amazing him. For there stood a handsome, brass-buttoned giant directing the heaviest traffic Gillis had ever seen; halting unnumbered tons of automobiles and trucks and wagons and pushcarts and street-cars; holding them at bay with one hand while he swept similar tons peremptorily on with the other; ruling the wide crossing with supreme self-assurance; and he, too, was a Negro!

Yet most of the vehicles that leaped or crouched at his bidding carried white passengers. One of these overdrove bounds a few feet and Gillis heard the officer's shrill whistle and gruff reproof, saw the driver's face turn red and his car draw back like a threatened pup. It was beyond belief—impossible. Black might be white, but it couldn't be that white!

"Done died an' woke up in Heaven," thought King Solomon, watching, fascinated; and after a while, as if the wonder of it were too great to believe simply by seeing, "Cullud policemans!" he said, half aloud; then repeated over and over, with greater and greater conviction, "Even got cullud policemans—even got cullud—"

"Where y'want to go, big boy?"

Gillis turned. A little, sharp-faced yellow man was addressing him. "Saw you was a stranger. Thought maybe I could help y'out."

King Solomon located and gratefully extended a slip of paper. "Wha' dis hyeh at, please, suh?"

The other studied it a moment, pushing back his hat and scratching his head. The hat was a tall-crowned, unindented brown felt; the head was brown patent-leather, its glistening brush-back flawless save for a suspicious crimpiness near the clean-grazed edges.

"See that second corner? Turn to the left when you get there. Number forty-five's about halfway the block."

"Thank y', suh."

"You from—Massachusetts?"

"No, suh, Nawth Ca'lina."

"Is 'at so? You look like a Northerner. Be with us long?"

"Till I die," grinned the flattered King Solomon.

"Stoppin' there?"

"Reckon I is. Man in Washin'ton 'lowed I'd find lodgin' at dis address."

"Good enough. If y' don't, maybe I can fix y' up. Harlem's pretty crowded. This is me." He proffered a card.

"Thank y', suh," said Gillis, and put the card in his pocket.

The little yellow man watched him plod flat-footedly on down the street, long awkward legs never quite straightened, shouldered extension-case bending him sidewise, wonder upon wonder halting or turning him about. Presently, as he proceeded, a pair of bright-green stockings caught and held his attention. Tony, the storekeeper, was crossing the sidewalk with a bushel basket of apples. There was a collision; the apples rolled; Tony exploded; King Solomon apologized. The little yellow man laughed shortly, took out a notebook, and put down the address he had seen on King Solomon's slip of paper.

"Guess you're the shine[1] I been waitin' for," he surmised.

As Gillis, approaching his destination, stopped to rest, a haunting notion grew into an insistent idea. "Dat li'l yaller nigger was a sho' 'nuff gen'man to show me de road. Seem lak I knowed him befo'—" he pondered. That receding brow, that sharp-ridged, spreading nose, that tight upper lip over the two big front teeth, that chinless jaw—He fumbled hurriedly for the card he had not looked at and eagerly made out the name.

"Mouse Uggam, sho' 'nuff! Well, dog-gone!"

II

Uggam sought out Tom Edwards, once a Pullman porter, now prosperous proprietor of a cabaret, and told him:—

"Chief, I got him: a baby jess in from the land o' cotton and so dumb he thinks ante bellum's an old woman."

"Where d'you find him?"

"Where you find all the jay birds[2] when they first hit Harlem—at the subway entrance. This one come up the stairs, batted his eyes once or twice, an' froze to the spot—with his mouth open. Sure sign he's from 'way down behind the sun an' ripe f' the pluckin'."

Edwards grinned a gold-studded, fat-jowled grin. "Gave him the usual line, I suppose?"

"Didn't miss. An' he fell like a ton o' bricks. 'Course I've got him spotted, but damn 'f I know jess how to switch 'em on to him."

"Get him a job around a store somewhere. Make out you're befriendin' him. Get his confidence."

"Sounds good. Ought to be easy. He's from my state. Maybe I know him or some of his people."

"Make out you do, anyhow. Then tell him some fairy tales that'll switch your trade to him. The cops'll follow the trade. We could even let Froggy flop into some dumb white cop's hands and 'confess' where he got it. See?"

"Chief, you got a head, no lie."

"Don't lose no time. And remember, hereafter, it's better to sacrifice a little than to get squealed on. Never refuse a customer. Give him a little credit. Humor him along till you can get rid of him safe. You don't know what that guy that died may have said; you don't know who's on to you now. And if they get you—I don't know you."

"They won't get me," said Uggam.

King Solomon Gillis sat meditating in a room half the size of his hencoop back home, with a single window opening into an airshaft.

An airshaft: cabbage and chitterlings cooking; liver and onions sizzling, sputtering; three player-pianos out-plunking each other; a man and woman calling each other vile things; a sick, neglected baby wailing; a phonograph broadcasting blues; dishes clacking; a girl crying heartbrokenly; waste noises, waste odors of a score of families, seeing issue through a common channel; pollution from bottom to top—a sewer of sounds and smells.

Contemplating this, King Solomon grinned and breathed, "Doggone!" A little later, still gazing into the sewer, he grinned again. "Green stockin's," he said; "loud green!" The sewer gradually grew darker. A window lighted up opposite, revealing a woman in camisole and petticoat, arranging her hair. King Solomon, staring vacantly, shook his head and grinned yet again. "Even got culled policemans!" he mumbled softly.

III

Uggam leaned out of the room's one window and spat maliciously into the dinginess of the airshaft. "Damn glad you got him," he commented, as Gillis finished his story. "They's a thousand shines in Harlem would change places with you in a minute jess f' the honor of killin' a cracker."

"But, I didn't go to do it. 'Twas a accident."

"That's the only part to keep secret."

"Know whut dey done? Dey killed five o' Mose Joplin's hawses 'fo he lef'. Put groun' glass in de feed-trough. Sam Cheevers come up on three of 'em one night pizenin' his well. Bleesom beat Crinshaw out o' sixty acres o' lan' an' a year's crops. Dass jess how 't is. Soon's a nigger make a li'l sump'n he better git to leavin'. An' 'fo long ev'ybody's goin' be lef'!"

"Hope to hell they don't all come here."

The doorbell of the apartment rang. A crescendo of footfalls in the hallway culminated in a sharp rap on Gillis's door. Gillis jumped. Nobody but a policeman would rap like that. Maybe the landlady had been listening and had called in the law. It came again, loud, quick, angry. King Solomon prayed that the policeman would be a Negro.

Uggam stepped over and opened the door. King Solomon's apprehensive eyes saw framed therein, instead of a gigantic officer, calling for him, a little blot of a creature, quite black against even the darkness of the hallway, except for a dirty, wide-striped silk shirt, collarless, with the sleeves rolled up.

"Ah hahve bill fo' Mr. Gillis." A high, strongly accented Jamaican voice, with its characteristic singsong intonation, interrupted King Solomon's sigh of relief.

"Bill? Bill fo' me? What kin' o' bill?"

"Wan bushel appels. T'ree seventy-fife."

"Apples? I ain' bought no apples." He took the paper and read aloud, laboriously, "Antonio Gabrielli to K. S. Gillis, Doctor—"

"Mr. Gabrielli say, you not pays him, he send policemon."

"What I had to do wid 'is apples?"

"You bumps into him yesterday, no? Scatter appels everywhere—on de sidewalk, in de gutter. Kids pick up an' run away. Others all spoil. So you pays."

Gillis appealed to Uggam. "How 'bout it, Mouse?"

"He's a damn liar. Tony picked up most of 'em; I seen him. Lemme look at that bill—Tony never wrote this thing. This baby's jess playin' you for a sucker."

"Ain' had no apples, ain' payin' fo' none," announced King Solomon, thus prompted. "Didn't have to come to Harlem to git cheated. Plenty o' dat right wha' I come fum."

But the West Indian warmly insisted. "You cahn't do daht, mon. Whaht you t'ink, 'ey? Dis mon loose 'is appels an' 'is money too?"

"What diff'ence it make to you, nigger?"

"Who you call nigger, mon? Ah hahve you understahn' "—

"Oh, well, white folks, den. What all you got t' do wid dis hyeh, anyhow?"

"Mr. Gabrielli send me to collect bill!"

"How I know dat?"

"Do Ah not bring bill? You t'ink Ah steal t'ree dollar, 'ey?"

"Three dollars an' sebenty-fi'cent," corrected Gillis. " 'Nuther thing: wha' you ever see me befo'? How you know dis is me?"

"Ah see you, sure. Ah help Mr. Gabrielli in de store. When you knocks down de baskette appels, Ah see. Ah follow you. Ah know you comes in dis house."

"Oh, you does? An' how come you know my name an' flat an' room so good? How come dat?"

"Ah fin' out. Sometime Ah brings up here vegetables from de store."

"Humph! Mus' be workin' on shares."

"You pays, 'ey? You pays me or de policemon?"

"Wait a minute," broke in Uggam, who had been thoughtfully contemplating the bill. "Now listen, big shorty. You haul hips on back to Tony. We got your menu all right"—he waved the bill—"but we don't eat your kind o' cookin', see?"

The West Indian flared. "Whaht it is to you, 'ey? You can not mind your own business? Ah hahve not spik to you!"

"No, brother. But this is my friend, an' I'll be john-browned if there's a monkey-chaser[3] in Harlem can gyp him if I know it, see? Bes' thing f' you to do is catch air, toot sweet.'"[4]

Sensing frustration, the little islander demanded the bill back. Uggam figured he could use the bill himself, maybe. The West Indian hotly persisted; he even menaced. Uggam pocketed the paper and invited him to take it. Wisely enough, the caller preferred to catch air.

When he had gone, King Solomon sought words of thanks.

"Bottle it,"[5] said Uggam. "The point is this: I figger you got a job."

"Job? No I ain't! Wh' at?"

"When you show Tony this bill, he'll hit the roof and fire that monk."

"Wha ef he do?"

"Then you up 'n ask f' the job. He'll be too grateful to refuse. I know Tony some, an' I'll be there to put in a good word. See?"

King Solomon considered this. "Sho' needs a job, but ain' after stealin' none."

"Stealin'? 'T wouldn't be stealin'. Stealin' 's what that damn monkey-chaser tried to do from you. This would be doin' Tony a favor an' gettin' y'self out o' the barrel. What's the hold-back?"

"What make you keep callin' him monkey-chaser?"

"West Indian. That's another thing. Any time y' can knife a monk, do it. They's too damn many of 'em here. They're an achin' pain."

"Jess de way white folks feels 'bout niggers."

"Damn that. How 'bout it? Y' want the job?"

"Hm—well—I'd ruther be a policeman."

"Policeman?" Uggam gasped.

"M—hm. Dass all I wants to be, a policeman, so I kin police all de white folks right plumb in jail!"

Uggam said seriously, "Well, y' might work up to that. But it takes time. An' y've got to eat while y're waitin'." He paused to let this penetrate. "Now, how 'bout this job at Tony's in the meantime? I should think y'd jump at it."

King Solomon was persuaded.

"Hm—well—reckon I does," he said slowly.

"Now y're tootin'!" Uggam's two big front teeth popped out in a grin of genuine pleasure. "Come on. Let's go."

IV

Spitting blood and crying with rage, the West Indian scrambled to his feet. For a moment he stood in front of the store gesticulating furiously and jabbering shrill threats and unintelligible curses. Then abruptly he stopped and took himself off.

King Solomon Gillis, mildly puzzled, watched him from Tony's doorway. "I jess give him a li'l shove," he said to himself, "an he roll' clean 'cross de sidewalk." And a little later, disgustedly, "Monkey-chaser!" he grunted, and went back to his sweeping.

"Well, big boy, how y' comin' on?"

Gillis dropped his broom. "Hay-o, Mouse. Wha' you been las' two-three days?"

"Oh, around. Gettin' on all right here? Had any trouble?"

"Deed I ain't—'ceptin' jess now I had to throw 'at li'l jigger out."

"Who? The monk?"

"M—hm. He sho' Lawd doan like me in his job. Look like he think I stole it from him, stiddy him tryin' to steal from me. Had to push him down sho' 'nuff 'fo I could git rid of 'im. Den he run off talkin' Wes' Indi'man an' shakin' his fis' at me."

"Ferget it." Uggam glanced about. "Where's Tony?"

"Boss man? He be back direckly."

"Listen—like to make two or three bucks a day extra?"

"Huh?"

"Two or three dollars a day more'n what you're gettin' already?"

"Ain' I near 'nuff in jail now?"

"Listen," King Solomon listened. Uggam hadn't been in France for nothing. Fact was, in France he'd learned about some valuable French medicine. He'd brought some back with him,—little white pills,—and while in Harlem had found a certain druggist who knew what they were and could supply all he could use. Now there were any number of people who would buy and pay well for as much of this French medicine as Uggam could get. It was good for what ailed them, and they didn't know how to get it except through him. But he had no store in which to set up an agency and hence no single place where his customers could go to get what they wanted. If he had, he could sell three or four times as much as he did.

King Solomon was in a position to help him how, same as he had helped King Solomon. He would leave a dozen packages of the medicine—just small envelopes that could all be carried in a coat pocket—

with King Solomon every day. Then he could simply send his customers to King Solomon at Tony's store. They'd make some trifling purchase, slip him a certain coupon which Uggam had given them, and King Solomon would wrap the little envelope of medicine with their purchase. Mustn't let Tony catch on, because he might object, and then the whole scheme would go gaflooey. Of course it wouldn't really be hurting Tony any. Wouldn't it increase the number of his customers?

Finally, at the end of each day, Uggam would meet King Solomon some place and give him a quarter for each coupon he held. There'd be at least ten or twelve a day—two and a half or three dollars plumb extra! Eighteen or twenty dollars a week!

"Dog-gone!" breathed Gillis.

"Does Tony ever leave you heer alone?"

"M—hm. Jess started dis mawnin'. Doan nobody much come round 'tween ten an' twelve, so he done took to doin' his buyin' right 'long 'bout dat time. Nobody hyeh but me fo' 'n hour or so."

"Good. I'll try to get my folks to come 'round here mostly while Tony's out, see?"

"I doan miss."

"Sure y' get the idea, now?" Uggam carefully explained it all again. By the time he had finished, King Solomon was wallowing in gratitude.

"Mouse, you sho' is been a friend to me. Why, 'f't had n' been fo' you—"

"Bottle it," said Uggam. "I'll be round to your room to-night with enough stuff for to-morrer, see? Be sure'n be there."

"Won't be nowha' else."

"An' remember, this is all jess between you 'n me."

"Nobody else but," vowed King Solomon.

Uggam grinned to himself as he went on his way. "Dumb Oscar! Wonder how much can we make before the cops nab him? French medicine—Hmph!"

V

Tony Gabrielli, an oblate Neapolitan of enormous equator, wabbled heavily out of his store and settled himself over a soap box.

Usually Tony enjoyed sitting out front thus in the evening, when his helper had gone home and his trade was slackest. He liked to watch the little Gabriellis playing over the sidewalk with the little Levys and Johnsons; the trios and quartettes of brightly dressed, dark-skinned girls merrily out for a stroll; the slovenly gaited, darker men, who eyed them up and down and commented to each other with an unsuppressed "Hot damn!" or "Oh, no, now!"

But to-night Tony was troubled. Something was different since the arrival of King Solomon Gillis. The new man had seemed to prove himself honest and trustworthy, it was true. Tony had tested him, as he always tested a new man, by apparently leaving him alone in charge for two or three mornings. Tony's store was a modification of the front rooms of his flat and was in direct communication with it by way of a glass-windowed door in the rear. Tony always managed to get back into his flat via the side-street entrance and watch the new man through this unobtrusive glass-windowed door. If anything excited his suspicion, like unwarranted interest in the cash register, he walked unexpectedly out of this door to surprise the offender in the act. Thereafter he would have no more such trouble. But he had not succeeded in seeing King Solomon steal even an apple.

What he had observed, however, was that the number of customers that came into the store during the morning's slack hour had pronouncedly increased in the last few days. Before, there had been three or four. Now there were twelve or fifteen. The mysterious thing about it was that their purchases totaled little more than those of the original three or four.

Yesterday and to-day Tony had elected to be in the store at the time when, on the other days, he had been out. But Gillis had not been overcharging or short-changing; for when Tony waited on the customers himself—strange faces all—he found that they bought something like a yeast cake or a five-cent loaf of bread. It was puzzling. Why should strangers leave their own neighborhoods and repeatedly come to him for a yeast cake or a loaf of bread? They were not new neighbors. New neighbors would have bought more variously and extensively and at different times of day. Living near by, they would have come in, the men often in shirtsleeves and slippers, the women in kimonos, with boudoir caps covering their lumpy heads. They would have sent in strange children for things like yeast cakes and loaves of bread. And why did not some of them come in at night when the new helper was off duty?

As for accosting Gillis on suspicion, Tony was too wise for that.

Patronage had a queer way of shifting itself in Harlem. You lost your temper and let slip a single "nègre." A week later you sold your business.

Spread over his soap box, with his pudgy hands clasped on his preposterous paunch, Tony sat and wondered. Two men came up, conspicuous for no other reason than that they were white. They displayed extreme nervousness, looking about as if afraid of being seen; and when one of them spoke to Tony it was in a husky, toneless, blowing voice, like the sound of a dirty phonograph record.

"Are you Antonio Gabrielli?"

"Yes, sure." Strange behavior for such lusty-looking fellows. He who had spoken unsmilingly winked first one eye then the other, and indicated by a gesture of his head that they should enter the store. His companion looked cautiously up and down the Avenue, while Tony, wondering what ailed them, rolled to his feet and puffingly led the way.

Inside, the spokesman snuffled, gave his shoulders a queer little hunch, and asked, "Can you fix us up, buddy?" The other glanced restlessly about the place as if he were constantly hearing unaccountable noises.

Tony thought he understood clearly now. "Booze, 'ey?" he smiled. "Sorry—I no got."

"Booze? Hell, no!" The voice dwindled to a throaty whisper. "Dope. Coke, milk, dice—anything. Name your price. Got to have it."

"Dope?" Tony was entirely at a loss. "What's a dis, dope?"

"Aw, lay off, brother. We're in on this. Here." He handed Tony a piece of paper. "Froggy gave us a coupon. Come on. You can't go wrong."

"I no got," insisted the perplexed Tony; nor could he be budged on that point.

Quite suddenly the manner of both men changed. "All right," said the first angrily, in a voice as robust as his body. "All right, you're clever, You no got. Well, you will get. You'll get twenty years!"

"Twenty year? Whadda you talk?"

"Wait a minute, Mac," said the second caller. "Maybe the wop's on the level. Look here, Tony, we're officers, see? Policemen." He produced a badge. "A couple of weeks ago a guy was brought in dying for the want of a shot, see? Dope—he needed some dope—like this—in his arm. See? Well, we tried to make him tell us where he'd been getting it, but he was too weak. He croaked next day. Evidently he hadn't had money enough to buy any more.

"Well, this morning a little nigger that goes by the name of Froggy was brought into the precinct pretty well doped up. When he finally came to, he swore he got the stuff here at your store. Of course, we've just been trying to trick you into giving yourself away, but you don't bite. Now what's your game? Know anything about this?"

Tony understood. "I dunno," he said slowly; and then his own problem, whose contemplation his callers had interrupted, occurred to him. "Sure!" he exclaimed. "Wait. Maybeso I know somet'ing."

"All right. Spill it."

"I got a new man, work-a for me." And he told them what he had noted since King Solomon Gillis came.

"Sounds interesting. Where is this guy?"

"Here in da store—all day."

"Be here to-morrow?"

"Sure. All day."

"All right. We'll drop in to-morrow and give him the eye. Maybe he's our man."

"Sure. Come ten o'clock. I show you," promised Tony.

VI

Even the oldest and rattiest cabarets in Harlem have sense of shame enough to hide themselves under the ground—for instance, Edwards's. To get into Edwards's you casually enter a dimly lighted corner saloon, apparently—only apparently—a subdued memory of brighter days. What was once the family entrance is now a side entrance for ladies. Supporting yourself against close walls, you crouchingly descend a narrow, twisted staircase until, with a final turn, you find yourself in a glaring, long, low basement. In a moment your eyes become accustomed to the haze of tobacco smoke. You see men and women seated at wire-legged, white-topped tables, which are covered with half-empty bottles and glasses; you trace the slow-jazz accompaniment you heard as you came down the stairs to a pianist, a cornetist, and a drummer on a little platform at the far end of the room. There is a cleared space from the foot of the stairs, where you are standing, to the platform where this orchestra is mounted, and in it a tall brown girl is swaying from side to side and rhythmically proclaiming that she has the world in a jug and the stopper in her hand. Behind a counter at your left sits a fat, bald, tea-colored Negro, and you wonder if this is Edwards— Edwards, who stands in with the police, with the political bosses, with the importers of wines and worse. A white-vested waiter hustles you to a seat and takes your order. The song's tempo changes to a quicker; the drum and the cornet rip out a fanfare, almost drowning the piano; the girl catches up her dress and begins to dance....

Gillis's wondering eyes had been roaming about. They stopped.

"Look, Mouse!" he whispered. "Look a-yonder!"

"Look at what?"

"Dog-gone if it ain' de self-same gal!"

"Wha' d' ye mean, self-same girl?"

"Over yonder, wi' de green stockin's. Dass de gal made me knock over dem apples fust day I come to town. 'Member? Been wishin' I could see her ev'y sence."

"What for?" Uggam wondered.

King Solomon grew confidential. "Ain but two things in dis world, Mouse, I really wants. One is to be a policeman. Been wantin' dat ev'y sence I seen dat cullud traffic-cop dat day. Other is to git myse'f a gal lak dat one over yonder!"

"You'll do it," laughed Uggam, "if you live long enough."

"Who dat wid her?"

"How'n hell do I know?"

"He cullud?"

"Don't look like it. Why? What of it?"

"Hm—nuthin—"

"How many coupons y' got to-night?"

"Ten." King Solomon handed them over.

"Y'ought to've slipt 'em to me under the table, but it's all right now, long as we got this table to ourselves. Here's y' medicine for to-morrer."

"Wha'?"

"Reach under the table."

Gillis secured and pocketed the medicine.

"An' here's two-fifty for a good day's work." Uggam passed the money over. Perhaps he grew careless; certainly the passing this time was above the table, in plain sight.

"Thanks, Mouse."

Two white men had been watching Gillis and Uggam from a table near by. In the tumult of merriment that rewarded the entertainer's most recent and daring effort, one of these men, with a word to the other, came over and took the vacant chair beside Gillis.

"Is your name Gillis?"

"Tain' nuthin' else."

Uggam's eyes narrowed.

The white man showed King Solomon a police officer's badge.

"You're wanted for dope-peddling. Will you come along without trouble?"

"Fo' what?"

"Violation of the narcotic law—dope-selling."

"Who—me?"

"Come on, now, lay off that stuff. I saw what happened just now myself." He addressed Uggam. "Do you know this fellow?"

"Nope. Never saw him before tonight."

"Didn't I just see him sell you something?"

"Guess you did. We happened to be sittin' here at the same table and got to talkin'. After a while I says I can't seem to sleep nights, so he offers me sump'n he says'll make me sleep, all right. I don't know what it is, but he says he uses it himself an' I offers to pay him what it cost him. That's how I come to take it. Guess he's got more in his pocket there now."

The detective reached deftly into the coat pocket of the dumfounded King Solomon and withdrew a packet of envelopes. He tore off a corner of one, emptied a half-dozen tiny white tablets into his palm, and sneered triumphantly. "You'll make a good witness," he told Uggam.

The entertainer was issuing an ultimatum to all sweet mammas who dared to monkey round her loving man. Her audience was absorbed and delighted, with the exception of one couple—the girl with the green stockings and her escort. They sat directly in the line of vision of King Solomon's wide eyes, which, in the calamity that had descended upon him, for the moment saw nothing.

"Are you coming without trouble?"

Mouse Uggam, his friend. Harlem. Land of plenty. City of refuge— city of refuge. If you live long enough—

Consciousness of what was happening between the pair across the room suddenly broke through Gillis's daze like flame through smoke. The man was trying to kiss the girl and she was resisting. Gillis jumped up. The detective, taking the act for an attempt at escape, jumped with him and was quick enough to intercept him. The second officer came at once to his fellow's aid, blowing his whistle several times as he came.

People overturned chairs getting out of the way, but nobody ran for the door. It was an old crowd. A fight was a treat; and the tall Negro could fight.

"Judas Priest!"

"Did you see that?"

"Damn!"

White—both white. Five of Mose Joplin's horses. Poisoning a well. A year's crops. Green stockings—white—white—

"That's the time, papa!"

"Do it, big boy!"

"Good night!"

Uggam watched tensely, with one eye on the door. The second cop had blown for help—

Downing one of the detectives a third time and turning to grapple again with the other, Gillis found himself face to face with a uniformed black policeman.

He stopped as if stunned. For a moment he simply stared. Into his mind swept his own words like a forgotten song, suddenly recalled:—

"Cullud policemans!"

The officer stood ready, awaiting his rush.

"Even—got—cullud—policemans—"

Very slowly King Solomon's arms relaxed; very slowly he stood erect; and the grin that came over his features had something exultant about it.

(1925)

NOTES

1. Shine: A black. Used by and about blacks only.
2. Jay bird: A simpleton.

3. Monkey-chaser: A West Indian black primarily, although the term could be used for blacks from any tropical country. Black Americans used this phrase pejoratively in the 1920s.

4. Toot sweet: A version of the French expression, *tout de suite* (immediately).

5. Bottle it: Be quiet; say no more.

Ringtail

The pavement flashed like a river in the sun. Over it slowly moved the churches' disgorged multitudes, brilliant, deliberate, proud as a pageant, a tumult of reds and blues and greens, oranges, yellows, and browns; from a window above, outrageous, intriguing, like music full of exotic disharmonies; but closer, grating, repellent, like an orchestra tuning up: this big broad-faced, fawn-colored woman in her wide, flappy leghorn hat with a long cerise ribbon streaming down over its side, and a dress of maize georgette; or that poor scrawny black girl, bareheaded, her patches of hair captured in squares, her beaded cobalt frock girdled with a sash of scarlet satin. But whether you saw with pleasure or pity, you could have no doubt of the display. Harlem's Seventh Avenue was dressed in its Sunday clothes.[1]

And so was Cyril Sebastian Best. To him this promenade was the crest of the week's wave of pleasure. Here was show and swagger and strut, and in these he knew none could outvie him. Find if you could a suit of tan gabardine that curved in at the waist and flared at the hips so gracefully as his own; try to equal his wide wing-collar, with its polka-dot bow-tie matching the border of the kerchief in his breast pocket, or his heavy straw hat with its terraced crown and thick saucer-shaped brim, or his white buckskin shoes with their pea-green trimmings, or his silver-topped ebony cane. He challenged the Avenue and found no rival to answer.

Cyril Sebastian Best was a British West Indian. From one of the unheard-of islands he had come to Trinidad. From Trinidad, growing weary of coin-diving, he had sailed to Southampton as kitchen boy on a freighter, acquiring en route great skill in dodging the Irish cook's missiles and returning his compliments. From Southampton he had shipped in another freighter to New York under a cook from Barbados, a man who compunctionlessly regarded all flesh as fit for carving; and Cyril had found the blade of his own innate craftiness, though honed to a hair-splitting edge, no match for an unerringly aimed cleaver. The trip's termination had undoubtedly saved his life; its last twenty-four hours he had spent hiding from the cook, and when the ship had cast anchor he had jumped overboard at night, swimming two miles to shore. From those who picked him up exhausted and restored him to bodily comfort he had stolen what he could get and made his way into New York.

There were British West Indians in Harlem who would have told Cyril Sebastian Best flatly to his face that they despised him—that he would not have dared even address them in the islands; who frequently reproved their American friends for judging all West Indians by the Cyril Sebastian Best standard. There were others who, simply because he was a British West Indian, gathered him to their bosoms in that regardless warmth with which the outsider ever welcomes his like.

Among these latter, the more numerous, Cyril accordingly expended. His self-esteem, his craftiness, his contentiousness, his acquisitiveness, all became virtues, certainly not eliminating or modifying any of them. He became fond of denying that he was "colored," insisting that he was "a British subject," hence by implication unquestionably superior to any merely American Negro. And when two years of contact convinced him that the American Negro was characteristically neither self-esteemed nor crafty nor contentious nor acquisitive, in short was quite virtueless, his conscious superiority became downright contempt.

It was with no effort to conceal his personal excellence that Cyril Sebastian Best proceeded up Seventh Avenue. All this turnout was but his fitting background, his proper setting; it pleased him for no other reason than that it rendered him the more conscious of himself—a diamond surrounded with rhinestones. It did not occur to him as he swung along, flourishing his bright black cane, that any of the frequent frank stares or surreptitious second glances that fell upon him could have any origin other than admiration—envy, of course, as its companion in the cases of the men. That his cocky air could be comic, that the extremeness of his outfit could be ridiculous, that the contrast between his clothes and his complexion could cause a lip to curl—none of these far winds rippled the complacency of his ego. He had studied the fashion books carefully. Like them, he was incontrovertibly correct. Like them, again, he was incontrovertibly British; while these Harlemites were just American Negroes. And then, beyond and above all this, he was Cyril Sebastian Best.

The group of loud-laughing young men near the corner he was approaching had not regard for the Sabbath, appreciation for the splendor of Seventh Avenue, or respect for any particular person who might pass within earshot. Indeed, they derived as great a degree of pleasure out of the weekly display as did Cyril Sebastian Best, but of a quite different sort. Instead of joining the procession, they preferred assembling at some point in its course and "giving the crowd the once-over." They enjoyed exchanging loud comments upon the passers-by, the slightest quip provoking shouts of laughter; and they possessed certain stock subtleties which were always sure to elicit merriment, such as the whistled tune of "There she goes, there she goes, all dressed up in her

Sunday clothes!" A really pretty girl usually won a surprised "Well, hush my mouth!" while a really pretty ankle always occasioned wild embraces of mock excitement.

An especially favored and carefully reserved trick was for one member of the group to push another into a stroller, the latter accomplice apologizing with elaborate deference, while the victim stood helpless between uncertainty and rage. In Harlem, however, an act of this kind required a modicum of selectivity. The group would never have attempted it on the heavy-set, walnut-visaged gentleman just passing, for all of his suede spats and crimson cravat; but when Cyril Sebastian Best lilted into view the temptation was beyond resistance.

"Push me!" Punch Anderson pleaded of his neighbor. "Not yet, Meg. Wait a minute. Now!"

The impact sent Cyril's cane capering toward the gutter; his hat described progressively narrower circles on the sidewalk; and before Punch could remove his own hat and frame his polite excuse Cyril's fulminant temper flashed. Some would have at least considered the possibility of innocent sincerity; others, wiser, would have said nothing, picked up their things, and passed on; but Cyril Sebastian Best reacted only to outraged vanity, and the resultant cloudburst of vituperation staggered even the well-informed Punch Anderson.

"Soft pedal, friend," he protested, grinning. "I'm apologizing, ain't I?"

More damnation. Epithets conceived over kitchen filth; curses born of the sea; worded fetor.

Punch's round-faced grin faded. He deliberately secured the West Indian's hat and cane and without a word handed them to him. Cyril snatched them out of Punch's hand as if from a leper and flung out a parting invective—a gem of obscenity. Punch's sense of humor died.

"Say that again, you black son of a simian, and somebody'll be holding an inquest over you!"

In the act of raising his hat to his head Cyril said it again. Punch's fist went through the crown of the hat to reach the West Indian's face.

A minute later Cyril, tears streaming, polka-dot kerchief growing rapidly crimson with repeated application, was hurrying through the unbearable stares of gaping promenaders, while in his ears seethed the insult: "Now get the hell out o' here, you ringtail monkey-chaser!"[2]

II

The entrance of the Rosina wears an expression of unmistakable hauteur and you know it immediately to be one of the most arrogant of apartment houses. You need not stand on the opposite side of the Avenue and observe the disdain with which the Rosina looks down upon her neighbors. You have only to pass between her distinguishing gray-granite pillars with their protective, flanking grille-work and pause for a hesitant moment in the spacious hall beyond: the overimmaculate tiled floors, the stiff, paneled mahogany walls, the frigid lights in their crystalline fixtures, the supercilious palms, all ask you at once who you are and what you want here. To reach the elevator you must make between two lordly, contemptuous wall-mirrors, which silently deride you and show you how out of place you are. If you are sufficiently courageous or obtuse, you gain the elevator and with growing discomfiture await the pleasure of the operator, who is just now occupied at the switchboard, listening in on some conversation that does not concern him. If you are sufficiently unimpressed or imprudent, you grumble or call aloud, and in that case you always eventually take to the stairs. Puff, blow, rage, and be damned. This is the Rosina. Who are you?

What more pleasurable occupation for Cyril Sebastian Best, then, than elevator- and switchboard-operator in the Rosina? If ever there was self-expression, this was it. He was the master of her halls, he was the incarnation of her spirit; in him her attitude became articulate—articulate with a Trinidadian accent, but distinctly intelligible, none the less. There were countless residents and their callers to be laughed at; there were endless silly phone-talks to be tapped at the switchboard; there were great mirrors before which he could be sure of the perfect trimness of his dapper gray-and-black uniform; there were relatively few passengers who absolutely required the use of the elevator, and most of those tipped well and frequently. It was a wonderful job.

Cyril's very conformity with his situation kept him ordinarily in the best of humor, the rendering of good service yielding him a certain satisfaction of his own. It was therefore with a considerable shock that one resident, flatteringly desirous, as she thought, of Cyril's aid in facilitating a connection, heard herself curtly answered, "Ah, tell de outside operator. Whaht you t'ink I keer?"—and that a familiar caller in the Rosina, upon being asked, "Whaht floor?" and answering pleasantly, "Third, as usual," heard himself rebuked with " 'As usual'! You t'ink I am a mindreader, 'ey?"

Clearly Cyril Sebastian Best was in no obliging mood to-day.

Nothing amused, nothing even interested him: neither the complexion of the very dark girl who persisted in using too much rouge with an alarmingly cyanotic result, nor the leprously overpowdered nose of the young lady who lived in fifty-nine and "passed" for white in her downtown position. He did not even grin at the pomposity of the big yellow preacher who, instead of purchasing ecclesiastic collars, simply put his lay ones on backward.

Cyril sat before the switchboard brooding, his memory raw with "monkey-chaser" and "ringtail." Now and then a transient spasm of passion contorted his features. In the intervals he was sullen and glum and absorbed in contemplated revenge.

"Cyril! Aren't you ever going to take me up? I'm starving to death!"

He looked up. Hilda Vogel's voice was too sweet, even in dissatisfaction, not to be heeded; and she was too pretty—fair, rougelessly rosy, with dimpled cheeks and elbows. How different from the picture just now in his mind!

Cyril had secret ambitions about Hilda. Like himself, she was foreign—from Bermuda; a far cry, to be sure, from Trinidad, but British just the same. And she was sympathetic. She laughed at his jests, she frankly complimented his neatness, she never froze his pleasantries with silence, nor sneered, nor put on airs. One day, during their frequent ascents, she had paused for as long as five minutes at her landing to listen to his description of the restaurant he was going to own someday soon. It couldn't be meaningless. She saw something in him. Why shouldn't he have ambitions about her?

"Cyril! How'd you hurt your lip?" she asked in the surprise of discovery as the car mounted.

Merely that she noticed elated him; but he would have bitten the lip off rather than tell her. "I bump' into de door doonsteers."

"Shame on you, Cyril. That's an old one. Do I look as dumb as that?"

He was silent for three floors.

"Goodness! It must have been something terrible. Oh well, if you ignore me—" And she began humming a ditty.

She had never been so personal before. Had his soul not been filled with bitterness, he might have betrayed some of those secret ambitions at once, right there between floors in the elevator. As it was he was content with a saner resolution: he would ask permission to call Wednesday night. He was "off" Wednesdays.

"You soun' quite happy," he observed, to make an opening, as he slid back the gate at her floor.

"You said it!" she answered gayly, stepping out; and before he could follow his opening her dimples deepened, her eyes twinkled mysteriously, and she added, "I may be in love—you'd never know!" Then she vanished down the hallway with a laugh, while the speechless Cyril wondered what she could mean.

III

In the flat's largest room a half-dozen young men played poker around a dining-table. A spreading gas-dome of maroon-and-orange stained glass hung low over the table, purring softly, confining its whitish halo to the circle of players, and leaving in dimness the several witnesses who peered over their shoulders. One player was startlingly white, with a heavy rash of brown freckles and short kinky red hair. Another was almost black, with the hair of an Indian and the features of a Moor. The rest ranged between.

A phonograph in a corner finished its blatant "If You Don't I Know Who Will," and someone called for the "West Indian Blues."

"That reminds me, Punch," said Meg Minor over his cards. "Remember that monk you hit Sunday?"

"Never hit anybody on Sunday in my life," grinned Punch across the table. "I'm a Christian."

"Punch hit a monk? Good-night! There's gonna be some carvin' done."

"Name your flowers, Punch!"

" 'Four Roses,' for Punch!"

Meg went on through the comments: "He's an elevator-boy at the Rosina up the Avenue."

"What'd you hit him for, Punch?"

"Deal me threes, Red," requested Punch, oblivious, while Meg told the others what had happened.

"Serves you right for actin' like a bunch of infants," judged Red. "Punch in the Post Office and you supposed to be studyin'—what the hell are you studyin' now, Meg?"

"Serves *us* right? It was the monk that got hit."

"Hmph! D'you think that's the end of it? Show me a monk that won't try to get even and I'll swallow the Woolworth Building."

"Well, we were just feeling kind o' crazy and happened to meet up with that bunch of don't-give-a-kitty kids. It was fun, only—"

"Bet fifteen cents on these four bullets," said Punch.

"Call!"

"Call!"

"You stole the last pot, bluffin'," calculated Eight-Ball, nicknamed for his complexion's resemblance to the pool ball of that number. He tossed a blue chip into the growing pile.

"Have to protect my ante," decided his neighbor, resignedly.

"I'm a dutiful nephew, too," followed Meg.

Punch threw down three aces and a joker and reached for the pile of chips.

"Four bullets sure 'nough!"

"An' I had a full house!"

"The luck o' the Nigrish. Had a straight myself."

"Luck, hell. Them's the four bullets that monk's gonna put into him."

"Right. Get enough for a decent burial, Punch."

"Deal, friend," grinned the unruffled Punch. "I'm up."

"On the level, Punch," resumed Meg, "keep your eyes open. That little ape looks evil to me."

"Aw, he's harmless."

"There ain't no such thing as a harmless monkey-chaser," objected Red. "If you've done anything to him, he'll get you sooner or later. He can't help it—he's just made that way, like a spring."

"I ain't got a thing for a monk to do, anyhow," interjected a spectator. "Hope Marcus Garvey[3] takes 'em all back to Africa with him. He'll sure have a shipload."

Eight-Ball finished riffling the cards and began to distribute them carefully. "You jigs[4] are worse 'n ofays,"[5] he accused. "You raise hell about prejudice, and look at you—doin' just what you're raisin' hell over yourselves."

"Maybe so," Red rejoined, "but that don't make me like monks any better."

"What don't you like about 'em?"

"There ain't nothin' I do like about 'em. They're too damn conceited. They're too aggressive. They talk funny. They look funny—I can tell one the minute I see him. They're always startin' an argument an' they always want the last word. An' there's too many of 'em here."

"Yeah," Eight-Ball dryly rejoined. "An' they stick too close together an' get ahead too fast. They put it all over us in too many ways. We could stand 'em pretty well if it wasn't for that. Same as ofays an' Jews."

"Aw, can the dumb argument," said Meg. "Open for a nickel."

"Raise a nickel."

"Who was the pretty pink you were dancin' with the other night, Punch?" inquired the observer behind him.

The lethargic Punch came to life. "Boy, wasn't she a sheba?[6] And I don't even know her name."

"Sheikin'[7] around some hey?"

"Nope. My sister Marian introduced me. But I'm so busy looking I don't catch the name, see? When I dance with her she finds out I don't know it and refuses to tell. I ask if I can come to see her and she says nothing doing—wouldn't think of letting a bird call who didn't even know her name."

"Really got you goin', hey?"

"Damn right, she did. I ask Marian her name afterwards and she won't come across either. Says she's promised not to tell and if I really want to locate the lady nothing'll stop me. Can y' beat it?"

"Why don't y' bribe Marian?"

"If you can bribe Marian I can be President."

"All right, heavy lover," interpolated Meg impatiently. "You in this game?"

Punch discovered then that he had discarded the three queens he had intended to keep, and had retained a deuce and a fivespot.

"Well, cut me in my neck!" he ejaculated. "Did you see what I did?"

The man behind him laughed. "Boy, you're just startin'," he said. "Wait till you locate the pink!"

The gloomy dinginess that dimmed the stuffy little front room of the Rosina's basement flat was offset not so much by the two or three one-bulb lights in surprisingly useless spots as by the glow of the argument, heated to incandescence. Payner, the house-superintendent, whose occupancy of these rooms constituted part of his salary, had not forgotten that he was a naturalized American of twenty years' standing, and no longer fresh from Montserrat; but Barbadian Gradyne had fallen fully into his native word-throttling, and Chester of Jamaica might have been chanting a loud response to prayer in the intervals when the others let his singsong have its say.

"No people become a great people," he now insisted, with his peculiar stressing of unaccented syllables, "except where it dominate. You t'ink de Negro ever dominate America? Pah!"

"Africa," Gradyne lumberingly supported him, "dat de only chance. Teng mo' years, mahn, dis Harl'm be jes like downg Georgia. Dis a white mahn's country!"

"Back to Africa!" snorted Payner. "Go on back, you b'ys. Me—I doan give a dahm f' all de Garveys an' all do Black Star liners[8] in Hell. I stay right here!"

"You t'ink only for you'self," charged Chester. "You t'ink about you' race an' you see I am right. Garvey is de Moses of his people."

"Maybeso. But I be dahm' if Moses git any my money. Back to Africa! How de hell I'm goin' back where I never been?"

Neither Gradyne's retaliative cudgel nor Chester's answering thrust achieved its mark, for at that moment Cyril Sebastian Best broke unceremoniously in and announced: "De house is pinch'!"[9]

Like a blast furnace's flame, the argument faded as swiftly as it had flared.

"Where you was raised, boy? Don't you got no manners a-tall?"

Cyril banged the door behind him stuck out his chest, and strutted across the room. "I tell you whaht I hahve got," he grinned.

"A hell of a nerve," grunted Gradyne.

"An' I tell you whaht I'm goin' get," Cyril proceeded. "I'm goin' get rich an' I'm goin' get married."

"How much you pays, 'ey?" asked Chester.

"Pays? For whaht?"

"For you' licker. You's drunk as hell."

"Den I stays drunk all 'e time. I got de sweetes' woman in de worl', boy—make a preacher lay 'is Bible downg!"

"Who it is?"

"Never min' who is it." But he described Hilda Vogel with all the hyperbole of enthusiasm.

Gradyne inspected him quizzically. "Dat gel mus' got two glass eyes," he grinned.

"Or else you have," Payner amended.

"How you know she care anyt'ing about you?" Chester asked.

"I know." Cyril was positive. "She tell me so dis ahfternoon in de elevator. I been makin' time all along, see? So dis ahfternoon when I get to de top floor I jes' staht to pop de question an' she look at me an' roll 'er eyes like dis, an' say, 'I may be in love!' an' run like hell downg de hall laughin'! Boy, I know!"

Payner and Chester and Gradyne all looked at him with pitying sympathy. Then Chester laughed.

"You cahn't tell anything by that, mahn."

"I cahn't, 'ey? Why not?"

"You had de poor girl too far up in de air!"

IV

"Did you see the awful thing Harriet wore?"

"Did I? Who in the world made it?"

"Noah's grandmother."

"And that King Tut bob—at her age!"

"Maybe she's had monkey glands—"

Cyril, listening in at the switchboard, found it very uninteresting and leaving off, deigned to take up three passengers who had been waiting for five minutes in the elevator. When he reached the street floor again, the instrument's familiar rattle was calling him back.

"Apartment sixty-one, please."

Something in the masculine voice made Cyril stiffen, something more than the fact it sought connection with Hilda Vogel's apartment. He plugged in and rang.

"Can I speak to Miss Vogel, please?"

"This is Miss Vogel."

"Miss Hilda Vogel?"

"Yes."

The masculine voice laughed.

"Thought you'd given me the air, didn't you?"

"Who is it, please?" Cyril noted eagerness in Hilda's voice.

"Give you one guess."

"My, you're conceited."

"Got a right to be. I'm taking the queeniest sheba in Harlem to a show to-night, after which we're going to Happy's and get acquainted."

"Indeed? Why tell me about it?"

"You're the sheba."

Hilda laughed. "You don't lose any time, do you, Mr.—Punch?"

"I don't dare, Miss—Hilda."

Cyril, bristling attention, shivered. Despite its different tone, he knew the voice. A hot wave of memory swept congealingly over him; he felt like a raw egg dropped in boiling water.

"How did you find out I was—me?"

"Oho! Now it's your turn to wonder!"

"Tell me."

"Sure—when I see you."

"I think you're horrid."

"Why?"

"Well, I've got to let you come now or I'll die of curiosity."

"Dark eyes, but a bright mind. When do I save your life?"

"Are you sure you want to?"

"Am I talking to you?"

"You don't know a thing about me."

"More'n you know about me. I looked you up in *Who's Who!*"

"Now you're being horrid again. What did you find?"

"You work in the Model Shop on the Avenue, you live with your ma and pa, and you're too young and innocent to go around with only girls, sheikless and unprotected."

"How do you know I'm sheikless?" Cyril's heart stumbled.

"You're not—now," said the audacious Punch.

The girl gasped. Then, "You didn't find out the most important thing."

"To wit and namely?"

"Where I am from."

"Nope. I'm more interested in where you're going."

"We're—" she hesitated gravely. "I'm—Do you—object to—foreigners?"

It was Punch's gasp. "What?"

"There! You see, I told you you didn't want to come."

"What are you talking about?"

"We're—I'm a Bermudan, you know."

Punch's ringing laugh stabbed the eavesdropping ears. "I thought you were an Eskimo, the way you froze me that night."

"You're not—prejudiced?"

"Who, me? Say, one of the finest boys down at the P.O. is from Bermuda. Always raving about it. Says it's Heaven. Guess it's the place angels come from."

She was reassured. "Not angels. Onions."

"I like onions," said Punch.

"What time are you coming?"

"Right away! Now!"

"No. Eight."

"Seven!"

"Well—seven-thirty."

"Right."

"Good-bye."

"Not on your life. So long, Hilda."

"So long, Punch."

"Seven-thirty."

"Seven-thirty."

The lift was full of impatient people audibly complaining of the delay. The only response from the ordinarily defiant Cyril was a terrific banging open and shut of the gates as he let them out, floor by floor. His lips were inverted and pressed tightly together, so that his whole mouth bulged, and his little eyes were reddened between their narrowed lids.

"I may be in love—you'd never know." He had thought she was encouraging him. He would have made sure that next day had there not been too many people in the car. Fortunately enough, he saw now; for she had been thinking of the ruffian whose blow still rent his spirit, whose words still scalded his pride: "Now get the hell out o'here, you ringtail—"

He had seen Counselor Absalom. Absalom had said he couldn't touch the case—no witnesses, no money, prolonged litigation. Absalom hadn't even been sympathetic. Street brawls were rather beneath Absalom.

Cyril slammed the top gate to and reversed the controlling lever. As the car began to drop, something startled him out of his grim abstraction: the gate was slowly sliding open. It had failed to catch, recoiling under the force with which he had shut it. Yet the car was moving normally. The safety device whereby motion was possible only when all the gates were shut had been rendered useless—perhaps by his own violence just now. He released the lever. The car halted. He pushed the lever down forward. The car ascended. He released it. The car halted again. He pushed the lever down backward. The car descended. Its movements were entirely unaffected.

Cyril paused, undecided. For a long moment he remained motionless. Then with a little grunt he rose again and carefully closed the open gate. His smile as he reached the ground floor was incarnate malevolence, triumphant.

V

Meg Minor was following a frizzly bobbed head and a bright-red sweater up the Avenue. In the twilight he wasn't sure he knew her; but even if he didn't—he might. Introductions were old stuff. If the spark of attraction gleamed, blow on it: you might kindle a blaze.

As he crossed a side street an ambulance suddenly leaped from nowhere and rushed at him with terrifying clangor. He jumped back, the driver swore loudly, and the machine swept around the corner into the direction Meg was going.

"Swore like he was sorry he didn't hit me," he grinned to himself. "Must be out making patients or something. Where's that danger signal I was pacing?"

The red sweater had stopped in the middle of the next block. So had the ambulance. When Meg reached the place, a gathering crowd was already beginning to obstruct passage. Since the sweater had halted, Meg saw no reason for going on himself, and so, edging as close to it as he could, he prayed that the forthcoming sight might make the girl faint into his arms.

He paid no attention to the growling buzz about him. There was a long wait. Then the buzz abruptly hushed and the crowd shifted, opening a lane to the ambulance. In the shift Meg, squirming still nearer to the red sweater, found himself on the edge of the lane.

Two men, one in white, came out of the house, bearing a stretcher covered with a blanket. As they passed, Meg, looking, felt his heart trip and his skin tingle. He stared forward.

"Punch! For God's sake—"

"Stand back, please!"

"It's Punch Anderson, Doc! What—what—is he—?" Meg pressed after the white coat. "Doc—good Lord, Doc—tell me what happened! He's my buddy, Doc!"

"Tried to hop a moving elevator. Both legs—compound fractures."

Doors slammed. The ambulance made off with a roar and a clamor. Meg stood still. He did not see the bright red sweater beside him or hear the girl asking if his friend would live. He was staring with mingled bewilderment and horror into the resplendent entrance of the Rosina. And, as he stared, the sound of the ambulance gong came back to his ears, peal upon peal, ever more distant, like receding derisive laughter.

(1925)

NOTES

1. Strolling was an integral part of life in Harlem, as described by James Weldon Johnson: "The masses of Harlem get a good deal of pleasure out of

things far too simple for most other folks. In the evenings of summer and on Sundays they get lots of enjoyment out of strolling. Strolling is almost a lost art in New York; at least, in the manner in which it is so generally practiced in Harlem. Strolling in Harlem does not mean merely walking along Lenox or upper Seventh Avenue or One Hundred and Thirty-fifth Street; it means that those streets are places for socializing. . . . One saunters along, he hails this one, exchanges a word or two with that one, stops for a short chat with the other one. . . . This is not simply going out for a walk; it is more like going out for adventure." *Black Manhattan* (New York: Atheneum, 1968), 162–63.

2. Ringtail monkey-chaser: Pejorative term for a West Indian, or someone from the tropics, who is dismissed even further by the expression, ring-tail, which meant a criminal or, at least, a tramp.

3. Marcus Garvey (1887–1940) was the major proponent and leader of the "Back to Africa" movement in the United States and later in England. Born in Jamaica, B.W.I., the group he headed and brought to fame was the Universal Negro Improvement Association. Many intellectuals derided Garvey, but his magnetic personality impressed the masses.

4. Jig: A black. A variant term for "boogy," which itself derives from a contraction of Booker T. Washington. Both terms were used by and of blacks only.

5. Ofay: A white. "Fay" is said to be the original term and ofay a contraction of "old" and "fay."

6. Sheba: A queen of a woman; a real "good-looker."

7. Sheikin': Chasing women; womanizing.

8. Black star liners: "Garvey made a four months' tour of the West Indies in a Black Star liner, gathering in many converts to the movement, but no freight for the vessel. Of course, the bubble burst. Neither Garvey nor any one with him knew how to operate ships. . . . So the Black Star Line . . . collapsed in December 1921. The Federal Government investigated Garvey's share-selling scheme and he was indicted and convicted on a charge of using the mails to defraud." (Johnson, *Black Manhattan*, pp. 255–56)

9. Pinch': A cheat.

High Yaller

The timekeeper's venomous whistle killed the ball in its flight, halfway to the basket. There was a triumphant bedlam. From the walls of Manhattan Casino impatient multitudes swarmed on to the immense floor, congratulating, consoling, gibing; pouring endlessly from the surrounding terrace, like long restrained torrents at last transcending a dam; sweeping tumultuously in from all sides, till the dance floor sank beneath a sounding flood of dark-skinned people, submerged to its furthest corners save the distant platform that gave the orchestra refuge, like a raft. A sudden blare of music cut the uproar. The turbulence gradually ordered itself into dense, crawling currents, sluggish as jammed traffic, while the din of voices at length reluctantly surrendered to the rhythmic swish-swash of shuffling feet.

Looking down from a balcony on that dark mass of heads, close together as buckshot, Evelyn Brown wondered how they all managed to enjoy it. Why must they always follow a basket-ball game with a dance?—the one pleasurable enough, the other mob-torture, she knew.

"Game?" challenged MacLoed.

She couldn't refuse her escort, of course. "If you are."

They descended and struck out like swimmers in the sea. MacLoed surrounded her as closely as a lifesaver. She knew that he had to, but she hated it—this mere hugging to music, this acute consciousness of her partner's body. The air was vile—hot, full of breath and choking perfume. You were forever avoiding, colliding, marking time on the same spot. So insulating was the crush that you might sway for several minutes near a familiar couple, even recognize their voices, yet catch only the merest glimpse of their vanishing faces.

Something of the sort was happening now. Evelyn heard someone say her name, and the mordant intonation with the succeeding spiteful snatch-phrases made her forget the physical unpleasantness of the moment.

"Evelyn Brown?—Hmph!—got yellow fever—I know better—color struck, I tell you—girls she goes around with—all lily whites—even the fellows—Mac to-day—pass for white anywhere—Jeff, Rickmond, Stanley Hall, all of 'em—You? Shoot! You don't count—you're crazy 'bout high yallers anyhow."

The words were engulfed. Evelyn had not needed to look. Mayme Jackson's voice was unmistakable.

The dance number ended on an unresolved, interrogative chord that

set off an explosion of applause. Jay Martin, who had just been defending Evelyn against Mayme's charge, spied the former's fluff of fair
hair through several intervening thicknesses of straight and straightened black, and, dragging Mayme by the arm, he made for the other
couple.

"Now say what you said about Evelyn!" he dared Mayme, mock-
maliciously, quite unaware that Evelyn already knew.

"Sweetest old thing in the world," came Mayme's tranquil purr.

"Rake in the chips," gasped Jay. "Your pot." He addressed Evelyn,
"How about the next wrestle?"

There was a ready exchange of partners. The orchestra struck up an
air from a popular Negro comedy: "Yaller Gal's Gone Out o' Style."
Soon the two couples were urged apart in increasingly divergent currents.

"Black sea," commented Jay.

But Evelyn was thoughtful. "Jay?"

"Nobody else."

"I heard what Mayme said."

"You did? Aw, heck—don't pay any attention to that kid. She's a
nut."

"I'm not so sure she isn't right, Jay."

"Right? About what?"

"I've been thinking over my best friends. They're practically all 'passing' fair. Any one of them could pass—for a foreigner, anyway."

"Me, for instance," he grinned. "Prince Woogy-boogy of Abyssinia."

"I'm afraid you prove the rule."

He was serious. "Well, what of it?"

"Oh, I don't mean I've done it intentionally. I never realized it till
just now. But, just as Mayme says, it looks bad."

"Hang what Mayme says. She's kind o' gone on yaller men, herself.
See the way she melted into Mac's shirtfront! Hung round his neck like
a chest-protector. Didn't drape herself over me that way."

"Jay! You're as bad as she is."

"That's what she said."

"What do you mean?"

"Claims I fall only for pinks."

"Oh, I didn't mean that."

"Neither did she. Point is, there aren't any more dark girls. Skin
bleach and rouge have wiped out the strain. The blacks have turned
sealskin, the sealskins are high-brown, the high-browns are all yaller,
and the yallers are pink. How's a bird going to fall for what ain't?"

They jazzed on a while in noisy silence. Evelyn's tone was surprisingly bitter when at last she spoke again:

"I wish I looked like Mayme." Astonished, Jay stared at her as she went on: "A washerwoman can make half a million dollars turning dark skins light. Why doesn't someone learn how to turn light skins dark?"

And now, in addition to staring, he saw her: the averted blue eyes, the fine lips about to quiver, the delicate high-bridged nose, the white cheeks, colorless save for the faintest touch, the incredible tawny, yellow-flecked, scintillant hair,—an almost crystal-line creature, as odd in this dark company as a single sapphire in jet. He was quick to comprehend. "I know a corner—let's sit out the rest," he suggested.

When they achieved their place in a far end of the terrace, the orchestra was outdoing itself in the encore. One of the members sang through a megaphone in a smoky, half-talking voice:

> Oh Miss Pink thought she knew her stuff,
> But Miss High Brown has called her bluff.

When the encore ended, the dancers demanded yet another. The rasp of syncopation and the ceaseless stridor of soles mingled, rose about the two refugees, seeming to wall them in, so that presently they felt alone together.

"Jay, can you imagine what it's like to be colored and look white?"

He tried to be trivial. "Very convenient at times, I should think."

"But oftener unbearable. That song—imagine—everyone looking at you—laughing at you. And Mayme Jackson—'yellow fever'! Can I help it?—Jeff—Rickmond—Stanley Hall—yes, they're light. But what can I do? I like the others. I'd be glad to go places with them. But they positively avoid me."

"I don't, Ev."

"No, you don't, Jay." But her bitterness recaptured her. "Oh, I've heard them talking: 'There goes Evelyn Brown—queen of the lily-whites—nothing brown about her but her name'!" A swiftly matured determination rendered her suddenly so grim that it seemed, fragile as she was, something about her must break. "Jay, no one's going to accuse me of jim-crowing again!"

"Shucks. What do you care as long as you don't mean to?"

"I'm not only not going to mean to. I'm not going to. I'm going to see to it that I don't."

"What the deuce—by cutting your gang?"

"No. By cultivating the others."

"Oh."

"Jay—will you help me?"

"Help you? Sure. How?"

"Come to see me oftener."

"Good night! Don't you see enough of me at the office every day?"

"Come oftener. Take me places when you're not too broke. Rush me!"

He grinned as he perceived her purpose. "Doggone good stunt!" he said slowly, with increasingly enthusiastic approval. "Blessed if I wouldn't like to see you put it over, Ev. It'll show Mayme something, anyhow."

"It'll show me something, too."

"You? What?"

She was about to answer when a sharp, indecent epithet rent the wall of noise that had until then isolated them. Looking involuntarily up, Jay saw two youngsters, quarreling vituperatively. They were too close to be ignored, and, since dancing was at its height, no one else was about.

"Excuse me a second," he said, rising before Evelyn could protest. The pair were but a few feet away. The evident aggressor was a hard-looking little black youth of indefinite age,—perhaps sixteen actual years, plus the accumulated bonus of worldly wisdom which New York pays its children. He grew worse, word by word. Approaching, Jay spoke sharply, in a low voice so that Evelyn might not hear:

"Cut out that gutter-talk, boy!"

"Aw, go to hell!"

Jay stopped, less amazed than aggravated. He knew his Harlem adolescent, but he was not quite sure what to do with it. Meanwhile he was being advised: "This is a horse-race, big boy. No jackasses allowed!"

He seized the lad firmly by the shoulder and said, "Son, if you don't cover that garbage-trap of yours—" but the boy flung away and defied him in a phrase both loud and ugly. Thoroughly angered, Jay clapped one hand over the offending mouth and, catching the youngster around the waist with the other, forcibly propelled him through a tangle of empty, spindle-legged chairs to a place where two big policemen, one black and one red, were complacently watching the dancers. Here he released him with "Now—talk."

The boy scowled with wrath and impotence. So outraged in the street, he would have found a stone to throw. Now only a retaliative speech was left him, and the nearness of the law attenuated even that:

"Aw 'ight! Showin' off before 'at ole 'fay gal, huh? Aw 'ight, y' pink-chaser. Ah'm goan put y' both in." And he sidled darkly off, pulling at his disadjusted collar.

Evelyn, out of earshot, followed it all with her eyes. "Mac wouldn't have done that," she mused as she saw Jay turn from the boy and start back toward her. "Mac would have pretended he didn't hear." And before Jay reached her, she had decided something: "I certainly like Jay Martin. He's so—white."

II

Over One Hundred and Thirty-fourth Street's sidewalks between Fifth and Lenox Avenues Jay Martin's roller-skates had rattled and whirred in the days when that was the northern boundary of Negro Harlem. He had grown as the colony grew, and now he could just recall the time when his father, a pioneer preacher, had been forever warning him never to cross Lenox Avenue and never to go beyond One Hundred and Thirty-fifth Street; a time when no Negroes lived on or near Seventh Avenue and when it would have been almost suicidal for one to appear unarmed on Irish Eighth.

School had been a succession of fist-fights with white boys who called him nigger, until, when he reached the upper grades, the colored boys began to outnumber the whites; from that time until high school, pitched battles superseded individual contests, and he ran home bruised less often. His high school record had been good, and his father, anxious to make a physician of him, had sent him on to college. At the end of his third year, however, the looming draft menace, combined with the chance of a commission in the army, had urged him into a training camp at Des Moines.

He had gone to France as a lieutenant. When he returned, unharmed, he found his father fatally ill and his mother helpless. Further study out of the question, he had taken his opportunity with a Negro real estate firm, and for five years now he had been actively concerned in black Harlem's extension, the spread whose beginnings his earlier years had witnessed.

About Evelyn, of course, there had been hypothesis:

"Looks might funny to me when a woman Jennie Browns' color has a yaller-headed young one white as Evelyn."

"Daddy was white, so I understan'."

"Huh. An' her mammy, too, mos' likely. 'At's de way dese rich white folks do. Comes a wile oat dey doan want, dey ups an' gives it to one de servants—to adopt."

"Oh, I dunno. How come she couldn't been married to some white man'nuther? Dey's plenty sich, right hyeh in Harlem."

"Plenty whut? Plenty common law, maybe. You know d' ain' no se'f-respectin' white man gonna—"

"Well, doan make no diff'nce. Cain' none of us go but so fur back in our fam'ly hist'ry 'fo we stops. An' doan nobody have t' ask us why we stops. We jes' stops. Evelyn's a good girl. Smart—works regular an' makes mo' out o' dem real estate niggers 'n she'd ever make in Miss Ann's kitchen. Bad's her mother's ashthma's gittin', no tellin' whut they'd do if 'twasn't f' Evelyn's job an' dem two women lodgers."

"Oh, I ain' sayin' nuthin' 'gins 'em. Only seem like to me—dey's a white man in de woodpile somewha'."

Her own singularity had become conscious early in Evelyn's life. There crept often into her mind of late an old, persistent recollection. She and Sookie Johnson, seven-year-old playmates, had been playing jacks on the front stoop. There arose a dispute as to whose turn it was. Sookie owned the ball and Evelyn the jacks; neither would surrender her possession to the other, and the game was deadlocked. Whereupon, the spiteful Sookie had resorted to abuse:

"Y' ole yaller thing, you! My mother say y' cain't 'speck nuthin' f'm yaller niggers nohow!"

Evelyn had thrown the jacks into Sookie's face and ran heartbroken to her mother. Why didn't she have kinky hair and dark brown skin like Sookie's? "Why, honey, you're beautiful," her mother had comforted her. "Folks 'll call you names long as you live. They're just jealous, that's all."

Thus fortified, Evelyn had come to maturity, finding her mother's prophecy ever and again true. "They're just jealous" was but a fortification, however; within it Evelyn's spirit was still vulnerable, and she knew that under constant fire this stronghold could not stand forever. Mayme Jackson's thrust-in-the-back culminated what Sookie's sneer had begun. Evelyn felt her mother's defence crumbling rapidly and alarmingly, and her appeal to Jay Martin was a rather desperate effort to establish a defence of her own.

They sat now in the front of her flat; a room too full of mock-mahogany furniture about to collapse; a room with gas light and a tacked-down carpet, with flower-figured wall-paper and a marble-topped walnut table in one corner, bearing a big brown morocco-bound Bible.

"Jay, will you?"

"Remember the time I pulled your hair in Sunday-School?"

"I'm going to pull your ears if you don't answer me!"

"Did you say something?"

"You make me tired."

"Aw, for Pete's sake, Ev, I can't take you to that dump."

"Have the last two weeks frozen your nerve?"

"No—but—"

"Well, this isn't like the others, you know. This is a colored place."

"But why go there? Let's go to Broadway's or Happy's."

"No, I want to see something new. Why isn't Hank's decent, anyway? It can't be any worse than the Hole in the Wall."

"Much worse. Regular rat-trap. No gentleman would take a lady———"

"You flatter us. Let's don't be a gentleman and lady tonight. I want to see the rat-trap."

"Why, Ev, the place was raided only last week!"

"You can't scare me that way. If it was it'll be all the safer this week."

"Lord! You girls know it all."

"I don't know anything about Hank's."

"But I'm trying to tell you—"

"Seeing is believing."

"There's nothing to see."

She introduced strategy. "All right. I guess Mac won't be so hard to persuade."

"Ev—please—for Pete's sake don't let anybody take you to that—"

"Jay, I'd really hate to have to go with anybody but you." He was growing helpless. "Just the tiniest peep into the place, Jay. We won't stay—cross my liver."

"Your mother wouldn't like it."

"Come here." She led him by the arm down the long hallway to the dining-room, where her mother was sewing.

"You may go any place you please, if you go with Jay," smiled Mrs. Brown.

Hank's at first glance, presented nothing unique: a sedate old house in an elderly row of houses with high entrances, several steps above the sidewalk; houses that had once been private, but now, trapped in an extending matrix of business, stoically accepted their fates as real estate offices, printing shops and law rooms. Here and there a card peeped around the corner of a window and whispered, "Rooms"; but not the most suspicious eye would have associated those timid invitations with the bold vertical electric sign projecting over the doorway of the one lighted building in the row. Great letters, one above another, blazed the word "Café"; smaller horizontal ones across the top read "Hank's," and others across the bottom "Cabaret."

"This doesn't look so bad," commented Evelyn as they approached. "Police station right in the same block."

"Yes—convenient."

Several men stood about on the sidewalk, smoking and talking. One of these, a white man, looked sharply at Jay and Evelyn as they mounted the steps and entered.

"Why, this is like any restaurant," said Evelyn. "Just a lot of tables and folks eating."

"Only a blind," explained Jay. "The real thing is downstairs."

A dinner-coated attendant came toward them. "I'm sorry. Everything's gone in the cabaret. Would you care to wait a few minutes?"

Jay, eager for an excuse to flee, looked at Evelyn; but the blue eyes said, "Please," and he nodded. "Very well."

"This way, then."

They were led up a narrow flight of padded stairs, along a carpeted hallway with several mysterious closed doors on either side, and finally into a little room near the end. Against one wall of the room was a table with two chairs, and against the opposite a flat couch with two or three cushions. Curtains draped the one window, facing the door. The table was bare except for a small lamp with a parchment shade of orange and black, yielding a warm, dim light.

"M—m!" exclaimed Evelyn. "Cozy!"

"We can serve you here if you like," suggested the attendant.

"No, thanks," Jay answered quickly. "We'll wait."

The attendant seemed to hesitate a moment. Then, "All right," he said. "I'll let you know as soon as there's space in the cabaret." He went out and closed the door.

Evelyn was alive with interest. "Spiffy, isn't it?" She sat down on one of the chairs and looked about. "Couldn't get lost, could you?"

Jay thoughtfully took the other chair.

"You might," he said absently.

"What are you talking about? Goodness, what a lot of fun you're having!"

"I don't like this, that's a fact."

"What's wrong?"

Jay looked and noted that the door locked from within. He went over to the window, pulled the shade aside a crack, and made out the skeleton of a fire-escape in the darkness outside.

"Oh, nothing," he said, returning to his seat. "Not a thing."

"Heavens, you give me the shivers! What is it?"

He was not eager to answer. "I'm not sure but—I believe—that bird thinks you're ofay."

"White? What difference would that make?"

"Well, I'll tell you, Ev. This place, like some you already know about, has a mixed patronage, see? Part jigs, part ofays. That's perfectly all right as long as the jigs keep to their own parties and the ofays to theirs. But as soon as they begin to come mixed, trouble starts. The colored men don't like to see white men with colored women and the white men don't like to see colored men with white women. So the management avoids it. I don't believe that house-man was telling the truth when he said there was no room in the cabaret. It's too early in the evening and it's not a busy night. Fact is, the place is probably half full of ofays, and he figured that if we went down there together some drunk would get fly and I'd bounce him on the nose and right away there'd be a hullabaloo. So he took a chance that maybe we were more interested in each other than in the cabaret anyhow, and sidetracked us off up here."

"But he said he'd let us know—"

"Of course. He thought we'd be tickled silly to be in one of these rooms alone but after I refused to be served up here, what else could he say? I don't think he has any more idea of coming back than Jack Johnson."

"Then what does he expect you to do?"

"Get tired waiting and beat it."

"Oh." A depressed silence. Then a tragic diminuendo: "Lord, what a misfit I am!"

He was contrite at once. "I'm a bum. I shouldn't have told you. I don't know—maybe I'm wrong. We're here, so let's wait awhile and see."

"Jay, if only I were one thing or the other! You can't imagine—"

He absolutely could not answer. From somewhere below a thin strain drifted to their ears, like a snicker: "Yaller Gal's Gone Out o' Style."

Jay rose. "Let's breeze. That shine isn't coming back."

"All right. I'm sorry to be such a nuisance."

"You're not the nuisance. It's—folks."

They went down the soft-carpeted hallway. Strange, low sounds behind the closed doors seemed to hush apprehensively as they approached and revive after they passed. Once a shrill laugh was abruptly cut off as if by a stifling hand. There was a thick atmosphere of suppression, a sense of unspoken fears and half-drawn breaths and whispers.

As they reached the head of the padded stairs, they saw someone hurrying up and drew aside to let him pass. It was a youth in a white coat, bent on some errand. He looked at them as he went by. They resumed their course and proceeded down the stairs; but the boy halted in his, and turned to look again. Immediately, he left off his errand, and waiting until he heard the front door close behind them, retraversed the staircase. A minute later he was on the sidewalk talking in an undertone to the white man who had so sharply observed Evelyn and Jay when they entered, and who now stood smoking still, following their departure with his eyes.

"Ah know 'at sucker," scowled the little black youth. "Collects rents f' Hale an' Barker. See 'at 'fay wid 'im? Seen 'im pick 'uh up pre' near two weeks ago at Manhattan Casino."

The white man puffed a minute, while the boy looked up at him, side-long, expectant. "Hale and Barker, huh?—Hmph! All right, Shorty. I'll keep my eye on 'im. If you're on, I'll fix y' up as usual."

" 'At's the time papa." And the boy too stood eyeing the disappearing pair, an imp of malice and satisfaction.

III

A young man leaned nonchalantly on the high foot of Jay's wooden bed, grinning goodnaturedly at him; a young man who looked exactly like Jay, feature for feature, with one important exception; his skin was white.

"Who in hell are you?" asked Jay.

"What you would be if you could," came the prompt, pleasant response.

"Liar."

"Straight stuff, brother. Think of the heights you might rise to if you were I."

"Hell!" grunted Jay.

"Eventually, of course. But I mean meanwhile. Why, now you'd be in a big firm downtown, on your way to wealth. Or you might be a practicing physician—your old man could have kept you out of the draft."

"Oh, well, I'm not doing so worse."

"No, nor so better. And then there's Evelyn."

"What about Evelyn? Why, I wouldn't even know her."

"You'd know somebody like her. Don't kid yourself, boy. You like 'em pink. Remember Paris?"

"You lie like a bookmaker. I like 'em intelligent. If they happen to be bright on the outside, too, why of course, I don't bar 'em."

"No—of course not." The sarcastic caller paused a thoughtful moment. "I've got a jawful of advice for you, old-timer."

"Swallow it and choke."

"Now listen. Don't you get to liking Evelyn, see. She's too damned white."

"What of it?"

"Be yourself, son. You ask me that, after these last two weeks?"

Jay reached up and wiped a mosquito from his forehead and smacked at another singing into his ear. They irritated him. "I'll like whoever I damn please?" he flared.

"Don't get high, now," soothed the other. "I'm only warning you. Pull up on the emergency before something hits you. That girl's too fair for comfort."

"But I like her."

The other disregarded this. "You're too dark, buddy. You're ultra-violet anyhow, alone. Beside her you become absolute black—invisible. The lady couldn't see you with an arc-lamp."

"Shucks! Evelyn doesn't care."

"You're wrong there. She does. She can't help it. But she doesn't want to, so she tries hard to make herself believe she doesn't. She takes up with you, tells herself how much she likes you, invites all sorts of embarrassments upon both of you. She might even marry you. It's like taking bad medicine she thinks she's got to take and telling herself it's sweet. She figures it's better to gulp it down than to sip it, and it's better to say it's sweet than to make faces."

"Well, maybe. But I'm just conceited enough to think she likes me."

"Of course she does. I'm not talking about you. I'm talking about your color. If you were I, now, she'd jump at you."

"Humph! I don't see her jumping at MacLoed."

"Mac isn't either of us, buddy. He hasn't got a thing but his looks, and Evelyn's too wise to fall for that alone."

"There are others."

"None who can make her forget what she's trying to do. She thinks it's a sort of duty to be colored, so she's going to make a thorough job of it—do it up brown, you might say. See? The only man that could unscramble her would be a real white man. She's not going to compromise."

"You're too deep for me. But I don't believe she cares about the color of a fellow's skin."

"You don't? Well, stay away from her anyhow."

"How come?"

"To save her feelings. Every time you two go out together you're in torture. Everybody stares at you—jigs and ofays both. You've tried it now for two weeks. What's happened? The first night you went to Coney Island and nearly got yourself mobbed. A couple of days later you went into an ice-cream parlor on One Hundred and Twenty-Fifth Street, a place where Evelyn goes anytime she likes, and the proprietor had the nerve to tell you your presence hurt his business. Then how about that crowd of jigs on the subway? And last night, when you wanted to get up and punch that shine waiter in the ear because he gave Evelyn the once over and then rolled his eyes at you behind her back, as much as to say, 'Oh boy! How I envy you!'—and she looking at him all the time in the mirror! Tonight caps it all. You go out to enjoy yourself in a 'colored' place, and get jim-crowed by a man of your own color who's afraid to let the two of you be seen. Do you think Evelyn enjoys a string of things like that?"

"She enjoys 'em as much as I do."

"But it isn't the same. When people look at you, it's just with surprise. All their look says is, 'Wonder what that nigger is doing with a white woman?' But when they look at her, it's with contempt. They say, 'Humph! What a cheap drab she must be to tag around with a nigger!' No matter whether it's true or not. Do you suppose she enjoys being looked at like that?"

Jay was silent. Sounds came from the street below into his open window; an empty Coney Island bus, rumbling, clattering, shrieking, eager to get in before daybreak; gay singing of a joy-riding chorus, swelling, consummating, dying away; the night-clear whistle of a lone, late straggler—"Yaller Gal's Out o' Style."

"What do you expect me to do about it?" he finally asked.

"Ease out. See less and less of her. When you breeze away for your vacation, forget to write."

"Simple, ain't it?"

"Quite." The devil straightened up. "And now that that's settled, suppose you go to sleep a while."

"Suppose you go to hell," suggested Jay glumly.

"With pleasure. See you again."

Jay closed his smarting eyes. His caller departed into the clothespress or the hall or up the airshaft, he wasn't sure where; he knew only that when again he looked about, he was alone.

Evelyn Brown, too, lay in bed, debating with a visitor—a sophisticated young woman who sat familiarly on the edge of the counterpane and hugged her knees as she talked, and who might have been Evelyn over again, save for a certain bearing of self-assurance which the latter entirely lacked.

"Well, you've tried it," said this visitor. "See what a mess you've made of it."

"I wish you'd let me alone."

"I think too much of you, dear. And you're thinking too much of Jay. Surely the last two weeks have shown you how impossible that is."

"Two weeks isn't a long enough test."

"Quite long enough. The only place you and Jay could be happy together would be on a desert island that nobody could find. You can't go to a single place together without sooner or later wishing the ground would swallow you."

"Oh, I'd get hardened to it."

"Would that be happiness? And even if you did, he wouldn't. You don't think he enjoys all this, do you?"

"No, I suppose not."

"No. And don't think he's dumb enough to put himself into it for life either."

"He cares enough to, I think."

"Then you've got to care enough not to let him."

"How?"

"Drop him."

"I can't."

"You must. Don't you see now why you lily-whites seek each other? It's self-protection. Whether you do it consciously or not, you're really trying to prevent painful embarrassment."

"But I can't just shut myself away from everyone who happens to be a little darker than I am. If I did it before I didn't realize it, and I wasn't to blame. But if I do it now, intentionally, I'm just drawing the color-line, and that wouldn't be right. What can I do?"

Her visitor smiled. "Do? Get out. Pass. What else?"

"That's impossible. There's mother. Wherever I'd go I'd have to take her, and she couldn't pass for anything but American Negro—"

Her protest was drowned in her visitor's laughter. It was harsh, strident laughter, like the suddenly stifled outburst she'd heard at Hank's that night. It was long, loud laughter that left the visitor breathless, panting pitiably.

Of a sudden Evelyn sat upright, fearfully aware that the laughter of her dream had merged into something real and close. She listened a moment. It was her mother in the next room. Asthma again.

She met both the women lodgers in the hall, frightened, helpless. "Did you hear her?"

Shortly Evelyn hurried from her mother's room, leaving the two women with her. She slipt on as little as she dared and sped out to get a physician.

A half hour passed before she returned with one. She noted a bright light in the front room and hastened to it thinking the two women had taken her mother there for air; but she found only the two of them, huddled together on the sofa, shivering in their bathrobes, with something close to panic in their eyes.

IV

Jimmy MacLoed, red-eyed, stretchy, disconsolate, and broke, all the event of a prolonged and fatal night of stud-poker, got up at noon-time, dressed, and strolled languidly into the street, wondering from whom he could bum four bits for breakfast. At the corner of One Hundred and Thirty-Fifth Street and the Avenue he encountered Jay Martin, hurrying to lunch. This was luck, for Jay always had bucks.

"See me go for breakfast?" he asked.

"No," grinned Jay, "but I'll add it to the five I'm by you already."

Dick's lunchroom seemed to have been designed so that the two waitresses could serve everybody without moving from where they stood. You could pass from the little front door to your stool before the counter without colliding with someone only when there was no one else there. Many a patron had unexpectedly thrust his knife further into his mouth than he intended because some damn fool, rushing out, squeezed between him and the wall. But one of the waitresses was pretty; and the ham with your eggs was cut thick, not shaved; and the French fried potatoes were really French fried, not boiled ones warmed over in grease. Jay and MacLoed considered themselves lucky to find two of the dozen stools still unoccupied.

They gave their orders and rested their elbows on the counter while the waitress that wasn't pretty threw down some pewter implements before them.

"Too bad about Evelyn's old lady, huh?" said MacLoed.

Jay became grave. "Too bad about Evelyn."

"Evelyn? Wha' d' y' mean?"

"Nobody's seen her since the funeral."

"No? Only three days. Maybe she's gone off for a rest."

"Didn't leave any notice at the office."

"Think she went dippy and jumped in the river or somethin'?"

"No, but I think she's jumped out of Harlem."

"You mean—passin'?"

"I don't know. The last time I saw her she was sick enough to do anything. Those two women roomers wouldn't stay in the house another night. None of her friends would either, even after her mother was safe in the undertaker's. She had three rotten days of it, except when my mother was there. Nobody much went to the funeral. I sent the only flowers. Next day, my mother went around to see how she was making out and found nobody home.—There hasn't been, since."

"Didn't leave word with nobody, huh?"

"Nope."

" 'S funny. 'D she have any relations?"

"Nope."

"Hm! Then that's what she's doin' all right."

"Passing?"

"Yea." Mac contemplated the ham and eggs that the homely waitress had just slid between his elbows. "Don't blame her. I'd do the same thing if I didn't have so damn much brownskin family."

"Why?"

"Why?—Why not? Wouldn't you?"

"Be white if I could?" Jay paid the waitress. "I don't know."

"The hell you don't. What would you be afraid of? Meetin' somebody? Hell! Don't see 'em. If they jump you, freeze 'em.—But you'd never meet anybody you knew. S'posin' you looked white and didn't have anything to stop you, what would be the hold-back?"

Jay chewed a minute thoughtfully. Then he looked at MacLoed as if wondering whether he was worth a reply. Finally he answered:

"Kids."

"Kids?" Mac ingested this with two pieces of the real French fried potatoes well swabbed in ham gravy. "You mean you might get married and have a little pickaninny to account for, huh? Well, you could get out o' that all right. Just tell her she'd been runnin' around with a nigger and quit."

Jay knew MacLoed too well to be shocked. "You might not want to quit," he said. "You might like her. Or you might have a conscience."

"Humph! Conscience and kids. Old stuff, buddy."

"And even if your scheme worked with a man who was passing, it wouldn't with a woman. She couldn't tell her white husband he'd been running around with a colored girl. That wouldn't explain the pickaninny."

"No.—The woman catches hell both ways, don't she?"

"It's a damned shame." Jay was speaking rather to himself than to MacLoed. "I know. I took her—places. That girl was white—as white as anybody could be. Lord only knows what she'll be now."

Three or four men had come in, standing in what little space they could find and reading the menu signs while they awaited seats. No one paid any particular attention to one of these who was "ofay." White patrons were not infrequent in Dick's. This one had moved close enough to Jay to hear his last statement. He touched him on the shoulder. As Jay turned the white man drew aside his coat, and Jay glimpsed a badge. When the officer motioned him to step outside, there was nothing else to do, and with an "Excuse me a minute, Mac—be right back," he preceded the other to the sidewalk.

Outside, Jay asked, "What's the idea?"

"Didn't want to start a row in that dump. Somebody might'a had a gun."

"What's the idea?"

"Let's walk down this way." Jay knew better than to refuse, though "this way" led toward the police station. "So you think it's a damned shame, do you? Well, I think it's a damned shame, too."

"What the devil are you talking about?"

"Come down out o' that tree, son. I'm talking about you and the white girl you picked up at Manhattan Casino a while back. You y'self said just now she's white. That about settles it."

"White? Why, I only meant—"

"I heard you. You said 'white.' White's white, ain't it?"

Presently: "What's the charge?"

"Don't play dumb, bud. There's been too damn much of this thing goin' on here. We're goin' to stop it."

Suddenly Jay Martin laughed.

The two walked on in silence.

V

From a point in the wide, deep balcony's dimness, Jay followed the quick-shifting scenes; not those on the screen at which he stared, but others, flashing out from his mind.

Coney Island. He and Evelyn arm in arm, inconsequent, hilarious, eating sticky popcorn out of the same bag, dipping in at the same time, gaily disputing the last piece. Their laughter suddenly chilled by an intentionally audible remark: "Look at that white girl with a nigger." A half-dozen lowering rowdies. Evelyn urging him away. People staring.

An ice-cream parlor. A rackety mechanical piano, tables with white tops and dappled wire legs; outside One Hundred and Twenty-fifth Street traffic shadowing past; Evelyn and he, wilted with the heat, waiting a couple of eternities for a waitress; he finally looking about impatiently, beckoning to one, who leers through him. The proprietor. "Of course we don't mind serving the lady, sir; but while we can't actually refuse, why—er—frankly your presence is unprofitable to us, sir." People staring.

The subway. He and Evelyn in a corner of the car. Above the rattle and bump of doors and clang of signal-gong, wild laughter, coarse, loud. Different. Negro laughter. Headlong into the car, stumbling over one another, a group of hilarious young colored people. Men contesting seats with women, and winning; women flouncing defiantly down on the men's knees. Conscious of the attention attracted by their loudness; pleased with it. Train starting, accelerating. Train-din rising. Negro-noise rising through and above it, like sharp pain through and above dull ache. "Oh, you high yaller!" Evelyn ashamed. People staring.

Finally a back room in the police station. Two or three red-faced ruffians in brass-buttoned uniforms, sneering, menacing, quite like those Coney Island rowdies. Himself, outraged, at bay, demanding to know on just what score he was there. Surly accusation, hot denial, scalding epithet—flame. A blow. Swift, violent struggle. "Now mebbe y'll leave white women alone!" Emptiness. After a time release; release raw with bodily anguish, raw with the recurrent sting of that cover-all charge of policemen, "resisting an officer."

What an enormity, blackness! From the demons and ogres and ravens of fairy tales on; storm-clouds, eclipses, night, the valley of the shadow, gloom, hell. White, the standard of goodness and perfection. Christ himself, white. All the angels. Imagine a black angel! A black angel with a flat nose and thick lips, laughing loudly. The devil! Standards, of course; but beneath the standards, what? An instinctive shrinking from the dark? He'd seen a little white child run in terror from his father once, the first black man the child had ever seen. Instinctive? He looked about. All this balcony full of fellow creatures instinctively shrinking from him. No help for it? Awful idea. Unbearable.

A general murmur of amusement refocussed his attention for a moment on the screen. Two chubby infants sat side by side on a doorstep; the one shiny black, with a head full of kinks and eyes of twinkling midnight; the other white, with eyes of gray and the noonday sun in its hair; both dimpled and grinning and happy. Kids. Old stuff, buddy. Evelyn—would she dare?

The thoughts that gathered and throbbed like an abscess were suddenly incised. Off to one side, a row or two ahead, he had caught sight of an oddly familiar face. The dimness seemed to lift mockingly, so that he should have no doubt. Evelyn, like an answer. Different, but— Evelyn. The attitude of the young man beside her was that of an escort, and something in his profile, in the fairness of his hair and skin, discernible even through the dusk, marked him to the staring Jay as unmistakably white. Watching with quickened pulse Jay saw the young man's hand move forward over Evelyn's arm, lying on the elbow-rest between them; move forward till it reached her own hand, which turned palm-upward to clasp it. Saw one white hand close firmly over the other.

He rose abruptly and made his way past stubborn knees to the aisle. The orchestra struck up a popular bit of Negro jazz. It fell on his ears like a guffaw: the familiar refrain of "Yaller Gal's Gone Out o' Style."

(1925)

The South Lingers On

Ezekiel Taylor, preacher of the gospel of Jesus Christ, walked slowly along One Hundred and Thirty-Third Street, conspicuously alien. He was little and old and bent. A short, bushy white beard framed his shiny black face and his tieless celluloid collar. A long, greasy, green-black Prince Albert, with lapels frayed and buttons worn through to their metal hung loosely from his shoulders. His trousers were big and baggy and limp, yet not enough so to hide the dejected bend of his knees.

A little boy noted the beard and gibed, "Hey, Santa Claus! 'Tain't Chris'mas yet!" And the little boy's playmates chorused, "Haw, haw! Lookit the colored Santa Claus!"

"For of such is the kingdom of heaven," mused Ezekiel Taylor. No. The kingdom of Harlem. Children turned into mockers. Satan in the hearts of infants. Harlem—city of the devil—outpost of hell.

Darkness settled, like the gloom in the old preacher's heart; darkness an hour late, for these sinners even tinkered with God's time, substituting their "daylight-saving." Wicked, yes. But sad too, as though they were desperately warding off the inescapable night of sorrow in which they must suffer for their sins. Harlem. What a field! What numberless souls to save!—These very taunting children who knew not even the simplest of the commandments—

But he was old and alone and defeated. The world had called to his best. It had offered money, and they had gone; first the young men whom he had fathered, whom he had brought up from infancy in his little Southern church; then their wives and children, whom they eventually sent for; and finally their parents, loath to leave their shepherd and their dear, decrepit shacks, but dependent and without choice.

"Whyn't y' come to New York?" old Deacon Gassoway had insisted. "Martin and Eli and Jim Lee and his fambly's all up da' now an' doin' fine. We'll all git together an' start a chu'ch of our own, an' you'll still be pastor an' it'll be jes' same as 'twas hyeh." Full of that hope, he had come. But where were they? He had captained his little ship till it sank;

This series of sketches appeared in Alain Locke's The New Negro (New York: Boni, 1925) as "Vestiges: Harlem Sketches." Section III was entitled "Mujutah"; section IV was called "Learnin"; and section V had the title "Revival."

he had clung to a splint and been tossed ashore; but the shore was cold, gray, hard and rock-strewn.

He had been in barren places before but God had been there too. Was Harlem then past hope? Was the connection between this place and heaven broken, so that the servant of God went hungry while little children ridiculed? Into his mind, like a reply, crept an old familiar hymn, and he found himself humming it softly:

> The Lord will provide,
> The Lord will provide,
> In some way or 'nother,
> The Lord will provide.
> It may not be in your way,
> It may not be in mine,
> But yet in His own way
> The Lord will provide.

Then suddenly, astonished, he stopped, listening. He had not been singing alone—a chorus of voices somewhere near had caught up his hymn. Its volume was gradually increasing. He looked about for a church. There was none. He covered his deaf ear so that it might not handicap his good one. The song seemed to issue from one of the private houses a little way down the street.

He approached with eager apprehension and stood wonderingly before a long flight of brownstone steps leading to an open entrance. The high first floor of the house, that to which the steps led, was brightly lighted, and the three front windows had their panes covered with colored tissue-paper designed to resemble church windows. Strongly, cheeringly the song came out to the listener:

> The Lord will provide,
> The Lord will provide,
> In some way or 'nother,
> The Lord will provide.

Ezekiel Taylor hesitated an incredulous moment, then smiling, he mounted the steps and went in.

The Reverend Shackleton Ealey had been inspired to preach the gospel by the draft laws of 1917. He remained in the profession not out of gratitude to its having kept him out of war, but because he found it a far less precarious mode of living than that devoted to poker, black-jack and dice. He was stocky and flat-faced and yellow, with many black freckles and the eyes of a dogfish. And he was clever enough not to conceal his origin, but to make capital out of his conversion from gambler to preacher and to confine himself to those less enlightened groups that thoroughly believed in the possibility of so sudden and complete a transformation.

The inflow of rural folk from the South was therefore fortune, and Reverend Shackleton Ealey spent hours in Pennsylvania station getting newly arrived migrants, urging them to visit his meeting-place and promising them the satisfaction of "that old-time religion." Many had come—and contributed.

This was prayer-meeting night. Reverend Ealey had his seat on a low platform at the distant end of the double room originally designed for a "parlor." From behind a pulpit-stand improvised out of soap-boxes and covered with calico, he counted his congregation and estimated his profit.

A stranger entered uncertainly, looked about a moment, and took a seat near the door. Reverend Shackleton Ealey appraised him: a little bent-over old man with a bushy white beard and a long Prince Albert coat. Perfect type—fertile soil. He must greet this stranger at the close of the meeting and effusively make him welcome.

But Sister Gassoway was already by the stranger's side, shaking his hand vigorously and with unmistakable joy; and during the next hymn she came over to old man Gassoway and whispered in his ear, where-upon he jumped up wide-eyed, looked around, and made broadly smiling toward the newcomer. Others turned to see, and many, on seeing, began to whisper excitedly into their neighbor's ear and turned to see again. The stranger was occasioning altogether too great a stir. Reverend Ealey decided to pray.

His prayer was a masterpiece. It besought of God protection for His people in a strange and wicked land; it called down His damnation upon those dens of iniquity, the dance halls, the theaters, the cabarets; it berated the poker-sharp, the blackjack player, the dice-roller; it de-nounced the drunkard, the bootlegger, the dope-peddler; and it ended in a sweeping tirade against the wolf-in-sheep's clothing, whatever his motive might be.

Another hymn and the meeting came to a close.

The stranger was surrounded before Reverend Ealey could reach him. When finally he approached the old preacher with extended hand and hollow-hearted smile, old man Gassoway was saying:

"Yas, suh, Rev'n Taylor, dass jes' whut we goin' do. Start makin' 'rangements tomorrer. Martin an' Jim Lee's over to Ebeneezer, but dey doan like it 'tall. Says hit's too hifalutin for 'em, de way dese Harlem culled folks wushup; Ain't got no Holy Ghos' in 'em, dass whut. Jes' come in an' set down an' git up an' go out. Never moans, never shouts, never even says 'amen.' Most of us is hyeh, an' we gonna git together an' start us a ch'ch of our own, wid you f' pastor, like we said. Yas, suh. Hyeh's Brother Ealey now. Brother Ealey, dis hyeh's our old preacher Rev'n Taylor. We was jes' tellin' him—"

The Reverend Shackleton Ealey had at last a genuine revelation—that the better-yielding half of his flock was on the wing. An old oath of frustration leaped to his lips—"God—" but he managed to bite it in the middle—"bless you, my brother," he growled.

II

"What makes you think you can cook?"

"Why, brother, I been in the neighborhood o' grub all my life!"

"Humph! Fly bird, you are."

"Pretty near all birds fly, friend."

"Yes—even black birds."

The applicant for the cook's job lost his joviality. "All right. I'm a black bird. You're a half-yaller hound. Step out in the air an' I'll fly down your dam' throat, so I can see if your insides is yaller, too!"

The clerk grinned. "You must do your cooking on the top of your head. Turn around and fly out that door there and see if the Hundred and Thirty-Fifth Street breeze won't cool you off some. We want a fireless cooker."

With an unmistakable suggestion as to how the clerk might dispose of his job the applicant rolled cloudily out of the employment office. The clerk called "Next!" and Jake Crinshaw, still convulsed with astonishment, nearly lost his turn.

"What kind of work are you looking for, buddy?"

"No purtickler kin', suh. Jes' work, dass all."

"Well, what can you do?"

"Mos' anything, I reckon."

"Drive a car?"

"No suh. Never done dat."

"Wait table?"

"Well, I never is."

"Run elevator?"

"No, suh."

"What have you been doing?"

"Farmin'."

"Farming? Where?"

"Jennin's Landin', Virginia. 'At's wha' all my folks is fum."

"How long you been here?"

"Ain' been hyeh a week yit. Still huntin' work." Jake answered rather apologetically. The question had been almost hostile.

"Oh—migrant." In the clerk's tone were patronization, some contempt, a little cynical amusement and complete comprehension. "Migrant" meant nothing to Jake; to the clerk it explained everything.

"M-hm. Did you try the office up above—between here and Seventh Avenue? They wanted two dozen laborers for a railroad camp upstate—pay your transportation, board and everything."

"Yas, suh—up there yestiddy, but de man say dey had all dey need. Tole me to try y'all down hyeh."

"M-hm. Well, I'm sorry, but we haven't anything for you this morning. Come in later in the week. Something may turn up."

"Yas, suh. Thank y' suh."

Jake made his discouraged way to the sidewalk and stood contemplating. His blue jumpers were clean and spotless—they had been his Sunday go-to-meeting ones at home. He wore big, broad, yellow shoes and a shapeless tan felt hat, beneath whose brim the hair was close cut, the neck shaved bare. He was very much dressed up.

The applicant who had preceded him approached. "What'd that yaller dog tell you, bud?"

"Tole me come in later."

"Huh! That's what they all say. Only way for a guy with guts to get anything in this town is to be a bigger crook 'n the next one." He pointed to two well-dressed young men idling on the curb. "See them two? They used to wait on a job where I was chef. Now look at 'em—prosperous! An' how 'd they get that way? Hmph! That one's a pimp an' th' other's a pickpocket. Take your choice." And the cynic departed.

But Jake had greater faith in Harlem. Its praises had been sounded too highly—there must be something.

He turned and looked at the signboard that had led him to enter the employment office. It was a wooden blackboard, on which was written in chalk: "Help wanted. All sorts of jobs. If we haven't it, leave your name and we'll find it." The clerk hadn't asked Jake *his* name.

A clanging, shrieking fire engine appeared from nowhere and swept terrifyingly past. It frightened Jake like the first locomotive he had seen as a child. He shrank back against the building. Another engine passed. No more. He felt better. No one minded the engines. No one noticed that he did. Harlem itself was a fire engine.

Jake could read the signs on the buildings across the street: "Harlem Commercial and Savings Bank"—"Hale and Clark, Real Estate"—"Restaurant and Delicatessen, J. W. Jackson, proprietor"—"The Music Shop"—"John Gilmore, Tonsorial Parlor." He looked up at the buildings. They were menacingly big and tall and close. There were no trees. No ground for trees to grow from. Sidewalks overflowing with children. Streets crammed full of street-cars and automobiles. Noise, hurry, bustle—fire engines.

Jake looked again at the signboard. Help wanted—all sorts. After a while he heaved a great sigh, turned slowly, and slouched wearily on, hoping to catch sight of another employment office with a signboard out front.

III

It was eleven o'clock at night. Majutah knew that Harry would be waiting on the doorstep downstairs. He knew better than to ring the bell so late—she had warned him. And there was no telephone. Grandmother wouldn't consent to having a telephone in the flat—she thought it would draw lightning. As if every other flat in the house didn't have one, as if lightning would strike all the others and leave theirs unharmed! Grandmother was such a nuisance with her old fogeyisms. If it weren't for her down-home ideas there'd be no trouble getting out now to go to the cabaret with Harry. As it was, Majutah would have to steal down the hall past Grandmother's room in the hope that she would be asleep.

Majutah looked to her attire. The bright red sandals and scarlet stockings, she fancied, made her feet look smaller and her legs bigger. This was desirable, since her black crepe dress, losing in width what style had added to its length, would not permit her to sit comfortably and cross her knees without occasioning ample display of everything below them. Her vanity-case mirror revealed how exactly the long pendant earrings matched her red coral beads and how perfectly becoming the new close bob was, and assured her for the tenth time that Egyptian rouge made her skin look lighter. She was ready.

Into the narrow hallway she tipped, steadying herself against the walls, and slowly approached the outside door at the end. Grandmother's room was the last off the hallway. Majutah reached it, slipped successfully past, and started silently to open the door to freedom.

"Jutie?"

How she hated to be called Jutie! Why couldn't the meddlesome old thing say Madge like everyone else?

"Ma'am?"

"Wha' you goin' dis time o' night?"

"Just downstairs to mail a letter."

"You easin' out mighty quiet, if dat's all you goin' do. Come 'eh. Lemme look at you."

Majutah slipped off her pendants and beads and laid them on the floor. She entered her grandmother's room, standing where the foot of the bed would hide her gay shoes and stockings. Useless precautions. The shrewd old woman inspected her granddaughter a minute in disapproving silence, then asked:

"Well, wha's de letter?"

"Hello, Madge," said Harry. "What held you up? You look mad enough to bite bricks."

"I am. Grandmother, of course. She's a pest. Always nosing and meddling. I'm grown, and the money I make supports both of us, and I'm sick of acting like a kid just to please her."

"How'd you manage?"

"I didn't manage. I just gave her a piece of my mind and came on out."

"Mustn't hurt the old lady's feelings. It's just her way of looking out for you."

"I don't need any looking out for—or advice either!"

"Excuse me. Which way—Happy's or Edmonds'?"

"Edmonds'—darn it!"

"Right."

It was two o'clock in the morning. Majutah's grandmother closed her Bible and turned down the oil lamp by which she preferred to read it. For a long time she sat thinking of Jutie—and of Harlem, this city of Satan. It was Harlem that had changed Jutie—this great, noisy, heartless, crowded place where you lived under the same roof with a hundred people you never knew; where night was alive and morning dead. It was Harlem—those brazen women with whom Jutie sewed, who swore and shimmied and laughed at the suggestion of going to church. Jutie wore red stockings. Jutie wore dresses that looked like nightgowns. Jutie painted her face and straightened her hair, instead of leaving it as God intended. Jutie—lied—often.

And while Madge laughed at a wanton song, her grandmother knelt by her bed and through the sinful babel of the airshaft, through her own silent tears, prayed to God in heaven for Jutie's lost soul.

IV

"Too much learnin' ain' good f' nobody. When I was her age I couldn't write my own name."

"You can't write much mo' 'n that now. Too much learnin'! Whoever heard o' sich a thing!"

Anna's father, disregarding experience in arguing with his wife, pressed his point. "Sho they's sich a thing as too much learnin'! 'At gal's gittin' so she don't b'lieve nuthin'!"

"Hmph! Didn't she jes' tell me las' night she didn' b'lieve they ever was any Adam an' Eve?"

"Well, I ain' so sho they ever was any myself! An' one thing is certain: If that gal o' mine wants to keep on studyin' an' go up there to that City College an' learn how to teach school an' be somebody, I'll work my fingers to the bone to help her do it! Now!"

"That ain' what I'm talkin' 'bout. You ain' worked no harder'n I is to help her git this far. Hyeh she is ready to graduate from high school. Think of it—high school! When we come along they didn' even *have* no high schools. Fus' thing y' know she be so far above us we can't reach her with a fence-rail. Then you'll wish you'd a listened to me. What I says is, she done gone far enough."

"Ain' no sich thing as far enough when you wants to go farther. 'Tain' as if it was gonna cost a whole lot. That's the trouble with you cullud folks now. Git so far an' stop—set down—through—don't want no mo'." Her disgust was boundless. "Y' got too much cotton field in you, that's what!"

The father grinned. "They sho' ain' no cotton field in yo' mouth, honey."

"No, they ain't. An' they ain' no need o' all this arguin' either, 'cause all that gal's got to do is come in hyeh right now an' put her arms 'roun' y' neck, an' you'd send her to Europe if she wanted to go!"

"Well, all I says is, when dey gits to denyin' de Bible hit's time to stop 'em."

"Well all I says is, if Cousin Sukie an' yo' no 'count brother, Jonathan, can send their gal all the way from Athens to them Howard's an' pay car-fare an' boa'd an' ev'ything, we can send our gal—"

She broke off as a door slammed. There was a rush, a delightful squeal, and both parents were being smothered in a cyclone of embraces by a wildly jubilant daughter.

"Mummy! Daddy! I won it! I won it!"

"What under the sun—?"

"The scholarship, Mummy! The scholarship!"

"No!"

"Yes, I did! I can go to Columbia! I can go to Teachers College! Isn't it great?"

Anna's mother turned triumphantly to her husband; but he was beaming at his daughter.

"Yo sho' is yo' daddy's chile. Teachers College! Why, that's wha' I been wantin' you to go all along!"

V

Rare sight in a close-built, top-heavy city—space. A wide open lot, extending along One Hundred and Thirty-Eighth Street almost from Lenox to Seventh Avenue; baring the mangy backs of a long row of One Hundred and Thirty-Ninth Street houses; disclosing their gaping, gasping windows, their shameless strings of half-laundered rags, which gulp up what little air the windows seek to inhale. Occupying the Lenox Avenue end of the lot, the so-called Garvey tabernacle, wide, low, squat, with its stingy little entrance; occupying the other, the church tent where summer camp meetings are held.

Pete and his buddy, Lucky, left their head-to-head game of coon-can[1] as darkness came on. Time to go out—had to save gas. Pete went to the window and looked down at the tent across the street.

"Looks like the side show of a circus. Ever been in?"

"Not me. I'm a preacher's son—got enough o' that stuff when I was a kid and couldn't protect myself."

"Ought to be a pretty good show when some o' them oldtime sisters get happy. Too early for the cabarets; let's go in a while, just for the hell of it."

"You sure are hard up for somethin' to do."

"Aw, come on. Somethin' funny's bound to happen. You might even get religion, you dam' bootlegger."

Lucky grinned. "Might meet some o' my customers, you mean."

Through the thick, musty heat imprisoned by the canvas shelter a man's voice rose, leading a spiritual. Other voices chimed eagerly in, some high, clear, sweet; some low, mellow, full,—all swelling, rounding out the refrain till it filled the place, so that it seemed the flimsy walls and roof must soon be torn from their moorings and swept aloft with the song:

> Where you running, sinner?
> Where you running, I say?
> Running from the fire—
> You can't cross here!

The preacher stood waiting for the song to melt away. There was a moment of abysmal silence, into which the thousand blasphemies filtering in from outside dropped unheeded.

The preacher was talking in deep, impressive tones. One old patriarch was already supplementing each statement with a matter-of-fact "amen!" of approval.

The preacher was describing hell. He was enumerating without exception the horrors that befall the damned: maddening thirst for the drunkard; for the gambler, insatiable flame, his own greed devouring his soul. The preacher's voice no longer talked—it sang; mournfully at first, monotonously up and down, up and down—a chant in minor mode; then more intensely, more excitedly; now fairly strident.

The amens of approval were no longer matter-of-fact, perfunctory. They were quick, spontaneous, escaping the lips of their own accord; they were frequent and loud and began to come from the edges of the assembly instead of just the front rows. The old men cried, "Help him, Lord!" "Preach the word!" "Glory!" taking no apparent heed of the awfulness of the description, and the old women continuously moaned aloud, nodding their bonneted heads or swaying rhythmically forward and back in their seats.

Suddenly the preacher stopped, leaving the old men and old women still noisy with spiritual momentum. He stood motionless till the last echo of approbation subsided, then repeated the text from which his discourse had taken origin; repeated it in a whisper, lugubrious, hoarse, almost inaudible: " 'In—hell—' " paused, then without warning, wildly shrieked, " '*In hell*—' " stopped—returned to his hoarse whisper—" 'he lifted up his eyes....' "

"What the hell you want to leave for?" Pete complained when he and Lucky reached the sidewalk. "That old bird would 'a' coughed up his gizzard in two more minutes. What's the idea?"

"Aw hell—I don't know.—You think that stuff's funny. You laugh at it. I don't, that's all." Lucky hesitated. The urge to speak outweighed the fear of being ridiculed. "Dam' 'f I know what it is—maybe because it makes me think of the old folks or somethin'—but—hell—it just sorter—gets me—"

Lucky turned abruptly away and started off. Pete watched him for a moment with a look that should have been astonished, outraged, incredulous—but wasn't. He overtook him, put an arm about his shoulders, and because he had to say something as they walked on, muttered reassuringly:

"Well—if you ain't the damndest fool—"

(1925)

NOTE

1. Coon-can: A two-handed card game popular among Southern Negroes (a rummy-like game).

The Promised Land

At a certain level of the airshaft two songs, issuing from opposite windows, met, mingled minor refrains, and rose together toward Negro Harlem's black sky; two futile prayers which spent themselves like mist ere they reached the roof. The one was a prayer for the love of man, the other a prayer for the love of God: "blues," and a spiritual.

The blues song would have drowned the spiritual had it not labored against a closed window. No such barrier stayed the spiritual. To be sure the singer was old, as her present posture emphasized: shoulders bent round, dim eyes and unsteady hands searching the pages of the Bible on her lap. But her voice was well sustained, and her song was none the less clear because it accompanied her endless thumbing of thin leaves.

Like her eyes and her fingers, her hymn sought comfort, sought while it almost despaired:—

> Bow low!—How low mus' I bow?
> Bow low!—How low mus' I bow?
> Bow low!—How low mus' I bow
> To enter in de promis' land?

Presently, as if there came no answer, she interrupted her quest and her song, turned out the gas, and sat back in the darkness to observe the progress of the rent party across the shaft.

A rent party is a public dance given in a private apartment. If, after letting out three of your five rooms to lodgers, your resources are still unequal to your rent, you make up the deficit by means of a rent party. You provide music, your friends provide advertisement, and your guests, by paying admission, provide what your resources lack.[1]

Such a party Mammy now witnessed. Through the window opposite her own she commanded most of one room and a corner of another in the adjacent flat. The window was indeed a screen upon which flashed a motion picture oddly alive and colorful. Boys whose loose trousers were too long for their legs and girls whose tight skirts were too short for theirs hugged each other close, keeping time to the rhythm of hoarsely phonographed blues.

Bright enough dresses, certainly: scarlet and green and glowing purple, rendering dark complexions darker, lending life to pale ones; dresses that, having lost half their volume, put all their color into the rest. Bright enough faces, too: boys wagging their heads and grinning, girls gayly laughing at their jokes.

But such a dance! The camel walk. Everybody "camelling." Had God wanted man to move like a camel He'd have put a hump in his back. Yet was there any sign of what God wanted in that scene across the shaft? Skins that He had made black bleached brown, brown ones bleached cream-color; hair that He had made long and kinky bobbed short and ironed dead straight. Young girls' arms about boys' shoulders, their own waists tightly clasped; bodies warmly fused, bending to the sensual waves of the "camel." Where was God in that?

Mammy watched as she had often watched before, with a dull wonder that such colossal wickedness should be allowed to prevail. The song that had mingled with hers now filtered through the closed window opposite and came along to her ears, bringing no reassurance. For all that it plumbed the nadir of woe, was it not a song of sin?

> Lawdy, Lawdy, I can't help but cry an' moan.
> Lawdy, Lawdy, I can't help but cry an' moan.
> My man done gone and lef' me—
>   gone an' lef' me all alone.

One couple swung into view which especially caught Mammy's attention, so completely had it abandoned itself to the dance. Mammy saw with a little quiver of alarm that the boy was her grandson, Sam. Wesley, her other grandson, was also in that company, and it was Wesley's girl with whom Sam was dancing. If Wesley ever saw Sam dancing like that with Ellie—

In the visible corner of the far room Mammy recognized Wesley's back. Wesley's shoulders, far less mobile than Sam's, were gradually turning as he faced about in the slow measure of the dance. In but a few seconds he would be looking at his cousin through the intervening doorway, would see Sam and Ellie's exaggerated movements, despite the people between. An old and mounting hostility between them would swiftly surge and flare—they would quarrel, perhaps they would fight. Mammy sat up, leaned tensely forward, whispered, "Lawd, have mercy!"

Unlike her earlier prayer, this one was apparently heard, for at that moment the blues halted and the dancing abruptly ceased. The change of partners, however, only momentarily relieved Mammy's qualms. Over her settled a deadly certainty that the clash had been merely postponed. There would be many more dances, one of which would rejoin Ellie and Sam as partners. The later that happened, the higher would everyone's spirits be, the wilder the dancing, and so the quicker and hotter Wesley's resentment. As the new dance began, Mammy grew

rapidly surer of what she foresaw. Soon her helplessness and the increasing effort to suppress her excitement welled almost beyond bearing. Her misgiving urged her to do something to prevent this long-
deferred crisis; but somehow she could only sit still and look on and
pray that this time for once her foresight would prove wrong.

Her apprehension became black emptiness into which memories,
rocket-wise, soared and burst: rumor of opportunity in the cities of the
North—certainly of ruin should rumor prove false; hope of young and
old men departing, of women and children gone after them—despair
of tranquil homes upheaved, of families ruthlessly scattered; the joy
she herself had felt when these two grandsons had finally sent for her—
the sorrow of being the last to leave the lopsided old Virginia home.

They were equally dear to Mammy, these two boys, and, until they
had come to New York, had been equally fond of each other. They had
grown up together, attended the four-months-a-year school together,
played hooky, fished, hunted rabbits, and got baptized together; and
finally, caught in the epidemic fever of migration that swept the dark-
skinned South, they had left home together to find their fortunes in
Harlem.

As life had thus brought some to seek wealth, so death, back home,
brought others to seek peace; but Mammy had been beckoned toward
neither goal, had simply been left quite alone. And rather because there
was nothing else to do than because they wanted or needed her, the
cousins, Wesley and Sam, had offered to let her housekeep for them
in a small flat in the great city.

Scarcely had she got over the shock of underground railroads, of
trains overhead, of mountainous buildings where people lived like
chickens, before she perceived that the city had done something to
Wesley and Sam. They had lost their comradeship, they just managed
to tolerate each other, and they compensated for this mere toleration
by goading each other persistently with strange, new malicious jibes:—

"Down-home boy lak you ain' got no business in no city nohow."

"Don ketch me th'owin' my money 'way on no numbers, though, uh
no baseball pool."

"Co'se not. You don' *make* no money. How you go'n'th'ow any 'way?"

Mammy soon saw what new feature of their life lay at the bottom of
this. To Sam, whose hands learned quickly, the city had been kind.
Starting as handy man in a garage, he had soon become a mechanic's
helper, and now at last was a mechanic with wages of sixty dollars a
week. Wesley, always more awkward, had found the city indifferent,
and so perforce had become his own boss, washing windows at fifteen
cents each. So Harlem, where there was insistent competition to test
and reward special skill, and where there was so much more for men
to quarrel about and resent, had quickly estranged these two unguarded

lads simply by paying the one twice as much as the other; had furnished
them thus with taunts that had not been possible back home, and now
kept them constantly wounding each other with the heedless cruelty
of children—wounds that would one day translate themselves from the
spirit into the flesh.

"Ellie? Ellie yo' gal? Whut business you got wid a gal? You could n'
buy a gal coffee n' a san'wich."

"Reckon you could buy huh champagne an' lobster."

"An' I don' mean maybe."

"Better put some dat money in accident 'nsurance den."

"What you talkin' 'bout?"

" 'Cause 'f I ketch you messin' roun' Ellie I'm sho' go'n' turn yo'
damper down. An' I don' mean maybe."

"Shuh! Listen t' dis boogy.² Man, my slowes' move's too fas' f' you."

"Not yo' slowes' move roun' Ellie ain't."

"One my thoughts 'd bust yo' haid wide open."

"Yeah? Well it don' do nuthin' to *yo*' haid but *swell* it."

Suddenly these remembered mockings leaped out of past into present. As one rudely waked starts up, so Mammy's fear now started out
of the stupor of memory. In the room across the airshaft Sam and Wesley
were facing each other, the fire of their hostility having driven the
onlookers back into an expectant surrounding circle. Mammy saw the
boys' lips move, and from their malignant countenances and the dismay
on the faces about them she knew that again bitter taunts were being
exchanged, this time in company where words quickly kindled action.
Hitherto her own presence had always restrained them. Now the only
spectators were hoodlums off the street, before whom the boys might
well wish to show off, at the same time squaring the urgent account of
a hundred bygone insults.

The antagonists stood toe to toe, Sam the more lithe, slightly taller,
Wesley broader and heavier. Their lips no longer moved, and Mammy
recognized that silent, critical moment in an encounter when the mere
forward swaying of a body is enough to free madness.

She jumped up, tried to cry out a warning, achieved but a groan:
"Good Lawd!" Her impotence became frenzy; she cast about wildly for
some means of diverting the inevitable. A soft golden glint caught and
held her eyes—the gilt edge of the Bible still in her hand, touched to
a glow by light from across the way.

The Bible was suddenly divine revelation, an answer. She hesitated
only long enough to note Sam's hand creeping toward his coat pocket.
"God fo'give me," she breathed; then drew back an arm grown oppor-
tunely strong, and hurled the Word with all her might through the pane
of the opposite window.

At the crash and jingle of glass she shrank back into the shadow of her own room; yet not so far back as to obscure the picture of her two grandsons, staring limply agape, now at each other, now at the Book at their feet.

II

Mammy asked Ellie point blank:—

"Which a one my boys you lak sho' nuff?"

And Ellie, a girl of the city, replied with a laugh and a toss of her bob:—

"Both of 'em. Why not?"

They sat in the kitchen of Mammy's three-room flat, of which the parlor served as the boys' bedroom and the third room on the airshaft as Mammy's own. Ellie and a chum occupied a similar apartment, the adjacent one, where the rent party had been given; and Ellie occasionally "ran in," ostensibly anxious to inquire after Mammy, actually hoping to see one of the boys and possibly make a date.

Mammy saw through these visits, of course, and had thought that Ellie's interest was in Wesley. But Ellie's behaviour with Sam at the party tinctured this conclusion with doubt. No girl, thought Mammy, who liked one man would behave like that with another—not with both present.

Hence, with characteristic directness, Mammy instituted investigation; and Ellie's side-stepping answer but whetted a suspicion already keen.

"You lak bofe of 'm d' same?" [sic]

"I'll say I do."

"Jes d' same?"

"Nothin' different."

"Hmph. Dat mean you don' really lak neither one of 'm, den."

"Oh, yes, I do. Pretty skee sheiks[3] for country jakes."

"Whut you lak 'bout 'm?"

"Well, different things. Sam's crazy and knows how to show a girl a good time, see? Wesley ain't so crazy, but he tries hard and you can depend on him. You wonder about Sam, you know about Wesley. Wesley's better-lookin', too."

"S'posin' you had to choose between 'm. Which a one you take?"

"Oh, Sam. Sam makes twice as much as Wesley."

The casualness of that answer made Mammy wince. To accustom yourself to some things is easy—to subways and "L's," to army-worn traffic, to hard grassless pavements, hot treeless sidewalks, cold distant starless skies; even to a fifth-story roost on the airshaft of a seven-story hencoop. But to accustom yourself to the philosophy of the metropolis, to its ruthless opportunism—that is hard.

"S'posin'," Mammy experimented, "dey bofe made zackly d' same? Which a one you take den?"

The questioning began to irritate Ellie. "Wha' d' y' mean, take? I ain't grabbin' after neither one of 'em, y' know."

"I mean ef dey bofe ast you to marry 'm."

"Oh, to marry 'em? And both drawin' the same pay? Why, Wesley, by all—" Ellie bit her lip, and withdrew into the cautious neutrality out of which the unexpected contemplation of matrimony had surprised her. "Or—well—either one—I don't know." This old woman was nearer to either boy than was she herself, she remembered. Both the bumpkins spent on her. Why reduce her chances for a good time by making a betraying choice? Play the boobs off against each other, let them both strut their stuff. Maybe a better catch then either would meanwhile gulp your bait. Then you could discard both these poor fish with a laugh. "You know what the song says, Mammy: 'Don't let no one man worry your mind.' "

Mammy looked at Ellie as she might have looked at the armadillo in the zoo—this strange, unbelievable creature who in the spring of her life subjected romance to utility. For Mammy saw that the girl really preferred Wesley to Sam, yet had no apology of word or manner in prospectively renouncing Wesley's character for Sam's superior pay. Young, pretty, live girls like Ellie should have to be told to consider their suitors' pay. With them it ought to be secondary to youth's more compelling absurdities. But here was a slip of a girl who spoke like a thrice-married widow of fifty.

Mammy accepted this as one of the mysteries of city breeding. Having done so, it was easy to prophesy. Ellie's willingness to take equally what Sam and Wesley had to give would be the crux of the boys' antagonism. Wesley claimed right of priority. Neither Ellie nor Sam cared a sneeze for such right. Ellie, city-wise, "liked them both." Into the mould of this situation all of the vague potent bitterness of the boys' recent hatred would be poured, to take definite form. The city had broken the bond between them. The city now fashioned them a bludgeon with which to shatter their common life.

"Listen, daughter. How come you carry on wid Sam lak dat las' night? Did n' you know 't would start trouble?"

"Carry on? Wha' d' y' mean, carry on? I only danced with 'im."

"Dat all? Den whut start d' trouble?"

"Wesley buttin' in, the dumbbell. Why don't somebody tell him something? He ain't down home now. This is New York."

"Uh-huh. Dis is New York. Dis is New York. An' ain't New York in God's worl'? Don' New York come under His eyes a-tall?"

This was quite out of Ellie's line. She shrugged and kept still. Mammy's voice, however, grew stronger with her pain.

"New York. Harlem. Thought all along 't was d' las' stop 'fo' Heaven. Canaan hitself. Reg'lar promis' lan'. Well, dat's jes' whut 't is—a promis' lan'. All it do is promise. Promise money lak growin' on trees—ain' even got d'trees. Promise wuk fo' dem whut want wuk—look at my boy, Wesley. Promise freedom fum d' whi' folks—white man be hyeh to-day, take d' las' penny fo' rent. You know why 't is? You know how come?"

Ellie stared. Mammy got up, stood erect with almost majestic dignity. "Hit's sin. Dat's whut 't is—sin. My people done fo'got dey God, grabbin' after money. I warn 'm 'fo' dey all lef'. Longin' fo' d' things o' dis worl' an' a-fo'gittin' d' Lawd Jesus. Broke up dey homes in d' country—lef' folks behind sick an' dyin'. So anxious. So scairt all d' money be gone 'fo' dey git hyeh. I tole 'm. Fust seek d' kingdom of God an' His right-eousness. But no. Everybody done gone crazy over gittin'. An' hit don' bring nothin' but misery in dis worl' an' hellfire in eternity. Hit's sin!"

"Soft pedal, Mammy. And hold the sermon, will you?"

"An' dat's another thing." The diminished tone only bared Mammy's intensity. "You-all so scairt o' d' Word o' God. Sam and Wesley done got d' same way sence dey been up hyeh. Seem lak hit make you oncomf'table. Make you squirm. Make you squirm wuss'n 'at low-down dancin' you do. Well, hit oughter. Garment o' righteousness don' b'long on no body o' sin."[4]

Ellie didn't quite get this, but she didn't like the way Mammy was looking at her. "Say, what's the idea?" she inquired.

"Idea?" Mammy grew calm, almost cold; focused her distraction on one problem: "Idea is, you either let *one* my boys alone or let 'em *bofe* alone. You heah? You cain't run wid d' hare an' hunt wid d' hounds. Dis hyeh 'either one' business'll have 'm both at each other's th'oats 'fo' another day. Lawd knows dey'd be better off ef you stayed 'way fum 'm bofe."

At this Ellie flared. "Well, of all the cockeyed nerve! Say, where do you think you get off? D' you s'pose I'm chasin' after your farmer boys?"

Mammy said nothing. It was Ellie's turn to wax loud.

"Pity, you old handkerchief-heads wouldn' stay down South where you belong. First you ask me to state my intentions. Then you tell me I started the argument at the party. Then you preach me a sermon on sin or clothes or somethin'. Then you tell *me* to let *them* alone—as if they didn't pester me dizzy. As if I was *chasin'* them. What are you trying to call me, anyhow? Do you think I'd chase any bozo[5] on earth?"

Mammy did not dream what vile accusation lay in the provincialism "chase." Unaware of what the word meant to Ellie, she commented promptly and bluntly:—

"You sho' ain' chasin' me."

Ellie sprang up, furious, inflamed less by the implication than by

Mammy's intuitively shrewd analysis. "Why, you dirty old devil—I ought to paste you one! If that's what you think you can all go to hell." She turned and strode hotly away, flinging back a smouldering "Damn you!" The hall door slammed behind her with a bang that jarred the floor.

Mammy stood bewildered a while; presently murmured, "She cuss' me—" Slowly she sank into her chair and looked around at the close kitchen walls; kept repeating, as if to convince herself, "Dat li'l chile— she cuss' me."

III

The three-room apartment boasted four windows, and on them, following Mammy's request, Wesley agreed to finish his fruitless day.

"I done done d' inside all right," she explained, "but I cain't make d' outside. I scairt to stick my haid out one o' dese winders. No sense in folks livin' in d' side of a cliff dis-a-way—'cep'n' hit's as near to d' heaven as dey'll ever git again."

Wesley, polishing glass, endeavored to stay the passing light of day with song, but even his song grew dark as the mood of blues settled gradually over it:—

> . . . cain't but cry an' moan.
> My gal done gone an' lef' me—gone an' lef' me all alone.

The words were not without significance. Usually Ellie greeted him with great show of eagerness; comforted him at the end of a poor day when he dropped in for a while before dinner; suggested some means of disposing of the day's return—which, of course, was too small to save. But today, after peeping out as usual, she had slammed the door in his face.

"Ellie—wha's a matter?"

Only a diminuendo of angry clicks, receding down her hallway.

Well, it had served him right. He'd been warned about these uppity Northern gals, these "gimme" gals. Always had their hands out, expecting something. Something for nothing. Taxis. Eats. Liquor. Big times. Back home a girl couldn't want so much because there wasn't so much to want. But here—no effort on his part in spending three days' earnings on Ellie in a single night. No effort on her part to save it, either. And in return a kiss and a promise—a promise to go out again with him some night. Gimme.

Probably sore because he'd started a row at her party last night. Well, was she his gal or wasn't she? A kiss. In the city a kiss has many meanings. Maybe she kissed Sam also. Maybe her kisses were a commodity.

He stopped polishing to look down on the street five stories below. Folks look funny at that distance and angle. All look alike. None human. Long thin feet alternately passing each other, arms circling awkwardly outside the feet, heads gliding squatly forward in the midst of arms and legs. People seen on end resemble spiders.

Ellie, maybe, was a spider, and he had been her fly. Having withdrawn his little substance, she now discarded his shell. Sam's turn now. Fly guy, Sam. Ought to swat him. Leave it to Ellie—she'll swat him for sixty bucks a week. Gimme.

"Don' set dey idle, son. Fust thing you know you'll lose yo' holt an' fall."

"Make no diff'unce ef I land on my haid."

"Git th'ough in d'kitchen nex'. Got to git supper. Sam be home tireckly."

"M-hm."

Wesley did the kitchen window and proceeded to Mammy's room. The airshaft was quite dark, so that he had to light the gas jet. He soaped his wet rag and clambered half through, turned, and clamped his heels as usual against the wall beneath the sill, thus leaving both hands free for work. He soaped the outside surface of the pane and, while waiting for it to dry, twisted about to look behind him at Ellie's window. It was still unrepaired; a newspaper covered the jagged opening in the pane. His enlarged shadow fell misshapen on the wall about the window and the jagged opening looked like a wound in his side.

Somewhere beyond the broken window a door banged loudly shut. Soon another, closer door did likewise.

Sam shuffled angrily into the kitchen and tossed something black on to the table, where it landed with a thump. Peering over her "specks," Mammy recognized her Bible. She reproved:—"Don't you know no better 'n to th'ow d' Word of d' Lawd aroun' lak dat? Better learn to keep it near yuh."

"Didn' th'ow it half as fur as you did."

"I th'owed it to keep you young fools fum doin' harm. You jes' th'owed it to be th'owin'."

"Da's aw right 'bout doin' harm. Ef I had busted Wesley, he could 'a' gone to d' free hospital. But you busted d' winder. Who go'n' pay fo' dat?"

"Lan'lawd oughter pay fo' it. He charge enough rent."

"Maybe he would, but sump'n done got into Ellie—she raisin' d' devil. 'Clare out she go'n' tell d' lan'lawd you th'owed it—yo' name's wrote in it. Dat mean I have to pay d' bill—lak I pay f' ev'ything else roun' hyeh."

"Dat all she say?"

"No. Say she go'n have you 'rested fo' disturbin' d' peace. Say sump'n 'bout slander too."

"Hmph!"

"Den she slam' d' do' in my face."

"Maybe dat'll help you stay 'way fum 'uh."

"Stay 'way fo' whut?"

"Cause she ain' got d' love o' God in huh heart, dat's fo' whut. An' neither is you. Hit's a bad combination."

"Ain' lookin' fo no love o' God. Lookin' fo' Wesley. Wha' he at?"

"Washin' my room winder. Let 'im 'lone."

"I'll let 'im 'lone, aw right. I'll th'ow 'im out it."

Only Wesley's legs were visible to Sam, entering the room. Wesley was wiping off the frosting of soap that he had allowed to dry on the pane. As he wiped, more of his body appeared through the glass thus made clear, and at last his troubled face. It showed surprise at the presence of Sam, who stood glowering accusation.

"What d' hell you been tellin' Ellie 'bout me?"

Even through intervening glass Wesley's anger was quick to respond. "What d' hell could I tell 'uh bad enough?"

"You been puttin' me in—else she wouldn' 'a' slam' no do' in my face."

"She slam' d' do' in yo' face?"

"Reckon you tole 'uh to do it."

Wesley's anger subsided. He repeated, with something akin to relief, eagerly,—

"Say she slam' d' do' in yo' face?"

"Did n' miss it."

Wesley threw back his head and filled the airshaft with loud laughter. To Sam it was galling, derisive, contemptuous laughter, laughter of victory. Anger, epithets, blows he could have exchanged, but laughter found him defenseless. In a hot flush of rage he drew back a foot and kicked viciously at Wesley's legs.

At the moment Wesley had only one leg pressed firmly back against the wall. It was this that received the blow, and the quick sharp pain loosened its grip. In swift effort to catch himself, Wesley snatched at the bottom edge of the lower frame, but with such desperate force that it slid instantly upward, so that his hold was broken by the upper. Grabbing wildly, Sam sprang forward, frightened into contrition—succeeded only in further dislodging his already unbalanced cousin. A brief mad scramble to save him—a futile clawing and slipping of hands—a cry—a moment's incredulous silence—silence that broke with a soft and terrible thud.

Sam shrank back and threw one hand up over his mouth like a child that has heard something forbidden; wheeled, to see Mammy stiff in the doorway, staring with stricken eyes. Hysteria gripped him.

"I didn' do it—I 'clare out 'fo' God, Mammy—" He turned back toward the window; backed off from it, crouching and trembling; faced again toward Mammy. Deprecation gave way to bravado. He whispered sharply, "Ef you tell anybody, I'll—" Then suddenly rushed with insane menace toward her as panic rushed through his brain, reached her, stopped—abruptly collapsed at her feet, shuddering with sobs.

Mammy, roused by a spirit which still hoped in the face of calamity, quickly bent down and shook the crumpled lad with sobering vigor. "Git up, son! Make has'e! Git up! Mammy seen yuh! Seen yuh try to ketch 'im! Make has'e to 'im! Maybe he's on'y hurt!"

The boy raised a countenance wretched with fear and doubt and weakness, but the strength and will in Mammy's eyes brought him to his senses.

"Make has'e, I tell yuh!"

He jumped up, his face still convulsed, and sped toward the outer door and the stairs.

IV

Again Mammy sat by her window, her fingers groping amid the thin leaves of her Bible.

Out of the airshaft sounds came to her, sounds of the land of promise. Noise of a rent party somewhere below from a tiny dwelling that had to be hired out if it was to be dwelt in at all—peculiar feature of a place where your own home wasn't your own. Noise of a money quarrel somewhere above, charges, taunts, disputes—fruit of a land where sudden wide differences in work and pay summoned disaster. Noise of sinful singing and dancing, pastime of Ellie's generation, breed of a city where children cursed and threatened the old and went free.

For Ellie still went her way rejoicing, heedless of what she had precipitated in a passing fit of temper. Sam in a week had forgotten—was with Ellie at this very rent party below. And when the white folks had come to investigate the unfortunate death by violence, Mammy had sworn with stiffened lips it was all an accident.

Into the airshaft crept her old hymn, lifting toward Harlem's black sky:—

Bow low!—How low mus' I bow
To enter in de promis' land?

(1927)

NOTES

1. The following observation was made by a social historian in the 1960s who was reexamining the history and growth of Harlem: "The white world saw rent parties as picturesque affairs—in reality they were a product of economic exploitation and they often degenerated into rowdy, bawdy and violent evenings." Gilbert Osofsky, *Harlem: The Making of a Ghetto* (New York: Harper & Row, 1966), 128.

2. Boogy: Negro. A contraction of Booker T., used only of and by Negroes.

3. Skee sheiks: "Skee" refers to whiskey or bootlegger; "sheik" is an irresistible, well-dressed man.

4. The mentioning of the "garment of righteousness" is particularly apropos in this scene; it comes from the Book of the Prophet Isaiah, 61:10: "I will greatly rejoice in the Lord, my soul shall be joyful in my God; for he hath clothed me with the garments of salvation, he hath covered me with the robe of righteousness, as a bridegroom decketh *himself* with ornaments, and as a bride adorneth *herself* with her jewels."

5. Bozo: A silly person; a funny fellow.

Blades of Steel

Negro Harlem's three broad highways form the letter H, Lenox and Seventh Avenues running parallel northward, united a little above their midpoints by east-and-west 135th Street.

Lenox Avenue is for the most part the boulevard of the unperfumed— "rats" they are often termed. Here during certain hours there is nothing unusual in the flashing of knives, the quick succession of pistol shots, the scream of a police whistle or a woman.

But Seventh Avenue is the promenade of high-toned "dickties" and strivers. It breathes a superior atmosphere, sings superior songs, laughs a superior laugh. Even were there no people, the difference would be clear: the middle of Lenox Avenue is adorned by street-car tracks, the middle of Seventh Avenue by parking.

These two highways, frontiers of the opposed extremes of dark-skinned social life, are separated by an intermediate any-man's land, across which they communicate chiefly by way of 135th Street. Accordingly 135th Street is the heart and soul of black Harlem; it is common ground, the natural scene of unusual contacts, a region that disregards class. It neutralizes, equilibrates, binds, rescues union out of diversity.

In a fraction of a mile of 135th Street there occurs every institution necessary to civilization, from a Carnegie library opposite a public school at one point to a police station beside an undertaker's parlor at another. But one institution outnumbers all others—an institution which, like the street itself, represents common ground: the barber shop overwhelmingly predominates.

Naturally on the day of the Barbers' Annual Ball this institution clipped off, among other things, several working hours. The barbers had their own necks to trim, their own knots[1] to conquer, their own jowls to shave and massage. The inevitable last-minute rush of prospective dancers, eager for eleventh-hour primping, would have kept the hosts themselves from appearing at the dance hall, in their best, on time. Hence the association had agreed that every member's door be closed and locked to-day at four.

Shortly before that hour in one of 135th Street's "tonsorial parlors," the head barber, for whom a half-dozen men were waiting, dismissed a patron and called "Next!" Already Eight-Ball Eddy Boyd, whose turn it was, had removed coat and collar and started toward the vacated chair.

"Make it boyish, Pop," he grinned to the fat and genial proprietor. "And long as you trimmin' me, lemme have two tickets for the stomp-down to-night."

Pop Overton smiled goldenly and assumed the grand manner. "You means to grace our function wid yo' attendance?"

The other's assent was typical Harlemese:—

"I don't mean to attend yo' function with my grace."

As Eight-Ball put one foot on the foot rest of the chair, someone pulled him back urgently.

"My turn, big shorty."

Eight-Ball turned, recognized Dirty Cozzens,[2] an enemy of several days' standing.

"My turn," disagreed he evenly.

"Yo' mistake," Dirty corrected, and moved to brush the smaller man aside.

The move was unsuccessful. The smaller man exhibited something of the stability of a fire plug which one attempts to boot off the sidewalk. Dirty had bumped him without anticipating such firm footing, and now himself recoiled, careening off toward the mirrored wall with its im-plement-laden ledge. There was a little giggling jingle of instruments as his elbow struck this ledge. Then there was silence. Of the two barbers, one stopped pushing his clippers, but left them resting against the customer's neck while he gaped; the other halted, his razor poised, his thumb in one corner of his patron's mouth. Those who sat waiting dropped their papers, their conversation, and their lower jaws. Every-body stared. Everybody knew Dirty Cozzens.

Eight-Ball stood pat, as if awaiting an apology for the other's rudeness. Dirty also remained where he had landed, his elbow still amid the paraphernalia on the ledge, his eyes glaring, as if to let everyone see how he had been wronged.

The two made a striking contrast. Dirty Cozzens was a peculiar ge-netic jest. Heredity had managed to withhold his rightful share of pig-ment even from his hair, which was pale buff. His eyes were gray, their lids rimmed red. His complexion had won him his nickname, "Dirty Yaller," of which "Dirty" was the familiar abbreviation. In every other particular his African ancestry had been preserved and accentuated. The buff hair was wooly, the nose flat with wide nostrils, the mouth big, bordered by so-called liver lips, unbelievably thick. Within the shadow of a black skin, even, Dirty would have been a caricature; with the complexion that he actually had he was a cartoon, a malicious cartoon without humor.

So had heredity handed him over to environment, and environment had done its worst; had put sly cunning into the eyes, had distorted the lips into a constant sneer, had set the head at a truculent forward thrust on the large, lank body. With its present evil face, his was a head that might well have adorned the sceptre of Satan.

His opponent was his antitheses. Eight-Ball had been nicknamed after that pool ball which is black, and his skin was as dark as it is possible for skin to be, smooth and clean as an infant's. The close-cut hair hugged the scalp evenly, the bright black eyes were alive with quick understanding, the nose was broad but sharp-ridged, with sensitive nostrils, the lips thin and firm above a courageous chin. He was beautifully small, neither heavy nor slight, of proud, erect bearing, perfect poise, and a silhouette-like clean-cutness.

In the silence, Dirty's fingers reaching along the marble ledge found and caressed a barber's tool; an instrument which is the subject of many a jest, but whose actual use involves no element of humor; a weapon which is as obsolete as a blunderbuss, even among those whose special heritage it is commonly supposed to be—as obsolete and as damaging. Dirty, skilled in the wielding of steel, would never have considered this instrument in a set encounter, but the Devil put the thing now in his hand. He decided it would be entertaining to run his enemy out of the shop.

Pop Overton saw the movement, and it lifted him out of his daze. He said:—

"Aimin' to shave yo'self, Dirty?"

"None yo' dam' business," snapped Dirty, still eyeing Eight-Ball.

"No," said Pop. " 'Tain't none my business. But hit's my razor."

Dirty threw himself together, but not erect,—"You seen what he done?"—moved then with slow menace across the distance between himself and Eight-Ball. "You seen it, didn' y'?"

"Now listen, big boy. Don't you go startin' nothin' in my shop, you hear?"

"I ain't startin' nothin'. I'm finishin' sump'n. Dis started a week ago. Hot nigger, dis black boy, but I'm go'n' turn his damper down."

Eight-Ball spoke: "Don't burn yo' fingers."

Dirty advanced another step, knees bent, one hand behind him. Had Eight-Ball retreated a single foot, Dirty would have tossed the razor aside with a contemptuous laugh; would have made a "fly crack" about fast black guaranteed not to run; would have swaggered out, proudly acknowledging that he had picked the quarrel. But Eight-Ball had not retreated. Eight-Ball had stood still and looked at him; had even taunted him: "Don't burn yo' fingers"; had watched him approach to arm's length without budging. Ought to take one swipe at him just to scare him good. Ought to make him jump anyhow—

Whatever might have happened didn't. Instead of the expected swift sweep of an arm, Dirty's next movement was a quick furtive bending of his elbow to slip the armed hand into his coat pocket; such a movement as might have greeted the entrance of an officer of the law.

As a flame flares just before it goes out, so the tension heightened, then dropped, when eyes discovered that the figure which had darkened the door was only that of a girl. She was a striking girl, however, who at once took the centre of the stage.

"Whew-ee!" she breathed. "Just made it. Hi, Pop. Hello Eighty. One minute to four! And the head barber waitin' for me! Some service, I scream—some service." Wherewith she clambered into the vacant chair and effervesced directions.

The waiting customers first ogled, then guffawed. It struck them as uproarious that two men should appear to be on the point of bloodshed over a mere turn and neither of them get it. But the girl seemed quite oblivious.

Eight-Ball greeted her, "Hello, Effie," grinned, and returned to his seat. Dirty shuffled to the wall opposite the mirrors, got his hat, and went toward the door. As he passed the head barber's chair he paused and spoke to the girl:—

"It was my turn, Miss Effie—but you kin have it." He smiled so that his thick lips broadened against his teeth, and he touched his hat and went out.

His departure released comment:—

"Nice felluh!"

"Doggone! Sposin' he really got mad over sump'n'!"

"He wasn't mad. He was jes' playin'."

"He better not play wi' me like dat."

"Take 'at thing out'n his hand and he'd run."

"Leave it in his hand and you'd run."

Then, to everyone's astonishment, before Pop Overton had assembled the proper implements, the girl jumped down from the chair, scattering stealthy glances which had been creeping toward the crimson garters just below her crossed knees.

"Whose turn was it?" she asked Pop.

"Eighty's."

"Thought so. Come on, Eighty. I got mine this morning."

"What's the idea?" wondered Eight-Ball.

"Wasn't it a fight?"

"Pretty near. How'd you know?"

"Anything wrong with these?"

A purely rhetorical question. There was certainly nothing wrong with Effie Wright's eyes—nor with her hair, nor with that rare, almost luminous dark complexion called "sealskin brown." One might complain that she was altogether too capable of taking care of herself, or that she was much too absorbed in Eight-Ball. Beyond that no sane judgment criticized.

Effie ran a beauty parlor directly across the street, and it was to this that she now referred.

"I was lookin' out the window over there. Saw you drive up in your boss's straight eight. Your friend was standin' in front of the saloon—he saw you, too, so he come in behind you. Pop's window's got too much advertisin' in it to see through, so I come on over. Seem like I spoiled the party."

"Ain't this sump'm?" Eight-Ball asked the world.

"Angels rush in when fools is almost dead," was Pop's proverb.

"Well, since you won't open a keg o' bay rum, I guess I'll breeze.—Say, Pop, got an extra safety-razor blade?—Yes.—Oh, a customer gimme a pair o' pumps to wear to the shindig to-night, and I got to whittle off here and there till I can get 'em on. Cheatin' the foot doctor.—A single-edged blade if you got it, Pop. Double-edged one cuts your fingers before it cuts anything else.—Thanks. Shall I lock the door on my way out?—Stop by before you haul it,[3] Eighty."

She was gone in a flurry of words.

"Can y' beat that, Pop?" Eight-Ball laughed.

"They ain't but two like her and she's both of 'em," admitted Pop. "But what's that Cozzens boy on you for?"

"We had a little argument in a dark-john game[4] a while back."

"Yes? Well, watch 'im, boy. Bad boogy[5] what knows he's bad. And don't think he won't cut. He will. Thass th' onliest kind o' fightin' he knows, and he sho' knows it. They's nineteen niggers 'round Harlem now totin' cuts he give 'em. They through pullin' knives, too, what I mean."

"He's that good, huh?"

"He's that bad. Served time fo' it, but he don't give a damn. Trouble is ain't nobody never carved him. Somebody ought to write shorthand on his face. That'd cure him."

"Yeah? Whyn't you shave him sometime, Pop?"

"Mine's accidental," answered Pop. "Somebody ought to carve him artistically."

"Well," Eight-Ball said thoughtfully, "maybe somebody will."

II

The Barbers' Ball does not pretend to be a "dickty" affair. It is announced, not by engraved cards through the mails, but by large printed placards in barber-shop windows. One is admitted, not by presenting a card of invitation, but by presenting a dollar bill in exchange for a ticket. It is a come-one-come-all occasion, where aspiring local politicians are likely to mount the platform between dances and make announcements and bow while influential bootleggers cheer. It was quite fitting, therefore, that this fête of, for, and in spite of the people should take place on 135th Street—this year in a second-floor dance hall just east of Lenox Avenue.

"Well, hush my mouth!" exclaimed Eight-Ball as he and Effie entered somewhat before midnight.

"Do tell!" agreed she.

For there were decorations. Nothing subdued and elegant, like the So-and-So's dance. Nothing "fly," like the Dirty Dozen's. Just color in dazzling quantity, presented through the inexpensive medium of crepe paper—scarlet, orange, brilliant green, embracing the lights, entwining the pillars, concealing the windows, transforming the orchestral platform into a float.

The orchestra also made no pretenses. It was a so-called "low-down" orchestra and it specialized in what are known as "shouts." Under the influence of this leisurely rhythm, steady, obsessing, untiring, you gradually forget all else. You can't make a misstep, you can't get uncomfortably warm, you can't grow weary—you simply fall more and more completely into the insistently joyous spirit of the thing until you are laughing and humming aloud like everyone else. You get happy in spite of yourself. This is the inevitable effect of shouts, to which the orchestra to-night largely confined its efforts.

The newcomers joined the gay, noisy dancers, finding their way not too swiftly around the crowded floor. Here someone advised them to "get off that dime!" and there someone else suggested that they "shake that thing!"

But the shout to which Eight-Ball and his girl inadvertently kept time had not yet saturated their emotions, and in spite of it they discussed less happy concerns.

"I been so mad I ain't had no dinner," said Eight-Ball.

"Bout what?"

"Notice I didn't bring the car tonight?"

"Yes. Boss usin' it?"

"No.—Know when I left your place this afternoon, after you showed me that trick?"

"Yes."

"Notice anything wrong with the car when I drove off?"

"Nope. Too busy watchin' the driver."

"I went about half a block and felt somethin' wrong. Pulled up and got out to look. Two flat tires."

"No!"

"Uh-huh. Front and back on the side away from the sidewalk."

"They was O.K. when you parked?"

とおさ

"Brand new."

"Blow-outs? Slow leaks?"

"No. Cuts."

"What are you ravin' about?"

"Both tires had a six-inch gash in 'em, made with a knife—"

"What!"

"Or a razor."

Effie stopped dancing. "The yellow son of a baboon!"

"Everybody says they ain't nothin' he can't do with a knife. Looks like they ain't nothin' he *won't* do."

The shout, the rhythmically jostling crowd, impelled them back into step.

"Eighty, you ought to half kill 'im. Of all the low, mean, gutter-rat tricks—you ought to lay 'im up f' a year."

"How you know I can?" he grinned.

"Can't y'?"

"I can't prove nothin' on him. Who seen him do it?"

"Nobody didn't have to see him. You know he did it."

"Nope, I can wait. He's sore. He'll keep on messin' around. Thinks he can't be had."

"He can be had, all right. All I'm 'fraid of is somebody else'll have 'im first. Everybody that knows that guy hates 'im and most of 'em's scared to boot. Whoever whittles 'im down will be a hero."

As the jazz relented, the object of her anger took form out of the crowd and approached.

"Evenin', Miss Effie," said he, ignoring Eight-Ball. "Been lookin' f' you. I give you my turn in d' barber shop to-day. How 'bout givin' me mine now?"

Effie looked through him at the decorations surrounding a post. As if she and Eight-Ball had been discussing the colors, she commented:—

"That's one color I'm glad they forgot—I can't stand anything yellow."

Dirty turned garnet; but before his chagrin became active resentment the music returned with a crash. Eight-Ball and Effie moved on past him, their anger partially appeased by knowing that Effie's tongue had cut like steel.

And now the shout more easily took hold on them, hammering them inexorably into its own mould. The increasing jam of people pressed them more closely into each other's arms. The husky mellowness of soft-throated saxophones against the trumpet's urge, the caress of plaintive blues melody against the thrill of strange disharmonies, the humor of capricious traps against the solidity of unfailing bass—to these contrasts the pair abandoned themselves. Harsh laughter, queer odors, the impact of the mob, became nothing. They closed their eyes and danced.

They might have danced for an hour, only half aware of the jumble of faces about, of their own jests and laughter, of the occasional intervals of rest. Then something woke them, and they suddenly realized that it was at them that people near by were laughing—that a little space cleared about them wherever they moved and people looked at them and laughed.

At first they were unconvinced and looked around them for something comic. Then Pop Overton appeared smiling roundly.

"Thought monkey backs was out o' style, son."

"What?"

"Did you have yo' coat cut to order?"

Effie switched Eight-Ball around and gasped while onlookers frankly smiled. A triangle of white shirt back, its apex between Eight-Ball's shoulder blades, shone through a vertical vent in his coat, a vent twice as long as any designed by a tailor. In the crush and abandonment of the dance a single downward stroke of a keen-edged instrument, light enough not to be noticed, had divided the back of the garment in two as cleanly as if it had been ripped down midseam. The white of the shirt gleamed through like a malicious grin.

As Eight-Ball examined himself unsmilingly, Pop Overton sobered. "I thought it was torn accidental," he said. "Judas Priest! I bet that—! Say, Eighty, fo' Gawd's sake don't start nothin' here. We ain't never had a row—!"

Eight-Ball and Effie, faces set, stood looking at each other in silence.

Dirty Cozzens stood in the shadow of the doorway beside that leading to the Barber's Ball, and in return for a generous drink unburdened himself to a buddy.

"It was in d' back room at Nappy's place. Dis li'l spade turns a black jack and wins d' deal, see? Well, he's a-rifflin' d' cards and talkin' all d' same time, and he says, 'You guys jes' git ready to loosen up, cause I'm gonna deal all d' dark johns home. I promis' my boss I wouldn' gamble no mo', but dis is jes' like pickin' up money in d' street.' Fly line, see? Den he starts dealin'. Well, I figgers dis guy's been so lucky and jes' turned a black jack for d' deal, it's time fo' his luck to change. So I ups and stops his bank fo' twenty bucks, see? And I be dam' if he don't deal himself another black jack—makin' two in a row!"

"Well, he picks up all d' money befo' we git our breath, see? Everybody laffs but me. I figger dey's a trick in it. Wouldn' you?"

"Sho' I would. Two black jacks in a row. Huh!"

"So I calls 'im crooked. But he jes' laffs and tells me to talk wid mo' money and less mouf. Natchelly dat makes me mad. A guy pulls a crooked deal and says sump'n like dat. Wouldn' you 'a' got mad?"

"Sho' I would. Sho', man."

"So I tells him to pass back my twenty, long as he said he wasn't gamblin'. Den he stops dealin' and asts me is I big enough to take it. Tryin' to start sump'n all d' time, see?"

"Sho' he was. Tryin' to staht sump'm."

"So I says I'll either take it out his pile or off his hips, see? But when I starts for him d' guys won't let me put it on him, see? Fact, dey puts me out d' game. So natchelly I jes' got to get me some o' dis li'l spade's meat, dass all. I got to. He can't git away wid nuthin' like dat."

"Tryin' to git away wi' sump'n. Huh!"

"Sho' he is. But I'll git 'im."

"What you aim to do?"

"I been primin' 'im fo' a fight."

"Dey claim he's pretty good wif 'is hands."

"Ain't gonna be no hands. See dis?"

He drew from his right-hand coat pocket what appeared to be a quite harmless pocketknife. He pressed it under his thumb and a steel blade leaped forth, quick as the tongue of a snake, a blade five inches long with a sweeping curve like a tiny scimitar. It was hollow-ground and honed to exquisite sharpness. A little catch fell into place at the junction of blade and handle, preventing the protruding blade from telescoping shut. The steel gleamed like eyes in the dark.

"Whew-ee!" admired the observer.

"He won't be d' fus' one I ever put it on. And here's how I figger. His boss is tight, see? Fired two guys already fo' roughin'. Dis boogy's got two new tires to account fo' now. And when his boss sees he been cut, he'll find out it's count o' some gamblin' scrape and fire him too. Dass where I laff. See?"

" 'Deed, boy, it's a shame fo' all dem brains to go to seed in yo' head. You could sell 'em and buy Europe, no stuff."

Then abruptly both shrank into deeper shadow as Eight-Ball and Effie came out.

III

Diagonally across the street from the dance hall stands Teddy's place, an establishment which stays open all night and draws all manner of men and women by the common appeal of good food. Oddly, it was once a mere bar-room lunch, and the mahogany bar counter still serves the majority of Teddy's patrons, those who are content to sit upon stools and rub elbows with anybody. But there is now a back room also, with a side entrance available from the street. Here there are round-top tables beside the walls, and here parties with ladies may be more elegantly served. It is really a "high-class" grill-room, and its relation to the bar counter lunchroom, the whole situated on democratic 135th Street, marks Teddy a man of considerable business acumen.

In one corner of the grillroom there is an excellent phonograph which plays a record repeatedly without changing. A song ends; you wait a few moments while the instrument is automatically rewound and adjusted; and the song begins again.

To-night the long-distance record was Tessie Smith's "Lord Have Mercy Blues," a curious mingling of the secular and the religious, in the tragic refrain of which the unfortunate victim of trouble after trouble resorts to prayer. The record was not playing loudly, but such was the quality of Tessie Smith's voice that you heard its persistent, half-humorous pain through louder, clearer sounds.

Just now there were no such sounds, for the room was almost empty. The theatre crowd had departed; the crowd from the dance halls had not yet arrived. Three or four couples sat about tête à tête, and near the phonograph Eight-Ball and Effie. Eight-Ball's back was turned toward the wall to hide the gape in his coat.

The phonograph wailed:—

> "My man was comin' to me—said he'd let me know by mail,
> My man was comin' to me—said he'd let me know by mail—
> The letter come and tole me
> They'd put my lovin' man in jail."

Grief, affliction, woe, told in a tone of most heartbroken despair; desolation with the merest tincture of humor—yet those who listened heard only the humor, considered only the jest.

> "Mercy—Lawd, have mercy!
> How come I always get bad news?
> Mercy—Lawd, I have mercy!
> How come I always got the blues?"

"Them's the blues I ought to be singin'," said Eight-Ball.

"You'll feel better after you eat," soothed the girl.

"I'll feel better after I get one good crack at that half-bleached buzzard."

"You ought to pick your comp'ny, Eighty."

Her tone surprised him. He encountered her look, mingled tenderness and reproach, and his eyes fell, ashamed.

"All right, kid. I'm off gamblin' for life.—But if that dude keeps messin' around—"

"Don't forget—he cuts."

"He better cut fast, then."

As if willing to oblige, Dirty Cozzens appeared at the door. He stood looking about, head hunched characteristically forward, right hand deep in his right coat pocket; calmly observed the relative desertion of the dining room; then slowly advanced across the open space in the centre of the floor.

Quickly Effie reached into her bag, drew something forth, put it into Eight-Ball's hand. The movement could have been seen, but the object passed was too small for the closest observation to make out. She might merely have been indulging in a heartening handclasp. Eight-Ball looked at her, first with puzzlement, then with understanding and resolution.

This time Dirty ignored Effie. This afternoon he might have had a chance with her; now he knew he had not. Then he had hidden his weapon from her; now he wanted her to see. That, too, had been largely bullying; this was serious challenge. Then he had sought but a momentary satisfaction; the satisfaction pending now would last, arising as it would out of the infliction of physical injury which would cost the victim his job. Let Effie share all of this—by all means let her see.

"Gimme my twenty bucks."

Eight-Ball looked up, allowed his gaze to pause here and there over his enemy's frame; then patted his left trousers pocket. "It's right here.— You big enough to take it?"

"Listen, lampblack. You been tryin' to git fly wid me ev'ry sence las' week, ain't y'? Put d' locks on me wid a crooked deal. Tried to start sump'm in d' barber shop to-day. Tole yo' woman to freeze me at d' dance to-night. Aw right. I'm warnin' y', see? I done warned you twice. I put my mark on yo' two shoes to-day and I put it on yo' coat to-night. D' nex' time I'm gonna put it on yo' black hide. See?"

Eight-Ball sat quite still, looking up at the lowering face.

"I tole y' I'd either take it out yo' pile or off yo' hips. Now put up or git up, you—"

Eight-Ball went up as if he'd been on a coil spring, suddenly released. Dirty staggered backward, but did not lose his footing.

Naturally none of Teddy's three waiters was in sight—it is unlikely that they would have interfered if they had been. Indeed, had they seen the initial blow of Eight-Ball,—a familiar patron,—they would have been satisfied to let him take care of himself. As for the other guests, they were interested, but not alarmed. One does not yell or run at such a time unless a pistol is drawn.

Recovering balance, Dirty Cozzens drew his right hand from his pocket. It is difficult to believe possible the expression of evil that now contorted his features. That expression, however, was not more evil than the glint of the miniature scimitar, whose handle his right hand grasped.

He held the weapon in what pocket-knife fighters consider best form—three fingers firmly encircling the handle, but the index finger extended along the posterior, dull edge of the blade, tending to direct, brace, and conceal it. A sufficient length of the curved point extended beyond the end of the index finger to permit the infliction of a dangerously deep wound.

Eight-Ball stood ready, leaning a little forward, arms lax, both palms open—and empty.

Dirty's scowl concentrated on Eight-Ball's hands, and that he did not move at once was probably due to his astonishment at seeing no weapon in them. Any such astonishment, however, promptly gave way to quick appreciation of an advantage, and he did what a knifer rarely does: he rushed, bringing his blade swiftly across and back in a crisscross sweep before him.

Eight-Ball neither side-stepped nor attempted to block the motion. Either might have been disastrous. Instead, he ducked by suddenly squatting, and, touching the floor with his left hand for balance, kicked suddenly out with his right foot. The sharp crack of his heel against his antagonist's shin must have almost broken it. Certainly he gained time to jump up and seize Dirty's wrist before it could execute a second descending arc.

One less skilled than Eight-Ball would have found this useless. From such a wrist-hold the knife hand is effectively liberated by simply inverting the weapon, which the fingers are still free to manipulate. The blade is thus brought back against its own wrist, and any fingers surrounding that wrist usually let go at once. Eighty had forestalled this contingency by a deft slipping of his grip upward over the fingers that held the knife handle. The hold that he now fastened upon those fingers was the same that had yanked two slashed balloon tires off their rims some hours before, and it held Dirty's fingers, crushed together around their knife, as securely as a pipe wrench holds a joint.

And now those who had watched this little fellow empty-handed win the advantage over an armed and bigger adversary saw a curious thing occur. Regularly in the ensuing scuffle Eight-Ball's right hand landed open-palmed against Dirty's face—landed again and again with a sounding smack; and for every time that it landed presently there appeared a short red line, slowly widening into a crimson wheal.

Before long Dirty, rendered helpless now and losing heart, raised his free hand to his face, and as his fingers passed across it the crimson wheals that they touched all ran together. He looked at the tips of those fingers, saw they were wet and red; his mouth fell open; the hand which Eight-Ball held went limp, the knife fell to the floor and Dirty Cozzens quailed, as craven now as he'd been evil a moment before.

He began to stammer things, to deprecate, to plead; but Eight-Ball was deaf. The muscles of the latter's left arm seemed about to burst through their sleeve, while the artificial vent in the back of the coat ripped upward to the collar, as with one tremendous twist he brought the other man to his knees.

In that mad moment of triumph no one may say what disproportionate stroke of vengeance might not have brought on real tragedy. But with that strange and terrible open palm raised a voice halted Eight-Ball's final blow:

"Mercy—Lawd, have mercy!"

Tessie Smith's voice, wailing out of an extremity of despair:—

"Letter come and tole me
They'd put my lovin' man in jail."

The entire engagement had occupied only the few moments during which the phonograph automatically prepared itself to repeat. Now the words came as warning and plea:—

"Mercy—Lawd, have mercy!"

Eight-Ball released Dirty Cozzens, stepped back, picked up a crumpled paper napkin from the table where Effie still sat.

"Wipe y' face with this. Go on 'round to the hospital." He urged Dirty, whimpering, out of the side door.

Then he turned back toward Effie, stood over the table a moment, returned her rather proud smile. Two of the men who had looked on came up. Said one:—

"Buddy, show me that trick, will you?"

Eight-Ball extended his right hand, palm downward, and spread the fingers wide open. Freed from its vise-like hiding place between firmly adjacent fingers, something fell upon the porcelain table top. It fell with a bright flash and a little clinking sound not unlike a quick laugh of surprise—the safety-razor blade which Effie had borrowed that afternoon from Pop Overton.

(1927)

NOTES

1. Knots: Kinky hair.
2. Note how this name rhymes with the "dirty dozens." The "dozens" is a verbal game, practised among blacks, based on negative talk about someone's

mother. The object is to better your opponent with cleverer insults. The "dozens" can be done in fun, or with venom and severe animosity.

3. Haul it: Go (depart) in great haste.
4. Dark-john game: Blackjack.
5. Boogy: Negro. A contraction of Booker T., used only of and by Negroes.

The Backslider

The meeting-house had once been a dwelling, no better, no worse than all the other houses in the row. It had dressed like them in curtains of lace, in half-drawn shades, in soft, seductive, crimson-shaded lights. But now, transfigured into a church, it wore the saintlier garb of a proper convert: an uncompromising halo from a globe-light over the doorway; windows stained with tissue-paper, red and green in squares. Its very voice had changed, no longer crooning balmy blues but shouting hallelujahs. If the Lord dwelt anywhere in Negro Harlem, surely He dwelt in this place.

So thought Ebenezer Grimes. Eben knew he had sinned and felt like it. He stood irresolute, staring fearfully up at the three narrow first-floor windows, mustering courage to mount the front steps, open the door and go in. But the halo glared at him balefully. The tissue-paper of red and green curled and shrank from its window-edges, leaving clear corners to transmit merciless slashes of yellow light. Surely not only the Lord was in this place, but His wrath as well.

Eben weighed the issues; compared these unmistakably divine manifestations with the terrors of Hell-fire; contrasted the momentary shame of public repentance with the eternal tortures of the damned. There could be but one decision, but, even so, it was with fear and trembling that he went up the steps into the halo, slowly pushed open the door and turned backwards into the meeting-room, pretending thereby to close the door the more carefully.

No sooner had he crept into a chair than he sensed surrounding tension. Prayer-meeting had not begun, and ordinarily there would have been noise—chairs scraping, feet shuffling, ripple of voices, splashes of laughter. But tonight there was heavy silence. Sister Gassoway over in the corner, big, shiny and round, would have been gyrating as usual on her perilous pedestal of a chair, diffusing cheer, bouncing with full-bosomed merriment. Tonight she was as ominously still as a large, billowy storm-cloud. Brother Hezekiah Mosby, sexton, usher and chorister, would have been busily flitting about like a worrisome little black fly, grinning, whispering, buzzing useless greetings, questions, confidences. Tonight he sat on the front row alone, silent, with folded arms. Beyond all these Eben recognized the most dismaying sign—not one of the saints turned to greet him, not one called the customary welcome, not one gave any indication of being so much as aware of his presence. Eben's heart dropped out of his chest. They knew. All of them knew.

Now Senior Deacon Crutchfield, assistant to the absent shepherd, mounted the low platform at the end of the room. Eben had only admiration for Deacon Crutchfield. He was a magnificent man, big, hearty, bass-voiced, with an engaging smile and a painfully powerful handshake. Eben longed for the power to squeeze a hand as did Deacon Crutchfield. And, incredibly enough, only two years ago Deacon Crutchfield had been, in his own words, a rat in the gutter, a thief in the night, a poor lost soul who had never even heard of the mercy of God. From rat in the gutter to Senior Deacon in two years—there was a career!

Eben contrasted himself—brought up, down home, in church from infancy; Sunday-school as far back as he could recall; finally conversion and baptism, years of faithful attendance; but now, in New York, instead of advancing to high office, miserably falling from grace, a sinful backslider.

"Let us read the word of the Lord," rumbled the voice of Deacon Crutchfield, who scowled straight at Eben with a light in his eyes curiously like the halo over the entrance. Eben heard the psalmist's distant thunder, nearing: " 'But the ungodly are like the chaff which the wind driveth away. Therefore the ungodly shall not stand in the judgment, nor sinners in the congregation of the righteous. For the Lord knoweth the way of the righteous, but the way of the ungodly shall perish.' " Here Deacon Crutchfield turned too many pages, but read on with triumphant satisfaction: " 'Let the sinners be consumed out of the earth, and let the wicked be no more! Bless thou the Lord, O my soul. Praise ye the Lord.' " Then in the vibrant quiet followed: "Brother Mosby, lead us in prayer." The deacon sat down.

No one will deny that public praying is a decidedly difficult accomplishment. It demands rare capabilities—unusual range of voice, accurate appraisal of the occasion, an appearance of having completely forgotten the audience—which is, of course, impossible—and ability to sound spontaneous even when everybody knows the prayer by heart. It demands, in short, technique.

In this peculiar art, Christendom has probably never seen the peer of Brother Hezekiah Mosby. His repertoire was inexhaustible and displayed the most extraordinary versatility; he could pop up and pray on an instant's notice at meeting, banquet or wake, and always with the proper wail or shout or moan or sing-song; you had but to hear his prayer to know the occasion.

Never had Eben heard Brother Hezekiah pray as he prayed tonight. He addressed God by at least three dozen different designations, obviating any possible failure of connection. In a sonorous voice that soared and sank like shifting diapasons, he called down the punishment of Heaven to humble the heads of the wicked. He omitted no competent agent of vengeance—"Thy divinable wrath—terrible right hand—re-

vengeable angel—diluvient thunder and lightning—the resuming fire
by night and the fumigant sword by day—" Nor did he neglect any
worthy object of destruction—"liar—thief—gambler—contamerating
drunkard—bootlegger—politician—" Abruptly he halted, surprising
his accompanying chorus of amens and glorys, which clamored on for
a moment, unable to cease so suddenly. Then, resuming, in a soft, weepy
tremolo: "If there do be one amongst us which are unworthy of Thy
mercy"—he rose to a passionate roar—"cast out the hypocrite, the *backslider* like the seven devils of old!"

The end of the prayer was submerged beneath a tide of approving
cries.

There was a lull, a moment of calm ere the final deluge broke. Deacon
Crutchfield rose, as also did Eben's pulserate.

"Brothers an' sisters, this bein' the reg'lar monthly business meetin',
it becomes our duty to take up certain matters. We will leave the best
till the last and take up the painfullest first.

"It comes to our ears on good authority that our former brother Ebenezer Grimes has been seen on two occasions comin' out of one of
Harlem's worst dens of iniquity, the Rodent cabaret." Silence with an
occasional rustle. "Both times was after midnight." Silence, save for
Eben's heart-beats. "And both times our former brother was unquestionably drunk." Silence intact. Deacon Crutchfield's flashing eyes now
engaged Eben's reluctant shifting ones. The awful question leaped forth:
"Young man, is these things true?"

Eben had planned to pray aloud, to confess his sins in his prayer, to
plead for pardon. But after Brother Hezekiah's masterpiece, any effort
of his would have been puny. Now, transfixed with this challenge of
Deacon Crutchfield, the backslider was rendered speechless. He
groaned as if the question had been a spear.

"Our former brother seems to have nothing to say. What is yo' pleasure?"

Brother Hezekiah popped up. "It are my painful duty, brothers 'n'
sisters, to relate that this hyer same young man up and took communion
Sunday!" There was a horrified gasp of unbelief, especially from those
who had seen him take it. To share communion after sinning—unfor-
givable! "Tha'fo', I move you, Brother Senior Deacon, that this onwor-
thy young man's name be hencefo'th an' fo'ever struck off'n our church
roll!"

Eben jumped up in a panic. They were putting him out of church.
A dozen protests stuck in his throat. Hell-fire—eternal damnation—
putting him out of church—

He sank weakly back, unable to state a defense. Some one objected—
called for a vote. They were voting. Voting on him. Ten ayes, for putting
him out. Ten noes, opposed. A tie, thank the Lord. There was hope
now. Maybe Deacon Crutchfield would save him. He tried to beseech

the Senior Deacon with his eyes, but the Senior Deacon was uttering terrible, righteous, decisive words:

"In case of a tie like this, brothers and sisters, it becomes the duty of the moderator, which is yo' humble servant, to cast his vote. Shall we strike this name off from our rolls?" An instant's exquisite uncertainty. Then, "The Lord bids me vote 'aye' !"

After a blurred, stunned moment, Eben rose and stumbled out.

Whither may that man go on whom God has turned His back? To the Devil, sooner or later. It happens in Harlem, as elsewhere, that God and the Devil are neighbors—it is but the briefest step from the One to the other. And so five minutes after his excommunication, Ebenezer Grimes was in the Rodent.

The Rodent is, of course, nothing but a transformed cellar—not too much transformed. It is very exclusive in its membership; no habitué is expected to have retained any vestige of good reputation, and those are its special favorites whose occupations are unknown or unmentioned. Its transient guests, therefore, are naturally people of excellent repute, who, attracted by its unconcealed vices, get a far more violent "kick" out of its smoky closeness, its wire-legged chairs, its threepiece, slow-jazz orchestra than ever they get out of the velvet pomp and splendor of more carefully disguised cellars. The Rodent has, in short, successfully capitalized its bad name. You simply can't plan a wicked night and leave the Rodent out.

To this place Eben had first been introduced as the unwitting victim of one of its regular practitioners in good standing, a certain "Spider" Webb, who anesthetized the "jay-bird"[1] with gin and successfully extracted his pay-envelop. The second time, Eben returned to see if any one had found his lost pay-envelop. He didn't discover the envelop, but he did discover Lil. Lil was the entertainer. He told her it really didn't matter anyhow—she was worth a dozen envelops. Rather intrigued by this brand-new line, she spent half an hour with him, just to see how green and grimy they could come. Then, warning him to keep better company than Spider Webb if he didn't want to lose all of his envelops, she tanked him up on corn and sent him staggering blissfully homeward.

This, then, was Eben's third call at the Rodent. It was dismally early. There was a waiter or two about. A bareheaded girl sat brooding at a table. Stripped of its song and smoke and laughter, the squat little room was as desolate as an empty coal-bin. To Eben the impish silhouettes on the walls became hunched, clubfooted menaces, and on the bare little platform, naked of its orchestra, Deacon Crutchfield might have been standing, pronouncing final sentence.

He dropped into a chair. The girl saw him, rose and came over to his table. "Hello, Eben."

He looked up. It was Lil. "Evenin', Miss Lil."

"You're early tonight."

"No place else to go."

She caught his tone, his limpness. "What's the grand tragedy?"

"Nothin'."

"Liar." She sat down. "Come on, spill it. Help take my mind off my own troubles."

"You in trouble too?"

"Never out. What is it, bucks?"

"No'm. Church."

"Church? For the love o' cream cheese!"

" 'Tain' no mystery," he said. "Somebody seen me both times I was hyeh. Seen me come out drunk. Dass all."

"That's all? Well, for cryin' out loud—what's the grand larceny? What if they did see you?"

"Oh—dey put me out o' church."

"Just for getting soaked a coupla times?"

"Un-huh."

"Why, the hypocrites!" And then she promptly and whole-heartedly threw herself into his problem. After a moment's ponderous thought she exclaimed: "Why, it's easy! It's a cinch! What kind of a church is this?"

"Baptis'."

"Huh. Bogus, you mean. Well, now, all you've got to do is find yourself another kind of church, see? One that's not so tight—one with a broader mind."

To Eben churches were of three classes, Baptist, Methodist, and others. "Methodist?" he ventured.

"Naw. They're just like the Baptist—horn rimmed. Get yourself into a regular kind with a long name, like Episcolopian or Utilitarian or something. They don't care what you do."

"How come you know so much 'bout 'em?"

She contemplated his curious eyes, his clean brown skin, his carefully parted, not too kinky hair. Then she contemplated the table top. "Well," she said presently, and Eben caught in her eyes shadows of tragedy older than his, "I don't usually brag about it, but my old man was a preacher ages ago. Not the fly kind they got nowadays, though. Nothing synthetic about him; real genuine stuff, vintage of 1850."

"Yea? He got a church now?"

"Nope. He's got a harp. Say, I know just the joint for you—Saint Augustine's, over by Morningside Heights. Boy, that's some swell dump, no perjury."

Eben stared with more interest than understanding.

"Know what I'm goan do?" he said, coming to.

"Somethin' dumb, I bet."

"Sent me straight to de Devil, didn' dey? All right, den. I'm goin'!"

"Halt, friend. You've arrived."

"All my life I been tryin' to do right. Seem like doin' right never was doin' nothin' but what you didn' want to do. Ev'ybody else doin' different. Ev'ybody doin' wrong—but me. Ev'ybody happy but me. Couldn' go fishin' Sundays down home, 'count o' Sunday-school or church. Couldn' steal peaches, couldn' fight, couldn' dance, couldn' do nothin' wuth doin' thout bein' scared o' missin' Heaven. Now 'tain' no need to worry 'bout Heaven—ain' goan git da' nohow. I kin dance all I doggone please! I kin cuss! Hot dam', I kin cuss! I kin fight—git even wid folks what does me wrong. Dat lil yaller² slew-face booger³ what stole my pay-envelop—I'm goan git 'im an' knock 'im from amazin' grace to a floatin' opportunity! Dey put me out? Well, dey done me a favor! I'm free—free as a dog-gone bird! An' I'm goan act like it too—you watch!"

"Take it slow and easy, cuckoo. Birds can be caged, you know."

He grew silent but no less intense. Before he'd had time to say a word, they'd voted on him. Ten ayes. Ten noes. Senior Deacon Crutchfield—had he, then, never done wrong? Yes—he'd had his fun, first. But it wasn't Deacon Crutchfield who'd sent him to Hell. "The Lord bids me vote 'aye'." The Lord—the Lord.

Eben's head suddenly fell on his arms.

"Snap out of it, bozo.⁴ We'll have spectators in a minute."

Eben exposed a bitter countenance. "Is dey put you out o' church too?"

"Tisn't what they've put me out of. It's what they're going to put me in."

"What's 'at?"

"Jail."

"Jail! Wha' fo'?"

"Debts." Eben sat up and gaped. "Cops'll be here any minute now. Sweet mamma'll have some escort, big boy. Liveried, what I mean. Lucky at that. A private room in prison beats a clothespress in a flat and costs less." She signed, prodigiously sardonic: "Hey-hey—bring on the bright brass buttons."

It did not occur to Lil that Eben, evergreen though he undoubtedly was, would think of taking her half-jest literally. But he did, and not without reason. Down home Eben had seen men sent beyond jail for less than debt.

Slowly inspiration came, yielding a simple solution. He could save Lil and vindicate himself—if he acted quickly enough.

Ebenezer Grimes walked rapidly in quest of a chance to steal.

The only concern, then, was time; the only danger delay. He reached the corner of the avenue and turned out of the side street's darkness into the glow of lighted shop-windows. Now he proceeded more deliberately, looking carefully into the shops, noting those which were closed and dark—a Universal Grocery, a clothing store, a real estate office, a barber shop. He went up to the window of the barber shop, intently peered into the dimness. On the ledge in front of the wall mirror gleamed a silver and porcelain cash-register. If he could get into the rear of the place, he could reach that cash register and empty it. The grocery, on investigation, presented a cash-register too. The others looked lean and barren. Two chances. He must get around back somehow.

Above the foundation of shops rose several layers of apartments, and between the shops at intervals gaped the narrow apartment-house entrances. One of these was beside the grocery, and into it Eben slipped. Eagerly he traversed the hallway, only to find that it ended blindly, without any door, and with only a ground-glass window, firmly nailed down. He came back and mounted the hall stairs that led to the flats above. At the rear of each floor's hallway he sought the window corresponding to the first. The second, third and fourth were immovable. The fifth went up with a bang. To Eben's satisfaction it opened on the balcony of a fire-escape.

With no notion of how rare a thing a full cash-register is, and quite unaware of his own futility, the new disciple of Satan awkwardly clambered through the window and began to scuffle none too quietly down the iron skeleton.

He was negotiating his second story, creeping past a kitchen which shared its balcony with the corresponding hall, when he observed that, of the few lighted windows above, one was just beyond the balcony rail. He halted and saw, too, that it was open. Then his new patron disclosed to his eyes, on the near edge of a bureau, a large, flat patent-leather purse, such as many women insist on carrying under the arm.

"Amazin' grace!" he whispered. "Ain't dis sump'n?"

Without looking into the darkness below, he measured the distance from the balcony rail to the nearer edge of the window and decided to acquire the purse. He got over the rail and, holding to it with one hand, leaned out as far as he could. The room was apparently empty. A half-minute later he had his prize and was scrambling back over the rail the way he had come.

Up the fire-escape he made his way, back through the still open window.

He dived down the stairs, still holding the purse in his hand. In the hallway below he brought up short, guiltily facing a man whose approach he had not heard. The purse was still in plain sight—the man's gaze was upon it. In the same moment that Eben saw the uselessness of hiding it, he recognized Spider Webb, the man who had caused his pay-envelop so strangely to disappear. Webb now recognized him also, and took a surprised step backward.

"You needn' run," grunted Eben. "Ain' got time to git you now. But next time we meets, when I git thoo you ain' goan be fit fo' hog-fodder."

He slipped the purse under his coat and brushed swiftly past.

"Not so good," thought Spider Webb. He wheeled and, unobserved, followed Eben down to the street. Eben turned the corner, but was not ten yards beyond it before Spider was pointing him out to a black policeman at the curb.

"Say, Ben, see that black bird there?"

"With both eyes."

"Step after him and find out what he's doin' with a woman's pocketbook. My guess is he snatched it. See?"

"Snatched a woman's pocketbook, huh? Where's the woman?"

"Never mind—get *him* first—before he fades."

"Right." At a rapid stride the officer made after Eben. Half-way down the block Eben cast a glance behind, saw the uniform approaching. He did not know that the officer was pursuing him, but he did know that distance was desirable and that, in any case, Lil's security depended on his speed. He began to run. The policeman began to run too.

Eben reached the Rodent's door and, too frightened to look back, plunged in. The officer was almost at his heels, intent now on making an arrest. Somehow in the precipitous descent Eben's feet managed to keep ahead of the rest of him. His momentum carried him headlong past two or three startled rounders who had come in during his absence, and landed him squarely in the center of the floor and the middle of one of Lil's songs.

Lil herself was well-nigh mowed down. "For the love o'—"

"Hyeh—take it—quick!" gasped Eben, thrusting out the the purse.

There was, perhaps, but one person in the room whose respirations were normal. That one said:

"Well, if it ain't Big Ben, the cream o' the force! What's the idea chasin' my friend around? He don't need exercise."

The policeman pointed at the purse with his night-stick. "He snatched that off a woman."

Lil rescued the purse from Eben's infirm grasp. "Oh, he did, did he? Where?"

"Up on the avenue."

"You see him do it?"

"No—Spider Webb did."

"That yellow insect? Why, if he saw Saint Peter at the gates of Heaven he'd swear he was chargin' admission. You believe him?"

"Sorry this is a friend o' yourn; but there's the bag y' see."

"Certainly. Right in mama's arms, where it belongs."

"Yours?"

"I didn't say your grandpa's."

"Why—but what's this bird doin' with it, then?"

"Be your age. I sent him for it, of course."

"Well—what was he runnin' for?"

"Because I told him to hurry, Sherlock."

The gendarme grinned and scratched his head. "Well, I'll be—'scuse me. I'm goin' to run that Spider Webb in for lyin', sure as I got a badge."

"If you don't, you hadn't ought to have no badge."

The officer left. Eben was limp as a mop. Lil dragged him to a corner and dropped him across a chair. The few spectators, fully recovered, were now intent on their own concerns.

"What's the bright notion?" demanded Lil.

"Didn' you say dey was goan put you in jail fo' debt?"

It took a good deal to amaze Lil, but this did it. Sixty seconds went by before she could ask. "Do you want to take it back now or later?"

"Take it back?"

"You ain't blind."

"You doan want it?"

"Listen, darkness." Lil's tone was not unkind. "Mamma plays with lots o' things, including fire. But mamma doesn't play with hot stuff, see? And she'd feel lots better if you didn't either. Take it back."

After a moment she got up and went to resume her song. Eben sat in a daze. He felt as if he'd poured kerosene on a fire and the fire had promptly gone out. As if he'd jumped off a bridge and landed back on the bridge again. Deacon Crutchfield's awful "Aye!" Lil's cold "Take it back." Forsaken by God and denied by the Devil. Lost.

Presently he, too, got up and crossed the floor. Then, without God or Devil, with only a purse full of money, he made his way up the stairs and out into the pitiless night.

Standing by the piano, Lil watched him disappear. "The poor sap would-a gone to jail for me," she wonderingly mused. "Phil, there's the kind of a bozo I'd—I'd join church for, no perjury."

Precisely how he returned the purse Eben never remembered. One thing he knew—somehow he got it back. It was two hours after he left the Rodent before he performed a clearly conscious act.

He would not have been jolted out of his stupor then had he not walked headlong into a crowd; and the impact of his blind collision was not nearly so reviving as the retaliative thrusts of comment from those whom he had bumped.

He found himself standing at the edge of a thick group of people, chiefly men in collarless shirts which bloused loosely over their belts;

a few women, some in kimonos, their hair tightly twisted in knots. Through the middle of this crowd an open space ran across the sidewalk, beginning at the steps of a brightly lighted house and ending at the curb. As if in anticipation of a procession, everyone craned his neck to keep this pathway in view, and Eben, craning, saw that at the curb end of the lane some sort of vehicle was backed up. He wondered about it. A moving-van? Too small; too late at night. An ambulance, then? That would explain the interest and excitement. Some one hurt, no doubt—about to be brought out on a stretcher. He craned still further. Strange sort of an ambulance—two vertical rails of shining brass; between them a rear entrance so narrow it made either wall look a foot thick; two or three steps below.

"Dog-gone!" he exclaimed. "One dem patrol-wagons!"

"Naw!" grunted a bystander. "Baby-carriage."

"Who dey after?"

"That's what we're all waitin' to see, Oscar."[5]

Eben was wide awake now. With an interest arising out of his own narrow escape from arrest, he pursued his questioning in the face of every discouragement. Laboriously he learned that the police were making a raid; that a raid was a legalized rampage upon blind pigs and gambling dens; that a blind pig was a place where you could buy bootleg liquor if you were wealthy enough; yes, that Harlem as a whole might be considered a prolific sow without eyes; but that the police rarely bestirred themselves save where bootleg and blackjack were wed; that everybody found in any such establishment was placed under arrest, lined up and marched out into the wagon; finally, that in the present case the next would be the third and last wagon-load, hence the close attention—the ringleaders always came out last, having proved the hardest to find.

There came now a stir and a hush. All eyes focused on the door of the house, a half-dozen steps above the sidewalk. A lone policeman stepped through the glowing doorway, a majestic silhouette, slowly descended the stairs and waved the crowd back with his stick. The crowd, of course, paid him no attention. Then the moment's lull broke into a murmur, and the doorway grew dark with heads—more policemen than Eben had ever seen at one time, roughly ushering out a fagged line of captives. Down the steps they passed in file, this one bareheaded, that one's hat hiding his eyes, this one coatless, that one's ears deep in his collar; some erect, some slouching, some requiring support.

Eben somehow envied them. They were at least loyal to their sins. A phrase of the old folks came to him: "It's mighty hard to be a loyal solder." His own case came before him—he had been dishonorably discharged from one army. All right—he had joined another. And now, having lost his very first fight, he was on the point of deserting. Why, he belonged in that very line of prisoners filing past; that was his army now.

Out of such wry delirium rose a crazy urge to join them.

Eben wriggled through the crowd, which was now too absorbed in the panorama to resent his jostling; reached the edge of the lane. As he did so, the last of the prisoners descended the steps and approached. Eben, rather mad, taut, half intent on slipping into line behind this last man, of a sudden fell back as abruptly as if an officer had turned and clubbed him. It seemed to him that he shrieked, but his cry was the phantom of a whisper:

"Senior Deacon Crutchfield! 'Mazin' grace!"

His wide eyes watched the senior deacon pass, saw him reach the curb, mount the steps of the patrol-wagon, suffer a policeman to push him none too gently, stoop, disappear within.

Senior Deacon Crutchfield! The patrolwagon roared and was gone. Senior Deacon Crutchfield! The crowd had melted away. Senior Deacon Crutchfield—gambler—bootlegger—hypocrite.

It took time for this to register. Eben wandered slowly along, trying to grasp what he had seen. Deep-rooted memories of old folks' words rose again to his rescue.

> Hypocrite, hypocrite God despise
> Always tellin' dem Christian lies.

Why—then it hadn't been God Who'd put him out of church; it had been Senior Deacon Crutchfield—nobody else. A hypocrite whom God despised.

Eben halted, confronting revelation: "I ain' never been forsook a-tall. 'Twas jess dem narrer-minded niggers—an' dat hypocrite a-blamin' it on de Lawd!"

He heaved a sigh of tremendous relief and grew interested in his whereabouts. Looking up, he discovered moonlight. And not a hundred yards away rose the spire of Saint Augustine's.

For a long time he gazed upon it as upon some lofty aim. "I did backslide on de Lawd," he penitently confessed, "but"—he grinned with the joy of redemption—"now 'm goan backslide on de Devil."

"Wonder," he added presently, "wonder ef Lil would backslide too."

(1927)

NOTES

1. Jay-bird: A simpleton.
2. Yaller: A light-skinned Negro.
3. Booger: A black (used by Negroes only).
4. Bozo: A silly person; a funny fellow.
5. Oscar: A dumbbell.

Fire by Night

For the cloud of the Lord was upon the tabernacle by day, and fire was on it by night.

Lenox Avenue arises in a park, flaunts a brief splendor, dies and is buried in a dump. From 110th Street it marches proudly northward with the broad grandeur of boulevard. Fatal pride. Within half a dozen blocks comes sudden hopeless calamity—a street-car line slips in from a side street, stealthily as from ambush, and with a whir, a rising roar, a crash, deals the highway its death-blow. Splits its spine. Ugly, cheap little shops attack it, cluster like scavenging vermin about it. Trucks crush blindly, brutally over it, subway eats wormily into it. Waste clutters over it, odors fume up from it, sewer-mouths gape like wounds in its back. Swift changes of complexion come—pallor—grayness—lividity. Then, less than a mile beyond its start, the Avenue turns quite black.

So mighty you feel, coming unwarned into this part of the colony. You shudder a little, perhaps, sensing more than merely a change of color; and rightly, for these sudden dark faces belong not to Negroes, simply, but to a distinct group of Negroes, mentioned even by their own as "bad." These are they whom police respect most and have learned it is best not to bother. These are the heirs of those who protected the colony in its infancy by their skill with pistols and knives and fists.

To be sure, there is little need of them now, the colony is mature and competent in ways beyond those of steel and flesh. But these "bad" Negroes linger yet, spending their heritage on each other, on dickties, the high-toned hated ones, or on 'fays, the indiscreet whites. They live in that forbidding strip whose western edge is black Lenox Avenue, whose northern end is the dump. Alien enough by day, this tameless corner of Negro Harlem is transformed by night into a quivering wilderness. Here strange songs ring, and queer cries sound, and life stumbles blindly toward death.

On one side of the Avenue, just beyond its change of color, you see this morning a triad of small frame houses, burned well toward the ground. What flame has left undone above, flood has accomplished below. Roofs and attics are a wretched seaming crush of ash and charcoal, while the unburned lower walls are thoroughly drenched and dripping still.

Even yesterday, ere last night's disaster, the triad looked miserable enough. They huddled together in the middle of the block, as if trapped between the brownstone walls approaching on either hand; as if caught and squeezed ever tighter and tighter till they cracked and puckered and caved. Roofs were sunken, windows stared vacantly, clapboards were wry and colorless.

Like a brace to save the three from collapse, a flat sign stretched across their front. "The Club," said the sign defensively. Beneath it a doorway opened at street level, and beyond this the three ground floors were thrown into one large, low-ceilinged room. Green-covered pool-tables squatted in rows, green-shaded drop-lamps showered light on them. Men stood beside them, chalking their cues, or leaned far over them, making hard shots; men in vests and silk-striped shirt-sleeves; big men with brown felts pushed back from their brows, small men with caps yanked down over one eye; mostly young men, war vets, consciously hard, the most worldly-wise and the most heedless Negroes on earth.

As evening advanced the Club grew more crowded; toward midnight the room was alive. Pool-balls clicked and chunked into pockets, cue-handles thump-thumped the floor for reracking. There was round kidding and rougher replying and curses and laughter through smoke.

A narrow platform ran along one wall, bearing occasional stools for spectators. On one of these hunched Rusty Pride, watching the whole affair glumly; watching it all with a self-disgust unrelieved by this place or these men.

"Me"—he mused—"I'm that eight-ball there. Black all over but one spot. God knows what, inside. Watch it now. Three times he's tried it for that side pocket. Easy shot. Soft shot. But it won't go in. It's me. Shoot, fool. What you wastin' time for squintin' and squirmin'? It won't go in. Shoot, I tell you. See? Hit the cushion and hopped. What's I tell you? Like my old man tryin' to shoot me into a hole. Hmph! That's good. My old man shootin' pool. Imagine. A Baptist preacher shootin' pool. That's good."

Some one came near. "Let's go Rusty. Last table's comin' up."

"Nothin' doin'," Rusty refused briefly.

"Spot you ten. Hundred points for two bits."

"No." Curt, briefer still.

"The hell with you, then." The speaker grinned and departed.

More musing. "The old man shooting me into a hole. Wild. Well, what of it? Who's tame in this man's town? Me—his son—disgracing him. Hmph. Did I ask to be his son? Join church. Church. Niggers prancing—raising hell and calling it religion. What does it matter what you call it? Or where you raise it? It's hell, that's all. Blues—spirituals.

Shimmy in a dance-hall—shout in a church. Religion. Join church. Acknowledge God—or else get out and find Him. That's what he said. Well, I got out. Nearly a year ago I got out. What did I find? Hell. Plenty of hell. That's all. God? He don't bother getting in people's way."

Some one else came up. "Come on, pool-shark. I'm yo' bait."

Rusty might have been deaf.

The challenger insisted. "Snap out of it, biggy, and get yo'self licked."

Rusty gave him a silent, virulent scowl; the challenger shrugged and passed on.

The eight-ball touched another and shied off as if alarmed at the contact. "Me again. Meeting Roma Lee today. Her of all people in this part of Harlem." One of those chance meetings from which he forever shrank. She had squealed a delightful recognition—run to him and thrown her arms about him there on the street, hugged him on Lenox Avenue where always he felt people's eyes. Impulsive kid, Roma.

"Rusty, for goodness' sake! Where did you come from?"

"Nowhere much." Shabby. No collar. Coat turned up to hide his bare neck. Shoes like old boxing-gloves.

"Been running on the railroad. Canada." Rag of a coat—both pockets ripped out at the corners. Hide 'em with your thumbs, fool. Two days' beard—chin like a brush.

"Gee, but it's good to see you! Going to the dance tonight?... Didn't know about it—the So-and-So's supper dance?... Then when are you coming round?... Married—me? Lord—who'd be goose enough? Waiting for you, silly."

Laughing at him. Well—but was she? Used to care some. Might yet. What of that moonlight sail? Wide Hudson—shore lights—a nook astern—jazz laughing somewhere ahead, white wake laughing behind. Something today in her eyes, something incredulous, pained, anxious, coming with a gleam instead of a twinkle. Laughing at him? Or shuddering? Or maybe crying a little underneath? Jackass!

Rusty withdrew himself from meditation with an effort. It was as though he were a well into which he himself had fallen, floundered a while, almost drowned. Many times in places like this he had fallen into the well, tripping usually over the memory of his father's final dictum. Now as before he reached in and pulled himself out with a tug. Just as he emerged, a little black figure rushed past him, catching his eye—a little cinder of a man with bare, crinkly scalp, shriveled face and uncovered ashen forearms. He had come in from the street on this midwinter night in an undershirt and trousers, and he sped past as if he'd been thrown. As if he'd been thrown at Turpin, the proprietor, who sat behind an iron cage in one back corner of the Club. Turpin, too, saw the flying cinder coming. His hand reached under the shelf on which he'd been leaning. The little man brought up in front of the cage. Only the nearest heard or cared what he said, and of these Rusty happened to be one.

"You sell my brother dat gin today?"

Turpin's hand, holding a pistol, came from beneath the shelf and rested upon its surface. Turpin, small, compact, cool and hard, looked the questioner up and down. "Talk sense, Chinaman," he advised.

"Well, you done kilt 'im."

Turpin grinned. "How often do you take it, friend?"

"Sole 'im bad gin, you did. Pizen gin. Now he's daid. Went blind, he did. Went blind, doubled up 'n' died."

"You sho' takes it calm."

"I could tell d' police ef'n I felt lak it. I could tell 'em you sole my brother pizen fo' licker and kilt 'im daid. Tell 'em you sole 'im bad gin."

"They's no sich thing as bad gin. All gin is good."

"Twouldn' do no good. Know whut dey'd say? Dey'd say any fool nigger whut drinks pizen licker's too dumb t' live anyhow."

"An' they'd be right."

"Aw right—dey'd be right. An' y'know whut I say? I say any chinch whut sells pizen licker's too low-down t'live. An' I'm right—dead right."

Turpin still caressed the gun. "Which means which?" he inquired with some deference.

"I see yo' gun. An' I ain' no fool." For a moment the accuser hesitated, as though, having confirmed his suspicion about the sale, he had no idea what to do next; as though something unforeseen, Turpin's gun, perhaps, prevented what otherwise would have occurred.

The doubt passed quickly. "Killin' you won't help none nohow," the little man contemplated. "But I got t' pay you fo' dat licker. You ain' been paid fo' it yit."

"Remarks," smiled Turpin pleasantly.

"I ain' no fool." The other spoke with a sort of meditative menace. He stiffened with quick decision now. "But ef'n you got mo' pizen licker to sell, sell it fas', you hyeh? 'Cause sumpin' tells me you ain' goan be sellin' it long."

Rusty listened beyond the first few words not because such scenes were strange to him, but because this one was different. In company like this some one was always accusing somebody of something, but the accuser was usually drunk. This man was certainly sober. Usually the words of the offended one were loud, befuddled and heedless. This man's words, though breathless, were low, clear and deliberate. The usual plaintiff would have libeled the defendant's several ancestors one by one, would have dared the defendant, ever more loudly, to raise

and point his gun; would have invited him outside his cage and promised to carve him like a turkey. This little shrunken fellow, however,
displayed no swagger, no bravado. He was agitated, indeed, but cool;
threatening, but intensely quiet, was not loud nor invective, nor especially self-assured; attracted hence no great attention. But Rusty,
watching, had the impression that every word was weighed, as though
some other spirit than his own was using this little man's body. His
gin-dead brother's spirit, perhaps.

Rusty snorted at this hypothesis as he'd snorted at his others. The
snort plunged him back into the wall. Acknowledge God. Everything
that met his eyes at the moment denied God. Everything argued Hell.
Turpin might have been Satan himself, surveying his cavorting imps,
and enjoying especially the acute torture of this particular rum-scorched
soul.

The cinder-man departed. Well, Turpin wasn't overcareful about the
quality of his gin. He made it himself. Up-stairs in that blank-looking
attic were tin cans full of alcohol. Rows of them. Occasionally Turpin
boasted of them, and of the gin he made. It might be good alcohol he
put into it, it might not. Turpin took the word of those from whom he
got it, too ignorant to do otherwise, too unscrupulous to care. An honest
moonshiner, a good business man, even, would at least have protected
his clients. Not Turpin. Gin was gin—a gallon of alcohol, a gallon of
water, a little extract of juniper—gin.

So Rusty brooded, ill with revolt, with revolts against his revolt.
Beasts like Turpin and the rest of these thugs. If he, Rusty Pride, were
that little shine, do you know what he would do?

He'd manage to get up-stairs to that alcohol—by way of the next roof
maybe. Get to that alcohol and dump it all over the place. Then he'd
set fire to it—and pray that Turpin, the thick little brute, would try to
save it and would get trapped while trying.

Pray. Hmph. "Now I lay me ... And look at me now. The old man
must be pretty lonesome living there all by himself. His own fault,
though. Oh, Lord, I want to go home! No, I'm hanged if I do."

A third challenger approached. "Well, blacker'n me, how 'bout
pushin a few around? You been takin up room long enough."

It was Stud Samson, Turpin's partner, a creature whom Rusty never
looked upon without revulsion. His coarse granular skin was dingy
yellow and scarred, and the only facial expression of which he was
capable was inevitably a grimace. Even at rest his features described a
leer, and this never changed save into a spreading, snaggle-toothed
distortion. His whole squat head, you could suppose, had been fashioned of yellow clay by a sculptor who, in a fit of disgust, had seized
chin and forehead between angry palms and compressed them with all
his might.

Rusty, already on edge with his thoughts, found himself summoned now out of the most turbulent reflections by Stud Samson's hoarse derision, to gaze upon that ugly face and hear its equally ugly hint. He had an impulse to get up and bury his fist in Samson's face, to smash it, shattering thus by proxy the evil it symbolized. The habit of repression turned this impulse into sarcasm. With an unpardonable look and scalding effrontery, Rusty said:

"Go get your face lifted."

Now of ordinary kidding the coproprietor of the Club was able to take his share. You could criticize his taste in gals, for example, or his taste in ties—if you grinned. You might even get away with "slipping" him "in the dozens,"[1] reminding him with impunity of his wooden-legged uncle or his grandmammy's cross-eyed cousin. If you grinned. There is in Harlem a term which signifies the last straw, the maddening limit, the one thing that won't be tolerated. It is expressed in the phrase "my cup runneth over" and is shortened to the one word "cup." Any contemptuous reference to Stud Samson's face was Stud Sampson's cup. Rusty had made such a reference, and Rusty had not grinned.

For a moment the Stud's face did seem to lift, to straighten out, to untwist; then it tightened into a knot, like a coiled spring suddenly released. "Say that ag'in an' I'll lift yo' jaw," came rasping out of the knot.

Rusty was in a complying mood. "I said," he repeated, unruffled, "to go try and get your face lifted. And while you're about it, you might have 'em straighten your hair."

Between this stimulus and Stud's reaction there was an appreciable latent period. Rusty had time to imagine the insult boring through Samson's thick head to his brain, then down and out to his muscles. The expected lunge came. Rusty in his chair on the platform, with his back against the wall, simply drew his knees up to his chin as Stud rushed and suddenly straightened his legs. Some seconds later Stud crawled dazzedly out from under the nearest pool-table.

"The fall of Samson!" commented a wag, and Stud, looking about, realized that the bystanders considered the joke on him. It is difficult at once to encounter a husky enemy and a dozen shouts of laughter. Stud Samson knew no fear like that of appearing ridiculous. The attitude of the onlookers, therefore, though it enraged him the more, yet tended to check his impending rush. Crouching a little, his arms hanging ape-like, he stood still and leered about him, and probably no one really knew whether he was trying to smile or to frown.

Nor did most of them ever find out, for in that moment of doubt a door banged open and some one rushed in with news. It was news that commanded attention. Players pulled up as they sighted their shots, arrested by the first word. Cues about to rap on the floor or mark off points overhead halted promptly just where they were, while those who held them gave ear. Within five seconds a single loud voice had taken the place of thirty.

"Gravy, you boogies![2] Yassuh! Le's go! Gravy an' I doan mean maybe! Keep yo' red flannel shirts on now. I'm tellin' you fas' as I kin. Dat dicky dance what I'm checkin' coats fuh at d' New Casino is 'bout to break up in a row. Three drunks tried to bust in. I lef' 'em fightin. Rich niggers, packed up fo' cabaret parties. 'Tain' two blocks away—all y' got to do is mix in an' grab it. Dey's fat rolls cryin' fo' a home!"

"Listen to d' man!" . . . "Gravy, he say!" . . . "Le's go f'm hyeh!" . . . "Hot dam', baby!" . . . "Git on d' gravy-train!"

Within a few moments the Club was miraculously empty. Only Rusty, Turpin and a player or two remained. Even Turpin's partner, Stud Samson, had departed with the marauders.

Rusty had at first no thought of joining them. His own melancholia had enshrouded him like mist. Even his upsetting of Stud had been instinctively defensive, and he had seemed to be observing himself as in a dream. Visionary likewise had been the dance announcement and the responding babel and hubbub. But as action and noise had blurred his surroundings and driven him into himself, so now unusual quiet rendered them clear and drew him out. He got up, looked about him, realized that excitement had just tramped out of the door. Excitement had become Rusty's tonic and dope; he never denied himself a dose. With a grin of anticipation he adjusted his cap, hunched up his collar and went trudging out of the Club.

A figure, surprised by the suddenness of his exit, shrank into an adjacent doorway as he turned up the street. Managing purposely to walk near this doorway, Rusty peered warily in as he passed. The eyes that met his glared through the shadow with a sort of subdued madness. They belonged to the cinder-man, who just now had uttered a smoldering threat to the sneering Turpin.

Rusty, hurrying on, found himself muttering: "Pizen gin—blind—doubled up 'n' died—you ain' been paid fo' it yet."

Between Lenox and Seventh Avenues lives Harlem's middle class, flanked on the east by rats, by dickties on the west. Accordingly, those who are middle in station are more or less middle in territory. This central strip is in truth the colony's backbone. Here live its laborers, haulers, truck-drivers, carpenters, chauffeurs, mechanics; here live its steady, dependable, year-around wage earners, family providers. Its businesses fringe and invest this strip and subsist largely upon it. But those who own the businesses and the strip have moved across Seventh Avenue, occupying the so-called private houses of the dickty upper two hundreds. When they move, they move westward and northward: Edgecombe, St. Nicholas, Morningside, even Riverside Drive will be reached one day.

This is middle ground—there are other plots like it, but none approaching it in extent. Accordingly, here Harlem's one tradition, the church, has its firmest foundation; and most of the remnant that still fears God will be found in these mountains of flats.

Here too, in occasional private houses, still reside many of those who minister to this class. Of these none is more widely known or loved than Zachary Pride, Rusty's father. "Daddy Pride" the children of his parish call him, while to their parents he is "The Rev'm." He is seventy years old, and his dark face is lined, his soft hair is white as a halo. But he has the bearing of one who has braved a thousand indignities, and in his face are a courage and faith undisturbed by the jazz all about him. He has knelt by a sick-bed and made God hear through the wild liquor party overhead. He has gone into a cellar when police declined and settled a clamorous argument. He believes in a God who can see and hear and a church that can teach and serve. The doctors of divinity in Harlem call him "a preacher of the old school."

They smile at his disregard of the proprieties; for instance, that cross on his church steeple. Every one knows that a Baptist church has no business with a cross on its steeple. It isn't proper. When Zachary Pride's congregation purchased this building, which had been an Episcopal mission, the first thing they should have done was to take down the cross. It had never even occurred to Zachary Pride to take down the cross.

His is a small gray church on a side street, not far from Lenox Avenue; and while it stands humble between the lofty dwellings on either side, it yet sends its spire and its criticized cross far above them.

This particular prayer-meeting night service had held later than usual, and the elderly shepherd was left unwontedly weary of mind. There had been financial questions to settle; coal was running low in the bins though ever so high on the bills; the notes on the newly installed organ promised to require far more than one rally; there was a leak in the roof and a spreading area of discoloration on the ceiling over the choir—plaster might drop in the middle of an anthem next Sunday if repairs were delayed; a dozen members on the sick-list were badly in need of help, and the sick-fund would be spread too thin if all received equal share. Then there was the problem of young folks— sin contagious as smallpox. Old members came with their burdens to him—he must help old Sister Mosby find the father of her granddaughter's coming baby; he must testify in court to the character of Len Wiggin's boy, the dupe of some thieving jail-dodgers; he must find jobs for a dozen derelict sons. . . .

Tonight, as usual, Zachary Pride was the last to leave. The church was near Lenox Avenue, but his house was a hundred yards away toward Seventh, on the opposite side of the street. Here he had lived since the church was bought years ago from white Christians for whom the region was growing altogether too dark. This house had been a home then. Sarah, his wife, and three bright youngsters had made it a home in those days. The children grew up—romped to bed one night and woke up the next morning grown. Jessie went out to a party against his persuasion—he refused to coerce—and caught cold. She never recovered. The War and the draft came along and swept the two boys off to sea. Zachary junior never came back, and his mother went—to find him. Russell—Rusty—returned unharmed, but not the same lad that had left—a swaggering, regardless, worldly-wise Rusty, who boasted acquaintance with Hell and the Devil, but laughed at God and religion.

The old preacher prayed for two years about it and finally reached a decision. There had been no quarrel, no unpleasant preface, no stern denunciation. The father had met his son at breakfast one morning—Rusty had been out all night—and had spoken quietly and earnestly.

"Son, you don't seem to like it here. You squirm under my eye—you chafe. You even laugh at my faith. Why not be free? You're twenty-three. Leave. Find God for yourself; and when you have found Him, come back."

It had cost something, that experiment; it had taken the faith of Abraham. All the old man's fleeing hopes had sought refuge in this boy.

Zachary Pride entered his house. The door closed behind him—a hollow sound. He had let the two upper floors to a couple who'd agreed to cook and clean for him. He was a roomer and boarder in his own house.

Yet never a moment did he doubt that Rusty would sometime return. He simply could not believe that his life would be stripped of this last little sweetness. All that made the place bearable to him was the thought of the boy's coming back, living here, free of that devil-born restlessness. He would marry some fine girl, perhaps; the house would again be a home. Some girl like Roma Lee, clear-eyed and impulsively honest.

It was Roma's aunt and uncle who rented the upper floors of the house, and with them Roma spent much of her time. She always asked about Rusty. Where was he? When would he be back? Nor was she merely being polite. Roma's questions were as genuine now as they had been a dozen years ago when she had asked Daddy Pride in Sunday-school if there really was a special nigger Heaven. She still called him "Daddy Pride," even.

He smiled and wished that it might really be Roma whom his son would choose. And after a while he knelt by his bed and prayed the prayer he'd prayed every night for a year:

"Reveal Thyself unto my boy, and in Thine own time bring him again to me; and let him be an example unto many that grope as the blind in darkness."

And at the moment of his prayer one man was threatening another with destruction for selling his brother bad gin; another was rushing to a pickpocket gang to herald a profit-sharing rough-house; and the suppliant's own son was upsetting an adversary by implanting both feet in his chest.

Harlem knows no dance-hall more elegant than the New Casino, which has looked upon crowds of every kind in their moments of greatest pretension. The Barbers' Ball, the Jumpsteady Club, the Dirty Dozen, the Backbiters—all hold forth in the New Casino two or three times a year. But, although this place is situated in the dictydom west of Seventh Avenue, only once has it been honored by the presence of the So-and-So Club, and the memory of what happened then is this lofty society's cup. Never will the So-and-So's Supper Dansant take place again in the Casino.

Had you arrived a half-hour before midnight, you could not have believed possible the storm that later broke. A magnificent liveried attendant stood at the curb in front of the door. Above him an elongated canopy extended from the sidewalk edge to the entrance. With utmost deference the attendant opened door after door of cab or limousine and out stepped handsome, dark-skinned blades, sharply arrayed in black and white, turning to hand down gorgeous women in bright-colored wraps or fur cloaks. From a brilliant mirror-walled foyer they ascended lateral stairways, railed with palms. Above they found a smaller lobby with a coat-checking room on either side. Wraps were left here, ladies' on one side, gentlemen's on the other; company then rejoined, and arm in arm stepped into the spacious ballroom.

And gasped. Only the So-and-So's could transform the Casino like this. There were no walls, but palisades of palms and banks of flowers. One guest braved his wife's glares to remark that it was the biggest funeral he'd ever seen; and later that night added grimly, "I told you so." There was no orchestra, but matchless music from somewhere behind the palms. There were no benches, but cushions thrown carelessly here and there on the plant tubs and a casual group of easy chairs in the center amid tubbed orange-trees. Above all, there was no glaring light; just a floor lamp or two in the central group and a shadowy glow from amid the palms, soft as the saxophone crooning the drowsy melody of a waltz. It was indeed to be a night of nights; the punch was full of promise; and the dancers' spirits and heads and feet grew rapidly light together.

In the lobby, near the ballroom door, sat members of the So-and-So dance committee, checking off names of invited guests on a list as they arrived. It was nearly midnight when three rather unsteady lads presented themselves to the committee—a tall, lanky yellow boy whose features were spattered with brown freckles as if he'd been sprayed with hot grease; a big-shouldered black fellow with a broad, flat face and a protrusive underlip; and a short, stocky, noisy, belligerent young man who unanimously elected himself spokesman. Each of the three had in him six drinks, and an equal number of devils. They had decided that the rent party which they'd been attending considerably cramped their style. They had further concluded that the So-and-So's stomp-down would be just about their speed. They had plenty of jack for their admission, they thought, and a decided taste for shimmying with sweet yaller gals. And so they walked past the liveried one at the entrance, stumbled upstairs and approached what appeared to be ticket-sellers, asking the price of admission.

But the So-and-So's represented an aristocracy too young to be very generous, and the strangers' question, with their absence of evening dress, betrayed them at once as Philistines.

"Private dance," said the chairman shortly.

This should have been sufficient dismissal; but a real hard Negro around six drinks . . .

"Listen, mistuh. Is anybody ast you what kind o' dance dis is?"

"You can't come in without an invitation."

The spokesman, unheading, turned to his companions. "Did I ast him what kind o' dance dis was?"

"We don't care what kind o' dance hit is."

Reassured, the spokesman turned back. "I ain't ast you what kind o' dance dis was, mistuh. I know what kind o' dance dis is. Dis is a dickty dance, dis is. Rich uppity boogies. Plenty bucks. Doctors, lawyers, and undertakers, what I mean, with nothin' but sweet an' pretty pinks. When dey leave hyeh dey go to a cabaret and stay all night. Big-time niggers, see? Well, we're big-time niggers, too. Me. I'm a doctor myself, see? An' my boy hyeh, he's a lawyer, he is. An' my other boy theh, he's a undertaker. And what we want to know ain't what kind o' dance dis is. What we want to know is how much does we put up to git in."

Another member of the committee interceded. "You'll have to go, boys. We don't sell tickets."

The intruder turned red eyes to this new opponent, looking him up and down. "Listen, mistuh. Is anybody ast you anything? Is dey? Huh? An' nobody talkin' to you. I'm talkin' to my doctor friend hyeh. I know dis nigger, I do. Him an I used to hop bells in de same hotel, we did. Now he doan know me. Dass all right, too. I ain' astin' him fo' nothin' but info'mation. He doan need yo' help. He kin talk, dumb as he is. He ain' been a dickty all his life."

The doctor began to realize why it would have been better to sacrifice appearances and have policemen at the door. He tried a bluff. "Call that officer inside there, Jim," he said.

"Yea, call 'im," growled the trespasser. "Tell 'im to bring his dice an' licker wid' 'im, too."

The chairman was desperate. "We've told you we aren't selling tickets!"

The contentious one grew calm, seeing the subject in a possible new light. "You doan sell no tickets?"

"No!"

"Nobody doan pay to go in?"

"No!"

"Well, ain't dat nice? Le's go, you niggers. Hit's free!"

"Free?"

"No 'tain't."

"Sho, 'tis. Didn' y' jess hyeh 'im say 'twas free?"

The trio started for the door. The second committeeman caught the leader by the arm. The leader halted.

"Go on in," urged his companions.

"What you stop fuh?"

"Mistuh, listen," arbitrated the intercepted one, "Doan you go gittin' so bran'new, see? You's second-hand, an' you has been worn, an' you sho kin be worn ag'in."

"That way out," said the So-and-So, giving the other a little shove.

"Mistuh, I ain't lookin' f' no trouble. But de las' man whut put his hand on my arm like dat is got his haid bound up like a Hindu."

So saying, the invader attempted to jostle past, but his obstacle stood firm. Followed a bit of a scuffle, the sharp crack of a blow to the face, and promptly a barroom battle was under way. The intruders were in that state of half-anesthesia where senses are dulled but actions are violent. Blows meant nothing to them, and, even sober, they would have enjoyed a fracas. The two committeemen were soon disposed of.

Guests near the door rushed to their aid, demanding explanations. The answers were hard, fists that hurt, while furious attempts at self-defense served merely to spread the commotion. Dickties dance well but fight poorly. Within three minutes men were engaged in the rumpus who had no idea why they were fighting nor whom they were supposed to strike, and who, even if they had, would not have known in the least how to make their blows tell.

The rough-looking lad in charge of the men's coat-room rushed out and down the stairs.

"Riot up yonder," he breathed to the doorman. "Stay put. I'll git d' cops quick."

And the dressed-up doorman, who had no thirst for battle, stayed very decidedly put, although he wondered mistily why the checker had not sped toward the police-station instead of the Club.

By a small, velvet-hung, unobtrusive doorway, the ladies' dressing-room was directly accessible to the ballroom; and, since the scantiest attire requires yet much attention, the traffic through this doorway was not inconsiderable. There were mirrors about this dressing-room, and comfortable wicker settees; there was a thick, soft carpet on the floor, and the arrangement was such that a second inside door joined this room with the ladies' coat-room, making it unnecessary for one to go out into the lobby to get one's wraps.

Roma Lee, a fresh little creature of rose and tan, bright with the thrill of her first big party, had slipped into this dressing-room to resurvey herself in a mirror. Nothing could have been more reassuring than what she saw—glossy black bob quite innocent of irons, dark eyes dancing, white teeth flashing, slim waist stressed by a filmy frock that gathered and flared at the hips.

Sally Epps, a scrawny, speckled, cream-colored girl with long skinny arms, unbelievably thin legs and enormous feet, who thoroughly enjoyed being colored and habitually wallowed in Harlemisms, came limping and grunting into the room behind Roma and kicked off both slippers.

"Great head o' the church, but them things burn! After this I'm wearin' nothin' but galoshes. Oh, baby, what a carpet! Spread out, feet, and radiate. Ladies, here's your original red-hot mamma—right from the ankles down. Bet this pair o' feet'd make a pan o' water bubble."

"They'd make a *tub* of water bubble, dear," smiled an observer, whose companion sniffed agreement.

Sally grinned and flopped into a chair as the disapproving pair went out, leaving her and Roma alone.

"Say, sweet and pretty, don't believe all that mirror tells you. Mirrors are the smoothest liars on earth. Fact is, you've got bad hair and a nose that was melted and thrown at you, and your knees are perfect strangers; while I, if you only notice, have the form of Venus de Nigro and a strawberry-shortcake complexion."

Roma came and sat on the arm of her friend's chair. "Sally, you're horribly colored and an awful goose."

"Hold on, flapper! Don't tell me I got web-feet."

"Hush and listen. Who do you think I saw today?"

"Adam and Eve fightin' over a fig-leaf."

"Rusty."

"Rusty Pride?"

"Rusty Pride."

"Where's that no'count tramp been?"

"He isn't a tramp. He's been running on the railroad to Canada all this time."

"Bootleggin', I bet. If there ever was a shine that was jail-house bound—"

"Sally!"

Sally stopped and stared. Stared from unbelief to wonder and from wonder to conviction.

"Romie, how long've you been likin' that triflin' scamp?"

"Liking him? Me? Don't be a nut. It was on Daddy Pride's account. You know Aunt Min sort of takes care of Daddy Pride since she rented most of his house. He's been worrying lately—wants Rusty home again. He's such a darling old man—I hate to see him so unhappy. I'd heard some of the boys say Rusty hung out around that Club place down on Lenox Avenue. So today I walked down that way to see if I could see him. Just curiosity. And I did."

"You did? And what of it?"

"That's all. I just saw him. It fell rather flat. I spoke to him, tried to show him I was glad to see him and all. Didn't seem to brighten him much. He looked as though he needed somebody to take care of him."

"How'd you like to have the job?"

"Oh, Sally, I hate to see him look like that!" Roma caught herself up and added, "I hate to see anybody look like that."

"Anybody. Of course. Well, ain't this sumpin' to print in the papers?"

"What do you mean?"

"I mean, baby, wasn't it just too sweet of you to think so much of the Rev'm Daddy Pride? That's what I mean. He'll certainly appreciate it. Such a darling old man! Well, can y' imagine this?"

Sally's ironic laugh halted at the sudden shrill yell of a woman. Both girls stopped to listen. The dance-music had broken off, and in its place came strange, startling sounds; first muffled, shuffling, breathing noises, swelling steadily into a crescendo more and more unmistakably evil; then cracks, thumps, claps, thuds against a continuous laborious stridor, growing by seconds, broken by half-oaths and shouts.

Sally jumped up and ran to the door that led to the dancing floor, drew the velvet draperies aside. "Great Gordon gin, it's a fight, Romie! If it ain't, I'm a Chinaman. Look!"

Well might they look. A crowd mobbed about the main doorway; people at the edges craning their necks; people rushing up from the far corners of the room; signs of a violent scramble at the entrance; certainty of a clamorous battle beyond it; people watching as the focus spread, now falling back from the central turbulence, now closing in anew.

Sally turned suddenly, made a dive for her discarded slippers. The tumult grew. "Romie, you wearin' your fur coat? Me too. We got to get 'em. Hear that fool woman holler somebody was stealin' coats? In two minutes this room'll be a bargain-counter.''

They were across the carpet and at the inner door of the coat-room, calling to the girl in charge. There was no girl in charge. Without waiting to determine her whereabouts, Sally got the lower movable half of the door open and crawled under the shelf over which wraps were normally delivered. Roma followed.

"Did you see where they put yours when they took it? Mine's—here it is! Sweet three hundred berries, come to your mama. Find it? Grab it—here come the harpies!''

The "harpies" had indeed come, had come in a drove: girls who had saved for two years to buy seal wraps; wives who had wheedled for months to get a caracal like Mrs. Jones'; women who had undertaken payment for their Persian lambs by installments and feared now to lose the entire bargain—all came rushing at once into the dressing-room, each elbowing, shouldering her way through the rest, attempting to get to the racks of cloaks. The inner door, its lower half already swinging open, presented no barrier at all; they swarmed under it, over it, through it, in among the rows of coats, which dangled untouched on their hangers; they grabbed and jerked and discarded and chattered; they quarreled and tussled and wept.

The outer door of the coat-room, through which guests' wraps were received on arrival, opened into the lobby, and so commanded the scene of the original scrimmage. Sally and Roma had by now reached this outer door, just beyond which riot raged. They found themselves thus between fighting, cursing men on one hand and hysterical women on the other; danger of physical injury beyond the door, scarcely less danger this side of it.

Sally kept saying, "Can you imagine this?" Roma was scared and silent. Ere they could decide either to stay or flee, a woman came rushing toward them.

"That's my coat!" she cried, seizing Sally's wrap and giving it a tug. "That's my coat! Take it off!"

"It won't be nobody's coat in a minute," observed Sally. "Get away. Shoo! Go chase yourself.''

"Mine, I say! I'd know it in a million!''

"Lady, it'll be your funeral if you tear it." But the frantic claimant fell to yanking and dragging, and Sally became very busy defending not only her wrap but herself.

Another woman had already spied Roma and was coming toward her with speed. One look and Roma made up her uncertain mind, ducked quickly under the door-shelf and out into the lobby.

She was now on the rim of the major fracas, which showed no sign of abating. She did not know, of course, that two dozen of those engaged were deliberately keeping up the tumult, slipping their hands into dress-suit pockets at every opportunity. She edged along the wall toward the head of the stairs, watching them wrestle, hardly knowing what she herself was doing. Then somewhere in the chaos of features she caught sight of Rusty Pride's face. He was grinning as he grasped and held a dickty in close embrace. The dickty wriggled and twisted and bucked; Rusty rode him as a buster rides a broncho, just held on and squeezed and grinned. Then Roma, staring, saw something shoot up into the air over Rusty—a chair in the hands of another dickty, poised to crash down on Rusty's head; and Roma screamed at the top of her lungs:

"Duck—Rusty—duck!"

Then she shut her eyes and leaned back against the wall.

The blank moment passed. She still carried her coat in her arms, and she realized of a sudden that some one had taken hold of it. When she saw the face of the creature that had done so, she almost laughed with fright. All this was a nightmare, and this creature was beyond doubt an ogre. It was a squat, yellow, flat face, leeringly toothsome, an incredible false-face that spoke.

"Papa'll take charge o' this little furpiece, sweetie. Turn it loose—and hold on to that holler." The yellow face developed arms which snatched the fur away from her; developed a body and legs which turned and made off toward the stairs. But in no time, unbelievingly, Roma saw the same body backing toward her, as though its departure had been a movie scene, which was now being run backwards. The uproar writhed about her like vapor, but out of the mist came one clear thing—Rusty grappling with the ogre, ogre's arms all clogged with fur, Rusty pressing the ogre back toward the place where he'd snatched the coat. The coat dropped—was kicked toward her. She stooped, caught it up. As she did so the ogre went sprawling into the nearest tangle of legs and feet, and Rusty himself was beside her, urging her out.

They almost fell down the stairs, Rusty explaining in staccato: "Stud Samson—rat—Club—thinks—I wanted—coat—" And Roma gathered between gasps that already the ogre and Rusty had been enemies; that they had fought at some time before, when Rusty had intensified the enmity by winning; that this last encounter must be Stud's cup, since, so far as he could see, Rusty's sole motive had been to deprive him of his spoil. Theft among thieves is unpardonable.

"Got to run—he'll be right on our heels—not a cop in sight—totes a gun, too—half-drunk and blood-mad—"

They struck sharp air, turned eastward toward the lights of Seventh Avenue. Not till they broke into its brightness and crossed did Rusty realize his thoughtlessness.

"Good night!" he groaned. "Right in the light. He's seen us—he's

seen us sure." Holding her arm he thrust her on, into the relative darkness of Harlem's middle strip. "Why the devil did I come this way?
Why the devil—"

They were now just beyond Seventh Avenue, going toward Lenox
along one of the numbered side streets. Rusty himself did not know
what refuge he was seeking. His folly in crossing the avenue, his fear
for Roma had paralyzed every mental resource. "I'm panicky," he
thought. He looked ahead—the Club was that way, offering certainly
no hopes. Stud Samson owned half the Club. He looked behind, into
the dimness beyond the Avenue, whence they had come. At that moment he saw a flash and heard a report like a five-ton truck, back-firing.
He stopped, caught Roma about the waist, turned, propelled her up the
stairs of the nearest house, into its glass-doored vestibule.

They shrank back into the darkest corner.

"What—was—was he shooting?"

"Darned if I know. May've been cops. Why the devil I came this
way—Maybe he saw your gray fur—he'd plug me, the fool. Look, you
get out and haul it—No, he'd think I was with you and plug anyhow.
I wouldn't care about myself if I could only get you to some safe place.
What the devil—oh, Lord!"

"Rusty—I couldn't leave you now. He might—"

There was a long moment, a moment of heavy breathing, a moment
in which they could imagine their pursuer coming nearer, red-minded,
gin-reckless, running perhaps from one stoop to the next, ready to
"plug" in the general direction of a gray fur coat, should he see one.

Then came from somewhere out in the dark a faint and far-away
shriek. It drew closer, grew louder, till they recognized the penetrating
scream, then the clangor and roar of headlong fire-engines.

"Firemen?" wondered Rusty. "Ought to be cops there by now. No.
It's the other way. It's Lenox Avenue."

But it was not the noise of the engines alone that grew sharper now
in consciousness. Something else was happening, something far more
subtle and portentous, something felt, still uncomprehended, that held
them expectant, like daybreak. Then from where they hid in the vestibule they saw that the sky, as much as they could see of it, was actually
growing brighter; first a faint, flickering yellow, then successive waves
of orange, pursuing each other like wind-flaws; and presently a steady,
flame-red glow whose heat they could almost sense through the cold.
And when they looked at each other they saw that their own faces
faintly reflected the glow.

"Good Lord!" breathed Rusty. "'Tisn't half a mile away. If Stud comes
past now, we're good-bygoners, that's all." And Roma heard him whisper over and over, "Lord, Lord," as if he were praying; nor did his eyes
search the street, as they had searched, but were fixed on the vivid sky.

Suddenly, something near caught Roma's eye. At first she shrank in alarm, then cried with relief: "Rusty—Rusty—it's all right now! He ran right past—that man—I saw him. He thinks it's his Club that's afire."

But Rusty seemed to have forgotten Stud Samson. He was still gazing into the sky; and now live wonder had recast his features and he was mumbling meaningless words:

"Pizen gin—doubled up 'n' died—you ain't been paid fo' it yit.... "

"Rusty—what are you saying?"

"Look, Romie!"

There was in his whisper discovery and awe, and he spoke without turning his head.

She pressed forward so that she, too, could see what held him so wholly absorbed. Together they stared. So might the children of Israel have stared upon the illumined tabernacle; so might Elijah have looked upon the approaching chariot of fire. High above the houses, black against the flame, a cross stood out in silhouette against the kindled sky; bold, untroubled, clear-cut, still—serenely terrible....

The door of the house in whose entrance they had hidden grew bright and opened behind them. A kindly warmth touched their cold cheeks. Surprised, they turned, then gaped at each other in utmost, blankest amazement.

Rusty's father stood smiling upon them as if he had known they were coming.

(1927)

NOTES

1. Slipping in the dozens: Verbal repartee, sometimes kidding, sometimes venomous, disparaging one's family.

2. Boogy: A Negro. A contraction of Booker T., used only of and by Negroes.

Common Meter

The Arcadia, on Harlem's Lenox Avenue, is "The World's Largest and Finest Ballroom—Admission Eighty-Five-Cents." Jazz is its holy spirit, which moves it continuously from nine till two every night. Observe above the brilliant entrance this legend in white fire:

TWO—ORCHESTRAS—TWO

Below this in red:

FESS BAXTER'S FIREMEN

Alongside in blue:

BUS WILLIAMS' BLUE DEVILS

Still lower in gold:

HEAR THEM OUTPLAY EACH OTHER

So much outside. Inside, a blazing lobby, flanked by marble stairways. Upstairs, an enormous dance hall the length of a city block. Low ceilings blushing pink with rows of inverted dome-lights. A broad dancing area, bounded on three sides by a wide soft-carpeted promenade, on the fourth by an ample platform accommodating the two orchestras.

People. Flesh. A fly-thick jam of dancers on the floor, grimly jostling each other; a milling herd of thirsty-eyed boys, moving slowly, searchingly over the carpeted promenade; a congregation of languid girls, lounging in rows of easy chairs here and there, bodies and faces unconcerned, dark eyes furtively alert. A restless multitude of empty, romance-hungry lives.

Bus Williams's jolly round brown face beamed down on the crowd as he directed his popular hit—*She's Still My Baby*:

> You take her out to walk
> And give her baby-talk,
> But talk or walk, walk or talk—
>   She's still my baby!

But the cheese-colored countenance of Fessenden Baxter, his professional rival, who with his orchestra occupied the adjacent half of the platform, was totally oblivious to *She's Still My Baby*.

Baxter had just caught sight of a girl, and catching sight of girls was one of his special accomplishments. Unbelief, wonder, amazement registered in turn on his blunt, bright features. He passed a hand over his straightened brown hair and bent to Perry Parker, his trumpetist.

"P.P., do you see what I see, or is it only the gin?"

"Both of us had the gin," said P.P., "so both of us sees the same thing."

"Judas Priest! Look at that figure, boy!"

"Never was no good at figures," said P.P.

"I've got to get me an armful of that baby."

"Lay off, papa," advised P.P.

"What do you mean, lay off?"

"Lay off. You and your boy got enough to fight over already, ain't you?"

"My boy?"

"Your boy, Bus."

"You mean that's Bus Williams' folks?"

"No lie. Miss Jean Ambrose, lord. The newest hostess. Bus got her the job."

Fess Baxter's eyes followed the girl. "Oh, he got her the job, did he?— Well, I'm going to fix it so she won't need any job. Woman like that's got no business working anywhere."

"Gin," murmured P.P.

"Gin hell," said Baxter. "Gunpowder wouldn't make a mama look as good as that."

"Gunpowder wouldn't make you look so damn good either."

"You hold the cat's tail," suggested Baxter.

"I'm tryin' to save yours," said P.P.

"Save your breath for that horn."

"Maybe," P.P. insisted, "she ain't so possible as she looks."

"Huh. They can all be taught."

"I've seen some that couldn't."

"Oh you have?—Well, P.P., my boy, remember, that's you."

*   *   *

Beyond the brass rail that limited the rectangular dance area at one lateral extreme there were many small round tables and clusters of chairs. Bus Williams and the youngest hostess occupied one of these tables while Fess Baxter's Firemen strutted their stuff.

Bus ignored the tall glass before him, apparently endeavoring to drain the girl's beauty with his eyes; a useless effort, since it lessened neither her loveliness nor his thirst. Indeed the more he looked the less able was he to stop looking. Oblivious, the girl was engrossed in the crowd. Her amber skin grew clearer and the roses imprisoned in it brighter as her merry black eyes danced over the jostling company.

"Think you'll like it?" he asked.

"Like it?" She was a child of Harlem and she spoke its language. "Boy, I'm having the time of my life. Imagine getting paid for this!"

"You ought to get a bonus for beauty."

"Nice time to think of that—after I'm hired."

"You look like a full course dinner—and I'm starved."

"Hold the personalities, papa."

"No stuff. Wish I could raise a loan on you. Baby—what a roll I'd tote."

"Thanks. Try that big farmer over there hootin' it with Sister Full-bosom. Boy, what a side-show they'd make!"

"Yea. But what I'm lookin' for is a leadin' lady."

"Yea? I got a picture of any lady leadin' you anywhere."

"You could, Jean."

"Be yourself, brother."

"I ain't bein' nobody else."

"Well, be somebody else, then."

"Remember the orphanage?"

"Time, papa. Stay out of my past."

"Sure—if you let me into your future."

"Speaking of the orphanage—?"

"You wouldn't know it now. They got new buildings all over the place."

"Somehow that fails to thrill me."

"You always were a knock-out, even in those days. You had the prettiest hair of any of the girls out there—and the sassiest hip-switch."

"Look at Fred and Adele Astaire over there. How long they been doing blackface?"

"I used to watch you even then. Know what I used to say?"

"Yea. 'Toot-a-toot-toot' on a bugle."

"That ain't all. I used to say to myself, 'Boy, when that sister grows up, I'm going to—.' "

Her eyes grew suddenly onyx and stopped him like an abruptly reversed traffic signal.

"What's the matter?" he said.

She smiled and began nibbling the straw in her glass.

"What's the matter, Jean?"

"Nothing, Innocence. Nothing. Your boy plays a devilish one-step, doesn't he?"

"Say. You think I'm jivin',¹ don't you?"

"No, darling. I think you're selling insurance."

"Think I'm gettin' previous, just because I got you the job."

"Funny, I never have much luck with jobs."

"Well, I don't care what you think, I'm going to say it."

"Let's dance."

"I used to say to myself, 'When that kid grows up, I'm going to ask her to marry me.' "

She called his bluff. "Well, I'm grown up."

"Marry me, will you, Jean?"

Her eyes relented a little in admiration of his audacity. Rarely did a sober aspirant have the courage to mention marriage.

"You're good, Bus. I mean, you're good."

"Every guy ain't a wolf, you know, Jean."

"No. Some are just ordinary meat-hounds."

From the change in his face she saw the depth of the thrust, saw pain where she had anticipated chagrin.

"Let's dance," she suggested again, a little more gently.

*   *   *

They had hardly begun when the number ended, and Fess Baxter stood before them, an ingratiating grin on his Swiss-cheese-colored face.

"Your turn, young fellow," he said to Bus.

"Thoughtful of you, reminding me," said Bus. "This is Mr. Baxter, Miss Ambrose."

"It's always been one of my ambitions," said Baxter, "to dance with a sure-enough angel."

"Just what I'd like to see you doin'," grinned Bus.

"Start up your stuff and watch us," said Baxter. "Step on it, brother. You're holding up traffic."

"Hope you get pinched for speedin'," said Bus, departing.

The Blue Devils were in good form tonight, were really "bearin' down" on their blues. Bus, their leader, however, was only going through the motions, waving his baton idly. His eyes followed Jean and Baxter, and it was nothing to his credit that the jazz maintained its spirit. Occasionally he lost the pair: a brace of young wild birds double-timed through the forest, miraculously avoiding the trees: an extremely ardent couple, welded together, did a decidedly localized mess-around; that gigantic black farmer whom Jean had pointed out sashayed into the line of vision, swung about, backed off, being fancy.

Abruptly, as if someone had caught and held his right arm, Bus' baton halted above his head. His men kept on playing under the impulse of their own momentum, but Bus was a creature apart. Slowly his baton drooped, like the crest of a proud bird, beaten. His eyes died on their object and all his features sagged. On the floor forty feet away, amid the surrounding clot of dancers, Jean and Baxter had stopped moving and were standing perfectly still. The girl had clasped her partner close about the shoulders with both arms. Her face was buried in his chest.

Baxter, who was facing the platform, looked up and saw Bus staring. He drew the girl closer, grinned, and shut one eye.

They stood so a moment or an hour till Bus dragged his eyes away. Automatically he resumed beating time. Every moment or so his baton wavered, slowed, and hurried to catch up. The blues were very low-down, the nakedest of jazz, a series of periodic wails against a background of steady, slow rhythm, each pounding pulse descending inevitably, like leaden strokes of fate. Bus found himself singing the words of this grief-stricken lamentation:

> Trouble—trouble has followed me all my days,
> Trouble—trouble has followed me all my days—
> Seems like trouble's gonna follow me always.

The mob demanded an encore, a mob that knew its blues and liked them blue. Bus complied. Each refrain became bluer as it was caught up by a different voice: the wailing clarinet, the weeping C sax, the moaning B-flat sax, the trombone, and Bus' own plaintive tenor:

> Baby—baby—my baby's gone away,
> Baby—baby—my baby's gone away—
> Seems like baby—my baby's gone to stay.

Presently the thing beat itself out, and Bus turned to acknowledge applause. He broke a bow off in half. Directly before the platform stood Jean alone, looking up at him.

He jumped down. "Dance?"

"No. Listen. You know what I said at the table?"

"At the table?"

"About—wolves?"

"Oh—that—?"

"Yea. I didn't mean anything personal. Honest, I didn't." Her eyes besought his. "You didn't think I meant anything personal, did you?"

"Course not," he laughed. "I know now you didn't mean anything." He laughed again. "Neither one of us meant anything."

With a wry little smile, he watched her slip off through the crowd.

*   *   *

From his side of the platform Bus overheard Fess Baxter talking to Perry Parker. Baxter had a custom of talking while he conducted, the jazz serving to blanket his words. The blanket was not quite heavy enough tonight.

"P.P., old pooter, she fell."

Parker was resting while the C sax took the lead. "She did?"

"No lie. She says, 'You don't leave me any time for cash customers.' "

"Yea?"

"Yea. And I says, 'I'm a cash customer, baby. Just name your price.' "

Instantly Bus was across the platform and at him, clutched him by the collar, bent him back over the edge of the platform; and it was clear from the look in Bus's eyes that he wasn't just being playful.

"Name her!"

"Hey—what the hell you doin'!"

"Name her or I'll drop you and jump in your face. I swear to—"

"Nellie!" gurgled Fessenden Baxter.

"Nellie who—damn it?"

"Nellie—Gray!"

"All right then!"

Baxter found himself again erect with dizzy suddenness.

The music had stopped, for the players had momentarily lost their breath. Baxter swore and impelled his men into action, surreptitiously adjusting his ruffled plumage.

The crowd had an idea what it was all about and many good-naturedly derided the victim as they passed:

" 'Smatter, Fess? Goin' in for toe-dancin'?"

"Nice back-dive, papa, but this ain't no swimmin'-pool."

Curry, the large, bald, yellow manager, also had an idea what it was all about and lost no time accosting Bus.

"Tryin' to start somethin'?"

"No. Tryin' to stop somethin'."

"Well, if you gonna stop it with your hands, stop it outside. I ain't got no permit for prize fights in here—'Course, if you guys can't get on together I can maybe struggle along without one of y' till I find somebody."

Bus said nothing.

"Listen. You birds fight it out with them jazz sticks, y' hear? Them's your weapons. Nex' Monday night's the jazz contest. You'll find out who's the best man next Monday night. Might win more'n a lovin' cup. And y' might lose more. Get me?"

He stood looking sleekly sarcastic a moment, then went to give Baxter like counsel.

*   *   *

Rumor spread through the Arcadia's regulars as night succeeded night.

A pair of buddies retired to the men's room to share a half-pint of gin. One said to the other between gulps:

"Lord today! Ain't them two roosters bearin' down on the jazz!"

"No lie. They mussa had some this same licker."

"Licker hell. Ain't you heard 'bout it?"

" 'Bout what?"

"They fightin', Oscar, fightin'."

"Gimme that bottle 'fo' you swaller it. Fightin'? What you mean fightin'?"

"Fightin' over that new mama."

"The honey-dew?"

"Right. They can't use knives and they can't use knucks. And so they got to fight it out with jazz."

"Yea? Hell of a way to fight."

"That's the only way they'd be any fight. Bus Williams'd knock that yaller boy's can off in a scrap."

"I know it. Y'ought-a-seen him grab him las' night."

"I did. They tell me she promised it to the one 'at wins this cup nex' Monday night."

"Yea? Wisht I knowed some music."

"Sho-nuff sheba[2] all right. I got a long shout[3] with her last night. Papa, a' she's got ever'thing!"

"Too damn easy on the eyes. Women like that ain't no good 'cep'n to start trouble."

"She sho' could start it for me. I'd 'a' been dancin' with her yet, but my two-bitses give out. Spent two hard-earned bucks dancin' with her, too."

"Shuh! Might as well th'ow yo' money in the street. What you git dancin' with them hostesses?"

"You right there, brother. All I got out o' that one was two dollars worth o' disappointment."

Two girl friends, lounging in adjacent easy chairs, discussed the situation.

"I can't see what she's got so much more'n anybody else."

"Me neither. I could look a lot better'n that if I didn't have to work all day."

"No lie. Scrubbin' floors never made no bathin' beauties."

"I heard Fess Baxter jivin' her while they was dancin'. He's got a line, no stuff."

"He'd never catch me with it."

"No, dearie. He's got two good eyes too, y'know."

"Maybe that's why he couldn't see you flaggin' 'im."

"Be yourself, sister. He says to her, 'Baby, when the boss hands me that cup—.' "

"Hates hisself, don't he?"

" 'When the boss hands me that cup,' he says, 'I'm gonna put it right in your arms.' "

"Yea. And I suppose he goes with the cup."

"So she laughs and says, 'Think you can beat him?' So he says, 'Beat him? Huh, that bozo[4] couldn't play a hand-organ.' "

"He don't mean her no good though, this Baxter."

"How do you know?"

"A kack[5] like that never means a woman no good. The other one ast her to step off with him."

"What!"

"Etta Pipp heard him. They was drinkin' and she was at the next table."

"Well, ain't that somethin'! Ast her to step off with him! What'd she say?"

"Etta couldn't hear no more."

"Jes' goes to show y'. What chance has a honest workin' girl got?"

Bus confided in Tappen, his drummer.

"Tap," he said, "ain't it funny how woman always seems to fall for a wolf?"

"No lie," Tap agreed. "When a guy gets too deep, he's long-gone."

"How do you account for it, Tap?"

"I don't. I jes' play 'em light. When I feel it gettin' heavy—boy, I run like hell."

"Tap, what would you do if you fell for a girl and saw her neckin' another guy?"

"I wouldn't fall," said Tappen, "so I wouldn't have to do nothin'."

"Well, but s'posin' you did?"

"Well, if she was my girl, I'd knock the can off both of 'em."

"S'posin' she wasn't your girl?"

"Well, if she wasn't my girl, it wouldn't be none o' my business."

"Yea, but a guy kind o' hates to see an old friend gettin' jived."

"Stay out, papa. Only way to protect yourself."

"S'posin' you didn't want to protect yourself? S'posin' you wanted to protect the woman?"

"Hmph! Who ever heard of a woman needin' protection?"

* * *

"Ladies and gentlemen!" sang Curry to the tense crowd that gorged the Arcadia. "Tonight is the night of the only contest of its kind in recorded history! On my left, Mr. Bus Williams, chief of the Blue Devils. On my right, Mr. Fessenden Baxter, leader of the Firemen. On this stand, the solid gold loving-cup. The winner will claim the jazz championship of the world!"

"And the sweet mama too, how 'bout it?" called a wag.

"Each outfit will play three numbers: a one-step, a fox-trot, and a blues number. With this stop watch which you see in my hand, I will time your applause after each number. The leader receiving the longest total applause wins the loving-cup!"

"Yea—and some lovin'-up wid it!"

"I will now toss a coin to see who plays the first number!"

"Toss it out here!"

"Bus Williams's Blue Devils, ladies and gentlemen, will play the first number!"

Bus's philosophy of jazz held tone to be merely the vehicle of rhythm. He spent much time devising new rhythmic patterns with which to vary his presentations. Accordingly he depended largely on Tappen, his master percussionist, who knew every rhythmic monkey-shine with which to delight a gaping throng.

Bus had conceived the present piece as a chase, in which an agile clarinet eluded impetuous and turbulent traps. The other instruments were to be observers, chorusing their excitement while they urged the principals on.

From the moment the piece started something was obviously wrong. The clarinet was elusive enough, but its agility was without purpose. Nothing pursued it. People stopped dancing in the middle of the number and turned puzzled faces toward the platform. The trap-drummer was going through the motions faithfully but to no avail. His traps were voiceless, emitted mere shadows of sound. He was a deaf mute making a speech.

Brief, perfunctory, disappointed applause rose and fell at the number's end. Curry announced its duration:

"Fifteen seconds flat!"

Fess Baxter, with great gusto, leaped to his post.

"The Firemen will play their first number!"

Bus was consulting Tappen.

"For the love o' Pete, Tap—?"

"Love o' hell. Look a' here."

Bus looked—first at the trapdrum, then at the bass; snapped them with a finger, thumped them with his knuckles. There was almost no sound; each drumsheet was dead, lax instead of taut, and the cause was immediately clear: each bore a short curved knife-cut following its edge a brief distance, a wound unnoticeable at a glance, but fatal to the instrument.

Bus looked at Tappen, Tappen looked at Bus.

"The cream-colored son of a buzzard!"

Fess Baxter, gleeful and oblivious, was directing a whirlwind number, sweeping the crowd about the floor at an exciting, exhausting pace, distorting, expanding, etherealizing their emotions with swift-changing dissonances. Contrary to Bus Williams's philosophy, Baxter considered rhythm a mere rack upon which to hang his tonal tricks. The present piece was dizzy with sudden disharmonies, unexpected twists of phrase, successive false resolutions. Incidentally, however, there was nothing wrong with Baxter's drums.

Boiling over, Bus would have started for him, but Tappen grabbed his coat.

"Hold it, papa. That's a sure way to lose. Maybe we can choke him yet."

"Yea—?"

"I'll play the wood. And I still got cymbals and sandpaper."

"Yea—and a triangle. Hell of a lot o' good they are."

"Can't quit," said Tappen.

"Well," said Bus.

Baxter's number ended in a furor.

"Three minutes and twenty seconds!" bellowed Curry as the applause eventually died out.

Bus began his second number, a fox-trot. In the midst of it he saw Jean dancing, beseeching him with bewildered dismay in her eyes, a look that at once crushed and crazed him. Tappen rapped on the rim of his trap drum, tapped his triangle, stamped the pedal that clapped the cymbals, but the result was a toneless and hollow clatter, a weightless noise that bounced back from the multitude instead of penetrating into it. The players also, distracted by the loss, were operating far below par, and not all their leader's frantic false enthusiasm could compensate for the gaping absence of bass. The very spine had been ripped out of their music, and Tappen's desperate efforts were but the hopeless flutterings of a stricken, limp, pulseless heart.

"Forty-five seconds!" Curry announced. "Making a total so far of one minute flat for the Blue Devils! The Firemen will now play their second number!"

The Firemen's fox-trot was Baxter's re-arrangement of Burleigh's "Jean, My Jean," and Baxter, riding his present advantage hard, stressed all that he had put into it of tonal ingenuity. The thing was delirious with strange harmonies, iridescent with odd color-changes, and its very flamboyance, its musical fine-writing and conceits delighted the dancers.

But it failed to delight Jean Ambrose, whom by its title it was intended to flatter. She rushed to Bus.

"What is it?" She was a-quiver.

"Drums gone. Somebody cut the pigskin the last minute."

"What? Somebody? Who?"

"Cut 'em with a knife close to the rim."

"Cut? He cut—? Oh, Bus!"

She flashed Baxter a look that would have crumpled his assurance had he seen it. "Can't you—Listen." She was at once wild and calm. "It's the bass. You got to have—I know! Make 'em stamp their feet! Your boys, I mean. That'll do it. All of 'em. Turn the blues into a shout."

"Yea? Gee. Maybe—"

"Try it! You've got to win this thing."

An uproar that seemed endless greeted Baxter's version of "Jean." The girl, back out on the floor, managed to smile as Baxter acknowledged the acclaim by gesturing toward her.

"The present score, ladies and gentlemen, is—for the Blue Devils, one minute even; for the Firemen, six minutes and thirty seconds? The Devils will now play their last number!" Curry's intonation of "last" moved the mob to laughter.

Into that laughter Bus grimly led his men like a captain leading his command into fire. He had chosen the parent of blue songs, the old St. Louis Blues, and he adduced every device that had ever adorned that classic. Clarinets wailed, saxophones moaned, trumpets wept wretchedly, trombones laughed bitterly, even the great bass horn sobbed dismally from the depths. And so perfectly did the misery in the music express the actual despair of the situation that the crowd was caught from the start. Soon dancers closed their eyes, forgot their jostling neighbors, lost themselves bodily in the easy sway of that slow, fateful measure, vaguely aware that some quality hitherto lost had at last been found. They were too wholly absorbed to note just how that quality had been found: that every player softly dropped his heel where each bass-drum beat would have come, giving each major impulse a body and breadth that no drum could have achieved. Zoom-zoom-zoom-zoom. It was not a mere sound; it was a vibrant throb that took hold of the crowd and rocked it.

They had been rocked thus before, this multitude. Two hundred years ago they had swayed to that same slow fateful measure, lifting their lamentation to heaven, pounding the earth with their feet, seeking the mercy of a new God through the medium of an old rhythm. Zoom— zoom. They had rocked so a thousand years ago in a city whose walls were jungle, forfending the wrath of a terrible black God who spoke in storm and pestilence, had swayed and wailed to that same slow period, beaten on a wild boar's skin stretched over the end of a hollow tree-trunk. Zoom—zoom—zoom—zoom. Not a sound but an emotion that laid hold on their bodies and swung them into the past. Blues—low-down blues indeed—blues that reached their souls' depths.

But slowly the color changed. Each player allowed his heel to drop less and less softly. Solo parts faded out, and the orchestra began to gather power as a whole. The rhythm persisted, the unfaltering common meter of blues, but the blueness itself, the sorrow, the despair, began to give way to hope. Ere long hope came to the verge of realization— mounted it—rose above it. The deep and regular impulses now vibrated like nearing thunder, a mighty, inescapable, all-embracing dominance, stressed by the contrast of wind-tone; an all-pervading atmosphere through which soared wild-winged birds. Rapturously, rhapsodically, the number rose to madness and at the height of its madness, burst into sudden silence.

Illusion broke. Dancers awoke, dropped to reality with a jolt. Suddenly the crowd appreciated that Bus Williams had returned to form, had put on a comeback, had struck off a masterpiece. And the crowd showed its appreciation. It applauded its palms sore.

Curry's suspense-ridden announcement ended:

"Total—for the Blue Devils, seven minutes and forty seconds! For the Firemen, six minutes and thirty seconds! Maybe that wasn't the Devils' last number after all! The Firemen will play *their* last number!"

It was needless for Baxter to attempt the depths and heights just attained by Bus Williams's Blue Devils. His speed, his subordination of rhythm to tone, his exotic coloring, all were useless in a low-down blues song. The crowd, moreover, had nestled upon the broad, sustaining bosom of a shout. Nothing else warmed them. The end of Baxter's last piece left them chilled and unsatisfied.

But if Baxter realized that he was beaten, his attitude failed to reveal it. Even when the major volume of applause died out in a few seconds, he maintained his self-assured grin. The reason was soon apparent: although the audience as a whole had stopped applauding, two small groups of assiduous handclappers, one at either extreme of the dancing-area, kept up a diminutive, violent clatter.

Again Bus and Tappen exchanged sardonic stares.

"Damn' if he ain't *paid* somebody to clap!"

Only the threatening hisses and boos of the majority terminated this clatter, whereupon Curry summed up:

"For Bus Williams's Blue Devils—seven minutes and forty seconds! For Fess Baxter's Firemen—eight minutes flat!"

He presented Baxter the loving-cup amid a hubbub of murmurs, handclaps, shouts, and hisses that drowned whatever he said. Then the hubbub hushed. Baxter was assisting Jean Ambrose to the platform. With a bow and a flourish he handed the girl the cup.

She held it for a moment in both arms, uncertain, hesitant. But there was nothing uncertain or hesitant in the mob's reaction. Feeble applause was overwhelmed in a deluge of disapprobation. Cries of "Crooked!" "Don't take it!" "Crown the cheat!" "He stole it!" stood out. Tappen put his finger in the slit in his trap-drum, ripped it to a gash, held up the mutilated instrument, and cried, "Look what he done to my traps!" A few hardboiled ruffians close to the platform moved menacingly toward the victor. "Grab 'im! Knock his can off!"

Jean's uncertainty abruptly vanished. She wheeled with the trophy in close embrace and sailed across the platform toward the defeated Bus Williams. She smiled into his astonished face and thrust the cup into his arms.

"Hot damn, mama! That's the time!" cried a jubilant voice from the floor, and instantly the gathering storm of menace broke into a cloudburst of delight. That romance-hungry multitude saw Bus Williams throw his baton into the air and gather the girl and the loving-cup both into his arms. And they went utterly wild—laughed, shouted, yelled and whistled till the walls of the Arcadia bulged.

Jazz emerged as the mad noise subsided: Bus Williams's Blue Devils playing "She's Still My Baby."

*   *   *

In the shelter of a nearby night-club Bus and his girl found a secluded corner.

"But you said you didn't mean—anything."

"I'm a awful liar sometimes. Specially when I see my girl givin' another guy a play."

"Giving who a play?"

"My boy, Baxter."

"When?"

"Out on the floor that first night. Baby, you draped yourself over him like a Spanish shawl. And there wasn't any movement to speak of."

Her brow cleared and she heaved a sigh. "Well, they say when a guy really falls he quits using his bean."

"He don't go blind, does he?"

"You did. Didn't you see that big farmer step on my foot? For a minute I thought I'd faint!"

(1930)

NOTES

1. Jivin': Fooling with flattery.
2. Sheba: A queen of a woman; a real "good-looker."
3. Shout: A slow one-step.
4. Bozo: A silly fellow; a funny person.
5. Kack: Extreme sarcasm for "dickty" (a swell; a high-toned person).

Dust

The long, low, black-and-silver roadster overtook a small clutter of cars waiting at a town crossing, snorted impatiently once or twice, and settled into a grumbling, disgusted purr. The people in the other cars stared, conferred among themselves, and stared again.

Pard grinned at the girl beside him. "Kills 'em to see us in a car like this. Know what they're saying?"

Billie smiled back. "Of course. 'Why, my *dear*, they're *colored*.' "

"No," said Pard. "One word: 'Niggers!' Leaves 'em speechless.—Look at that barmaid in the flivver[1]—can't get her mouth shut."

The signal changed, the cars moved forward. Pard said: "Now, damn it, eat niggers' dust."

Easily the mighty motor swept them in and out past car after car till they were far in the lead.

"Too bad," said Billie.

"What?"

"There isn't any dust."

With open country and a rolling straight-away they settled down to an even forty. A warm breeze sang round the windshield, ruffling the brown girl's hair with gentle fingers—glossy black hair which the low sun touched to a glow. She looked thoughtfully out over the Connecticut landscape. Wide meadows swept past or stretched gently away, lifting into distant hills; the hills dodged behind one another, and the sun dodged behind the high hills. She looked at the proud dark face of her companion, still grim with the joy of outstripping white folks.

"Horrible thing, prejudice," she said. "Does you all up. Puffs you all out of shape."

"Not if you have a safety-valve. This buggy's mine. Take everything on the road. Only fun fays[2] give me."

"It's such bitter fun."

"Deep, though. Satisfying. If hating's their game, I can hate right along with 'em. They hate me—sure. But I out-hate 'em. I hate 'em so much I like it."

"No. You like covering them with dust."

"Sure."

"Even when there isn't any dust."

A sudden, loud, almost articulate warning cried startlingly out behind them. Pard instinctively swung over, and a bright yellow sport coupe, of a make as powerful as his own roadster, eased effortlessly past. The interval between the two cars widened rapidly; the other motor's abrupt guffaw dwindled to a receding chuckle.

"Billy [sic], did you see that?"

"He's doing sixty."

"The license-plate, I mean."

"Green and white."

"Georgia?"

"Georgia—the dirty—"

"Lord protect us now," prayed Billie, knowing what was coming.

"Lord protect him," Pard corrected, his face again grimly bitter. "Hold fast."

His foot went down on the gas; the roadster jumped forward like a cruelly spurred horse, then laid back its ears and flattened itself out in a wild, headlong, heedless run.

Already the car ahead was lost around a left bend in the road. Pard took the bend blindly on its inside margin at fifty miles an hour, while Billie closed her eyes. When she looked again the yellow machine was vanishing to the right at the end of a half-mile straight-away. This they clipped off at seventy, taking the next curve, which was luckily shallow, at fifty-five.

The other car re-appeared; the interval had merely been maintained, not diminished. But the road now chose to climb the low ground-rises rather than side-step them so that, save for occasional depressions, it was now visible straight ahead for two miles. And it was clear.

The yellow sport-coupe, unaware of pursuit, maintained its even sixty. Pard's speedometer passed seventy-five. As his fifteen-mile-an-hour advantage devoured the stretch between him and his object, his lips formed rancorous words:

"No damn cracker—do that to me ... die first ... "

Billie yelled, "If you mean that, let me out!"

"Lyncher.... Atta baby—go get 'im—Red-necked hill-billy... Ought to run him off the road anyhow—every cracker less is a nigger more.... Listen.... "

As they drew nearer, the other engine's voice came back to them no longer a derisive chuckle but a deepening, desperate snarl.

"Holler, damn it. Holler and burn—like a black man down in Georgia—"

"Let up, Pard! Sharp curve ahead—"

The Georgia car, now a mere hundred yards in the lead, was slowing around the turn. Pard took the limit of approach before his foot sought the brake; his tires screeched in a straight skid, protesting the sudden change.

The sound seemed definitely to warn the yellow coupe of hostile approach from behind, whereupon it flung off the turn and engaged the next stretch in deadly earnest. This again was long straight highway, flatter than the other and flanked on either side by low, broad pasture-lands level with the road.

"Here we go," said Pard. Billie hung on, praying. The engine roared insanely, the wind whipped harshly past, swiftly, steadily the lead diminished. Perhaps three-quarters of a mile remained of the stretch when Pard, looking beyond the Georgia car ahead, saw the road split in a fork.

"Got to beat him to that fork. Next town's coming."

"And some cars, maybe," said Billie, thanking God for clear roads thus far.

"Come on, baby!" Pard jammed his foot down and held hard with both hands.

Billie squeezed her lids together. The stridor of the yellow car grew, beat painfully in her ears. "Bye-bye, cracker!" An irresistible impulse forced the girl's eyes open to observe impending disaster: Either car was flinging itself precipitately at the fork, Pard's roadster now a length ahead, to the left; both took the left bend of the fork; when, fifty yards ahead, a third car came out of a blind left intersection and stopped dead halfway across the road, startled to a standstill by the mad on-rushing pair.

Both jammed on brakes, Pard bearing right, directly into his competitor's path. The latter swung off the road with a crash into the grassy triangle between the two bends of the fork, managing by the grace of heaven and consummate skill not to flip upside down. Either car came to a standstill, Pard's fifty yards up the highway, the other in the middle of the field.

Billie was trembling. "Pard—go back—he must be hurt—"

No question now of hatred. Pard wheeled and drove back through the grass to the coupe. As they stopped, the yellow door opened, the driver backed stiffly out, and turned to present to their astonished eyes as black a face as ever came out of Georgia.

A deep breath all around. Then, "Are you—hurt? Billie managed; and, "I'm sorry," from Pard— "I'll pay for any damage—"

A far hill covered the face of the sun, like a hand concealing a grin.

(1931)

NOTES

1. Flivver: American slang for an old or cheap car.
2. Fays: White people. *Fay* is said to be the original term, although ofay is sometimes used (a contraction of "old" and "fay").

Guardian of the Law

Grammie's third-story window commanded the turbulent block. For her dark Harlem's 133rd Street was a stage upon which she looked as from an upper box. It was time now for the hero to enter. An anticipative half-smile on her lively little old face, she waited, looking brightly toward the 7th Avenue wing. Across her mind comment pursued comment like successive windflaws sweeping the surface of a pool:

"He'll be along presently. Watch these noisy young ones tone down. Yesterday he was jes' like 'em. Yellin'. Fightin'. Roller-skatin' over folks' corns. Stealin' apples off Tony, the peddler. Hookin' rides on trucks and taxis, scarin' the very kinks out my head. Now look—grown. Look like his grandpa that day he won the log-rollin' back home— Watch out, you little monkey you! 'Nother inch and you'd 'a' been squashed like a persimmon. Devlish young ones—!"

But there was something wrong about that.

"Hmph! Listen at you, you crazy old loon, you. Was they ever a devlisher young one than you fifty years ago? Fight? Done forgot all 'bout the time you bit Zeke Logan's ear half off 'cause he call' you a little yaller weasel. Steal? How 'bout the way you and Peace used to steal Gram Frankie's cider-wine and corncakes and puff up with colic like balloons? Scare yo' folks? 'Member the day you swum Uncle Jake's mare Steppit 'cross the widest part o' Deep Bayou, with yo' laigs drawn up and yo' feet crossed befo' you, same as if you was squattin' in front o' the fireplace? Jes' 'cause the black imp o' Satan, Jesse, up and dared you.—Young ones—"

But the hero had entered.

"Hot you! Hyeh he come!—Swing along, you proud young scamp, you!—Who'd a thought I'd live to see the day—?"

"Hey there, sweetheart!" A young bronze giant in a policeman's uniform had halted directly across the street and was waving cheerily up at her.

Grammie leaned forward, her quick smile answering his merry grin. "None o' yo' freshness, rookie. I's a lady, if it's any news to you."

"It's my job to look out for ladies, baby. How 'bout a little supper with me tonight?"

"Little is all I get any night, much as you eats."

"Stewed chicken and dumplin's would touch my heart."

"Yo' heart must be in yo' mouth."

"Sho is. Scared I might get corn beef and cabbage."

"Reckon cabbage'd tarnish them brass buttons or sump'm."

"The law demands chicken and dumplin's."

"Go 'long, boy and thank God for whatever you get."

"The law—"

"I'll fan the law with a hickory switch."

"All right, y' gangster. And I'll run you in for killin' an appetite, too." Officer Sam shook a threatening finger, turned and strolled away.

Fine boy. Much of a man. Much more than that no-'count Grip Beasely who lost the appointment Sam won. 'Course every crow thinks her young ones the blackest, but Grip would have been just one more hoodlum in uniform. Couldn't help it—too much Harlem in him. Too smart. Never depending on hard work for anything—always outsmarting somebody. Pulling wires, for instance, while Sam studied. It didn't work, though. Sam passed both tests high up, while Grip fell behind in the written. Of course he got close to Sam on the appointment-list, but Sam got the appointment, was now doing his six months' probation; all vacancies were filled and Grip was shut out.

Grip sort of held that against Sam. Though maybe Judy had a lot to do with it, too. Sweet child, Judy, with that red-brown skin and those big black eyes of hers. Little monkey turned Grip down flat and said she was Sam's girl, exclusively. Should have said it before Sam got the appointment, instead of waiting till after. Judy, of course, felt it might make Sam work harder if she withheld her decision till afterwards, but Grip naturally thought she chose Sam just because he got to be a cop.

"I don' trust that Grip—he's go'n' try to make it hard for my chile, sho's you born. Got some smart scheme up his sleeve right now, I know.—Well—guess that chicken's mos' done—time to put in the dumplin's."

Grammie rose, grunting a little with the stiffness of her lame knee, and approached a bureau on top of which lay a box of snuff. It was a small rectangular pasteboard box in one corner of which she had, after her custom, punched a hole with a safety-pin, and by the same device slightly enlarged the aperture to allow the dark brown powder to be shaken out in a thin stream as needed. But as she reached for it now, a sudden sharp pain shot through the lame knee, causing her to catch her weight on the bureau top; her fingers inadvertently compressed the snuff-box and a jet of brown powder shot across the white bureau-scarf.

"Now jes' look at that," she grumbled. "They's an excuse fo' a pain in the knee, but wastin' snuff and ruinin' linen is tom-foolishness." The pain passed. "Reckon it's a sin to dip snuff anyhow." She picked up the box. "But I likes it."

She returned to the window for a last look at her grandson. Instead of strolling down the street, he had stopped, facing the house on the first floor of which Grip Beasely lived. She saw him stand a moment as if puzzled, then suddenly break for the stoop and dash up the stairs and into the entrance.

"What under the sun—?"

Her bewilderment lasted but briefly.

"Sump'n wrong. That Grip is up to sump'm, sho." She looked about, peered out again toward Beasely's door. "Lemme get out o' hyeh." She caught up an old cloak that quite enveloped her slight form and with amazing agility, hurried out of the apartment and down the hall stairway.

"These chilun'll run me into my grave with their foolishness. I'm go'n shake that Grip's back teeth loose yet—the imp o' Satan!"

Along and across the street she sped with no sign of a lame knee, up the stoop and into the entrance of the house where Beasely dwelt. On the right of the passage, just within the entrance, was the door to Grip Beasely's flat. Grammie seized the knob, shook it, and stood back impatiently resolute. No answer. She discovered and pushed a button in the doorframe. She waited. Still no answer. The upper panel of the doorway was of glass, not thick plate-glass, but a common frosted window-glass that rattled when the door moved. "Lord help me if I'm right and forgive me if I'm wrong," she breathed, and raised her right foot to the lower edge of the flimsy panel, paused for balance, then thrust vigorously forward, heel first.

There was less crash and clatter than she expected. Through the jagged aperture she negotiated the snap-lock and was quickly inside. The room was unoccupied save by a few mistreated old mock-mahogany pieces of furniture on a gray, worn, dirty carpet, and a battered piano whose key-board grinned evilly at her from a distant dim corner. She halted, cocked her snowy head to one side, peered toward the rear of the apartment. The jangle of glass had drawn no investigation. Far down the obscurity of the narrow hallway, which ran lengthwise from parlor to kitchen, she heard voices and a laugh—an unpleasant, triumphant laugh.

Slowly and cautiously, she started toward that sound, wary of possible ambush from the intermediate rooms opening on the hallway. Deliberately she tip-toed forward, steadying herself with one hand against the wall.

"Mus' got my chile where he can't move—"

The first hall-room was open, the gray space beyond it lifeless. But now, sharpened by contrast, there came to her perceptions a decided, if intangible, animation somewhere beyond, a definite impression of subdued excitement in one of the rooms further along, somewhat like the far murmur of storm-wind in prairie grass. As she was about to pass the second chamber, the door of which was closed, she heard a chair scrape suddenly against a bare floor. An unexpected close crack of thunder could not have stiffened her to quicker attention.

Close to the door she crouched. The agitation, the voices further down the hall were now even more decided, and again Grammie heard that laugh. But for the moment she was arrested by the consciousness of something important here in this room at whose closed door she listened. It was very dark. Carefully she reached down feeling for the knob. Her hand encountered a key. The door had been locked from the outside and the key left in. She turned the key slowly, then suddenly threw the door open.

The airshaft-window was wide, and astride its sill, dimly outlined in a gray patch of light, was a girl. Her eyes, looking back over her shoulder, were wide with mingled terror and defiance.

"Judy!" went Grammie's sharp whisper. "What you doin', chile?"

"Grammie!"

"Sh! What you doin' in hyeh?"

"How—how'd you get in? Where are they?"

"Who?"

"Grip—Grip and Cawley."

"Cawley?—Who he?"

Judy abandoned the window sill. "Grip's friend.—I was leavin' for your house. Grip came up to our flat and begged me to come see his sister—said she was sick in bed. I did, but his sister wasn't here, and he and this Cawley shut the door and held me in the parlor till Sam came along. They were watchin' for him. When I saw Sam I yelled for him. I didn't know, but that was just what they wanted. They knew they couldn't get him in here any other way. But before Sam realized who yelled, Cawley yanked me away and dragged me down the hall. He put me in here. Said—"

"Sh!—Whisper, chile. Quick—"

"Said if I kept quiet it would just be a joke, but if I didn't it wouldn't. He locked me in. Then I heard 'em all go past down the hall. Grip said, 'No monkey-business, rookie—this thing's loaded.' So I was scared too yell again—Sam would've forgot Grip's gun and got himself shot."

Grammie stepped quickly to the window. Although this was the street foor, the air-well dropped a full story below to the level of the basement. "What was you aimin' to do?"

"Jump to the bottom, go through the cellar, and get help."

"Hmph.—Go on out the front door. Get a police—get all the polices [sic] you see—and come a-runnin'."

Before Judy got to the front door, Grammie had traversed the rest of the hall and was outside the room where things were happening. A third time she heard Grip Beasely's laugh. Knowing now what it meant transformed her into the same furious child who, fifty years ago, had bitten Zeke Logan's ear half off. She flung the door wide and stood framed on the threshold, a small, terrible angel of vengeance.

Cawley, his back to the door, was now holding the gun on Sam, who was seated, hands raised, on a chair. Grip was standing beyond Sam, holding a whiskey bottle, and as the door opened, he was growling, "Will you or won't you?"

"What kind o' foolishness is this?" Grammie stepped forward. Cawley turned his head in surprise to look over his shoulder. Grammie's hand shot forward toward that astonished countenance, and suddenly Cawley swore and dropped the gun, as both hands came up to cover his face.

The alert defiance in Officer Sam's eyes had been watching for just this instant's opening. His training as an officer had been brief but sufficient to teach him not to charge a loaded muzzle. Now, however, one of his raised hands quickly smacked the bottle out of Grip's fingers so viciously that it spattered with a wet crash against the wall. The other became a fist which traveled a short distance to reach the point of Beasely's jaw, and in as much as Officer Sam was at the same time lifting his one hundred and ninety pounds off the chair, there was considerable emphasis upon that point.

Cawley, one hand clamped over his face, was groping his way out, Grammie nimbly side-stepping to let him pass. But Beasely was too husky a young animal to be floored by a single blow. His hundred and ninety pounds were more closely packed than Sam's; he was shorter and broader with disproportionately long arms. And he had no physical fear. With Sam's blow he staggered back, shook his head as if in vigorous denial that any such thing had happened, then lunged precipitately forward. The next moment saw him and Officer Sam embracing each other with enthusiasm.

Grammie momentarily ignored them, stooped and picked up the pistol, considered it briefly, and deliberately tossed it into the hallway behind her. Then she stood and beheld the tussle, offering above the adversaries' stridor, shuffle, thumps and thwacks such advice and comment as she found indicated:

"Sam, you fool you, turn 'im loose so you can hit 'im. You huggin' im like you love 'im. Let him do the huggin'—you hit.—That's better, see? He can outhug you but you can outhit him.—I declare that po' chile look mo' like a gorilla 'n he do like a man. Look out—he'll bite you if he get a chance!—Now—that's it—that's it—now you got 'im. Tho'w 'im down and sit o' 'im. Fine.—You got to bounce up and down on 'im ev'y now and then, y' know, else he'll get his wind back.— 'Twon' be long 'fo'—hyeh they is now!"

Here they were indeed, a breathless Judy and two looming envoys of the law, one black, one yellow, both extremely interested.

"The other one went in yonder," said Grammie.

The other one was sought, found, and ungently returned to the scene of major activity, where Officer Sam was explaining:

"Judy yells and I rush in, excited and empty-handed. My bosom-friend, Grip here, has gun a-plenty, see? When I pop in, he's behind me. I start down the hall to this back room. Cawley comes up and takes his turn with the gun. I don't get what it's all about till Grip offers me a drink. The idea is to souse me, take my shield and gun, and turn me in. If I don't come around agreeable, I get beaned and the same thing happens anyhow."

"What's it to him?"

"He's in line for my job. I'm still a rookie. If I'm jammed and they break me, he pulls a fast wire and gets in.—So what happens? You'd be surprised. Just as I'm forgettin' there's a rod in the picture and figurin' on a quick dumb move, along comes—"

"A cockaroach."

"Huh?" said everybody.

"A cockaroach," Grammie repeated positively. "Kitchen's right next door, y' see. This cockaroach 'd got on Cawley's collar—right hyeh." She reached up and put her finger on the spot. "Y' all know how cockaroaches is. They likes to crawl between things—crazy 'bout cracks and such. So this one crawled right over Cawley's collar and got down between his collar and his neck. Natchelly it itches and natchelly Cawley scratches. And natchelly that takes Cawley's mind off what he was doin', y' see. Sam's lookin' fo' a chance like that. He grabs this Grip hyeh, pulls him 'round between hisself and that Cawley. Cawley can't shoot now 'thout hittin' Grip, y' see. So Sam jes' taps this Grip on his chin to stun him a little, so he won' suffer in case he gets hurt—Sam always was a tender-hearted chile—and then shoves him into this Cawley. Natchelly Cawley loses his balance, so Sam can take the gun 'way from him and th'ow it out in the hall. Too bad but he accidentally hit him in the nose doin' it, so he made him go in the kitchen yonder and bathe his face in cold water. And when y' all got hyeh, that Sam was a'kneelin' over Grip tryin' his best to bring him to."

"Well I be dog-goned!" said the yellow cop.

"Mus'n cuss, chile," Grammie reproached him. "Cussin's a sin."

" 'Scuse me, ma'am—But how'd you know all this?"

"Sam jes' now tol' me. Y'see I was passin' by the front do' when Judy run out to get y'all. She tol' me not to come in. Natchelly that made me curious, so in I come. I knowed nuthin' wasn' go'n' hurt me.—But by time I got in back hyeh, seem like ev'ything was over."

"Good boy, Sammy!" commended the black policeman. "That's hoppin' off a rough spot."

Officer Sam looked at Grammie; Grammie looked back at him and with her live eyes dared him to upset her account. And Officer Sam said, "Well, I don' guess he'd a' shot the thing off, sho' nough."

"If you jump at a guy with a gun, he'll shoot. He can't help it," the black one said.

But now Grip's breath had returned sufficiently for him to protest, "Hey, what kind of a lousy frame—?"

"Keep yo' teeth shut," advised the yellow one, "fo' I snatch yo' tongue out."

"This is my house!—He come in here of his own free will, 'cause his gal—"

That was the end of the Beasely defense. The immediately subsequent proceedings kept both Grip and Cawley busy avoiding dismemberment. With no effort to contume Sam's gentleness, the two officers urged the culprits forth.

Grammie, Judy, and Sam brought up the rear. Grammie's foot struck a hard object on the floor. Sam stooped in the darkness and picked up Grip's gun. He said,

"You ought to have this for a souvenir."

"Who me?" Grammie drew away. "Deed, chile, you couldn't pay me to touch one o' them things—I'm scared to death of 'em." Then— "Judy!—Bless my soul—I b'lieve my chicken done cooked dry! Come on, chile, less hurry—"

But it hadn't. In a small immaculate kitchen which might have been adequate for Grammie and Judy, but which Sam's magnitude filled to overflowing, supper was under way. "They'll put them birds under the jail," said Sam.

"You Judy," Grammie scolded, as she helped Sam to more chicken and dumplings, "You ought to be 'shamed o' yo'self."

Judy's black eyes twinkled. "Why, Grammie?"

" 'Cause you told sump'm that wasn't so."

"When?"

"You promised that Cawley you'd keep quiet if they didn't do nuthin' to Sam. And 'stead o' keepin' quiet, you'd 'a' jumped out that window and busted yo' fool laigs, and walked on yo' hands through the cellar, I reckon, till you got where you could holler fo' help. Only I stopped you.—Now what kind o' keepin' a promise is that?"

Judy and Sam exchanged grins. "Yes, ma'am," Judy said.

"And as fo' you, Sam—look a'hyeh—did you tell 'em any different at the jail-house—'bout that cockaroach?"

"No ma'am," grinned Officer Sam. "Didn' want 'em to think you and Judy would both—uh—uh—"

"You young scamp, if you call me a tain'-so, I'll never make you another chicken-dumplin' as long as you cullud." She eyed him sternly.

"You jes' ain' got no sense. Hyeh you is a rookie, on yo' six months' probation, when the boss-men can drop you fo' anything you do, drop you without givin' no explanation. And you gettin' ready to up and tell 'em that yo' grandmammy—yo' grandmammy!—had to come along and help you out. Humph!"

"Twould 'a' been true, wouldn't it?"

"They's a time and place fo' ev'thing. That wasn't no time for the truth."

"But Grammie—" began Judy.

"Hush up!" said Grammie. "When y'all get old as I is, y'all can lie too." She considered this a moment, then added, "But not befo'."

"What I want to know," said Sam, "is what did you hit Cawley with?"

Grammie could masquerade severity no longer. Her bright eyes became those of a mischievous child, she chuckled quite impishly. Into her bosom she reached, withdrew a small pastboard [sic] box, and, exhibiting the hole in its corner, said with relish:

"I squirted his eyes full o' snuff."

(1933)

Miss Cynthie

For the first time in her life somebody had called her "madam." She had been standing, bewildered but unafraid, while innumerable Red Caps appropriated piece after piece of the baggage arrayed on the platform. Neither her brief seventy years' journey through life nor her long two days' travel northward had dimmed the live brightness of her eyes, which, for all their bewilderment, had accurately selected her own treasures out of the row of luggage and guarded them vigilantly.

"These yours, madam?"

The biggest Red Cap of all was smiling at her. He looked for all the world like Doc Crinshaw's oldest son back home. Her little brown face relaxed; she smiled back at him.

"They got to be. You all done took all the others."

He laughed aloud. Then—"Carry 'em in for you?"

She contemplated his bulk. "Reckon you can manage it—puny little feller like you?"

Thereupon they were friends. Still grinning broadly, he surrounded himself with her impedimenta, the enormous brown extension-case on one shoulder, the big straw suitcase in the opposite hand, the carpet-bag under one arm. She herself held fast to the umbrella.

"Always like to have sump'm in my hand when I walk. Can't never tell when you'll run across a snake."

"There aren't any snakes in the city."

"There's snakes everywhere, chile."

They began the tedious hike up the interminable platform. She was small and quick. Her carriage was surprisingly erect, her gait astonishingly spry. She said:

"You liked to took my breath back yonder, boy, callin' me 'madam.' Back home everybody call me 'Miss Cynthie.' Even my own chillun. Even their chillun. Black folks, white folks too. 'Miss Cynthie.' Well, when you come up with that 'madam' o' yourn, I say to myself, 'Now, I wonder who that chile's a-grinnin' at? 'Madam' stand for mist'ess o' the house, and I sho' ain' mist'ess o' nothin' in this hyeh New York."

"Well, you see, we call everybody 'madam.' "

"Everybody?—Hm." The bright eyes twinkled. "Seem like that'd worry me some—if I was a man."

He acknowledged his slip and observed, "I see this isn't your first trip to New York."

"First trip any place, son. First time I been over fifty mile from Waxhaw. Only travelin' I've done is in my head. Ain' seen many places, but I's seen a passel o' people. Reckon places is pretty much alike after people been in 'em awhile."

"Yes, ma'am. I guess that's right."

"You ain' no reg'lar bag-toter, is you?"

"Ma'am?"

"You talk too good."

"Well, I only do this in vacation-time. I'm still in school."

"You is. What you aimin' to be?"

"I'm studying medicine."

"You is?" She beamed. "Aimin' to be a doctor, huh? Thank the Lord for that. That's what I always wanted my David to be. My grandchile hyeh in New York. He's to meet me hyeh now."

"I bet you'll have a great time."

"Mussn't bet, chile. That's sinful. I tole him 'fo' he left home, I say, 'Son, you the only one o' the chillun what's got a chance to amount to sump'm. Don' th'ow it away. Be a preacher or a doctor. Work yo' way up and don' stop short. If the Lord don' see fit for you to doctor the soul, then doctor the body. If you don' get to be a reg'lar doctor, be a tooth-doctor. If you jes' can't make that, be a foot-doctor. And if you don' get that fur, be a undertaker. That's the least you must be. That ain' so bad. Keep you acquainted with the house of the Lord. Always mind the house o' the Lord—whatever you do, do like a church-steeple: aim high and go straight.' "

"Did he get to be a doctor?"

"Don' b'lieve he did. Too late startin', I reckon. But he'd done succeeded at sump'm. Mus' be at least a undertaker, 'cause he started sendin' the homefolks money, and he come home las' year dressed like Judge Pettiford's boy what went off to school in Virginia. Wouldn't tell none of us 'zackly what he was doin', but he said he wouldn' never be happy till I come and see for myself. So hyeh I is." Something softened her voice. "His mammy died befo' he knowed her. But he was always sech a good chile—" The something was apprehension. "Hope he is a undertaker."

They were mounting a flight of steep stairs leading to an exit-gate, about which clustered a few people still hoping to catch sight of arriving friends. Among these a tall young brown-skinned man in a light grey suit suddenly waved his panama and yelled, "Hey, Miss Cynthie!"

Miss Cynthie stopped, looked up, and waved back with a delighted umbrella. The Red Cap's eyes lifted too. His lower jaw sagged.

"Is that your grandson?"

"It sho' is," she said and distanced him for the rest of the climb. The grandson, with an abandonment that superbly ignored on-lookers, folded the little woman in an exultant, smothering embrace. As soon as she could, she pushed him off with breathless mock impatience.

"Go 'way, you fool, you. Aimin' to squeeze my soul out my body befo' I can get a look at this place?" She shook herself into the semblance of composure. "Well. You don' look hungry, anyhow."

"Ho-ho! Miss Cynthie in New York! Can y'imagine this? Come on. I'm parked on Eighth Avenue."

The Red Cap delivered the outlandish luggage into a robin's egg-blue open Packard with scarlet wheels, accepted the grandson's dollar and smile, and stood watching the car roar away up Eighth Avenue.

Another Red Cap came up. "Got a break, hey, boy?"

"Dave Tappen himself—can you beat that?"

"The old lady hasn't seen the station yet—starin' at him."

"That's not the half of it, bozo.[1] That's Dave Tappen's grandmother. And what do you s'pose she hopes?"

"What?"

"She hopes that Dave has turned out to be a successful undertaker!"

"Undertaker? Undertaker!"

They stared at each other a gaping moment, then doubled up with laughter.

"Look—through there—that's the Chrysler Building. Oh, hell-elujah! I meant to bring you up Broadway—"

"David—"

"Ma'am?"

"This hyeh wagon yourn?"

"Nobody else's. Sweet buggy, ain't it?"

"David—you ain't turned out to be one of them moonshiners, is you?"

"Moonshiners—? Moon—Ho! No indeed, Miss Cynthie. I got a better racket 'n that."

"Better which?"

"Game. Business. Pick-up."

"Tell me, David. What is yo' racket?"

"Can't spill it yet, Miss Cynthie. Rather show you. Tomorrow night you'll know the worst. Can't you make out till tomorrow night?"

"David, you know I always wanted you to be a doctor, even if 'twasn' nothin' but a foot-doctor. The very leas' I wanted you to be was a undertaker."

"Undertaker! Oh, Miss Cynthie!—with my sunny disposition?"

"Then you ain' even a undertaker?"

"Listen, Miss Cynthie. Just forget 'bout what I am for awhile. Just till tomorrow night. I want you to see for yourself. Tellin' you will spoil it. Now stop askin', you hear?—because I'm not answerin'—I'm surprisin' you. Now don't expect anybody you meet to tell you. It'll mess up the whole works. Understand? Now give the big city a break. There's the elevated train going up Columbus Avenue. Ain't that hot stuff?''

Miss Cynthie looked. "Humph!" she said. "Tain' half high as that trestle two mile from Waxhaw.''

She thoroughly enjoyed the ride up Central Park West. The stagger lights, the extent of the park, the high, close, kingly dwellings, remarkable because their stoves cooled them in summer as well as heated them in winter, all drew nods of mild interest. But what gave her special delight was not these: It was that David's car so effortlessly sped past the headlong drove of vehicles racing northward.

They stopped for a red light; when they started again their machine leaped forward with a triumphant eagerness that drew from her an unsuppressed "Hot you, David! That's it!"

He grinned appreciatively. "Why, you're a regular New Yorker already.''

"New Yorker nothin'! I done the same thing fifty years ago—befo' I knowed they was a New York.''

"What!"

"Deed so. Didn' I use to tell you 'bout my young mare, Betty? Chile, I'd hitch Betty up to yo' grandpa's buggy and pass anything on the road. Betty never knowed what another horse's dust smelt like. No 'ndeedy. Shuh, boy, this ain' nothin' new to me. Why that broke-down Fo'd yo' uncle Jake's got ain' nothin'—nothin' but a sorry mess. Done got so slow I jes' won' ride in it—I declare I'd rather walk. But this hyeh thing, now, this is right nice.'' She settled back in complete, complacent comfort, and they sped on, swift and silent.

Suddenly she sat erect with abrupt discovery.

"David—well—bless my soul!"

"What's the matter, Miss Cynthie?"

Then he saw what had caught her attention. They were traveling up Seventh Avenue now, and something was miraculously different. Not the road; that was as broad as ever, wide, white gleaming in the sun. Not the houses; they were lofty still, lordly, disdainful, supercillious. Not the cars; they continued to race impatiently onward, innumerable, precipitate, tumultuous. Something else, something at once obvious and subtle, insistent, pervasive, compelling.

"David—this mus' be Harlem!"

"Good Lord, Miss Cynthie—!"

"Don' use the name of the Lord in vain, David.''

"But I mean—gee!—you're no fun at all. You get everything before a guy can tell you.''

"You got plenty to tell me, David. But don' nobody need to tell me this. Look a yonder."

Not just a change of complexion. A completely dissimilar atmosphere. Sidewalks teeming with leisurely strollers, at once strangely dark and bright. Boys in white trousers, berets, and green shirts, with slickened black heads and proud swagger. Bareheaded girls in crisp organdie dresses, purple, canary, gay scarlet. And laughter, abandoned strong Negro laughter, some falling full on the ear, some not heard at all, yet sensed—the warm life-breath of the tireless carnival to which Harlem's heart quickens in summer.

"This is it," admitted David. "Get a good eyeful. Here's One Hundred and Twenty-fifth Street—regular little Broadway. And here's the Alhambra,[2] and up ahead we'll pass the Lafayette."[3]

"What's them?"

"Theatres."

"Theatres? Theatres. Humph! Look, David—is that a colored folks church?" They were passing a fine gray-stone edifice.

"That? Oh. Sure it is. So's this one on this side."

"No! Well, ain' that fine? Splendid big church like that for colored folks."

Taking his cue from this, her first tribute to the city, he said, "You ain't seen nothing yet. Wait a minute."

They swung left through a side-street and turned right on a boulevard. "What do you think o' that?" And he pointed to the quarter-million-dollar St. Mark's.[4]

"That a colored church, too?"

" 'Tain' no white one. And they built it themselves, you know. Nobody's hand-me down gift."

She heaved a great happy sigh. "Oh, yes, it was a gift, David. It was a gift from on high." Then, "Look a hyeh—which a one you belong to?"

"Me? Why, I don't belong to any—that is, none o' these. Mine's over in another section. Y'see, mine's Baptist. These are all Methodist. See?"

"M-m. Uh-huh. I see."

They circled a square and slipped into a quiet narrow street overlooking a park, stopping before the tallest of the apartment houses in the single commanding row.

Alighting, Miss Cynthie gave this imposing structure one sidewise, upward glance, and said, "Y'all live like bees in a hive, don't y'?—I boun' the women does all the work, too." A moment later, "So this is a elevator? Feel like I'm glory-bound sho' nuff."

Along a tiled corridor and into David's apartment. Rooms leading into rooms. Luxurious couches, easy-chairs, a brown-walnut grand piano, gay-shaded floor lamps, panelled walls, deep rugs, treacherous glass-wood floors—and a smiling golden-skinned girl in a gingham house-dress, approaching with outstretched hands.

"This is Ruth, Miss Cynthie."

"Miss Cynthie!" said Ruth.

They clasped hands. "Been wantin' to see David's girl ever since he first wrote us 'bout her."

"Come—here's your room this way. Here's the bath. Get out of your things and get comfy. You must be worn out with the trip."

"Worn out? Worn out? Shuh. How you gon' get worn out on a train? Now if 'twas a horse, maybe, or Jake's no-'count Fo'd—but a train— didn' but one thing bother me on that train."

"What?"

"When the man made them beds down, I jes' couldn' manage to undress same as at home. Why, s'posin' sump'm bus' the train open— where'd you be? Naked as a jay-bird in dew-berry time."

David took in her things and left her to get comfortable. He returned, and Ruth, despite his reassuring embrace, whispered:

"Dave, you cain't fool old folks—why don't you go ahead and tell her about yourself? Think of the shock she's going to get—at her age."

David shook his head. "She'll get over the shock if she's there looking on. If we just told her, she'd never understand. We've got to railroad her into it. Then she'll be happy."

"She's nice. But she's got the same ideas as all old folks—"

"Yea—but with her you can change 'em. Specifically if everything is really all right. I know her. She's for church and all, but she believes in good times too, if they're right. Why, when I was a kid—" He broke off. "Listen!"

Miss Cynthie's voice came quite distinctly to them, singing a jaunty little rhyme:

> Oh I danced with the gal with the hole in her stockin',
> And her toe kep' a-kickin' and her heel kep' a-knockin'—
>
> Come up, Jesse, and get a drink o' gin,
> 'Cause you near to the heaven as you'll ever get ag'in.

"She taught me that when I wasn't knee-high to a cricket," David said.

Miss Cynthie still sang softly and merrily:

> Then I danced with the gal with the dimple in her cheek,
> And if she'd a' kep' a-smilin', I'd a' danced for a week—

"God forgive me," prayed Miss Cynthie as she discovered David's purpose the following night. She let him and Ruth lead her, like an early Christian martyr, into the Lafayette Theatre. The blinding glare of the lobby produced a merciful self-anaesthesia, and she entered the sudden dimness of the interior as involuntarily as in a dream—

Attendants outdid each other for Mr. Dave Tappen. She heard him tell them, "Fix us up till we go on," and found herself sitting between Ruth and David in the front row of a lower box. A miraculous device of the devil, a motion-picture that talked, was just ending. At her feet the orchestra was assembling. The motion-picture faded out amid a scattered round of applause. Lights blazed and the orchestra burst into an ungodly rumpus.

She looked out over the seated multitude, scanning row upon row of illumined faces, black faces, white faces, yellow, tan, brown, bald heads, bobbed heads, kinky and straight heads; and upon every countenance, expectancy—scowling expectancy in this case, smiling in that, complacent here, amused there, commentative elsewhere, but everywhere suspense, abeyance, anticipation.

Half a dozen people were ushered down the nearer aisle to reserved seats in the second row. Some of them caught sight of David and Ruth and waved to them. The chairs immediately behind them in the box were being shifted. "Hello, Tap!" Miss Cynthie saw David turn, rise, and shake hands with two men. One of them was large, bald and pink, emanating good cheer; the other short, thin, sallow with thick black hair and a sour mien. Ruth also acknowledged their greeting. "This is my grandmother," David said proudly. "Miss Cynthie, meet my managers, Lou and Lee Goldman." "Pleased to meet you," managed Miss Cynthie. "Great lad, this boy of yours," said Lou Goldman. "Great little partner he's got, too," added Lee. They also settled back expectantly.

"Here we go!"

The curtain rose to reveal a cotton-field at dawn. Pickers in blue denim overalls, bandanas, and wide-brimmed straws, or in gingham aprons and sun-bonnets, were singing as they worked. Their voices, from clearest soprano to richest bass, blended in low concordances, first simply humming a series of harmonies, until, gradually, came words, like figures forming in mist. As the sound grew, the mist cleared, the words came round and full, and the sun rose bringing light as if in answer to the song. The chorus swelled, the radiance grew, the two, as if emanating from a single source, fused their crescendos, till at last they achieved a joint transcendence of tonal and visual brightness.

"Swell opener," said Lee Goldman.

"Ripe," agreed Lou.

David and Ruth arose. "Stay here and enjoy the show, Miss Cynthie. You'll see us again in a minute."

"Go to it, kids," said Lou Goldman.

"Yea—burn 'em up," said Lee.

Miss Cynthie hardly noted that she had been left, so absorbed was she in the spectacle. To her, the theatre had always been the antithesis of the church. As the one was the refuge of righteousness, so the other was the stronghold of transgression. But this first scene awakened memories, captured and held her attention by offering a blend of truth and novelty. Having thus baited her interest, the show now proceeded to play it like the trout through swift-flowing waters of wickedness. Resist as it might, her mind was caught and drawn into the impious subsequences.

The very music that had just rounded out so majestically now distorted itself into ragtime. The singers came forward and turned to dancers; boys, a crazy, swaying background, threw up their arms and kicked out their legs in a rhythmic jamboree; girls, an agile, brazen foreground, caught their skirts up to their hips and displayed their copper calves, knees, thighs, in shameless, incredible steps. Miss Cynthie turned dismayed eyes upon the audience, to discover that mob of sinners devouring it all with fond satisfaction. Then the dancers separated and with final abandon flung themselves off the stage in both directions.

Lee Goldman commented through the applause, "They work easy, them babies."

"Yea," said Lou. "Savin' the hot stuff for later."

Two black faced cotton-pickers appropriated the scene, indulging in dialogue that their hearers found uproarious,[sic]

"Ah'm tired."

"Ah'm hongry."

"Dis job jes' wears me out."

"Starves me to death."

"Ah'm so tired—you know what Ah'd like to do?"

"What?"

"Ah'd like to go to sleep and dream I was sleepin'."

"What good dat do?"

"Den I could wake up and still be 'sleep.'

"Well y' know what Ah'd like to do?"

"No. What?"

"Ah'd like to swaller me a hog and a hen."

"What good dat do?"

"Den Ah'd always be full o' ham and eggs."

"Ham? Shuh. Don't you know a hog has to be smoked 'fo' he's a ham?"

"Well, if I swaller him, he'll have a smoke all around him, won' he?"

Presently Miss Cynthie was smiling like everyone else, but her smile soon fled. For the comics departed, and the dancing girls returned, this time in scant travesties on their earlier voluminous costumes—tiny sunbonnets perched jauntily on one side of their glistening bobs, bandanas reduced to scarlet neck-ribbons, waists mere brassieres, skirts mere gingham sashes.

And now Miss Cynthie's whole body stiffened with a new and surpassing shock; her bright eyes first widened with unbelief, then slowly grew dull with misery. In the midst of a sudden great volley of applause her grandson had broken through that bevy of agile wantons and begun to sing.

He too was dressed as a cotton-picker, but a Beau Brummel among cotton-pickers; his hat bore a pleated green band, his bandana was silk, his overalls blue satin, his shoes black patent leather. His eyes flashed, his teeth gleamed, his body swayed, his arms waved, his words came fast and clear. As he sang, his companions danced a concerted tap, uniformly wild, ecstatic. When he stopped singing, he himself began to dance, and without sacrificing crispness of execution, seemed to absorb into himself every measure of the energy which the girls, now merely standing off and swaying, had relinquished.

"Look at that boy go," said Lee Goldman.

"He ain't started yet," said Lou.

But surrounding comment, Dave's virtuosity, the eager enthusiasm of the audience were all alike lost on Miss Cynthie. She sat with stricken eyes watching this boy whom she'd raised from a babe, taught right from wrong, brought up in the church, and endowed with her prayers, this child whom she had dreamed of seeing a preacher, a regular doctor, a tooth-doctor, a foot-doctor, at the very least an undertaker—sat watching him disport himself for the benefit of a sinsick, flesh-hungry mob of lost souls, not one of whom knew or cared to know the loving kindness of God; sat watching a David she'd never foreseen, turned tool of the devil, disciple of lust, unholy prince among sinners.

For a long time she sat there watching with wretched eyes, saw portrayed on the stage David's arrival in Harlem, his escape from "old friends" who tried to dupe him; saw him working as a trap-drummer in a night-club, where he fell in love with Ruth, a dancer; not the gentle Ruth Miss Cynthie knew, but a wild and shameless young savage who danced like seven devils—in only a girdle and breast-plates; saw the two of them join in a song and dance act that eventually made them Broadway headliners, an act presented in toto as the pre-finale of this show. And not any of the melodies, not any of the sketches, not all the comic philosophy of the tired-and-hungry duo, gave her figure a moment's relaxation or brightened the dull defeat in her staring eyes. She sat apart, alone in the box, the symbol, the epitome of supreme failure. Let the rest of the theatre be riotous, clamoring for more and more of Dave Tappen, "Tap," the greatest tapster of all time, idol of uptown and downtown New York. For her, they were lauding simply an exhibition of sin which centered about her David.

"This'll run a year on Broadway," said Lee Goldman.

"Then we'll take it to Paris."

Encores and curtains with Ruth, and at last David came out on the stage alone. The clamor dwindled. And now he did something quite unfamiliar to even the most consistent of his followers. Softly, delicately, he began to tap a routine designed to fit a particular song. When he had established the rhythm, he began to sing the song:

> Oh I danced with the gal with the hole in her stockin',
> And her toe kep' a-kickin' and her heel kep' a-knockin'
>
> Come up, Jesse, and get a drink o'gin,
> 'Cause you near to the heaven as you'll ever get ag'in—

As he danced and sang this song, frequently smiling across at Miss Cynthie, a visible change transformed her. She leaned forward incredulously, listened intently, then settled back in limp wonder. Her bewildered eyes turned on the crowd, on those serried rows of shriftless sinners. And she found in their faces now an overwhelmingly curious thing: a grin, a universal grin, a gleeful and sinless grin such as not the nakedest chorus in the performance had produced. In a few seconds, with her own song, David had dwarfed into unimportance, wiped off their faces, swept out of their minds every trace of what had seemed to be sin; had reduced it all to mere trivial detail and revealed these revelers as a crowd of children, enjoying the guileless antics of another child. And Miss Cynthie whispered her discovery aloud:

"Bless my soul! They didn't mean nothin' ... They jes' didn' see no harm in it—"

> Then I danced with the gal with the dimple in her cheek,
> And if she'd a' kep' a-smilin' I'd a' danced for a week—
>
> Come up, Jesse—

The crowd laughed, clapped their hands, whistled. Someone threw David a bright yellow flower. "From Broadway!"

He caught the flower. A hush fell. He said:

"I'm really happy tonight, folks. Y'see this flower. Means success, don't it? Well, listen. The one who is really responsible for my success is here tonight with me. Now what do you think o'that?"

The hush deepened.

"Y'know folks, I'm sump'm like Adam—I never had no mother. But I've got a grandmother. Down home everybody calls her Miss Cynthie. And everybody loves her. Take that song I just did for you. Miss Cynthie taught me that when I wasn't knee-high to a cricket. But that wasn't all she taught me. For [sic] back as I can remember, she used to always say one thing: 'Son, do like a church steeple—aim high and go straight.' And for doin' it—" he grinned, contemplating the flower—"I get this."

He strode across to the edge of the stage that touched Miss Cynthie's box. He held up the flower.

"So y'see folks, this isn't mine. It's really Miss Cynthie's." He leaned over to hand it to her. Miss Cynthie's last trace of doubt was swept away. She drew a deep breath of revelation; her bewilderment vanished, her redoubtable composure returned, her eyes lighted up; and no one but David, still holding the flower toward her, heard her sharply whispered reprimand:

"Keep it, you fool you. Where's yo' manners—givin' 'way what somebody give you?"

David grinned:

"Take it, tyro. What you tryin' to do—crab my act?"

Thereupon, Miss Cynthie, smiling at him with bright, meaningful eyes, leaned over without rising from her chair, jerked a tiny twig off the stem of the flower, then sat decisively back, resolutely folding her arms, with only a leaf in her hand.

"This'll do me," she said.

The finale didn't matter. People filed out of the theatre. Miss Cynthie sat awaiting her children, her foot absently patting time to the orchestra's jazz recessional. Perhaps she was thinking, "God moves in a mysterious way," but her lips were unquestionably forming the words:

> —danced with the gal—hole in her stockin'—
> —toe kep' a-kickin'—heel kep' a-knockin'—

(1933)

NOTES

1. Bozo: A silly person; a funny fellow.

2. Alhambra: A theater at 126th Street and Seventh Avenue where, in 1926, Florence Mills appeared in the musical written for her and for which she was famous: "Blackbirds."

3. A theater in Harlem where, during the 1920s, Negro sketches, plays, and musicals were presented. "The intermediate and experimental theatrical period developed mainly in two Harlem theatres, the Lafayette and the Lincoln. Within several years both these houses had good stock-companies, and for quite a while their repertories consisted chiefly of downtown successes." [James Weldon Johnson, *Black Manhattan* (New York: Atheneum, 1968), 172.] The Lafayette was not as sedate as Johnson would have one believe, however. As Nathan Huggins points out in his book, *Harlem Renaissance*, "These Negro shows were little different from those downtown, except they were a little more

raucous, broad, and dirty" (p. 291). Some people, like Wallace Thurman, felt blacks were being exploited. In his novel, *The Blacker the Berry*, Thurman calls the Lafayette "the Jew's gift to Harlem colored folks" (New York: The Macaulay Co., 1929, pp. 200–1).

4. St. Mark's: Methodist Episcopal church which, at the writing of this story, had finally moved into Harlem. Many black churches, like St. Mary's, originated in black areas downtown and gradually moved northward with the shifting black population. During the 1890s, for example, St. Mark's was located on West 53rd Street.

John Archer's Nose

EDITOR'S INTRODUCTION TO "JOHN ARCHER'S NOSE"

"John Archer's Nose," as Rudolph Fisher's single published detective short story, is unique only because of his death; he had planned to write more, as indicated by his desire to write a series of Dart-Archer novels and, presumably, stories. As he discussed in an interview during 1933: "An archer, of course, is a bowman, one who shoots an arrow. Dart is another word for arrow. Dr. Archer and Detective Dart, therefore, stand in the relationship of a bowman and his arrow; the vision of the former gives direction and aim to the action of the latter."[1] And, of course, this is how the murder in "John Archer's Nose" is solved, with the doctor and detective working in tandem in areas that are fundamental to their respective professions. If it seems that Dr. Archer is the smarter of the two (and he is; perhaps Dr. Fisher would have discovered this later), one might postulate that Fisher was experimenting with some of the tried-and-true methods of detective fiction. There is precedent, of course, for the combination of amateur sleuth and official policeman (who is *not* a bungler) in such a work as *Clouds of Witness* by Dorothy Sayers or in the short story, "The Cyprian Bees," by Anthony Wynne.

The avid reader of mystery stories knows without the help of critics that the "plot's the thing." Without a solution to a situation, a story, the mystery tale is a failure. Plot, as E. M. Forster has pointed out, is not the same as the story: "... a story [is] a narrative of events arranged in their time-sequence. A plot is also a narrative of events, the emphasis falling on causality. 'The king died and then the queen died' is a story. 'The king died, and then the queen died of grief' is a plot."[2] Forster is a good reference when considering the mystery story, for he goes on to say that "this element of surprise or mystery—the detective element as it is sometimes rather emptily called—is of great importance in a plot.... To appreciate a mystery, part of the mind must be left behind, brooding, while the other part goes marching on."[3] A story that is of the mystery tale genre, then, with the emphasis upon plot, should be examined with this fictional feature in mind. What other features of detective fiction should the critical reader consider?

In his book about the detective story and the crime novel, Julian Symons indicates some characteristics that seem to be borne out in the reading of Fisher's mystery story. The detective, for instance, is the protector against evil (this has not been true always). When the body, in "John Archer's Nose," is discovered to be dead, Perry Dart, the detective, says to the dead man's sister: "Then, it's lucky I came.... Perhaps I can help you." Very polite, very reassuring, not tough or threatening, although he can be when necessary (and later, indeed, is hard on the family in the story).

The detective, also, as "Society's agent ... was the single character allowed to have high intellectual attainments."[4] Dart shares this feature, of course, with his friend, Dr. Archer. Actually, although Fisher stated he envisioned Dart and Archer as equals, it is evident from this story that Dart could not have solved the crime without Archer whereas Archer most certainly could have managed the entire detection on his own. This is an obvious weakness in the story which time, and greater practice in writing this genre, might have helped Fisher to correct.

A convention, an important one, that was followed in the story was, to be sure, that the criminal "should be part of the same social group that contained the other suspects."[5] And it must follow that the criminal is not someone unknown to the reader, although Fisher skirts on close to dangerous ground here with having his crazed criminal—in crime fiction known as the Most Unlikely Person—being such a shadowy, silent individual. There is logic behind the killing, to be sure, but there is also very little sympathy for the other suspects who turn out to be the killer's untouched victims.

The victim, of course, must be a person for whom there is little concern, a person whose loss is either a relief (because he was evil, or about to die—as in Fisher's story), or a person who is simply unattractive for one reason or another. This is also why the attempt on the girl's life has to be unsuccessful, for she would have been a loss the reader would regret.

As Symons and other writers concerning the detective story have emphasized, the clues are a salient feature of the genre—"the essential clue, the unique significant detail that unlocks the mystery. The detective story makes a distinction between essential and non-essential facts."[6] Here, Fisher adheres closely to convention, even giving a title that serves as a major clue. The reader suspects the title is important as a clue, but the connection between this and the solution to the crime still casts the title as only one of the clues.

Fisher is true to form in a social sense and close to his own tastes in that he does not emphasize the seamy or violent side of Harlem. He is more interested in atmosphere—the mystery of a setting, even though familiar to some of the readers of his fiction, that had never before been used for detective fiction with an all-black cast. As Fisher stated in an interview:

> Darkness and mystery go together, don't they? The children of the night—and I say this in all seriousness—are children of mystery. The very setting is mystery—outsiders know nothing of Harlem life as it really is.... And much of it is perfectly in tune with the best of mystery tradition—variety, color, mysticism, superstition, malice and violence.[7]

Fisher depicts some violence, and there is a sense that it exists, but his approach is still almost genteel in the eyes of today's reader.

The two men who solve the crime, Detective Sergeant Perry Dart and Dr. John Archer are gentlemen, bachelors who enjoy one another's company in a clubby manner. Fisher has Dr. Archer cast in the role of the amateur detective so beloved of the English novelists—the amateur who can enter where angels and professional police dare not tread or, upon entering, are thwarted by suspects who refuse to confide in them. Both men conform, in reactions, to their metier: Dart always expects the worst and is suspicious; Archer exhibits compassion, has a lively interest in people per se, and is the more reflective of the two. Their different approach to dealing with people is illustrated in the following section near the beginning of the story:

> "That ain't what I meant!" flared the wife.
> "We don't know who did it either."
> "Oh. [Dart speaking] And you are not anxious to find out—as quickly as possible?"
> Dr. Archer mediated. "Sergeant Dart naturally felt that in performing his duty he would also be serving you all. He regrets, of course, the intrusion upon your—er—moment of sorrow."
> "A sorrow which all of you do not seem to share alike," appended Dart, who believed in making people so angry that they would blurt out the truth.

The clues, the complications, the characters intertwine to move the story along in true detective fiction fashion, deftly and with a certain amount of swiftness. The formulaic quality must have appealed greatly to Fisher, for another writer of the genre aptly observed: "It possesses an Aristotelian perfection of beginning, middle and end. A definite and single problem is set, worked out, and solved."[8]

It appears also that Fisher's detective story touches the fringes of various types of detective fiction without giving allegiance to any one mode: The detective is intelligent, tough, gentlemanly, suspicious, trusting at times, and willing to share his investigation with an amateur. Indeed, Dart fairly insists that Archer participate in unravelling the crime, not merely because of his position as attending physician but also because he senses their interlocking relationship whereby one depends upon the other through an author-imposed definition of their beings: like siamese twins joined, the one can do something the other cannot, although each is capable of similar actions with the unjoined limbs; yet, they are unalterably tied to one another for the completion of self and actions. Fisher, of course, nearly defeats his own aims by the doctor's endowments of a superior mind. Nevertheless, Fisher's intention—as pointed out earlier—was to have a union between the two that was to be a long-term bonding.

It must not be forgotten, also, that Fisher wishes to be instructive—he is never too far from the didactic element—for the story points out the fatal consequences of a reliance on superstitious beliefs. (This story appeared in a Negro journal, of which there was only one issue; Fisher, then, presumed most of his readers would be Negroes, although this would not have changed his point of view.) As a story modeled on the traditional story, where Archer-Dart solve the crime through investigating clues and where these two are the most significant characters, Fisher placed himself in a position of being a forerunner to other black writers, such as Chester Himes, who created black investigators of entirely another breed.

It might be observed as well that at the conclusion of "John Archer's Nose" we have Aristotle's reversal (*peripeteia*) and recognition (*anagnorisis*) in the sense that Geoffrey Hartman points out as being quite applicable to the mystery story:

> The reversal in detective stories is more like an unmasking; and the recognition that takes place when the mask falls is not prepared for by dramatic irony. It is a belated, almost last minute affair, subordinating the reader's intelligence to such hero-detectives as Ross Macdonald's Archer, who is no Apollo, but who does roam the California scene with cleansing or catalyzing effect.[9]

Hartman's essay does not concentrate on these matters, however, but explores cogently the notion of *tòpathos*—suffering, or a "painful action" that dominates the minds of the characters and infuses the story with a central focus for which reversal and recognition are handmaidens. If we consider how instructive Fisher wishes to be, added to his moral stance, it is not inconceivable that he was attempting to create a tale imbued with a sense of Aristotelian pathos.

In conclusion, it has to be noted again that Rudolph Fisher's detective fiction has been ignored in literary history, even by black critics. In a collection of essays devoted to detective fiction,[10] with a 1976 imprint, there is no mention of Fisher. Indeed, the impression given is there was no writer of black detective fiction before Chester Himes—"none except the detective whom Harry Faggett, a black college teacher, glamorized in the *Baltimore Afro-American* newspaper but could not sell to a major publisher."[11] This unintentional neglect only adds to the interest the present-day reader can bring to both the novel, *The Conjure-Man Dies*, and the short story, "John Archer's Nose," where Fisher places the intelligence and wit of his amateur and professional sleuths against the evil and superstition of killers in Harlem.

NOTES

1. John Louis Clarke, "Mystery Novel Writer Is Interviewed over the Radio," *Pittsburgh Courier*, (January 21, 1933).
2. E. M. Forster, *Aspects of the Novel* (New York: Harcourt, c1954), 86.
3. Ibid., 87.
4. Julian Symons, *Mortal Consequences: A History—From Detective Story to the Crime Novel* (New York: Harper & Row, 1972), 11.
5. Ibid., 102.
6. William O. Aydelotte, "The Detective Story as a Historical Source," in *Dimensions of Detective Fiction*, edited by Larry N. Landrum, et al. (n.p.: Popular Press, 1976), 70.
7. Clarke, "Mystery Novel Writer."
8. Dorothy Sayers, ed., "Introduction," *The Omnibus of Crime* (New York: Harcourt, 1929), 31.
9. Geoffrey H. Hartman, "Literature High and Low: The Case of the Mystery Story," in his *The Fate of Reading and Other Essays* (Chicago: University of Chicago Press, 1975), 203.
10. Larry N. Landrum, et al., *Dimensions of Detective Fiction* (n.p.: Popular Press, 1976).

11. Darwin T. Turner, "The Rocky Steele Novels of John B. West," in Landrum, et al., *Dimensions*, 141.

Whenever Detective Sergeant Perry Dart felt especially weary of the foibles and follies of his Harlem, he knew where to find stimulation: he could always count on his friend, Dr. John Archer. Spiritually the two bachelors were as opposite as the two halves of a circle—and as complementary. The detective had only to seek out the physician at the latter's office-apartment, flop into a chair, and make an observation. His tall, lean comrade in crime, sober of face but twinkling of eye, would produce a bottle, fill glasses, hold a match first to Dart's cigar then to his own, and murmur a word of disagreement. Promptly an argument would be on.

Tonight however the formula had failed to work. It was shortly after midnight, an excellent hour for profound argumentation, and the sounds from the avenue outside, still alive with the gay crowds that a warm spring night invariably calls forth, hardly penetrated into the consulting-room where they sat. But Dart's provocative remark had evoked no disagreement.

"Your folks," Dart had said, "are the most superstitious idiots on the face of the earth."

The characteristic response would have been:

"Perry, you'll have to cut out drinking. It's curdling your milk of human kindness." Or, "*My* folks?—Really!" Or, "Avoid unscientific generalizations, my dear Sherlock. They are ninety-nine and six-thirteenths percent wrong by actual measurement."

But tonight the physician simply looked at him and said nothing. Dart prodded further:

"They can be as dark as me or as light as you, but their ignorance is the same damned color wherever you find it—black."

That should have brought some demurring comment on the leprechauns of the Irish, the totems of the Indians, or the prayer-wheels of the Tibetans. Still the doctor said nothing.

"So you won't talk, hey?"

Whereupon John Archer said quietly:

"I believe you're right."

Dart's leg came off its perch across his chair-arm. He set down his glass untasted on the doctor's desk, leaned forward, staring.

"Heresy, b'gosh!—I'll have you read out of church. What the hell? Don't you know you aren't supposed to agree with me?"

"Spare me, your grace." The twinkle which kindled for an instant in Dr. Archer's eyes flickered quickly out. "I've had a cogent example today of what you complain of."

"Superstition?"

"Of a very dark hue."

"State the case. Let's see if you can exonerate yourself."

"I lost a kid."

Dart reached for his glass. "Didn't know you had one."

"A patient, you jackass."

Dart grinned. "Didn't know you had a patient, either."

"That's not funny. Neither was this. Beautiful, plump little brown rascal—eighteen months old—perfectly developed, bright-eyed, alert—and it passes out in a convulsion, and I was standing there looking on—helpless."

"If it was so perfect, what killed it?"

"Superstition."

"Humph. Anything for an alibi, hey?"

"Superstition," repeated Archer in a tone which stilled his friend's banter. "That baby ought to be alive and well, now."

"What's the gag line?"

"Status lymphaticus."

"Hell. And I was just getting serious."

"That's as serious as anything could be. The kid had a retained thymus."

"I'll bite. What's a retained thymus?"

"A big gland here in the chest. Usually disappears after birth. Sometimes doesn't. Untreated, it produces this status lymphaticus—convulsions—death."

"Why didn't you treat it?"

"I did what I could. Been seeing it for some time. Could have cleared it up over night. What I couldn't treat was the superstition of the parents."

"Oh."

"Specially the father. The kid should have had X-ray treatments. Melt the thing away. These kids, literally choking to death in a fit, clear up and recover—zip—like that. Most spectacular thing in medicine. But the old man wouldn't hear of it. None of this new-fangled stuff for *his* only child."

"I see."

"You can't see. I haven't told you yet. I noticed today, for the first time, a small, evil-smelling packet on a string around the baby's neck. In spite of the shock immediately following death, my curiosity got the better of me. I suppose there was also a natural impulse to—well—change the subject, sort of. I asked what it was."

"You would."

"The father didn't answer. He'd gone cataleptic. He simply stood there, looking. It seemed to me he was looking rather at the packet than at the child, and if ever there was the light of madness in a man's eyes, it was in his. The mother, grief-stricken though she was, managed to pull herself together long enough to answer."

"What was it?"

"Fried hair."

"What?"

"Fried hair.—No—not just kinky hair, straightened with hot irons and grease, as the term usually implies. That packet—I examined it— contained a wad of human hair, fried, if you please, in snake oil."

Dart expelled a large volume of disgusted smoke. "The fools."

"A charm. The father had got it that morning from some conjure-woman. Guaranteed to cure the baby's fits."

"He'd try that in preference to X-rays."

"And his name," the doctor concluded with a reflective smile, "was Bright—Solomon Bright."

After a moment of silence, Dart said:

"Well—your sins are forgiven. No wonder you agreed with me."

"Did I?" Having unburdened his story, John Archer's habit of heckling, aided by a normal desire to dismiss an unpleasant memory, began now to assert itself. The twinkle returned to his eyes. "I am of course in error. A single graphic example, while impressive, does not warrant a general conclusion. Such reasoning, as pointed out by no less an authority than the great Bacon—"

"I prefer ham," cut in Dart as the 'phone rang. His friend, murmuring something to the effect that "like begets like," reached for the instrument.

"Hello... Yes... Yes. I can come at once. Where? 15 West 134th Street, Apartment 51... Yes—right away."

Deliberately he replaced the receiver. "I'm going to post a reward," he said wearily, "for the first person who calls a doctor and says, 'Doctor, take your time.' Right away—right away—"

He rose, put away the bottle, reached for hat and bag.

"Want to come along?"

"You're not really going right away?"

"In spite of my better judgment. That girl was scared."

"O.K. All I've got to do before morning is sleep."

"Don't count on it. Got your gun?"

"Gun? Of course. But what for?"

"Just a hunch. Come on."

"Hunch?" Dart jumped up to follow. "Say—what is this? A shooting?"

"Not yet." They reached the street.

"So what?"

"Girl said her brother's been stabbed."

"Yea?—here—let's use my car!"

"Righto. But lay off that siren. It gives me the itch."

"Well, scratch," Dart said as his phaeton leaped forward. "You've got fingernails, haven't you?" And with deliberate perversity he made the siren howl.

In three minutes they reached their destination and were panting up endless stairs.

"It's a cowardly trick, that siren," breathed the doctor.

"Why?"

"Just a stunt to scare all the bad men away from the scene of the crime."

"Well, it wouldn't work up here. This high up, they couldn't hear a thing in the street."

"You're getting old. It's only five flights."

Dart's retort was cut off by the appearance of a girl's form at the head of the stairway.

"Dr. Archer?" Her voice was trembling. "This way.—Please—hurry—"

They followed her into the hallway of an apartment. They caught a glimpse of a man and woman as they passed the front living-room. The girl stopped and directed them with wide, frightened eyes into a bed-chamber off the hall. They stepped past her into the chamber, Dart pausing automatically to look about before following the physician in.

An old lady sat motionless beside the bed, her distorted face a spasm of grief. She looked up at the doctor, a pitifully frantic appeal in her eyes, then looked back toward the bed without speaking.

Dr. Archer dropped his bag and bent over the patient, a lean-faced boy of perhaps twenty. He lay on his left side facing the wall, his knees slightly drawn up in a sleeping posture. But his eyes were open and fixed. The doctor grasped his thin shoulders and pulled him gently a little way, to reveal a wide stain of blood on the bedclothing below; pulled him a little farther over, bent in a moment's inspection, then summoned Dart with a movement of his head. Together they observed the black-pearl handle of a knife, protruding from the chest. The boy had been stabbed through his pajama coat, and the blade was unquestionably in his heart.

Dr. Archer released the shoulder. The body rolled softly back to its original posture. The physician stood erect.

"Are you his mother?" he asked the old lady.

Dumbly, she nodded.

"You saw the knife, of course?"

"I seen it," she said in almost a whisper, and with an effort added, "I I didn't pull it out for fear of startin' him bleedin' ag'in."

"He won't bleed any more," Dr. Archer said gently. "He hasn't bled for an hour—maybe two."

The girl behind them gasped sharply. "You mean he's been—dead—that long?"

"At least. The blood stain beneath him is dry."

A sob escaped the old lady. "Sonny—"

"Oh Ma—!" The girl moved to the old lady's side, encircled her with compassionate arms.

"I knowed it," the old lady whispered. "I knowed it—the minute seen him, I knowed—"

Dr. Archer terminated a long silence by addressing the girl. "It was you who called me?"

She nodded.

"When you said your brother had been stabbed, I knew the case would have to be reported to the police. Detective Sergeant Dart was with me at the time. I thought it might save embarrassment if he came along."

The girl looked at Dart and after a moment nodded again.

"I understand—But we—we don't know who did it."

A quick glance passed between the two men.

"Then it's lucky I came," Dart said. "Perhaps I can help you."

"Yes.—Yes perhaps you can."

"Whose knife is that?"

"His own."

"His own?—Where did you last see it?"

"On the bureau by the head of the bed."

"When?"

"This afternoon, when I was cleaning up."

"Tell me how you found him."

"Just like that. I'd been out. I came in and along the hall on the way to my room. I noticed his door was closed. He hasn't been coming in till much later recently. I stopped to speak to him—he hadn't been well.—I opened the door and spoke. He didn't answer. I pushed on the light. He looked funny. I went over to him and saw the blood—"

"Shall we go into another room?"

"Yes, please. Come, Ma—"

Stiffly, with the girl's assistance, the mother got to her feet and permitted herself to be guided toward the door. There, she paused, turned and looked back at the still figure lying on the bed. Her eyes were dry, but the depth of her shocked grief was unmistakable. Then, almost inaudibly, she said a curious thing:

"God forgive me."

And slowly she turned again and stumbled forward.

Again Dart and Archer exchanged glances. The former's brows lifted. The latter shook his head thoughtfully as he picked up his bag. As the girl and her mother went out, he stood erect and sniffed. He went over to the room's one window, which was open, near the foot of the bed. Dart followed. Together they looked out into the darkness of an airshaft. Above, one more story and the edge of the roof. Below, an occasional lighted window and a blend of diverse sounds welling up: a baby wailing, someone coughing spasmodically, a radio rasping labored jazz, a woman's laugh, quickly stifled.

"God forgive her what?" said Dart.

The doctor sniffed again. "It didn't come from out there."

"What didn't?"

"What I smelt."

"All I smell is a rat."

"This is far more subtle."

"Smell up the answer to my question."

The physician sniffed again, said nothing, turned and started out. He and Dart overtook the others in the hallway. A moment later, they were all in the living-room.

The man and woman, whom they had seen in passing, waited there, looking toward them expectantly. The woman, clad in gold-figured black silk Chinese pajamas, was well under thirty, slender, with yellow skin which retained a decided make-up even at this hour. Her boyish bob was reddish with frequent "frying," and her eyes were cold and hard. The man, in shirt-sleeves and slippers, was approximately the same age, of medium build and that complexion known as "riny"— light, sallow skin and sand-colored kinky hair. His eyes were green.

The girl got the old lady into a chair before speaking. Then, in a dull, absent sort of way, she said:

"This is the doctor. He's already turned the case over to this gentleman that came with him."

"And who," the woman inquired, "is this gentleman that came with him?"

"A policeman, a detective."

"Humph!" commented the woman.

"Fast work," added the man unpleasantly.

"Thank you," returned Dart, eyeing him coolly. "May I know to whom I owe the compliment?"

The man matched his stare before answering.

"I am Ben Dewey. This is my wife. Petal there is my sister. Sonny was my brother." There was unnecessary insolence in the enumeration.

" 'Was' your brother?"

"Yes, was." Mr. Dewey was evidently not hard to incense. He bristled.

"Then you are already aware of his—misfortune?"

"Of course."

"In fact, you were aware of it before Dr. Archer arrived."

"What do you mean?"

"I mean that no one has stated your brother's condition since we came into this room. You were not in the bed room when Dr. Archer did state it. Yet you know it."

Ben Dewey glared. "Certainly I know it."

"How?"

The elder brother's wife interrupted. "This is hardly the time, Mr. Detective, for a lot of questions."

Dart looked at her. "I see," he said quietly. "I have been in error. Miss Petal said, in the other room just now, 'We don't know who did it.' Naturally, I assumed that her 'we' included all the members of the family. I see now that she meant only herself and her mother. So, Mrs. Dewey, if you or your husband will be kind enough to name the guilty party, we can easily avoid a 'lot of questions.' "

"That ain't what I meant!" flared the wife. "We don't know who did it either."

"Oh. And you are not anxious to find out—as quickly as possible?"

Dr. Archer mediated. "Sergeant Dart naturally felt that in performing his duty he would also be serving you all. He regrets, of course, the intrusion upon your—er—moment of sorrow."

"A sorrow which all of you do not seem to share alike," appended Dart, who believed in making people so angry that they would blurt out the truth. "May I use your phone?"

He went to the instrument, resting on a table near the hall door, called the precinct station, reported the case, asked for a medical examiner, and declined assistants.

"I'm sure the family would prefer to have me act alone for the time being."

Only Dr. Archer realized what these words meant: that within five minutes half a dozen men would be just outside the door of the apartment, ready to break in at the sergeant's first signal.

But Dart turned and smiled at the brother and his wife. "Am I right in assuming that?" he asked courteously.

"Yes—of course," Ben said, somewhat subdued.

Swiftly the courteous smile vanished. The detective's voice was incisive and hard. "Then perhaps you will tell me how you knew so well that your brother was dead."

"Why—I saw him. I saw the knife in—"

"When?"

"When Petal screamed. Letty and I had gone to bed. And when Petal screamed, naturally we jumped up and rushed into Sonny's room, where she was. She was standing there looking at him. I went over to him and looked. I guess I shook him. Anybody could see—"

"What time was that?"

"Just a few minutes ago. Just before the doctor was called. I told her to call him."

"About ten minutes ago, then?"

"Yes."

"How many times did your sister scream?"

"Only once."

"You're sure?"

"Yes."

"You had retired. You heard one scream. You jumped up and went straight to it."

"Why not?"

"Extraordinary sense of direction, that's all.—Whose knife is that?"

"Sonny's."

"How do you know?"

"I've seen him with it. Couldn't miss that black pearl handle."

"Who else was in the house at the time?"

"No one but Ma. She was already in the room when we got there. She's got an extraordinary sense of direction, too."

"Any one else here during the evening?"

"No—not that I know of. My wife and I have been in practically all evening."

"Practically?"

"I mean she was in all evening. I went out for a few minutes—down to the corner for a pack of cigarettes."

"What time?"

"About ten o'clock."

"And you've heard nothing—no suspicious sounds of any kind?"

"No. At least I didn't. Did you, Letty?"

"All I heard was Sonny himself coming in."

"What time was that?"

" 'Bout nine o'clock. He went in his room and stayed there."

"Just what was everyone doing at that time?"

"The rest of us were in the back of the flat—except Petal. She'd gone out. Ben and I were in the kitchen. I was washing the dishes, he was sitting at the table, smoking. We'd just finished eating supper."

"Your usual supper hour?"

"Ben doesn't get home from the Post Office till late."

"Where was Mother Dewey?"

"In the dining-room reading the paper."

"Anyone else here now?"

"Not that I know of."

"Do you mind if we look?"

"If I minded, would that stop you?"

Dart indulged in an appraising pause, then said:

"It might. I should hate to embarrass you."

"Embarrass me!—Go ahead—I've nothing to hide."

"That's good. Doc, if you can spare the time, will you take a look around with me?"

Dr. Archer nodded with his tongue in his cheek. Dart knew very well that a cash-in-advance major operation could not have dragged the physician away.

"Before we do, though," the detective said, "let me say this: Here are four of you, all closely related to the victim, all surely more or less familiar with his habits and associates. Yet not one of you offers so much as a suggestion as to who might have done this."

"You haven't given us time," remarked Letty Dewey.

Dart looked at his watch. "I've given you five minutes."

"Who's been doing all the talking?"

"All right. Take your turn now. Who do you think did it?"

"I haven't the remotest idea."

"M-m—so you said before—while I was doing all the talking."—He smiled. "Strange that none of you should have the remotest idea. The shock, no doubt. I should rather expect a flood of accusations. Unless, of course, there is some very good reason to the contrary."

"What do you mean?"

"I mean—" the detective was pleasantly casual—"unless you are protecting each other. In which case, if I may remind you, you become accessory.—Come on, Doc. No doubt the family would like a little private conference."

During the next few minutes the two went through the apartment. Alert against surprise, they missed no potential hiding-place, satisfying themselves that nobody had modestly secreted himself in some out-of-the-way corner. The place possessed no apparent entrance or exit other than its one outside door, and there was nothing unusual about its arrangement of rooms, several bedchambers off a central hallway, with the living-room at the front end and a kitchen and dining-room at the back.

Characteristically, the doctor indulged in wordy and somewhat irrelevant reflection during the tour of inspection. Exchanges of comment punctuated their progress.

"Back here," Dr. Archer said, "I don't get it. But up there where they are, I do. And in the boy's room, I did."

"Get what—that smell?"

"M-m. Peculiar—very. Curious thing, odors. Discernible in higher dilution than any other material stimulus. Ridiculous that we don't make greater use of them."

"I never noticed any particular restriction of 'em in Harlem."

On the dining-room table a Harlem newspaper was spread out. Dart glanced at the page, which was bordered with advertisements.

"Here it is again," he said, pointing. " 'Do you want success in love, business, a profession?' These 'ads' are all that keep this sheet going. Your folks' superstition—"

Dr. Archer's eyes traveled down the column but he seemed to ignore the interruption.

"Odors *should* be restricted," he pursued. "They should be captured, classified, and numbered like the lines of the spectrum. We let them run wild—"

"Check."

"And sacrifice a wealth of information. In a language of a quarter of a million words, we haven't a single specific direct denotation of a smell."

"Oh, no?"

"No. Whatever you're thinking of, it is an indirect and non-specific denotation, liking the odor in mind to something else. We are content with 'fragrant' and 'foul' or general terms of that character, or at best 'alcoholic' or 'moldy,' which are obviously indirect. We haven't even such general terms as apply to colors—red, green, and blue. We name what we see but don't name what we smell."

"Which is just as well."

"On the contrary, if we could designate each smell by number—"

"We'd know right off who killed Sonny."

"Perhaps. I daresay every crime has its peculiar odor."

"Old stuff. They used bloodhounds in *Uncle Tom's Cabin.*"

"We could use one here."

"Do tell?"

"This crime has a specific smell—"

"It stinks all right."

"—which I think we should find significant if we could place it."

"Rave on, Aristotle."

"Two smells, in fact. First, alcohol."

"We brought that with us."

"No. Another vintage I'm sure. Didn't you get it in the boy's bed room?"

"Not especially."

"It's [sic] meaning was clear enough. The boy was stabbed while sleeping under the effect of alcohol."

"How'd you sneak up on that answer?"

"There was no sign of struggle. He'd simply drawn up his knees a little and died."

"Don't tell me you smelt alcohol on a dead man's breath."

"No. What I smelt was the alcoholic breath he'd expelled into that room before he died. Enough to leave a discernible—er—fragrance for over an hour afterward."

"Hm—Stabbed in his sleep."

"But that simply accounts for the lack of struggle and the tranquil posture of the corpse. It does indicate, of course, that for a boy of twenty Sonny was developing bad habits—a fact corroborated by his sister's remark about late hours. But that's all. This other odor which I get from time to time I consider far more important. It might even lead to the identity of the killer—if we could trace it."

"Then keep sniffing, Fido. Y' know, I had a dog like you once. Only he didn't do a lot of talking about what he smelt."

"Too bad he couldn't talk, Sergeant. You could have learned a great deal from him."

As they approached the front door the bell rang. Dart stepped to the door and opened it. A large pink-faced man carrying a doctor's bag stood puffing on the threshold. He blinked through his glasses and grinned.

"Dr. Finkelbaum!" exclaimed the detective. "Some service! Come in. You know Dr. Archer." He looked quickly out into the corridor, noted his men, grinned, signaled silence, stepped back.

"Sure. Hello, doctor," greeted the newcomer. "Whew! Thank your stars you're not a medical examiner."

"You must have been uptown already," said Dr. Archer.

"Yea. Little love affair over on Lenox Avenue. I always phone in before leaving the neighborhood—they don't do things by halves up here. Where's the stiff?"

"In the second room," said Dart. "Come on, I'll show you."

"At least," murmured Dr. Archer, "it was in there a moment ago."

Despite his skepticism, which derived from sudden mysterious disappearances of corpses on two previous occasions in his experience, they found the contents of Sonny's bedchamber unchanged.

"Who did this?" inquired the medical examiner.

"At present," Dart said, "there are four denials—his mother, his sister, his brother, and his brother's wife."

"All in the family, eh?"

"I haven't finished talking to them yet. You and Dr. Archer carry on here. I'll go back and try some more browbeating."

"Righto."

Now Dart returned to the living-room. The four people seemed not to have moved. The brother stood in the middle of the floor, meditating. The wife sat in a chair, bristling. The girl was on the arm of another chair in which her elderly mother still slumped, staring forward with eyes that saw nothing—or perhaps everything.

The detective looked about. "Finished your conference?"

"Conference about what?" said Ben.

"The national debt. What's happened since I left here?"

"Nothing."

"No conversation at all?"

"No."

"Then who used this telephone?"

"Why—nobody."

"No? I suppose it moved itself? I left it like this, with the mouthpiece facing the door. Now the mouthpiece faces the center of the room. One of the miracles of modern science or what?"

Nobody spoke.

"Now listen." There was a menacing placidity in the detective's voice. "This conspiracy of silence stuff may make it hard for me, but it's going to make it a lot harder for you. You people are going to talk. Personally, I don't care whether you talk here or around at the precinct. But whatever you're holding out for, it's no use. The circumstances warrant arresting all of you, right now."

"We've answered your questions," said Letty angrily. "Do you want us to lie and say one of us did it—just to make your job easier?"

"Lawd—Lawd!" whispered the old lady and Petal's arm went about her again, vainly comforting.

"Who else lives here?" Dart asked suddenly.

As if sparing them the necessity of answering, the outside door clicked and opened. Dart turned to see a young man enter the hallway. The young man looked toward them, his pale face a picture of bewilderment, closed the door behind him, mechanically put his key back into his pocket, and came into the living-room.

"What's up," he asked. "What do those guys want outside?"

"Guys outside?" Ben looked at Dart. "So the joint's pinched?"

"Not yet," returned Dart. "It's up to you people." He addressed the newcomer. "Who are you?"

"Me?—I'm Red Brown. I live here."

"Really? Odd nobody's mentioned you."

"He hasn't been here all day," said Letty.

"What's happened?" insisted Red Brown. "Who is this guy?"

"He's a policeman," Petal answered. "Somebody stabbed—Sonny."

"Stabbed Sonny—!" Dart saw the boy's wide eyes turn swiftly from Petal and fix themselves on Ben.

"A flesh wound," the detective said quickly.

"Oh," said Red, still staring with a touch of horror at Ben. His look could not have been clearer had he accused the elder brother in words.

"You and Sonny are good friends?" pursued Dart.

"Yea—buddies. We room together."

"It might make it easier for Ben if you told me why he stabbed his brother."

Red's look, still fixed, darkened.

"Why should I make it easier for him?"

There was silence, sudden and tense. Ben drew a deep sharp breath, amazement changing to rage.

"Why—you stinking little pup!"

He charged forward. Letty yelled, "Ben!" Red, obvious child of the city, ducked low and sidewise, thrusting out one leg, over which his assailant tripped and crashed to the floor. Dart stepped forward and grabbed Ben as he struggled up. There was no breaking the detective's hold.

"Easy. What do you want to do—prove he's right?"

"Let me go and I'll prove plenty! I'll make him—"

"It's a lie!" breathed Letty. "Ben didn't kill him."

Unexpectedly Dart released Ben.

"All right," said he. "Get to proving. But don't let me have to bean you."

The impulse to assault was spent. Ben pulled himself together.

"What's the idea?" he glowered at Red. "I even call up the poolroom where you work, trying to keep you out of this. And you walk in and try to make me out a murderer."

"Murderer?" Red looked about, engaged Dart. "You—you said—flesh wound."

"Yes," the detective returned drily. "The flesh of his heart."

"Gee! Gee, Ben. I didn't know you'd killed him."

"I didn't kill him! Why do you keep saying so?"

Red looked from Ben to Letty, encountering a glare of the most intense hatred Dart had ever seen. The woman would obviously have tried to claw his eyes out had not circumstances restrained her.

"Go on," she said through her teeth. "Tell your tale."

Her menace held the boy silent for an uncertain moment. It was outweighed by the cooler threat of Dart's next words:

"Not scared to talk, are you, Red?"

"Scared? No, I ain't scared. But murder—gee!"

"You and Sonny were buddies, weren't you?"

"Yea—that's right."

"Slept in the same bed."

"Yea."

"Supposing it had been you in that bed instead of Sonny?"

"Yea—it might 'a been."

"Sonny wouldn't have let you down, would he?"

"He never did."

"All right. Speak up. What do you know?"

"I know—I mean—maybe—maybe Ben figured there was somethin' goin on between Sonny and—." He did not look at Letty now.

"Was there?"

"Wouldn't matter whether there was or not—if Ben thought so."

"True enough. Well, Mr. Dewey, what about that?"

Ben Dewey did not answer—seemed not to have heard the detective's last word. His mouth hung open as he stared dumbfounded at his wife.

His wife, however, still transfixed Red with gleaming eyes.

"It should have been you instead of Sonny," she said evenly. "You rat."

Abruptly Dart remembered the presence of the old lady and the girl. He turned toward them, somewhat contrite for not having spared them the shock of this last disclosure, but got a shock of his own which silenced his intended apology: The girl's face held precisely the expression of stunned unbelief that he had expected to find. But the old lady sat huddled in the same posture that she had held throughout the questioning. Her steadfast gaze was still far away, and apparently she had not heard or seen a single item of what had just transpired in the room.

Dart stepped into the hall to meet Dr. Archer and the medical examiner, as they returned from the death room.

"I'm through," said Dr. Finkelbaum. "Immediate autopsy on this. Here's the knife." He handed Dart the instrument, wrapped in a dressing. "I don't believe—"

Dart interrupted him with a quick gesture, then said loudly enough to be heard by those in the living-room:

"You don't believe it could have been suicide, do you doctor?"

"Suicide? I should say not." The medical examiner caught Dart's cue and matched his tone. "He wasn't left-handed, was he?"

Dart turned back, asking through the living-room doorway, "Was your brother left-handed, Mr. Dewey?"

Ben had not taken his eyes off Letty.

"Seems like he was," he said in a low voice, which included his wife in his indictment.

"Is that true, Miss Petal?"

"No, sir. He was right-handed."

"Then it wasn't suicide," said the medical examiner. "The site of the wound and the angle of the thrust rule out a right hand. The depth of it makes even a left hand unlikely."

"Thanks, doctor. We can forget the fact that it was his own knife."

"Absolutely."

"And," Dart winked as he added, "we can expect to find the killer's fingerprints on this black pearl handle, don't you think?"

"Oh, unquestionably," replied Dr. Finkelbaum. "That handle will name the guilty party even if he wore a glove. The new method, you know."

"So I thought," said Dart. "Well, on your way?"

"Yep. I'll get him downtown and let you have a report first thing in the morning. See you later, gentlemen."

"I'm afraid you will," murmured Dr. Archer.

Dr. Finkelbaum departed. Dr. Archer and the detective conferred a brief moment in inaudible tones, then entered the living-room.

"Mr. Dewey," said Dart, "do you deny having committed this crime in the face of circumstances?"

"What circumstances?"

"The existence of ample motive, as testified by Red Brown, here, and an ample opportunity, as testified by your wife."

"What do you mean, opportunity?"

"She corroborated your statement that at about ten o'clock you went out for a few minutes on the pretext of getting a pack of cigarettes."

"I did go out and I got the cigarettes."

"The time when you say you went out happens to correspond with the time when the doctors say the crime was committed."

"And if I was out, how could I have done it?"

"You couldn't. But suppose you weren't out? Suppose you went down the hall, opened and shut the front door, crept back silently into Sonny's room—only a few steps—did what you had to do, and after the proper lapse of time, crept back to the front door, opened and shut it again, and walked back up the hall as if you had been out the whole time? Your wife says that you went out. But she can not swear that you actually left the apartment."

"Of course I can!" said Letty sharply.

"Yes? Then, Mrs. Dewey, you must have been in the hallway the whole time Mr. Dewey was out. You can not see the length of that hallway from any room in this house. The only way you can swear there was nobody in it throughout that time is to swear that you were in it throughout that time. Could you swear that?"

Letty hesitated only a moment before answering hotly, "Yes!"

"Careful, Mrs. Dewey. Why should you stand idle for ten minutes alone in an empty hallway?"

"I—I was measuring it for wallpaper."

"Strange. I noted that it had recently been re-papered."

"I didn't like the new paper. I was planning to have it changed."

"I see. Then you insist that you were in that hallway all that time?"

"Yes."

"And that Mr. Dewey was not?"

"Yes."

"And that no one else was?"

"No one."

"Madam, you have accused yourself."

"Wh—what?"

"You have just accused yourself of killing your brother-in-law."

"What are you talking about?"

"I'll make it plainer. The only doorway to Sonny's room is on the hall. Assuming that the doctors are right about the time of death, and assuming that the killer used the only door, which is on the hallway you so carefully kept under observation, no one but yourself was within striking distance at the time Sonny was stabbed. You follow my reasoning?"

"Why—"

"Therefore by your own statement—which you are willing to swear to—you must have killed him yourself."

"I never said any such thing!"

"You wish to retract your statement?"

"I—I—"

"And admit that your husband may have been in the hallway?"

Completely confused and dismayed, the woman burst into tears.

But disloyal or not, this was Ben Dewey's wife; he came to her rescue:

"Wait a minute, officer. At least you had a reason for accusing me. What would she want to do that for?"

"I'd rather not guess, Mr. Dewey. But it shouldn't be hard."

Only Letty's sobs broke the next moment's silence. Finally Ben said in a dull, low voice:

"She didn't do it."

"Did you?" asked Dart quickly.

"No. I didn't either. It's—it's all cockeyed."

The man's change of attitude from arrogance to humility was more touching than the woman's tears.

"Are we under arrest?"

Dart's answer was surprising. "No."

"No?"

"No. You are free to go about as usual. You will all hold yourselves ready for questioning at any time, of course. But I shall not make an arrest until this knife is examined."

Letty stopped sobbing to follow the general trend of eyes toward the gauze-wrapped knife in Dart's hand.

"Here is the answer," said the detective, looking about and raising the object. "Of course—a confession would save us a bit of time and trouble."

Nobody uttered a word.

"Well—in the morning we'll know. Dr. Archer put this in your bag, please. And do you mind keeping it for me until morning? I've got a bit of checking up to do meanwhile."

"Not at all." The doctor took the knife, placed it carefully in a side pocket of his bag. "It'll be safe there till you come for it."

"Of course. Thanks a lot. We'll be going now."

The two started out. Dart halted as his companion went on toward the outside door.

"I might say before going, Mr. Dewey," he remarked, "that anything that happens to Red Brown here will make things look even worse for you and your wife. Both of you threatened him, if I remember."

"I can take care of myself," said Red Brown coolly.

"I'm glad to know that," returned Dart. "And—oh yes, I'd like to see you all here in the morning at nine. That's all. Good night."

"From your instructions to your men," observed Dr. Archer, as he and the detective rode back toward his office, "I gather the purpose of not making an arrest."

"It's the only way," Dart said. "Let 'em go and keep an eye on 'em. Their actions will always tell more than their words. I hadn't got anywhere until Red Brown looked at brother Ben. Yet he didn't say a word."

"And," Dr. Archer continued, "I gather also that Exhibit A, which rests enshrouded in my bag, is to be a decoy."

"Sure. That was all stuff—about prints and the new method. Probably not a thing on that knife but they don't know that. Somebody's going to try and get that lethal weapon back."

"But—" the doctor's words disregarded the detective's interruptions—"what I fail to gather is the reason for dragging in me and my bag."

"You dragged me in, didn't you?"

"I see. One good murder deserves another."

"No. Look. The thing had to be planted where the guilty person figured it could be recovered. They wouldn't attempt to get it away from me. But you're different."

"Different from you?"

"Exactly."

"It's a relief to know that."

"You're no happier over it than I am."

"You'll be nearby, I trust?"

"Under your bed, if you like."

"No. The girl might come for it."

"That's just why I'll be nearby. Leave you alone and she'll get it."

"Shouldn't be at all surprised. Lovely little thing."

"But not too little."

"Nor too lovely."

"Aren't you ashamed of yourself?"

"Not at all. You see—"

"Yea, I see. Never mind the long explanation. Adam saw, too."

"Ah, but what did Adam see? An apple. Only an apple."

"Well, if it's the girl—which it won't be—she'd better bring an apple along—to keep the doctor away."

"Sergeant, how you admire me. What makes you think it won't be the girl?"

"You don't think she killed her brother, do you?"

"I hope not. But I wouldn't—er—express an opinion in cash."

"Couldn't you just say you wouldn't bet on it?"

"Never use a word of one syllable, sergeant, when you can find one of six."

"Why wouldn't you bet on it? She's just a kid. A rather nice kid."

"How did you find out?"

Dart ignored him. "She screamed. She telephoned for you."

"Nice girls of nineteen have been known to do such things."

"Kill their sweethearts, maybe—their ex-sweethearts. Not their brothers."

"True. Usually it is the brother who kill's [sic] his sister's sweetheart, isn't it? Whereupon the sweetheart is known as a betrayer."

"Yea. Family honor. Course I've never seen it, but—"

"Cynic. Here we are."

But Dart drove on past the doctor's apartment.

"Whither, pray?"

"Get smart. They may recognize the detective's license-plates. Around the corner'll be better."

"And me with no roller-skates."

Shortly they returned to the apartment on foot, and soon were engaged in smooth hypotheses, well oiled.

"One of these things is going to fool us yet," meditated the physician between sips.

"They all fool us."

"Modesty ill becomes you, Perry. I mean the party who obviously did the thing from the outset sometimes does it."

"That party is always obvious from the outset—when it's all over. What I'd like to see is a case in which the party who is obvious from the outset is obvious at the outset."

"The trouble is with the obviousness—the kind of obviousness. One person is obviously guilty because everything points to him. Another is obviously guilty because nothing points to him. In the present case, Ben is the one example, Red the other."

"You're drinking. How can a man be guilty because nothing points to him?"

"Because, of course, too perfect an alibi is no alibi, just as too perfect a case is no case. Perfection doesn't exist. Hence the perfect thing is false."

"This is false whiskey."

"May it continue to deceive us. Consider this: Can you imagine a lad like Red Brown living in a house with a girl like Petal not being—er—affected?"

"So what?"

"I was thinking of the brother-sweetheart complex you suggested."

"With the brother getting the worst of it? But Letty said Red had been out all day. How could Red—?"

"Just as you said Ben could. Only he didn't slam the front door."

"Of course Letty was lying about being in the hall all that time. Maybe Red could have sneaked in and out, at that. But that's taking it pretty far. Nothing that we know indicates Red."

"Nothing except that he's altogether too un-indicated."

"Well, if you really want to get fancy, listen to this."

"Go ahead."

"Red knows that Letty is two-timing."

"Yes."

"Ben doesn't."

"No."

"If Ben finds it out, it's her hips."

"Yes."

"She's rather partial to her hips."

"Naturally."

"A blab from either Sonny or Red—and bye-bye."

"Hips."

"So, tired of Sonny and afraid of Red, she decides on what is known a murder for elimination."

"Murder of Sonny?"

"No. Of Red. With Sonny implicated by his knife."

"Go on. How'd she get Sonny and Red mixed?"

"She heard Sonny come in—'way down the hall where she couldn't see. But Sonny, having developed bad habits, never comes in so early. She believes this is Red. When Ben steps out, she slips into the dark room and hurriedly acts in self-defense."

"Hip-defense."

"M-m. Only it happens to be Sonny."

"Well, what about it?"

"Utterly fantastic. Yet not utterly impossible."

"O.K. Your turn."

"You leave me the most fantastic possibility of all."

"The old lady?"

"No. The mother." The doctor paused a moment, then said, "There's quite a difference. Can you imagine anything that would make a mother kill her son?"

"That smell you mentioned, maybe."

"No. Seriously."

"I don't know. It's pretty hard to believe. But it could happen, I suppose. By mistake, for instance. Suppose the old lady thought it was Red—just as Letty might have. Red—leading her child down the road to hell. . . . That would explain why she said, "God forgive me!""

"Let's forget your 'mistake' for a while."

"Well then, look. When I was walking a beat, a woman came to me once and begged me to put her son in jail. He was a dope. She said when she saw him like that, she wanted to kill him."

"But did she?"

"No. But why can't mother-love turn to hate like any other love?"

"I guess the fact that it doesn't is what makes it mother-love."

"What about those hospital cases where unmarried girls try to smother their kids—and sometimes succeed?"

"Quite different, I should say. Those girls aren't yet mothers, emotionally. They're just parents, biologically. With a wholly unwanted and recently very painful obstruction between themselves and happiness. Mother-love must develop, like anything else. It grows as the child grows, becomes a personal bond only as the child becomes a person."

"All right. But mothers can go crazy."

"Yes. There are cases of that kind."

"That old lady acted kind o' crazy, I thought."

"Probably just grief. Or concern over the whereabouts of Sonny's soul."

"Maybe. I wouldn't press the point. But as long as we're guessing, I don't want to slight anybody."

"I did have a case once where, I believe, a fairly sane mother would have killed her son if she'd been able. He was a lad about Sonny's age, with a sarcoma of the jaw. It involved half his head—he suffered terrifically. Death was just a matter of time. She repeatedly begged me to give him an overdose of morphine."

"What prevented her from killing him?"

"I sent him to a hospital."

"Well—"

"Yes, I know. Sonny could have had a sort of moral sarcoma—eating up his soul, if you like. The sight of him going down and down might have been more than his mother could bear. But unless she was actually insane at the moment, she'd keep hoping and praying for a change—a turn for the better. That hope would prevent any drastic action. After all, sarcoma of the soul is not incurable."

"The only way it could be his mother, then, is if she went temporarily off her nut?"

"Exquisitely phrased, my friend. Have another drink."

Dr. Archer's apartment, which combined office and residence, was on the ground floor of a five-story house. Its front door was immediately within and to one side of the house entrance, off a large rectangular foyer at the rear of which a marble staircase wound upward and around an elevator-shaft. At this hour the elevator was not running.

Inside, the front rooms of the apartment constituted the physician's office—waiting-room, consultation-room, laboratory. Beyond these were a living-room, bedroom and kitchen.

It was agreed that Dart should occupy the bedroom for the rest of the night, while Dr. Archer made the best of the living-room couch. Dart could thus remain behind the scene of any forthcoming action, observe unseen, and step forward when occasion demanded.

Neither undressed, each lying down in shirt-sleeves and trousers. In the event of a caller, Dart agreed that, barring physical danger, he would not interfere unless the doctor summoned him.

"Still hoping it'll be the girl, hey?" grinned the detective.

"Nothing would amaze me more," returned Archer. "Go on—lie down. This is my party." He stretched his considerable length on the couch. Dart went into the adjacent bedroom, leaving the intervening door ajar.

As if some unseen director had awaited this moment, the apartment bell promptly rang, first briefly, timidly, then longer, with resolute determination. "I didn't want to sleep anyway," murmured the doctor. "Keep your ears open. Here goes."

He went through the office rooms to the front door, cracked the little trap-window designed against rent-collectors and other robbers, snapped it to with a gasp of astonishment, unlocked and opened the door.

His preliminary glance was corroborated. Before him stood Petal, bareheaded, with a handbag under her arm.

"I know it's late," she was saying, a little breathlessly, "but—"

"Not at all. Come in."

"Thank you." She looked behind her.

He closed the door quickly. "Someone following you?"

"I—I thought so. Just—nervousness I hope."

"Come back this way."

She followed him through the waiting-room into the consulting office. He slipped on an office coat from a rack.

"Who would be following you at this hour?" he asked, giving her a chair and seating himself at his desk.

"Detectives, maybe."

"Hardly. You're the last person to be suspected in this affair."

She was silent a moment. Her eyes rested on the doctor's bag, which sat conspicuously on top of his desk. Then she began still breathlessly to talk. She leaned forward in her chair, dark eyes wide and bright, gentle breasts rising and falling, small fingers moving restlessly over the flat handbag on her lap.

"Are—are we alone?"

He smiled. "Would you care to look about?"

She accepted this with a feeble reflection of his smile.

"I came here to—to warn you. About Ben."

"Ben?"

"He's—wild. He blames you. He says if you hadn't brought in that detective, he wouldn't be in a jam."

"But that's ridiculous. The thing couldn't have been covered up. The same facts would have been brought out sooner or later."

"I know. But he—he's a little crazy, I guess. Finding out about Letty and everything. He thinks he could have managed."

"Managed—what?"

"Keeping the thing quiet."

"Why should he want to keep it quiet?"

"I don't know. His job—his wife—it's all such a mess. I guess he wants to take it out on somebody and he can't—on Sonny."

"I see. What does he intend to do?"

"He's coming here and hold you up for that knife. If you refuse to give it to him—he'll take it."

"How?"

"He has a pistol. He has to have it when he's loading mail, you know. The way he is now, he'd use it."

"In which case he might be actually guilty of a crime of which he is now only suspected."

"Yes. He might kill you."

"And naturally you want to save him from that."

"Him—and you."

"Hm. . . . What do you suggest?"

"Give me the knife."

He smiled. "But I've promised Sergeant Dart to turn it over to him in the morning."

"I know. But I'll give it back to you, I swear I will."

"My dear child, I couldn't do that. Don't you see—it would make my position very awkward? Obstructing the due course of justice and all that?"

"Oh,—I was afraid you wouldn't.—Please! Don't you see? It may mean your life—and Ben's. I tell you he's crazy."

"How is it that he didn't get here first?"

"He had to stay with Ma. She passed out. I'm supposed to be out looking for medicine. As soon as I get back, he's coming."

"As soon as you get back. Well, that makes it simple."

"What do you mean?"

"Don't go back. Stay here. Sergeant Dart will come for the knife at eight o'clock in the morning. It's three now. When it has been examined, he will come back for us. It will be too late for Ben to do anything to me then."

"Stay here the rest of the night?"

"You'll be quite safe. I should hardly be—ungrateful for your effort to protect me."

"But—but—what about Ma's medicine?"

"If she simply fainted, she's in no danger."

"I couldn't stay away. If anything happened to Ma—"

The physician meditated.

"Well," he said after a moment, "strange how the simplest solution is often the last to occur to one. I can easily take care of both the danger to myself and the further implication of your brother."

"How?" Petal asked eagerly.

"By just spending the rest of the night elsewhere. Parts unknown."

"Oh."

"Come. That will settle everything. You run along now. Get your mother's medicine. When brother Ben arrives I'll be far, far away."

Reluctantly the girl arose. Suddenly she swayed, threw a hand up to her face, and slumped back down into the chair. Dr. Archer sprang forward. She was quite limp. He felt her pulse and grinned. She stirred, opened her eyes, smiled wanly.

"A little water—?" she murmured.

He filled a paper cup from a washstand faucet in the corner and brought it to her.

"It's so warm," she protested.

"I'll get a bit of ice."

He went through the next room into the kitchen, put ice in a glass, filled it and returned. She had not apparently moved, but the flap of his bag on the desk was unsecured at one end. She drank the water.

"Thank you. That's so much better. I'm sorry. I feel all right now."

Again she arose and now preceded him through the waiting-room. At the front door she turned and smiled. She was really very pretty.

"You've been swell," she said. "I guess everything will turn out all right now."

"I hope so. You've done bravely."

She looked at him, turned quickly away as if eluding some hidden meaning in his words, and stepped across the threshold. As she did so, the bang of a pistol shot shook the foyer. Archer reached out, seized the girl's arm, yanked her back, slammed the door. He secured its lock, then hustled her back into the consulting-room.

There, both drew breath.

"Somebody means business. Sit down."

She obeyed wordless, while he went back to reassure Dart. When he returned a moment later, he found a thoroughly frightened girl.

"I—I heard it hit the side of the doorway," she breathed. "Who—who'd shoot at me?"

"I can't imagine who'd shoot at either of us. Even your brother would try to get what he came for before shooting."

"It was at me," she insisted. "You were still inside the room. It was from the stairs at the back."

"Well. Looks as if we both have to stay here a while now."

"There's no other way out?"

"Yes. The kitchen. But that door opens on the same foyer."

She gave a sigh of despair. Slowly her eyes filled.

"Spoils your whole scheme, doesn't it?"

She said nothing.

"Don't feel too bad about it. It was spoiled already."

Her wet eyes lifted, questioning.

"Look in your bag," he said.

She opened the handbag, took out a gauze-wrapped object.

"Unwrap it."

She obeyed. The knife was not Sonny's pearl-handled weapon, but a shining surgeon's scalpel.

"I anticipated some such attempt as you made, of course. The real thing is already under inspection."

He felt almost ashamed at her look.

After a brief silence, she shrugged hopelessly. "Well—I tried."

He stood before her. "I wish you'd tell me the whole story."

"I can't. It's too awful."

"I'd really like to help you if I could."

"You could give me the knife."

"What could you do with it now? You don't dare leave, with somebody shooting at you."

"If Ben comes—"

"Ben has surely had time to come—come to his senses, anyway. Don't you see what it would mean? If Ben would go so far as to kill—as you claim—to get that knife, it can only mean one thing: He knows whom it would implicate." He paused, continued: "That might be himself."

Inspiration kindled her eyes for a brief instant. Before he was sure he saw it, the lids drooped.

"Or," he leaned a little closer, "would it be Letty? Letty, who killed Sonny for betraying her, then begged her husband to forgive her and recover the one thing that would identify her?"

She looked up at him, dropped her eyes again, and said:

"Neither."

"Who then?"

"Me."

"You!"

"Me." She drew deep breath. "Don't you think I know what it means for me to come here and try to get that thing? Why make it hard? It means I killed Sonny, that's all. It means I told them tonight after you left. Ben would have come here and done anything to get the knife, to save me. But Ma passed out when I told. And I ran out while Ben was holding her, saying I'd get something for her. And then I came here. ... Why should I let Ben risk his neck for something I did?"

Dr. Archer sat down. "Petal, you're lying."

"No. It's true. I did it. I didn't know it was Sonny. I didn't go out as Letty said. I hid in the room closet. I thought it was Red that came in. When he went to sleep I came out of the closet. It was dark .... I meant to—to hang on to the knife, but I couldn't pull it out." She halted, went on: "Then I went out, quietly. It was Ma who really discovered him as I came back in, later. That's why I screamed so when—" She halted again.

"But Petal—why?"

"Can't you guess?" she said, low.

"Good Lord!" He sat back in his chair. "If that's a lie, it's a good one."

"It's not a lie. You said you'd help me if you could. Will you give me the knife now? Just long enough to let me clean the handle?"

He was silent.

"It's my life I'm asking for."

"No, Petal," he said gently. "The beauty of your story is that if it stands up you might get off very lightly. Juries are funny about a woman's honor. It's certainly not a question of your life."

"Lightly! What good is a jailbird's life?"

"I can't believe this."

She stood up, her bag dropping to the floor.

"Look at me," she said. He looked. "I'll do anything you want me to, any time, from now till I die, if you'll give me the knife for five minutes. Anything on earth."

And, whatever her falsehood up to that moment, he had no doubt of her sincerity now.

"Sit down, Petal."

She sat down and began to cry softly.

"It's a lie. But it's a grand lie."

"Why do you keep saying that?"

"Because it's so. Don't you see how inconsistent you are?"

She stopped crying.

"Look," he went on. "You come to me, whom you know nothing about except that I'm a doctor. Nothing personal at all. You say you've killed for the sake of your—let us say—honor. Yet the same honor, which you prize highly enough to commit murder for, you offer to sacrifice to me if I will save you from the consequences of what you've done for it. Does that make sense?"

She did not answer.

"How can you hold so cheap now a thing which you held so dear a few hours ago?"

"I'm not. It's worth all it ever was. Something else is worth more, that's all."

"How you must love your brother."

"Myself."

"No. You wouldn't do this for yourself. If you were the only one involved, you'd still be defending your honor—not trading it in."

"Please—you said you'd help me."

"I'm going to help you—though not in the way you suggest—nor at the price."

"Then—how?"

"You'll have to leave that to me, Petal."

There was complete defeat in her voice. "It certainly looks that way."

"Now call your home and say that you've been detained by the police, but will be there in the morning. Tell Ben you were detained for trying to see me. That will keep him safe at home."

She obeyed, replaced the receiver, turned to him. "Now what?"

"Now lie down on that sofa and rest till morning. I'll be in the next room, there."

With utmost dejection in every movement, she went toward the sofa. John Archer turned and went out, back through the living-room into the bed-room where Dart waited, and went into whispered close communion with the detective.

An hour later he came softly back to the consulting-room, cracked the door, looked through. Petal lay face-down on the sofa, her shoulders shaking with silent sobs.

During that hour of whispered conference, the physician and the detective had engaged in one of their characteristic disagreements.

"You yourself said," Dart reminded the doctor, "that the party who is obviously guilty *is* guilty. That party is Ben. He is the only one with sufficient motive. This Letty and Petal stuff is hooey. Women don't kill guys that trick 'em any more. They sue 'em. But men still kill guys that trick their wives."

"You're barking up the wrong sycamore, Perry. Ben didn't know anything about Letty's two-timing—delightful phrase, 'two-timing'— till Red spilt it over two hours *after* the stabbing. The way you say he acted proves that. Why, he was still staring dumbfounded at Letty when the medical examiner and I came back on the scene. Men may kill guys that trick their wives—if I may borrow your elegant diction—but surely not till after they know the worst. It is still customary, is it not, for a cause to precede its effect?"

"You needn't get nasty. Maybe there was some other motive."

"You wouldn't abandon your motive, would you, Sergeant? 'Love is all,' 'Seek the woman' and all that?"

"It's been known to play a part," said the other drily.

"I wish I could place that smell."

"I wish you could place it, too—as far away as possible."

"Let's see now. I got it in the dead boy's room when we first went in. But I didn't get it when the medical examiner and I went in."

"So?"

"So it must have been upon someone who was present the first time and absent the second."

"Yea."

"Don't growl—you're not the hound you think you are. That would mean it was on one of four people—Sonny, Petal, Ma, or you."

"Wake me up when this is over."

"Then I got it in the front of the flat during the first period of questioning. So it couldn't have been Sonny. And I did not get it anywhere else in the flat when you and I were looking around. Hence it couldn't have been you."

"Nope. I use Life-Buoy."

"That leaves Petal and Ma. But I didn't get it when Petal greeted us at the head of the stairs, nor while I was talking to her just now. I actually leaned close to her to be sure."

"You leaned close to her—why?"

"To be sure."

"Oh. To be sure."

"That leaves Ma."

"Hmph. So Ma killed Sonny. I begin to smell something myself."

"I didn't say the bearer of the odor killed Sonny."

"No. You only said the odor would lead to the killer. You had a hunch."

"I've still got it—bigger than ever. Ma may not have killed Sonny, but I'll bet you champagne to Rochelle salts that if it hadn't been for Ma, Sonny wouldn't have been killed."

"It's a bet. And the one that wins has to drink his winnings on the spot."

"In other words, Ma is inextricably bound up in the answer to this little riddle."

"Anything besides an odor leading you on?"

"Yes. There are two things I can believe out of Petal's story: First, Petal is awfully anxious to protect somebody. Second, Ben—who was coming here also if Petal had returned home—is also very anxious to protect somebody. There was time for plenty of talk after we left, so it's unlikely that Ben and Petal are concerned over two different people. Ben and Petal, brother and sister, are trying to protect the *same* person. It wouldn't be Red, whom Ben tried to beat. It wouldn't be Letty, whom Petal has shown no special affection for. But it would be Ma, their mother, the one person in the picture whom both love."

"Are you trying to say that Ma killed her own son, and that Ben and Petal know she did?"

"Not exactly. I'm saying that Ben and Petal believe that that knife will incriminate Ma."

Dart became serious for a moment. "I get it. Ben's ignorance of Letty's two-timing eliminates him. Petal's inconsistency eliminates her. Yet each of them wants the knife, because it may incriminate Ma."

"Beautifully summarized, professor. With the aid of a smell."

"Where do you want to smell next?"

"At their apartment in the morning. Have everybody there—and a few trusty fallen arches. I'm going to locate that odor if it asphyxiates me."

"Y' know, maybe I ought to put you on a leash."

"Have the leash ready. I'll get you somebody to put on it."

In the morning about eight-thirty the two men and the girl had coffee together, Dart pretending to have just arrived. Petal exhibited a forced cheerfulness that in no wise concealed the despair in her eyes.

Even the hard habits of long police experience had not wholly stifled the detective's chivalry, and in an effort to match the girl's courageous masquerade, he said lightly:

"You know, this case is no cinch. I'm beginning to believe some of your folks must walk in their sleep."

As if struck, the girl jumped up. It was as if the tide of her terror, which had receded during the early morning hours, suddenly swung back with his remark, lifting her against her will to her feet. Controlling herself with the greatest effort, she turned from the table and disappeared into the next room.

"Gee!" said Dart. "Bull's eye—in the dark."

"M-m," murmured Archer. "Ma. But I hope I'm wrong."

"I hope so, too."

Petal reappeared.

"I'm sorry. I'm so upset."

"Better finish your coffee," said the doctor.

"My fault," Dart apologized. "I might have let you out a few more minutes."

"It's all right—about me. But there's someone I wish you would let out—as far as you can."

"Who?"

"Ma."

"I don't understand. Surely you don't mean that your mother—"

"No. Of course not. But—perhaps I should have mentioned it sooner—but it's not something we talk much about. You ought to know it though."

"I'll certainly try to protect your confidence."

"My mother is—well—not entirely—right."

"You mean she's—insane?"

"She goes off—has spells in which she doesn't know what she's saying. You saw how she was last night—she just sat there."

"But," the physician put in, "anybody—any mother, certainly— might act that way under the circumstances. The shock must have been terrific."

"Yes, but it is more than that. Ma has—I don't know—she sees things. As long as she's quiet it doesn't matter. But when she starts talking, she says the most impossible things. When you see her again, she's likely to have a complete story of all this. She's likely to say anybody did it—anybody." Her voice dropped. "Even herself."

The two men looked at her, Dart quizzically, Archer gravely.

"That's why I'm asking you to—let her out. If ever she had reason to be unresponsible for what she says, it's now."

"Quite so," the doctor said. "I'm sure Sergeant Dart will give your mother every consideration."

Dart nodded, "Don't worry, young lady. Policemen are people, too, you know."

"I just thought I'd better tell you beforehand."

"Glad you did. Now let's get around to your place and see if we can't clear up the whole thing. Some of the boys are to meet me there at nine. Perhaps something has developed that will put your mind at rest."

"Perhaps," said the girl with no trace of conviction or hope.

When, a few minutes later, they reached the Dewey apartment, they found a bluecoat in the corridor outside the door and two of Dart's subordinates already awaiting him, with the other members of the family, in the living-room.

"Isn't Red Brown here?" was the detective's first question.

"No," Ben told him. "He left right after you did last night and hasn't come back."

"The first law of nature," murmured Dr. Archer.

"Yea," Dart agreed, "but who is he protecting himself from—Mr. and Mrs. Dewey here or the law?"

"It could be both," remarked the tight-lipped Letty.

"Or neither," the doctor added. "He's probably stayed out all night before. And I doubt that I should care to occupy Sonny's bed under the circumstances."

"I told him to be here," Dart said. "This doesn't look too good for him."

One of the headquarters men called Dart aside.

"Autopsy report," he said, low. "Tuberculosis both lungs. Due to go anyway, sooner or later."

"M-m."

"Here's the knife."

"Anything on it?"

"Nothing."

And the detective, knowing that every Dewey's eyes had followed where their ears could not reach, pretended a satisfaction which only valuable information could have given.

"Thanks," said he aloud. "This is all I've been waiting for."

He surveyed the four members of the household—Ma, seated in the same chair she had occupied last night, much as if she had not left it since; Petal, again protectively by her side; Letty, still disagreeably defiant, standing beside Ben, her scowling husband. But the far-away expression was no longer in Ma's eyes; she was staring now at the detective with the same fearful expectancy as the others.

After a moment of complete silence, Dart, looking meditatively at the knife which he balanced in his hand, said almost casually:

"If I were the guilty party, I think I'd speak now."

Ma Dewey drew a quick breath so sharply that all eyes turned upon her.

"Yes," she said in a dull but resolute voice. "Yes. That's right. It's time to speak."

"Ma!" cried Petal and Ben together.

"Hush, chillun. You all don' know. I got to tell it. It's got to come out."

"Yes, Mrs. Dewey?"

"Oh Ma!" the girl sobbed, while Ben's shoulders dropped suddenly and Letty gave a sardonic shrug.

"I don't know," Ma said, "what you all's found on that knife. It don't matter. One thing I do know—my hand—this hand—" she extended a clenched, withered fist—"had hold o' that knife when it went into Sonny's heart."

Petal turned desperate, appealing eyes to Dart. No one else moved or spoke.

"I told the chillun las' night after you all had lef'."

Dr. Archer gave Petal a glance that at last comprehended all she had tried to accomplish in his office last night.

"You all don' know," the old lady resumed with a deliberate calmness of voice that held no hint of insanity. "You don' know what it means to a mother to see a child goin' down and down. Sonny was my youngest child, my baby. He was sick, body and soul."

She stopped a moment, went doggedly on.

"He got to runnin' around with the wrong crowd here in Harlem. Took to drinkin' and comin' in all hours o' the night—or not at all. Nothin' I say or do seem to have no effect on him. Then I see he's beginnin' to fall off—gettin' thinner by the minute. Well, I made him go 'round to the hospital and let them doctors examine him. They say he got the T.B. in his lungs and if he don' go 'way to a cemetarium he'll die in a year. And I knowed it was so, 'cause his father died o' the same thing."

She was looking back over the years now, and into her eyes came last night's distant stare.

"But he wouldn' go. Jes' like his father. Say if he go'n' die he go'n die at home and have a good time befo' he go. I tried ev'ything—prayer, charms—God and the devil. But I'd done seen his father go and I reckon I didn' have no faith in neither one. And I begun to think how his father suffered befo' he went, and look like when I thought 'bout Sonny goin' through the same thing I couldn' stand it. Seem like sump'm kep' tellin' me, 'Don' let him suffer like that.' "

"It weighed on my mind. When I went to sleep nights I kep' dreamin' 'bout it. 'Bout how I could save him from goin' through all that sufferin' befo' he actually come down to it. And las' night I had sech a dream. I seen myself kneelin' by my bed, prayin' for strength to save him from what was in store for him—strength to make his death quick and easy, 'stead o' slow and mis'able. Then I seen myself get up and slip into the hall and make into Sonny's room like sump'm was leadin' me. Same sump'm say, 'If he die in his sleep he won' feel it.' Same sump'm took my hand and moved it 'long the bureau-top till it hit Sonny's knife. I felt myself pick it up and move over to the bed ... and strike. . . . "

Her voice dwindled to a strained whisper.

"That's all. When I opened my eyes, I was in my own bed. I thought it was jes' another dream. . . . Now I know better. It happened. I killed him."

She had straightened up in her chair as she spoke. Now she slumped back as if her strength was spent.

Dr. Archer went quickly to her. Dart saw him lean over her, grow abruptly rigid, then fumble at the bosom of her dress, loosening her clothing. After a moment, the doctor stood erect and turned around, and upon his face was the light of discovery.

"She's all right," he said. "Wait a minute. Don't do anything till I get back."

He went into the hallway, calling back, "Petal, just fan your mother a bit. She'll be all right"—and disappeared toward the dining-room at the rear of the apartment.

In a few moments, during which attention centered on reviving Ma Dewey, he returned with a newspaper in his hand.

"This was on the dining-room table, open at this page, last night," he said proffering the paper to Dart. "Read it. I'll be right back."

He turned and went out again, this time leaving the apartment altogether, by way of its front door.

Dart looked after his vanished figure a moment, wondering perhaps if his friend might not also be acting in a trance. Then his eyes fell on the page which advertised columns of guaranteed charms.

Before he could find just what it was Dr. Archer had wanted him to read, a curious sound made him look up. From the hallway, in the direction of the rear, came a succession of sharp raps.

"What's that?" whispered Letty, awe-struck.

Dart stepped into the hallway, Ben, Letty, and the two officers crowding into the living-room doorway behind him. Again came the sharp succession of taps, and this time there was no mistaking their source. They came from within the closed door of Sonny's room.

Letty stifled a cry as Dart turned and asked.

"Who's in that room?"

"Nobody," Ben answered, bewildered. "They took Sonny away last night—the door's locked."

Again came the taps.

"Where's the key?"

Ben produced a key, Dart seized it, quickly unlocked the door and flung it wide.

Dr. Archer stood smiling in the doorway.

"What the hell?" said Dart.

"Unquestionably," returned his friend. "May I give an order to your two men?"

He wrote something on his prescription pad and handed it to one of the two men behind Dart. The latter read it.

"O.K., Doc. Come on, Bud."

They departed.

"As I remarked before," Dart growled, "what the hell?"

The physician backed into the room. "The missing link," he said blandly.

"Red Brown?"

"You heard Ma Dewey's story?"

"Of course I heard it."

"She was quite right. She did kill Sonny. But not in the way she believes. I'm just working out the details. See you in the living-room. Lock this door again, will you?" And he shut the door between himself and the detective.

With consummate self-control Dart suppressed comment and question and obeyed.

Then he went back into the living-room with the others. The local newspaper was still in his hand, somewhat crumpled. He smoothed the pages.

"Take it easy, everybody," he advised the members of the family, with whom he was now alone. "We'll wait for Dr. Archer and Red Brown." And he began to peruse in earnest the columns of ads:

BLACK CAT LODESTONE

Draw anything you want to you.
Free—Hot foot and attracting
   Powders with your order.
Pay the postman only $1.95 on delivery
and it is all yours to keep and enjoy
forever.
   Burn Lucky Stars and surround
yourself with good fortune.
      Win Your Loved One
Let us send you our Sacred Controlling
Love Powder.
   Do you suffer from lack of Friends,
Money, Health?
      Oriental Wishing Ring

He had read to the bottom of the right-hand column before something caught his eye, an address which seemed somehow familiar.

15 West 134th Street, Apt. 51—

"Why, that's here!"

He re-read the advertisement:

Faith Charm

Faith can move mountains.
Develop your faith by using our
special charm.

Secret formula. Bound to bring
health and happiness to the wearer.

"Say!"

The front door rattled. Dart stepped out and and admitted Dr. Archer. "What kind of hide-and-seek is this?"

"It isn't," smiled the physician. "It's a practical demonstration in entrances and exits. It shows that even if Sonny's door had been locked, his assailant could have entered and left his room undetected."

"How."[sic]

"The next apartment is empty. Its entrance is not locked—you know how vacant apartments are hereabouts: the tenants bring their own locks and take them when they move. One room has a window on the same airshaft with Sonny's, at right angles to it, close enough to step across—if you don't look down."

"You jackass! You'd risk your hindquarters like that?"

"Sergeant—please."

"But what's the use? We've got the old lady's confession, haven't we?"

"Yes."

"And you admitted she did it—you were working out details. Good grief—would she go around to the next apartment and climb across an airshaft—at her age? What do you want me to believe?"

"Believe in the value of an odor, old snoop. Come on."

They re-entered the living-room. Dr. Archer went to Ma Dewey.

"Tell me, Mother Dewey, where do you keep the oil?"

She looked up at him. "I don't keep it. I gets it jes' as I needs it."

"When did you last need it?"

"Yestiddy mornin'."

"After it had failed so long to help Sonny?"

"I didn' have faith. I'd done seen his father die. But somebody else might 'a' had faith."

"Curious," reflected the doctor, "but common."

Dart's patience gave out.

"Would you cut out the clowning and state in plain English what this is all about?"

"I mean the mixture of Christian faith and primitive mysticism. But I suppose every religion is a confusion of superstitions."

The doorbell saved Dart from exploding. He went to the door and flung it open with unnecessary violence.

His two subordinates stood before him, holding between them a stranger—a sullen little black man whose eyes smoldered malevolence.

As they brought him into the living-room, those eyes first encountered Ben. Their malevolence kindled to a blaze. The captive writhed from the hands that held him and leaped upon the brother, and there was no mistaking his intention.

His captors got hold of him again almost before Ben realized what had happened.

"Who the devil's this?" Dart asked the physician.

"Someone for your leash. The man that killed Sonny."

"Yea—" panted the captive. "I got him. And—" indicating Petal—"I come near gettin' her las' night. And if you turn me loose, I'll get *him*." Vainly he struggled toward Ben.

"Three for one," said the doctor. "Rather unfair, isn't it, Mr. Bright?"

"She took all *we* had, didn' she? Give my wife that thing what killed *our* kid. We got to pay her back—all for all."

"Solomon Bright," breathed Dart. "The guy that lost his kid yesterday."

Dr. Archer said to the man, "What good will it do to pay Mother Dewey back?"

The little man turned red eyes on the quiet-voiced physician. "They ain' no other way to get our chile back, is they?"

Dr. Archer gave a gesture of despair, then said to Dart:

"Mother Dewey made the charm yesterday."

"'Twasn' no charm," Solomon Bright glowered. " 'Twas a curse. Cast a spell on our chile, tha's what it done."

"It's [sic] odor," John Archer went on, "was characteristic. But I couldn't place it till Mother Dewey fainted just now and I saw the cord around her neck. On the end of it hangs the same sort of packet, that I saw on Mr. Bright's baby."

Dart nodded. "I get it.... When she made that charm, she was unwittingly killing her own son. This bird's poison."

"Grief-crazed—doesn't realize what he's doing. Look at him."

"Realize or no realize, he killed Sonny."

"No," said the doctor. "Superstition killed Sonny." He sighed. "But I doubt that we'll ever capture that."

(1935)

Ezekiel

EDITOR'S INTRODUCTION TO "EZEKIEL" AND "EZEKIEL LEARNS"

Fisher approached the writing of his two published stories for children in the same fashion as he did his adult stories—a view of a person's first encounter with Harlem, an adjustment to its ways, and the use of setting to teach a moral as well as to perform its primary function as background. Both stories appeared in *Junior Red Cross News*, a periodical certainly that had mostly white readership, and the setting and characters must have seemed as different to the young readers as Harlem was to Ezekiel. He comes to New York City like a young King Solomon Gillis—having to "stare and blink and gasp" as he sees the city for the first time. Ezekiel's education, however, is in the hands of the "good guys" of Harlem—his uncle and his two new young friends, both of whom exhibit the virtues of friendliness and sharing. True to Fisher's code of casting, the boys Ezekiel meets are contrasts in color—one dark, one light. The typical Fisher ingredients have been transferred to the child's story.

In the sequel to the first story, the young boy from Fisher's southern town of Waxhaw[1] (Miss Cynthie's town, for instance), displays his adaptive knowledge of his new home and also demonstrates the virtues of honesty and loyalty. And since Fisher wants to educate his young white reading audience, he inserts a section about the journeys into the cultural side of New York City that Ezekiel's uncle exposes him to: The white reader is instructed to understand that blacks do more than remain huddled in Harlem, that blacks live very much as whites in many ways.

As stories, these two are only mildly interesting because of their predictability and the failure of Fisher to create any really interesting characters. The young villain in "Ezekiel Learns" is perhaps the only one who stands out as an interesting character; of course, he is not supposed to be the one the reader will remember. Badness, like evil, carries its own fascination and often outshines virtue. As little moral tales, however, Fisher has managed to clothe his points in two stories that could benefit the uninitiated young white reader into the 1933 scene.[2]

NOTES

1. For some reason, the printed version says Waxhaw, Georgia, although Waxhaw is in North Carolina. This must be an error on the part of the magazine, for Fisher indicates North Carolina in his other stories for characters from Waxhaw (e.g., Gillis in "The City of Refuge"). Furthermore, the atlas lists only a Waxhaw, North Carolina.

2. A third story, "Ezekiel Goes to School," never appeared although it was accepted by *Junior Red Cross News*.

It was Ezekiel's first day in Harlem, the Negro colony of New York City. He had arrived the night before, after a long trip north from Waxhaw, Georgia, where the dozen years of his life up to now had been spent. But last night he had been unable to see anything clearly. The enormous Pennsylvania Railroad Station, the multitude of hurrying people, the terrifying subway trains, the heavy traffic of the streets, the glittering clusters of electric lights all had been too much for him to appreciate so suddenly. Last night he had been able only to stare and blink and gasp.

Now, however, the bright sunlight of the calmer morning allowed him somewhat to gather his bearings and observe this strange new place with less bewilderment. Even so, it was still all very much like a mystifying dream.

He was seated on the front stoop of a tall apartment house on One Hundred and Thirty-fifth Street. His uncle, to whom he had been sent so that he might attend the excellent New York schools, had brought Ezekiel downstairs. He was going to wait there on the stoop until his uncle returned. It might be an hour, but Ezekiel musn't go away. If he got lost in Harlem he might never find his way back. Ezekiel had promised faithfully to stay, and so now he sat and looked about him.

Never had he seen so many tall dwellings, side by side, with no elbow-room between. There was only one low building in the whole row, and even that was taller than anybody's house back home. Where were the trees, the grass, the flowers? He looked at the broad concrete sidewalk, at the wide asphalt pavement of the street, with its shining car-tracks down the middle, and wondered if one could dig up the hard level road and plant things and have them grow.

A little way down the street two boys were playing an odd game on the sidewalk. They knelt in turn and went through motions like shooting marbles, only it was not marbles they shot but little round things like checkers. And how they laughed and chattered as they played!

With a curiosity he could not resist, Ezekiel slipped down off his seat on the stoop and slowly moved toward the two boys playing the strange game. Trained as he was to the strictest obedience, he hesitated once or twice as a wave of guilt came over him. He knew he ought to stay on the stoop as his uncle had told him, and once he looked back to be sure that the stoop was still there within reach. But the new interest conquered his conscience and led him farther away, until in a few moments he found himself standing over the two boys.

He saw now that they were playing with the little round metal caps of soda-pop bottles. The two took turns, kneeling and shooting the caps by flipping out a finger and striking them, sending them sliding in the desired direction. On the sidewalk a number of chalk lines had been drawn to form squares, and the game seemed to depend on how the caps were shot into the squares.

Ezekiel watched a while, his shyness overcoming the constant impulse to ask questions about the game. The two boys at first paid no attention to him, so absorbed were they in the game and each other. The two were evidently the best of friends.

Soon the light one made a winning shot and looked up at Ezekiel with a grin so proud and friendly that the newcomer from the South lost some of his shyness.

"What do you call that game?" he asked.

"Lodi," said the winner promptly. "Ever play it?"

"No," said Ezekiel.

"Got a lodi?" asked the darker boy.

"No," Ezekiel answered. "Wish I had."

"Here," said the first boy. "I'll lend you one." He reached into his pants pocket and extracted a half-dozen bottle-caps. Selecting one which was somewhat battered, he handed it over to the eager and delighted Ezekiel, with the admonition, "But you've got to give it back to me, you know."

"Yes indeedy," promised Ezekiel.

The two Harlem boys were only too glad to show the stranger how to play. They took pride in their greater knowledge, Ezekiel was an apt and grateful pupil, and three players made a better game than two. Before long they were all having a marvelous time, laughing, shooting, arguing, explaining, shooting and laughing again.

Suddenly there was a clamor of bells directly across the street from where they were playing, then the roar of a mighty engine and an abrupt ear-piercing shriek that frightened Ezekiel almost out of his wits. The game stopped. The other two boys became highly excited.

"Fire!" they shouted. "Wonder where it is?"

Thereupon, before Ezekiel's startled eyes, appeared the most amazing thing he had ever seen. Out of the wide entrance of the one low building across the street came a raging, demon-like machine straight toward them. Ezekiel stood rooted to the spot, expecting to be destroyed, but the machine, when halfway to them, turned in some miraculous fashion and started away up the street. It was red and silver in the sun, it had long yellow wooden ladders along its sides and two drivers, one in front and one high on top of the ladder, behind. It seemed as long as the subway train on which Ezekiel had ridden last night, and it made infinitely more speed and noise. Even after it had turned the distant corner and disappeared, the scream of its whistles came back shrill and clear.

Other fire engines soon were heard at a distance and were seen passing the corner where the first had turned. Then the boys noted that people were running toward an invisible point somewhere near that corner, and at that point the clamor of engines seemed quite suddenly to cease. Immediately their excitement became greater.

"It's on the Avenue!—Must be right around the corner!—Come on!— Come on!—Let's go!"

Off they sped, the three of them, in the wake of the hook-and-ladder. But as Ezekiel passed the stoop were he had promised his uncle to remain, he halted.

"Come on!" called his new friends, outdistancing him. "Come on, boy! Hurry up!"

For a moment the impulse to follow them was almost too great to resist. Then Ezekiel saw that they were already too far ahead of him now anyway; he could not possibly catch up with them.

Sadly he returned to his stoop and dejectedly resumed his seat. What would they think of him? After they had accepted him as one of them, lent him a lodi, and taught him to play their game, what would they think when he so unaccountably deserted them? It was quite plain what they would think. They would think him a coward. They would never take him back as one of them. They would demand their lodi and never play with him again.

What would be left for him then? Why, he wouldn't dare show his face in the street. He would have to spend all his play-hours indoors, lest he be pointed out to other boys and girls as a coward. Perhaps he wouldn't even dare go to school after traveling so many miles to do so. His schoolmates would avoid him. No one would associate with a coward. Yes, he would have to spend his time in his uncle's apartment upstairs. Nothing could be more awful—staring down from lonely windows into the street, a dizzy distance below, or staring into the airshaft, that horrible channel that separated one tall house from the next, a place full of unpleasant noises and odors, one glance into which this morning had been quite enough for him.

Ezekiel felt like crying. Why hadn't he had courage to go on? Was he afraid of being lost? The boys would have shown him the way back— he need not have feared that. Then why hadn't he stuck by them?

A long time he sat there downheartedly, certain that his obedience to his uncle had brought him sorrow. He wondered if his uncle could play lodi. But nobody's uncle would kneel down on a sidewalk to shoot a lodi. Presently he became aware that fire engine noises were again in the air. And in another moment the hook-and-ladder machine reappeared, heading back for its station. As he watched it swing around and slowly back into the engine-house, he wondered what manner of machines these were that could put out a fire so quickly—with ladders.

Then a tremor of fear shot through him as he saw the two boys returning. They would ridicule him, call him coward. They might dare him to fight.

Truly enough, they did laugh when they saw him. But to his great astonishment it was not a laugh of ridicule but of admiration. And when he heard what they said, he heaved a great sigh of relief and joy.

"Boy, you did right," said the darker lad.

"Indeed you did," said the light one. "You've got plenty of sense. It was only a false alarm. Come on—let's play lodi."

(1932)

Ezekiel Learns

Within less than a month Ezekiel had become accustomed to the strange sights of the great city. Only a short time ago he would have tingled with fright at the shriek and clamor of fire-machines roaring down his street; would have gaped in awe at the blaring brass bands that so often led proud parades of uniformed societies past his apartment house; would have fled in dismay into the refuge of his own hallway at the occasional riots between oddly excited mobs and grimly determined policemen. But now he took all this for granted, much as if it had been designed for his own entertainment.

For had he not now witnessed all the miracles of greater New York? His uncle, to whom he had recently been sent from Georgia, had taken him downtown on the rumbling subway and shown him the tallest buildings in the world; had even taken him into one, where they entered an elevator that shot upward like a sky-rocket, and, from the topmost story, viewed all of Manhattan isle, spreading away below them like a relief map; had taken him then to the famous Aquarium and shown him the most curious creatures of the sea; then out in a boat to the Statue of Liberty, whose raised arm was really a lofty tower which you could climb by a circular staircase; then back to Manhattan and uptown again to the Museum of Natural History, which contained wax figures and mammoth skeletons and mummies thousands of years old. His uncle had further given him a whole day in the enormous Bronx Park Zoo, where he saw in the flesh all the incredible animals that peopled his books. Could Harlem, then, which was merely a part of all this, was indeed merely New York's Negro colony, be expected to show him anything more extraordinary than what he had already seen?

Yet today Harlem did show him such a thing, a thing which he recalled as remarkable long after all the rest had lost its glamor. And oddly enough it was not a thing that happened in the rumbling sub or the rattling el, or in a tall building, a museum or a zoo. It was something that happened within himself, impelling him into action, and showing him for the first time that, stranger though he still was, he could yet meet and solve a problem if he had to. Today Harlem gave him his first glimpse into himself.

He had been playing marbles with four other boys, each, like himself, about a dozen years old. He knew them all by name: Riny, Sam, Spinky, and Fats. But it was Riny whom he liked best, for it was Riny who had invited him to join a game of lodi on his very first day in Harlem, and who had taught him to play and made him feel at ease while he was yet a newcomer. Riny derived his nickname from his appearance, for he possessed that light, freckled skin and rough sandy hair which other dark folk refer to as "riny." On the other hand, it was Spink whom Ezekiel cared for least. For Spink was a loudmouthed, quarrelsome fellow who always insisted on having his own way and so hated to be opposed or to lose in any contest that he never yielded even the simplest point without some protest or ill-tempered argument.

Such was the case at the moment. Riny had just made an unusually successful shot. Spink promptly objected, insisting that Riny had cheated by shooting from a position nearer than that in which his aggie had previously fallen. But Riny only grinned good-humoredly and said:

"Aw, boy, you're always raising a howl. If you saw I was cheating, why didn't you holler before I shot?"

And he calmly picked the marbles to which he was entitled.

This so infuriated Spink that for a moment Ezekiel thought there would be a fight. But when Spink saw that he was alone in his accusation and that none of the others was supporting him, he hotly withdrew from the game, proclaiming that he'd be jim-swiggered if he'd play with a crowd that permitted such unfair advantages.

To his chagrin, the others accepted this decision without seeming to mind at all and coolly went on playing without him. Indeed they seemed, if anything, relieved to be rid of him, and this angered him all the more. He stood off to one side looking on sullenly, clearly smoldering in resentment; and it made Ezekiel uncomfortable to see that anyone could be so unnecessarily incensed. He did not understand that what inflamed Spink most was not the loss of the marbles, but the wound to his pride—that nothing stings like being ignored. But he did see that an expression of unbelievable malice was suffusing Spink's thin dark face, an expression so baleful, indeed, that Ezekiel, who was the only one watching, felt as though Spink might at any moment pick up a brick and hurl it into their midst.

A moment later Spink moved away and vanished around the nearby corner; and Ezekiel, seeing the black look which the departing boy threw over his shoulder, instinctively realized that Spink was up to some spiteful mischief. And so Ezekiel was now more apprehensive than ever. The others were wholly absorbed in the game, now silent as they tensely watched a shot, now laughing in honest praise for skill or good-natured derision for failure. But so intently did Ezekiel watch the corner around which Spink had disappeared that the others had to call his attention whenever his turn arrived.

Suddenly Spink came running back from around the corner, and before anyone knew what had happened he had rejoined the group. A

moment later the game stopped as a big fat man, whom they all recognized as the owner of the corner fruit store, came puffing around the
same corner apparently in pursuit. He was too fat and awkward to run,
but he was doing his best, waddling hurriedly forward, breathing hard,
and bouncing his great paunch before him like a medicine ball.

He reached the staring group of boys and halted, blowing like a steam
engine. His black eyes glared.

"Who steala da plum?" he demanded in a gruff and terrible voice.
"Who steala da plum?"

He surveyed them uncertainly a moment. Spink had moved close to
Riny. The man's eyes fell upon him. "You—you steala!" he accused
and started for Spink.

"No, mister!" Spink cried quickly. "Not me—another boy! He just
ran past—up that way—honest!" He pointed up the street.

Then Ezekiel saw a curious thing. For he, having been on the lookout,
knew that no other boy had just run past, and so he did not look, as
did all the others, in the direction in which Spink was pointing. Instead
he looked in amazement at Spink who had made the false statement,
and so saw what no one else saw: that Spink, with a deft, quick movement, still pointing with one hand, used the other to slip something
into Riny's coat pocket.

"No!" bellowed the huckster. "You—you steala! I see! I breaka you'
neck—"

"Nobody here took it," Spink insisted, backing off. "We've been playing marbles—haven't we fellows? Sure. Here—search us—we're not
afraid. Go on—search us."

"What's dis—search?" The big man looked from one to another. "I
find, I breaka—"

"Go ahead and look in our pockets. We didn't take it. Put your arms
up, fellows. Let him look in your pockets!"

Everyone obeyed but Ezekiel, who was for the moment too
dumbfounded to move. For now he saw Spink's plan of revenge. Spink
had taken the plum himself. That was what he had slipped into Riny's
pocket just now. The huckster would find the plum in the unsuspecting
Riny's pocket, and Riny would take the consequences while Spink
looked on in vengeful glee.

The man reached for Fats, who, hands righteously held high, happened to be nearest to him. As he did so Ezekiel started to shout the
truth aloud, but something kept him silent. Long afterwards he realized
the wisdom of this instinctive silence; for if he had revealed the plum's
hiding-place, the huckster would have refused to consider how it got
there. What would he have cared if someone else *had* put it in Riny's
pocket? They were all alike to him, these young rascals, working together, no doubt, and whoever had it would be guilty and must be made

an example of to prevent others from doing the same thing. But at the moment Ezekiel was simply obeying the ingrained aversion every boy has to "squealing" on another.

Yet he had to do something, for he was the only one who knew the truth, and Riny, his friend, was in danger. For a moment he stood there, panic-stricken. Only a moment, however. Before the stout vendor had finished feeling roughly through Fats' clothing, Ezekiel found himself doing something he would never have dreamed possible. Quickly he moved toward Riny and Spink, both standing with upraised arms, and thrust himself between them. The huckster was now searching Sam. The other boys' eyes were glued on his great angry form. Ezekiel, with desperate stealth, reached into Riny's coat pocket with one hand, extracted the plum, transferred it behind his back to his other hand, and slipped it into the pocket of Spink. Then he, too, innocently raised both arms high and calmly waited to be searched.

The vender disgustedly turned from a fruitless search of Sam, whereupon Ezekiel stepped forward and submitted himself. Not to be outdone in a show of innocence, Spink followed Ezekiel's example. Finishing with Ezekiel, the huckster laid hold of Spink's pockets.

Suddenly he became quite motionless, then cried, "Aha!" so fiercely that Spink shrank. Then out of one of Spink's pockets the searcher brought a small, round, purple plum.

"What I tella you!" he shouted triumphantly, and grabbed the thunderstruck Spink before he could wheel and run. Holding the plum in one hand and yanking the howling boy along by the other, he waddled away toward his corner, where stood a tall policeman.

Of course the policeman would only give Spink a thorough scare and turn him loose; or, at the worse, take him home to his parents and urge proper punishment. But this was not the chief concern of the boys who remained behind. What astonished them was Spink's unbelievable stupidity.

"Why in the world would he tell the man to search when he knew he had the thing in his pocket all along?"

So queried Riny and Sam and Fats and shook their bewildered heads.

But Ezekiel, in the suffusing warmth of a new self-assurance, only grinned and said with townbred nonchalance:

"Aw forget him. Come on—let's play marbles."

(1933)

BIBLIOGRAPHY

The following selective bibliography contains information about Rudolph Fisher's published and unpublished writings. In addition, articles and parts of books discussing the work of Fisher are presented. Some items are annotated.

A. BY FISHER

Short Stories and Fictional Sketches

1. "The Backslider." *McClure's Magazine* 59, no. 2 (August 1927): 16–17, 101–4.
2. "Blades of Steel." *Atlantic Monthly* 140 (August 1927): 183–92.
3. "The City of Refuge." *Atlantic Monthly* 135 (February 1925): 178–87.
4. "Common Meter," Part 1. *Baltimore Afro-American* (February 8, 1930): 11. Part 2. *Baltimore Afro-American* (February 15, 1930): 11.
5. "Dust." *Opportunity* 9, no. 2 (February 1931): 46–47.
6. "Ezekiel." *Junior Red Cross News* 13 (March 1932): 151–53.
7. "Ezekiel Learns." *Junior Red Cross News* 14, no. 6 (February 1933): 123–25.
8. "Fire by Night." *McClure's Magazine* 59, no. 6 (December 1927): 64–67, 98–102.
9. "Guardian of the Law." *Opportunity* 11, no. 3 (March 1933): 82–85, 90.
10. "High Yaller." Part 1. *Crisis* 30, no. 6 (October 1925): 281–86. Part 2. *Crisis* 31, no. 1 (November 1925): 33–38.
11. "John Archer's Nose." *The Metropolitan; A Monthly Review* 1, no. 1 (January 1935): 10–12, 47–50, 52, 67, 69–71, 73–75, 80.
12. "Miss Cynthie." *Story* 3, no. 13 (June 1933): 3–15.
13. "The Promised Land." *Atlantic Monthly* 139 (January 1927): 37–45.
14. "Ringtail." *Atlantic Monthly* 135 (May 1925): 652–60.

15. "The South Lingers On." *Survey Graphic* 53, no. 11 (March 1, 1925): 644–47.

    In this special issue devoted to the Negro, these same sketches, minus one, appeared in Alain Locke's *The New Negro* under the title of "Vestiges."

16. "Vestiges: Harlem Sketches." Edited by Alain Locke, *The New Negro*. New York: Boni, 1925, pp. 75–84.

    See note above.

Non-Fiction

17. "The Caucasian Storms Harlem." *American Mercury* 11 (August 1927): 393–98.

18. "The Resistance of Different Concentrations of Bacteriophage to Ultraviolet Rays" (with Earl B. McKinley). *The Journal of Infectious Diseases* (March 1927): 399–403.

Novels

19. *The Conjure Man Dies*. New York: Covici, Friede, 1932.

    This novel, the first detective novel by a black, was reprinted in 1971 (Arno Press). The team of Detective Dart and Dr. John Archer make their first appearance here.

20. *The Walls of Jericho*. New York: Knopf, 1928.

    I quote myself in describing this novel (from my book, *Silence to the Drums*, p. 66): "Thematically, Fisher was concerned with the idea of black unity and the discovery of self. He uses the Bible story of Joshua to reinforce his concern for the black man's search for his true nature that will permit him to disengage himself from the deceptions of the past." This book was also reprinted (Arno Press, 1969).

Book Reviews

21. Cullen, Countee. *One Way to Heaven*. New York: Harper and Bros., 1932. In *New York Herald Tribune Books*, February 28, 1932, p. 3.

22. Fauset, Jessie. *Chinaberry Tree*. New York: Stokes, 1931. In *New York Herald Tribune Books*, January 17, 1932, p. 6.

23. Heyward, DuBose. *Mamba's Daughters*. New York: Doubleday, 1929. In *The Book League Monthly* 2, no. 1 (May 1929): 201–2.

24. McKay, Claude. *Gingertown*. New York: Harper and Bros., 1932. In *New York Herald Tribune Books*, March 27, 1932, p. 3.

25. Schuyler, George S. *Black No More*. New York: Macaulay, 1931. In *New York Herald Tribune Books*, February 1, 1931, p. 5.

26. Thurman, Wallace. *Infants of the Spring*. New York: Macaulay, 1932. In *New York Herald Tribune Books*, February 21, 1932, p. 16.

Unpublished Writings

27. (story) "Across the Airshaft"
28. (story) "The Lindy Hop"
29. (story) "Lost Love Blues"
30. (story) "Passing for Black" or "False Face" or ["Incident in Harlem"?]
    The above four undated stories are in manuscript at Brown University (Archives). Three versions of "The Lindy Hop" are in this collection. No. 30 has all of its titles crossed out, including one in pencil which appears to be "Incident in Harlem."
31. (play) "Golden Slippers"
32. "One Month's Wages"
33. "Perfect Understanding"
34. "Skeetes"
35. (play) "The Vici Kid"
    The above five stories and plays appear on a list, in Fisher's widow's possession, of unpublished materials.
36. "War Hero"
    This story, part of which was seen by me, has penciled on it, "last story." This is probably true, inasmuch as the author's sister wrote: "Even during his last illness in December of 1934, whenever his strength permitted, he worked on a story which had been requested by *Esquire* depicting the exploits of a Negro soldier during World War I."
37. "Complexion of Negro Night Clubs." Purchased by *Harper's Bazaar*.
38. "Ezekiel Goes to School." Purchased by *Junior Red Cross News*.
39. "Shadow of White." Purchased by *Survey Graphic*.
    "Shadow of White" has confused scholars for years because it has appeared on several bibliographies even though it was never published.
    These three items are mentioned at various times in the bibliographies by Pearl Fisher as being purchased but not published. The whereabouts of the manuscripts for these titles is unknown to me at this printing.

B. ABOUT FISHER

Articles

40. Arden, Eugene. "The Early Harlem Novel." *Phylon* 20 (Spring 1959): 25–31.
41. Chamberlain, John. "The Negro as Writer." *The Bookman* 70, no. 6 (February 1930): 603–11.
42. Clarke, John Louis. "Mystery Writer Is Interviewed over the Radio." *Pittsburgh Courier*, January 21, 1933.
43. Deutsch, Leonard J. "A Corrected Bibliography for Rudolph Fisher." *Bulletin of Bibliography* 35, no. 1 (January–March 1978): 30–33.
    This bibliography includes items not listed in this present bibliography and also mentions references to Fisher stories that have been anthologized. A "Must" bibliography, despite some omissions (e.g., items 44

and 49 in this one) and errors (e.g., Isaac Anderson's review was in the *New York Times*, not in the *New York Evening Post*).

44. Friedmann, Thomas. "The Good Guys in the Black Hats: Color Coding in Rudolf [sic] Fisher's 'Common Meter.' " *Studies in Black Literature* 7, no. 1 (Winter 1976): 8–9.

45. Henry, Oliver Louis. "Rudolph Fisher: An Evaluation." *Crisis* 78, no. 5 (July 1971): 149–54.

46. Lomax, Michael L. "Fantasies of Affirmation: The 1920s Novel of Negro Life." *CLA Journal* 16, no. 2 (December 1972): 232–46.

47. McCluskey, Jr., John. "Healing Songs: Secular Music in the Short Fiction of Rudolph Fisher." *CLA Journal* 26, no. 2 (December 1982): 191–203.

48. Perry, Margaret. "A Fisher of Black Life." *Harlem Renaissance Re-examined*, edited by Victor Kramer. New York: AMS Press, due in 1987.

49. Schmuhl, Robert. "Treating the Harlem Human Condition." *Negro History Bulletin* 37 (Janaury 1974): 196–97.

50. Tignor, Eleanor Q. "A Bibliography of the Short Fiction of Rudolph Fisher." *The Langston Hughes Review* 1 (1982): 24.

51. ———. "Rudolph Fisher." *Afro-American Writers from the Harlem Renaissance to 1940 (Dictionary of Literary Biography*, vol. 51), edited by Trudier Harris. Detroit: Gale, 1986.

52. ———. "Rudolph Fisher: Harlem Novelist." *The Langston Hughes Review* 1 (1982): 13–22.

53. ———. "The Short Fiction of Rudolph Fisher." *The Langston Hughes Review* 1 (1982): 18–23.

54. Turpin, Waters E. "Four Short Fiction Writers of the Harlem Renaissance—Their Legacy of Achievement." *CLA Journal* 11 (September 1967): 59–72.

Parts of Books, Dissertations

55. Bone, Robert A. *Down Home: A History of Afro-American Short Fiction from Its Beginnings to the End of the Harlem Renaissance.* New York: G.P. Putnam's Sons, 1975.

56. ———. *The Negro Novel in America*, rev. ed. New Haven: Yale University Press, 1965.

57. Bontemps, Arna, ed. *The Harlem Renaissance Remembered.* New York: Dodd, Mead, 1972.

58. Brawley, Benjamin. *The Negro Genius.* New York: Dodd, Mead, 1937.

59. Brown, Sterling. *The Negro in American Fiction.* c1937. Reprint. Port Washington, N.Y.: Kennikat Press, 1968.

60. Davis, Arthur P. *From the Dark Tower: Afro-American Writers 1900–1960.* Washington, D.C.: Howard University Press, 1974.

   The book mentions the manuscript copies of the unpublished stories at Brown University, which Professor Davis did not receive in microfilm form, as he stated in his bibliography. The statement should have read "could be secured in microfilm form," but Professor Davis discovered this was not possible either.

61. Ford, Nick Aaron. "The Negro Author's Use of Propaganda in Imaginative Literature." Ph.D. diss. State University of Iowa, 1945.
62. Gayle, Addison, Jr. *The Way of the New World: The Black Novel in America.* New York: Doubleday, 1975.
63. Gloster, Hugh M. *Negro Voices in American Fiction.* Chapel Hill: University of North Carolina Press, 1948.
64. Gross, Theodore L. *The Heroic Ideal in American Literature.* New York: The Free Press, 1971.
65. Hemenway, Robert. *The Black Novelist.* Columbus, Ohio: Charles E. Merrill Publishing Co., 1970.
66. Huggins, Nathan Irvin. *Harlem Renaissance.* New York: Oxford University Press, 1971.
67. Perry, Margaret. *Silence to the Drums: A Survey of the the Literature of the Harlem Renaissance.* Westport, Conn.: Greenwood Press, 1976.
    This book discusses Fisher's short stories as well as his novels.
68. Queen, Eleanor Claudine. "A Study of Rudolph Fisher's Prose Fiction." Master's thesis, Howard University, 1961.
    A copy of this is in the Moorland-Springarn Collection at Howard University.
69. Singh, Amritjit. *The Novels of the Harlem Renaissance: Twelve Black Writers 1923–1933.* University Park: Pennsylvania State University Press, 1976.

Reviews of Fisher's Novels

The Conjure-Man Dies

70. *Boston Transcript,* August 3, 1932, p. 3. Reviewer: William Soskin.
71. *Crisis* 39, no. 9 (September 1932): 293.
72. *New York Evening Post,* July 30, 1932, p. 7. Reviewer: Rumana McManis.
73. *New York Evening Post,* July 30, 1932, p. 7. Reviewer: William Soskin.
    Of these two items (nos. 72 and 73) only the Soskin is a bona fide review. McManis merely annotates Fisher's book under the column entitled "Murder Chart."
74. *New York Herald Tribune,* August 14, 1932, p. 8. Reviewer: Will Cuppy.
75. *New York Times Book Review,* July 31, 1932, p. 13. Reviewer: Isaac Anderson.
76. *Opportunity* 10, no. 10 (October 1932): 320. Reviewer: Arthur P. Davis.
77. *Philadelphia Tribune,* September 29, 1932. Reviewer: Joseph V. Baker.
78. *Pittsburgh Courier,* September 24, 1932. Reviewer: Roseanne Charlton.
79. *Saturday Review of Literature* 9 (August 13, 1932): 47.
80. *Time* 20, no. 5 (August 1, 1932): 39.

The Walls of Jericho

81. *Baltimore-Afro-American,* August 11, 1928.
82. *Chicago Whip,* October 6, 1928. Reviewer: Mary White Ovington.
83. *Cleveland Open Shelf,* December 1928, p. 136.
84. *Crisis* 35 (November 1928): 374. Reviewer: W. E. B. Du Bois.

85. *New York Amsterdam News*, August 8, 1928. Reviewer: Aubrey Bowser.
86. *New Statesman*, August 5, 1928, p. 7. Reviewer: Walter White.
87. *New York Herald Tribune Books*, August 26, 1928, p. 5. Reviewer: Eric Walrond.
88. *New York Times Book Review*, August 5, 1928, p. 6.
89. *New York World*, August 5, 1928, p. 7. Reviewer: W. F. White.
90. *Opportunity* 6, no. 11 (November 1928): 346. Reviewer: B. A. Botkin.
91. *Saturday Review* (London) 146 (August 25, 1928): 250.
92. *Saturday Review of Literature* 5 (September 8, 1928): 110.
93. *Spectator* 141 (August 25, 1928): 252.
94. *Times Literary Supplement* (London), September 6, 1928, p. 630.

Index

Numbers in italics indicate full text pages.

About the Editor

MARGARET PERRY is Director of Libraries at Valparaiso University, Indiana. She is the author of *A Bio-Bibliography of Countee P. Cullen, 1903-1946, Silence to the Drums: A Survey of the Literature of the Harlem Renaissance* (Greenwood Press, 1971, 1976), and *The Harlem Renaissance: An Annotated Bibliography and Commentary.* She has written numerous short stories and has contributed articles to numerous professional journals and books including the *Dictionary of Literary Biography, American Libraries,* (Ball State University) *Forum, Panache,* and *Phylon.*